I052436

**It was bad enough his father wanted him to spy for him, but this…**

Vasili, the scrawny Greek who lived down the hall, opened his door and saw Mack on the phone. He pulled his head and wattled neck back inside, a sluggish turtle retreating into its shell. The sight took the edge off Mack's anger.

"I guess I've got no choice but to visit the Kilkennys and try to get the inside dope for your hero campaign. Tommy deserves the honor, though I still can't believe he'd go along with it if he were here."

Sim interrupted, not chuckling now. "So stop delaying. Go see Ellen and Blarney Bob. We must move ahead on this."

"But I can't just barge in on them and start nosing around. They must be devastated—and in mourning. They've lost their only son. Janice has lost her brother."

The prolonged silence on the other end surprised Mack. Was his father actually paying attention to what he was saying? He tried to recall the last time *that* had happened.

Sim's voice, slightly subdued now, came back on the line. "Our last meeting ended so hastily, I didn't mention it to you…"

"Mention what?"

"I told you only a very few people are aware of Thomas Kilkenny's death and the circumstances surrounding it." He let out a little cough. "The members of the Kilkenny family are not among them."

The terrible truth and his father's voice registered at the same moment.

"*You* must inform the Kilkennys of their son's death."

*Chicago, 1942. Can a reclusive and cynical factory janitor prevent the IRA from changing history?*

With US participation in World War II getting underway, John Mackenzie Simmons III "Mack" is in a difficult position. His draft status is 4F. He has lost an eye in a drunk-driving accident two years earlier, transforming him into a self-proclaimed "one-eyed freak." The driver was Mack's best friend, Thomas Kilkenny. After the accident, Tommy suddenly joins the US Army Air Corps, becoming a skilled pilot of a B-17 bomber. When Tommy dies in combat, Mack's wealthy and powerful father wants to make Tommy the war's first American hero to help promote the war. But first, they have to know if Tommy's father, a corrupt Chicago alderman, is involved in criminal activities hampering the war effort and won't stand up to scrutiny. Mack's father orders him to find out. But as Mack digs for the truth, he uncovers much more than gangland connections, stumbling upon an IRA plot that could change the course of the war.

war, as well as end Mack's life. Intense, poignant, and compelling, *A Necessary Hero* combines intrigue, suspense, and action to create a story that will grab you by the throat and hold you all the way through. *~ Regan Murphy, The Review Team of Taylor Jones & Regan Murphy*

# ACKNOWLEDGMENTS

The support and patience of many people contributed to this book. I owe a debt of gratitude to Fred Shafer and to my fellow participants in Fred's extraordinary novel-writing workshop for their patience, support, and insightful comments. And of course, many thanks to my agent Donna Eastman and her colleagues at Parkeast Literary and to the thoughtful editors and staff at Black Opal Books.

# A Necessary Hero

G. W. Kennedy

*A Black Opal Books Publication*

GENRE: HISTORICAL FICTION/WAR & MILITARY/THRILLER



A NECESSARY HERO
Copyright © 2018 by G. W. Kennedy
Cover Design by Jackson Cover Designs
All cover art copyright © 2018
All Rights Reserved
Print ISBN: 978-1-626949-75-1

First Publication: AUGUST 2018



Published by Black Opal Books **http://www.blackopalbooks.com**

# Part 1

# Flyboy and Hermit

"Perhaps it is good for us to have to face disaster, because we have been so optimistic and almost arrogant in our expectation of constant success. Now we shall have to find the courage to meet defeat and fight right on to victory. That means a steadiness of purpose and of will, which is not one of our strong points." ~ *Eleanor Roosevelt, February 1942*

# Chapter 1

*February 1942*:

"My father is a horse's ass."

It was an insult, Mack thought, his father would appreciate if Mack ever actually called him that. It was a slur his father had used himself a thousand times. Some neighbor or legal client or fellow Yale Club member he'd run afoul of "is more than an insufferable ninny—he's a horse's ass!" They're the fightin' words of Winnetka, an all-purpose insult within the North Shore set.

During one of Mack's rare voluntary visits home to see how his mother was doing, his father's usage went: "Mack, no one could possibly think worse of you for being Four F. No one who counts anyway. Any man who would place *you* among those slackers who perforate their own eardrums or claim to be perverts to get out of the draft, why he's just the scum of the earth. Nothing but a horse's ass!"

Then, the conversation ran its usual course, whether the visit was voluntary or a command performance. His father—John Mackenzie Simmons II (never "Junior," familiarly "Sim")—slid into the subject of other 4Fs in the Simmons family's social circle who were serving their country in honorable positions that didn't directly involve the armed forces.

Mack (technically John Mackenzie Simmons III) said

one more time that he "didn't want a phony paper-pusher's job as Assistant to the Assistant Secretary in the War Department Office of Bayonets and Rubbish Control."

Then good old Dad ended the father-son talk by calling him a horse's ass for working at such a "demeaning" job, by which Mack knew he meant embarrassing to his father professionally. For Mack, the position as a night janitor at the Steckel Avenue Plant, one of America's largest producers of engines for B-17 Flying Fortresses, unquestionably contributed to the war effort at least as much as any Assistant Secretary. But, unable to think of anything better to say or do, he stormed out of the family's Winnetka manse, nearly bowling over Mr. Dineen, the family's elderly butler.

Navigating his rusty Model A from the North Shore to the West Side of Chicago, Mack saw the fateful "4F" floating like a balloon in front of him. 4F: "physically, psychologically, or morally unfit for military duty." It was the combo of number and letter no man wanted to own up to, far down the ladder from 1A, where all real men wanted to be, at least until they got to boot camp, not to mention getting within range of a gun-toting Nip or Kraut.

Mack's cross-every-T, dot-every-I father liked to point out that they were at war with Mussolini and the Italian Fascists too. "They're the descendants of Imperial Rome, a tough bunch," he said with a sage nod. But, Mack thought but didn't say, *the Eye-talians haven't rolled their tanks halfway across Russia or bombed the living daylights out of our fleet at Pearl Harbor.*

As the winter of '42 wore on and the number of strapping, seemingly 1A-worthy gents usually found on the streets of Chicago began dwindling, Mack found himself getting the stink-eye more and more often. Uncle Sam was pulling in the youth of America, patriotic volunteers and reluctant draftees alike—another way of saying healthy young men, some large percentage of whom were going to be turned into armless or legless or eyeless veterans of the newly-minted war.

After locating a parking spot on Austin Boulevard a block from Mrs. McLady's rooming house, Mack dodged past a half dozen pedestrians, stone-faced older guys in worn Sunday suits and a young mother or older sister herding a pair of prancing little girls, twins in matching pink frocks and wool coats. Everyone ignored him.

Mack wanted to buttonhole the ones secretly thinking, "Why the hell aren't *you* in the army when they've got my son—my boyfriend—my husband, dad, or brother?"

He wanted to tell them, "I'm not a shirker or a draft dodger. I am large and strong enough to have played football at the University of Chicago before the hyper-intellectuals took over and the Maroons still had a team."

There was, Mack thought, more to him, and less, than met the eye of a man or woman on the street. The "more" part was the scrollwork of scars forming a relief map of some fantastic island across his back and ass. As for the lesser component, he had just one of something, an item generally viewed as critical, instead of two. Not kidneys, kneecaps, earlobes, nostrils, buttocks, elbows, or balls, not even little-piggy-went-to-market toes. You had to look for a while into Mack's unscarred face then move your own head a little so that his eye would follow—the one he was born with, a singular noun—not the glass eye, officially his ocular prosthesis. Even those in the know had to look carefully because it was a masterpiece of ocular prosthetic art, the iris and pupil painstakingly sized and matched to the pale blue and clear white of the functioning peeper. Surprisingly, both Mack and his father agreed the prosthesis was far superior to a pirate's eye patch. Who knew what wound lurked underneath?

So, in the country of the blind, Mack might be king, but he wasn't welcome in the army of the two-eyed. Something about lacking the depth perception required to aim a rifle at the vital organs of his fellow man, not to mention the tendency of the artificial orb to pop out of its socket under duress.

In addition to conferring 4F status, Mack came to understand that having one real eye and one well-crafted fake made him a subtle variety of freak, but a freak nonetheless. People initially saw what they expected, a run-of-the-mill American male. Then came the shock of recognition—Jesus Christ, this guy's got only one eye!—ringing down the curtain of separation, of otherness. It's what made working the graveyard shift so appealing. It wasn't exactly living in a cave, but the eleven p.m. to seven a.m. shift was as close as you could get to a hermit's existence in wartime America, working in the dead of night then going to ground in the daytime, when people saw more clearly.

Of course, as Mack's speculations on the subject always ended, if the Buick's gas tank hadn't been down past Empty when Tommy rolled the car, none of this would be any problem at all. He and Tommy would both be blackened corpses like the ambushed dead in the oily waters of Pearl Harbor. But nobody except history majors and Hawaiians had heard of Pearl Harbor when Thomas Kilkenny rolled his father's Buick Limited, running on fumes, two days before Christmas 1939.

# Chapter 2

*December 1939:*

Memories of that night kept coming back, seeping in like water sneaking through a pipe with a hairline crack. The Christmas lights flashing past, fat snowflakes smacking against the Buick's windshield, tiny collisions gentle as babies' kisses. Sweating in his overcoat inside the overheated car, the warm burn of the bourbon sliding down to join the beer already in Mack's belly as he and Tommy passed the flask back and forth. It still felt romantic and slightly rebellious to pull out a hip flask, so in those days, Mack followed Tommy's lead and always carried one.

He and Tommy had run into each other at Chester's in Hyde Park. It was a favorite hangout for fellows in his peculiar circle—hangers-on who, when asked, could identify themselves as history graduate students at the University of Chicago, a respectable-sounding, if essentially empty, occupation. It was a way of saying they were doing something when they were actually vetoing proposed occupations. In Mack's case, that meant refusing to follow in his father's footsteps at Yale Law or becoming an earnest history instructor in a corduroy jacket at a Midwestern college. No legal eagle or Mr. Chips for him.

Mack and Tommy found their favorite table, off in a corner beyond the end of the bar. Their talk rambled from women and football to the approaching end of the decade.

"The 'Dirty Thirties,'" Mack said. "First, the Depression, bread lines, crackpots like Father Coughlin, the Dust Bowl, now this goddamn war in Europe. Things have got to get better in the 'forties. They can't get any worse."

"Mack, I thought you were a history major." Tommy drank off the last of his beer. "Things can *always* get worse."

Tommy wore a loose-fitting white sweater over dark slacks. As always, his clothes fit perfectly, as if he were modeling them in the Marshall Field's catalogue. He was your "definitive black Irish type," as the relentlessly categorical scholars at UofC would put it, his straight ebony hair combed back from a high, pale forehead. They were both tall and wide-shouldered, likely recognizable as former footballers among the pasty-faced scholars of Robert Maynard Hutchins's new-fangled university. Slim at the waist, wide at the shoulders, Tommy had been the swivel-hipped tailback—star of the woebegone team. Mack was a rawboned lineman, the guy who clears the way for the gridiron hero, a blonde-headed Abe Lincoln, not as heroically homely, but still looking like a man assembled from spare parts.

At Chester's, as the winter evening wore on, a number of Hyde Park females stopped by their table, drawn to Tommy like moths to a flame. Undergrad girls taking a break from the intellectual life to model shoulder-padded dresses *a la* Joan Crawford and Southern-belle hair styles inspired by Scarlett O'Hara. High-school girls from the neighborhood trying out their cigarette-smoking techniques—one with tight blonde ringlets and full red lips faintly resembled Bette Davis. Mack didn't know any of them, but Tommy did, or pretended to. More beer came and went. As the bar population dwindled, and only the two of them manned the table, their talk rambled back to the stalled war.

"Hitler's gotten what he wanted—Poland and a treaty with Stalin. He'll make peace and consolidate his gains. That's what Napoleon did."

"You're right, Mack," said Tommy after a long swallow. "Then Bonaparte over-played his hand and invaded Russia."

"*Der Fuhrer* only pretends to be a screaming lunatic. He knows as well as we do how attacking Russia went for Napoleon. This is like when Hitler seized Czechoslovakia, only this time, the Limeys and the Frogs had to declare war because they'd been too frightened to do it before. It's all just posturing, dogs growling over a bone. A phony war, like the papers say."

Tommy took a thoughtful sip of beer. "Everyone thinks they know what will happen because of what happened in the past."

"Of course, that's what we do..."

"Who's 'we'?" Tommy interrupted. He slid his beer mug across a puddle on the black surface of the table, creating a thin wash. "Humans? Only historians?"

"Yes. Both. We all look to the past to understand the present and to at least have an idea of the future. Why the hell did you major in history if you don't believe that?"

Tommy gazed across the smoky barroom and shook his head. "Step-by-step evolution isn't the way things happen at all. It's only a comforting illusion Spengler and his buddies stole from Darwin—sentient critters get smarter 'til they turn into Homo Sapiens, clams get bigger over umpty-ump millions of years, and eventually, giants emerge with shells like bathtubs. More adventurous, more unlucky types become extinct."

"What's wrong with that? We all know civilizations rise and fall. It *is* like evolution..."

"Bullshit!" Tommy's table-slapping vehemence caught the attention of Gilbert the Great, Chester's fat, phlegmatic bartender, who swiveled his massive head in their direction. "That's not the way things happen at all," Tommy continued. "Real change is sudden and unexpected: Mount Vesuvius erupts, a cow knocks over a lantern and Chicago burns. Just look at assassins—they change history all the time. A crazy Serb gets off a lucky shot at Franz Ferdinand, and Europe goes crazy." Tommy poured the rest of his beer down his throat, barely swallowing.

"It's true right across the board, big and small events," he continued, after a soft burp. "The Red Sox owner wants to finance a play, and Babe Ruth suddenly gets traded to the Yankees."

"Those *are* all historical people and events. You can analyze them, understand what happened and why."

"Mack, that's our Historians' Mythology. We only understand, and barely at that, what's already happened. In France, they don't study anything later than Napoleon. For more recent happenings, like our own goddamn century, it's too soon for serious scholars to get involved. History with a capital-H is ass-backwards—by definition! Henry Ford said it better than Marx or Spengler or Toynbee. History *is* bunk!"

When Tommy got wound up like this, sliding into the rhythms of his dad's political speeches, it was more fun to let him go than to argue. Besides, the beer was thickening Mack's tongue, which didn't prevent him from draining his glass and waving to Gilbert the Great for two more steins.

"War is what proves me right," Tommy continued more quietly. "This war is phony right now, I'll admit, but no one, not the greatest historian alive, has any notion of what's to come. Just ask anybody who lived in Dublin during the Easter Rising or the Jews in Germany or the helpless folks the Nazis bombed in Guernica or Warsaw. You wake up one morning—the landscape is unrecognizable, and all your old assumptions have become laughable superstitions. Your native town—it could even be Winnetka—is smoking rubble. Your family? Who knows where they are? Evolution is for fools and romantics. War is the lens that lets us see what really creates our lives and circumstances!"

Mack gave Tommy a few seconds to enjoy the imagined applause of his theatrical crescendo. "Okay, Professor Catastrophe, just for the sake of argument, let's pretend this 'phony war' turns out like the little tiff in 1914 and pulls in us Yanks. Will you join up? Theoretically speaking, of course."

"It's a given, Mack," he replied with surprising seriousness. "When the Germans invaded Poland, my dear mother *and* Blarney Bob both said, in their own ways, that if we ever go to war, I should join up right away. Bob will wangle a safe spot for me on the General Staff, or whatever the hell they call it in the navy. Being in uniform will be 'a necessity for any successful political career.' Those were Mother's exact words."

Tommy glanced around, as if his parents might be eavesdropping. "What about you-all, Colonel Simmons? Sho-ly you got the makin's of an officer and a gentleman." His Southern-fried accent resembled Foghorn Leghorn, the Looney-Tunes rooster.

"The subject hasn't come up, General Cornpone. But if my father wants to pull strings to grab me a safe posting, I may enlist as a regular doughboy just to spite him." It was the first thinking he'd ever done on the subject.

They clinked mugs and drained the rest of their beer. Chester's was completely depopulated now—even Gilbert had left his post—but swirling cigarette smoke still filled the room.

Finally, Tommy said, "Mack, me boy, what I really want to do tonight is shoot some craps. Do you wanta shoot craps?"

"I sure as hell do!" Drinking made him ready for anything. So why not jump from barroom philosophizing to a crap game?

Mack staggered, but only a little. Paling around with Tommy had completed his education as a drinker. The pair steered a fairly straight course along 57th Street to Tommy's—or, technically, Blarney Bob's—brand-spanking-new Buick Limited. Its headlamps stared straight ahead into the night, unfazed by the weather. Snow had been falling on and off all day, and it was coming down hard now.

"There's a roadhouse out in the country, somewhere near Harvey—it's called Minnie's. My sources tell me Minnie's back room is home to one of Chicagoland's great floating crap games."

"By 'sources,' you must mean Alderman Robert Patrick Kilkenny, familiarly known as Blarney Bob, or perhaps his sidekick Victor Schlegel—the Schlegel who's not the German historian." Mack stifled a hiccup. "You'll notice I never mentioned Dominic O'Nore, who never speaks and therefore couldn't be a source for anything."

"The correct answer is B. Good old un-historic Victor was at the house when I picked up the car. He says get to Minnie's fast, her place is about to be raided 'cause she cut back her payments to the Sheriff." He took a swig from the flask and handed it back to Mack. "You know," Tommy said, "you really are a pretty smart guy."

"Sir," Mack replied with a belch after a belt of the sweet liquor collided with the pool of suds, "I attend the University of Chicago. Ergo, I must be one damned smart, ultra-intelligent fellow."

In Mac's memory, this continuing banter, which seemed witty at the time, melted together with clambering into the car and setting out through the worsening snow to find Minnie's place.

Mack wasn't paying attention as they left the city and nearest southern suburbs, noticing only a lonesome Mobil gas station they'd passed before. To Mack's bleary eyes, the flying red horse on the sign looked about to soar into the billowing snow. The station had been open the first time they went by, and he'd thought of suggesting a stop for gas until a mouthful of whiskey drove the thought away.

"Victor said it's someplace around here, near Dixie

Highway," slurred Tommy, a hint of desperation in his voice.

"Of course, you didn't write down the directions."

"You sound like my mother." Tommy tapped his forehead. "It's all in my steel-trap mind—Ah, here's where we turn. Ralston Road."

The Buick made a wide, skidding left turn. Nothing was visible except hurtling snowflakes: no headlights, no lights from houses or farms beside the road. Mack learned much later that the absence of roadside lights was because Ralston Road gradually climbed an embankment that carried it over fields that flooded in the spring.

Everything else was a collection of jigsaw-puzzle pieces: Tommy's gasp at the deer or shadow of a deer or pink elephant on the road ahead; the scream of brakes; Mack's shouted "Goddamn it!" when warm liquid from the flask dribbled down his chin; the Buick becoming airborne, spinning on its front-to-back axis.

Snowflakes seemed to fall upward then down again. Mack's body took blows from every direction, what footballers called a cement-mixer beating, when all the opposing players seem to clobber you at once.

The aerial thrill ride didn't last long. A Buick Limited is one of the world's worst flying machines—an airborne Great Dane, the *Titanic* taking off instead of going under. *Such a beautiful machine*, Mack thought in a weird, slow-motion monologue, *and it's about to be wrecked—hubcaps flying off to rust in the melting snow, smooth black fenders crumpled like paper, those ultra-modern headlights— hydraulically controlled, the magazine ads said—dangling in the icy wind.* Just before the thrill ride ended, his head shattered the passenger-side window, which knocked him out cold. His father became convinced the concussion changed his personality.

Other details came together slowly and long after the fact. The door on the driver's side somehow popped open then closed again, depositing Tommy in a deep snow bank next to the road. His overcoat was neatly ripped in half across the back, but he was otherwise undamaged.

By an odd coincidence, Mack's own overcoat and blood-soaked shirt were torn in just the same way. It was surmised that a sleeve became entangled with the knob that capped the gearshift and yanked it off. During the final spin down the embankment to Farmer McBean's field, the exposed end of the gearshift came into violent contact with Mack's left eye-socket.

# Chapter 3

The men Dominic O'Nore had killed didn't add up to a large number—ten or so, if you counted the assassinations where he was one of two or three gunmen. Except for Victor Schlegel, he hadn't known any of the dead or borne any real hatred toward them.

Besides Dominic's animus toward Schlegel, the arrogant fellow met *his* end in Chicago, not back home like the others Dominic introduced to the Hereafter. What's more, his death wasn't carried out according to the IRA rules that governed such matters, rigid as the order of the Mass.

Then there was the matter of the weapon. Dominic noticed it among the IRA goods stored in the special room in the alderman's cellar. A shotgun—nothing out of the way there, of course—but the front half of this one's twin barrels was neatly sawed away. The weapon now fit comfortably under a long coat, or even inside a deep pocket without much showing. Just the thing wanted for edging close to a bloody Brit policeman in a dodgy part of Belfast or a Dublin Free State traitor crossing a bridge over the Liffey.

Dominic was shifting small boxes of ammunition into a single large crate so Devlin's men could get in and out fast and get the ammo and weapons on the road to Boston and on a freighter bound for Cork or Dublin. Then, the scrawny weasel appeared at the door of the cellar room. Dominic thought Schlegel was on his way out to face the snow after the long session with the alderman. Before heading for the cellar, Dominic had seen the tubercular fellow put on a wide-brimmed fedora and shrug into his belted overcoat with the showy fur collar, trying to appear posh and failing miserably. But there stood Victor Schlegel, blinking in the raw glare of the overhead bulb and sweating into his fraudulent gentleman's coat.

"The alderman and I have decided. There will be no more of this goddamned Irish business," Schlegel said in a rasping voice that seemed to drag a rusty saw blade across Dominic's skull. "Get rid of this shit and bring no more into the house." The loathsome fellow was so famished-looking and gray-faced he resembled a cadaver out for a stroll. Schlegel puffed on a cigarette that Dominic hadn't noticed but knew was there because Victor was never without one. "Bob don't have the stomach for telling you himself, so he got smashed and convinced me to take on the job. Which I've just done."

Schlegel spat on the dirty concrete floor, a tiny raindrop, as though his shrunken frame couldn't put forth any more spittle. "I know you never speak, Dominic, so I won't ask if you understand, 'cause I damned well know you do. Just make sure these goods are gone—" He waved the hand without the cigarette to take in the whole cramped room. "—when I come by to wish Bob a Happy New Year." He wiped his brow with a fresh white handkerchief that appeared from inside the fur-collared coat. He turned on his heel and was gone, his steps silent as an alley cat's.

Dominic patiently stood still as a statue, grasping the ammo box he'd been holding when Schlegel came in, until he heard the front door open and close. He trotted upstairs for his own coat—something a bloody Eskimo would wear but necessary in the Arctic outpost of Chicago—and to check on the alderman, snoozing noisily, as he'd expected, on the living-room couch. Dominic ran back down the stairs and loaded the sawed-off shotgun, which slid nicely into the deep side pocket of his black-wool coat. The garment and the weapon felt made for each other.

Schlegel's footprints in the new-fallen snow showed like the harbor lights of Dublin. Dominic didn't need tracks to follow. Schlegel was still in sight, turning the corner onto Jeffery Boulevard. Dominic hurried at first to close the distance between them, but Schlegel wasn't walking fast and never looked back. A few more blocks would take Victor to the house of his sister Marie. In fact, Dominic would no doubt be driving him there if Thomas hadn't sweet-talked his da' into lending him the car. A wholly unwelcome picture of Marie Schlegel conjured itself up: a bloated, even homelier version of Victor.

Dominic allowed Schlegel to get halfway down the block, well away from 75th Street and the Kilkenny house but not yet reaching the point where the posh homes of South Shore gave way to shops and the twenty-four-hour service station at the corner of 77th. Dominic deemed he'd gotten close enough and blessed his luck that the snow was keeping everyone inside. He stopped, quickly caught his breath (for he remained fit as a soldier), and called after Victor.

"Mr. Schlegel! Wait, please! I've a message from Alderman Kilkenny—"

Schlegel stopped in his tracks. Spun around, looking surprised but still calm. "My God, Dominic, you *can* talk, after all!" Schlegel flipped his cigarette into a snow bank, where it sizzled into ash.

Dominic nodded. Snowflakes, now heavy and wet, kissed his hairless skull. Then, not being a fellow to draw out missions of this kind, he pumped the shotgun once and shot Victor Schlegel, aiming for the middle of his chest. The unfamiliar weapon kicked back with the force of an angry mule, throwing his aim off a bit and leaving a bad bruise on the inside bend of Dominic's elbow. Pellets clicked against a tree in the parkway.

Schlegel writhed on the snow-covered sidewalk like a maddened snake, long streaks of blood mingling with the shredded tan fabric of his coat, though the fur collar was untouched, the fedora still on his head as if clamped there. Dominic pumped the shotgun one more time. He dispatched Schlegel with a blast from three feet away that turned the fancy collar—fox fur, Dominic noted upon closer inspection—into bits of reddish gauze. They hung in the air among the hurtling snowflakes, both back-lit by the spotlights illuminating the life-sized crèche that stood on Dr. Desmond McCarthy's broad front lawn.

Dominic hadn't noticed the sound of the first shot. But the echo of the second seemed to bounce off the house fronts during his whole, purposefully slow walk back to Blarney Bob's.

Dominic knew there would be bad blood between himself and the alderman. But Dominic had already made it clear that Blarney Bob couldn't serve two masters, a point Jesus Himself had made. Because the alderman inexplicably thought of Victor Schlegel as a friend and confidant, Dominic knew Bob would use his contacts with the police and the state's attorney to push away the murder investigation. It would not be a difficult task. Everyone but the alderman shared Dominic's opinion that Schlegel was the scum of the Earth. For his part, Dominic vowed to himself never to breathe a word to the hard men back home that the alderman had, for a drunken moment at least, seen the Chicago Outfit as his first loyalty. Forgotten The Cause.

# Chapter 4



*May 1940*:

Mack was serving out yet another stay at Passavant Hospital, his face swaddled in a second skin of bandages. But even with a one-eyed squint half-blocked by ointment-stiffened gauze, Mack noted how the crisp khaki jacket of an army officer set off Thomas Kilkenny's wide shoulders. A swooning nurse, old as their mothers, had noticed too, wandering in behind Tommy as he stepped into the tiny room.

Tommy had visited once or twice right after the accident—same hospital, different room—but Mack had been too groggy from pain and anesthesia to remember much. More accurately, he thought, he remembered too much, a strange brew of probably-real memories, bizarre dreams, and peculiar admixtures of the two. Assorted doctors, his mother, his sister Felicia, metamorphosed into UofC grad students and fellow football players, some in full Chicago Maroons uniform. Tommy, dressed in pre-enlistment chinos and corduroy jacket, swam to his bed through a watery blizzard, as Passavant Hospital became the quaint structure inside a gigantic snow globe.

His father dropped in between court dates. Sim's voice temporarily cut through the fog, as he interrogated the attending doc with the quiet forcefulness that made Sim

Simmons a legendary divorce lawyer. Of course, he got more out of the tight-lipped MD than Mack was able to: "We're waiting for the infection to clear up. It's all we can do."

Blarney Bob sailed by—just once?—glad-handing the nurses, who gabbled afterward about a murder the night of the accident. Mack struggled to grasp the connection before their voices dissolved into a cacophony of clucks. What caught his addled attention wasn't Blarney Bob so much as his silent bodyguard Dominic O'Nore. Mack had never seen Dominic's broad, map-of-Ireland face away from the Kilkenny house. The bodyguard's thick black silhouette, more statue than man, filled the door and cast an impossibly wide shadow across the room.

Someone—not Blarney Bob and surely not the always-silent Dominic—passed along the rumor that Tommy had enlisted in the army air corps. Jumping the gun, Mack thought in a lucid moment: we aren't in the war yet. The bearer of the news might've been Felicia, even though Mack thought he remembered that Tommy had ended their passionate romance.

Just before the first release from Passavant, an orderly had shown him an item from the *Tribune*. "Same day as you," he muttered as he pushed the wheelchair down the hall. "One of the night nurses thought you'd be interested."

Most of the clipping, dated the day after the accident, was taken up by a gangland-slaying shot of Victor Schlegel lying flat on his back in the bloody snow, Christmas lights in the background, fedora still planted on his head. The caption noted that the Outfit fixer had been gunned down a scant four blocks from the home of "the notorious Alderman Robert ('Blarney Bob') Kilkenny." Mack had run into Schlegel a time or two at the Kilkennys' but never had a conversation with him, though he'd heard him muttering with the alderman, proof *he* could actually speak. Mack's only lasting impression was that Schlegel's cadaverous frame and creased face made him the ugliest human being Mack had ever encountered.

Looking at the clipping, though, Mack felt a connection. Two freaks who nearly shared space in the *Trib's* obit column, historically linked by the same date of death. Maybe Schlegel's freakishness had been transferred to him. After all, the Outfit bag man and Mack's left eye met their ends at nearly the same moment on that snowy evening. Stranger things have happened, right? Well, okay, probably not.

"Still in the land of the living, I see," the real Tommy said this time around, with no greeting or introduction. His booming voice woke up the admiring nurse. As Mack looked over Tommy's shoulder, she looked around with a start and backed out of the room.

Tommy dodged past the visitors' armchair, strode to the bed, and gave Mack's shoulder a sharp squeeze through the thin cotton hospital gown. Pokes and prods defined their physical contact, except for back-and-fanny slaps on the football field. There, the armor of helmets and pads took the onus off men touching one another, even when they were close as brothers.

Tommy gazed out the narrow window on the far side of the bed. "Great view of the lake. All you have to do is stand on your head on the window sill. You're probably not up to that yet, assuming you can see. Can you?"

He stared into Mack's face and soberly repeated the question. "Can you see, Mack?"

"I can see okay, but with all these mummy-wrappings, it's sometimes like looking through a blizzard." Mack quietly winced at the word "blizzard"—just an accidental turn of phrase? Nothing to do with the snowy, drunken search for Minnie's crap game. But didn't Dr. Freud say there are no accidents?

"For example," Mack continued, "I can see those wings on your lapel. You really are a flyboy now?"

"Getting ready to be one. I got straight A's on the eye-hand coordination tests. A natural-born pilot, they say."

"I always knew you were a natural-born something or other," Mack said, wondering how he'd do on those eye-hand tests.

"People usually fill that in with 'son of a bitch.'"

"Me boy, I've told you to *nivver* talk of yer sainted mother in that trifling way!" Mack felt his mimicry of Blarney Bob's Irish brogue succeeded reasonably well. They laughed like noisy school kids.

"I phoned your house," Tommy said more quietly. "Once I convinced the butler who I was, he said you've been in and out of the hospital for months. I thought you'd be home for good by now."

"The wound heals up and then gets infected again. Kindly old Doc Bennett says we're gradually winning the battle, though."

"That's what Chamberlain says about what's going on in France. The medicos don't talk about 'strategic retreats,' do they?"

"They can lie as well as any politician, I guess. But I do feel it getting better. When the socket gets infected, it itches—and I'm less itchy these days."

"Then, you can get to scratching some of those other itches!" He pointed to Mack's crotch, and they started laughing again.

"What are you flying? From what we read in the papers, our air corps would last about ten minutes against the Luftwaffe. Are you fellas still using those old barnstorming crates from the Great War?"

"Well, some of our trainers are pretty long in the tooth…"

"One reporter for the *Trib* said your planes are so old, 'air corps' should be pronounced c-o-r-p-s-e." The Blizzard Syndrome again. Some convoluted revenge? *You put me here in freak-show limbo, Mr. Eye-Hand Coordination, now think about dying yourself.*

"No, no, those days are long gone," Tommy replied

earnestly, clearly not picking up any buried meaning. "We're not training to fight the Red Baron any more. I'm slated for a Flying Fortress—best bomber in the world. Not even the Luftwaffe has anything like it!"

Tommy leaned forward, his black eyes inches from Mack's gauze-covered face. "And you wouldn't believe what it's like to fly, Mack, even in a trainer. It's another world altogether. They talk about being 'free as a bird,' but it's much better than that. You're cut loose from everything, like being on your own planet, your own star!"

Any theories that Tommy's peacetime enlistment was some kind of penance melted away in the heat of his enthusiasm. Tommy always had a talent for landing on his feet.

The middle-aged nurse stepped back into the room. Shaking her head, she pointed to her watch, all business now. "Visiting hours are over. I've already given you boys extra time."

Tommy stood, came to attention, and threw her a snappy salute. "Yes, ma'am. Will do!" She smiled broadly but didn't leave.

He reached down and squeezed Mack's shoulder again, not as hard as before. "I'm only passing through today, changing trains, but I'll get a real leave after flight school—a whole week! We'll get together then. Paint the town red, just like the old days. I'll let you know when—so you can give the women of Chicago fair warning!"

"I'll be ready," Mack replied, mustering his entire stock of enthusiasm.

"Mack, you were born ready. It won't be long. That's why they call us assembly-line flyboys 'ninety-day wonders.'"

Thomas Kilkenny marched out of the room as the nurse gazed after him.

⋙⋘

Returning home after completing the paperwork for Mack's final release from Passavant Hospital, Sim Simmons looked through the mail Mr. Dineen had left on his desk. It included four sizable checks, two from no-longer-married husbands, two from newly liberated wives. Some divorce lawyers specialized exclusively in male or female clients, but Sim had equal success with aggrieved partners of both sexes.

For some reason, slicing open the last envelope with his tarnished silver letter opener made Sim think of his wayward son. One would've thought a nearly fatal accident, one that had cost him an eye, would have sobered up Mack, not just his drinking binges but his broader life as well. Sim would've been perfectly satisfied if Mack had decided to return to the University of Chicago, for law school this time, instead of more useless history courses. (Solidly North-Shore Northwestern Law would have been even better than the disturbingly radical UofC) Instead, the accident pushed his son further away, to an even deeper retreat into the sullen withdrawal that had defined their father-son connection before the ridiculous drunken accident.

Sim endorsed the checks and locked them in his briefcase for deposit to his firm's account at the Northern Trust. Usually, the thought of adding to his considerable wealth gave Sim warm gratification, proving once again that he stood at the top of his profession. This time, though, he felt nothing but a stiffening chill spreading outward from his chest.

# Chapter 5

A few months after their last meeting at Passavant, Mack received a letter from Tommy, the first of a dozen or so—more, Mack decided, than he sent to his family. The letter was banged out with surprisingly few corrections on a typewriter with a clogged-up "p" that looked like half a lollypop.

*December 10, 1940*
*Larkin Air Field*
*Butler, California*

*Dear Cyclops:*
*Kilkenny, Winogrand, Smithfield, Ianelli, Sorenson, Gluck. The crew of our bird sounds like something from a phony war movie like* Rainbow Division *or* The Fighting 69th. *You know—red-blooded American boys from every corner of this great nation, proving that We're All in This Together just like 1917. Exactly what "This" might be isn't clear to any of us out here in the Ninth Circle of Hades, also known as the City of Butler, California. The locals always call it by the official name as if the magic words "City of Butler" will somehow make this godforsaken burg more than fly shit on the empty map of the Mojave Desert.*

*Half the guys here joined up because of Roosevelt's draft. (A peacetime draft—there's a contradiction of terms, if I ever heard one.) I'll wager Willkie got a passel of absentee votes from our little corner of the Golden State. Most of the other inmates here were too old for CCC camp and still had no job. They heard Uncle Sam gives you three squares a day, a place to sleep indoors some of the time, and even a tiny paycheck. That's all they needed to know about US foreign policy and legitimate war aims if we ever get into the fight.*

*The spots you see on the paper are drops of sweat I couldn't wipe away in time. I'm heading for the officers' canteen—a swank spot, as you can imagine—for a Coke or maybe a beer...*

*I'm back in my humble quarters—believe me, the enlisted men's barracks are humbler yet. The thermometer next to our door only goes up to 100 degrees. You can see the heat rise in sheets off the dead-black mountains.*

*Officially, it's Larkin Air Base, training headquarters for Continental Bomber Command. The name fits. We're dropping a hell of a lot of bombs onto the North American continent. Of course, they're fakes—sandbags actually—because we don't have enough real bombs to waste them on practice runs. Dropping sand onto the desert from 5000 feet—I can't think of a better metaphor for army life.*

*That's not to say that heat and numbing boredom define our lives here. As the old timers say, the army always means long dull stretches punctuated by abject terror. (They don't say "punctuated" or "abject"—usually, it's about shitting in your pants!) My own shit-in-the-pants moment came a week ago on a training flight. We were practicing close-formation flying, supposed to head for Death Valley, go around a landmark called Blackjack Mountain, and fly back to base. There were five 17s flying in a V, like migrating geese. Our bird was at the trailing end, on the right. As we got close to the turnaround point, the plane in front began losing altitude, fast. I yelled, "Burnaby, what the fuck..." Before I could finish, Mitch Burnaby, who'd arrived with his crew only a day or two before, said, calm as can be, "Don't worry, Tommy, I know there's a goddamned mountain there." Five seconds later, Burnaby's B-17 crashed, a couple of hundred feet below the summit. A dozen flyboys, men I'd had breakfast with that morning, gone in an instant, right in front of us—a fireball and an explosion that's still ringing in my ears. Usually, we're throwing insults and bullshit back and forth on a flight like that. But, after Captain Tuckman reported the crash, nobody said a word. Back at Larkin, we raised a toast to Burnaby and his crew at the officers club. Most of us stayed around and pounded down more beer.*

*A couple of days later, Bob Hope put on a USO show at Fort Ord, and they bussed in some of us from out here in the sand dunes. We were stuck on the edge of the mob of horny, entertainment-starved guys when Hope strolled out, golf club in hand. I don't remember his gags, but they all made fun of the heat, the food, the brass, the "military way" in general. What hit me was the easy way he spoke and how the fellows, brass hats included, drank it all in. Hope wasn't just performing. He was teaching us how to go to war. Pretend war is only a lunatic game of chance, a giant Irish Sweepstakes. If you take it too seriously, you're dead.*

*It worked for our crew after Burnaby's crash. "He must've had one helluva hard-on not to see that fucking mountain," our waist gunner Joe Ianelli said the next time we went up. "I'll bet that son of a bitch came just as he crashed." Nobody chastised him. We all laughed like he was Bob Hope. For my part, I laughed so hard I nearly shit in my pants all over again.*

*I don't think Hope has ever been to war. And I read that he's not even an American, born a Limey, a bloody Brit, as my da' would say. But Hope's got some kind of antenna that's telling him what to say to Americans facing the random catastrophe of war. Stay loose, don't stop joking— that's how to keep the nightmares away.*

*Since Ianelli's joke, one Bob Hope could never tell in public, no one has mentioned Burnaby or speculated about why his bird went down—not a word. No historians here.*

*Apologies for going on about this. My point was that sometimes you've got to step away from training for war. Right now, I'm going to step away and look for a cotton swab and some alcohol to clean the goddamned "p" on this machine. For some inscrutable army reason, it's the only typewriter we've got—Capt. Tuckman wrote up the official report on Burnaby's crash on it—but nobody cleans the damn thing.*

*Cyclops, we are brothers to the end,*
*Tommy*


Cyclops. It was pure Tommy. The man captured in a word, jaunty and boyish, clever and erudite, but with enough understanding of the damage he'd caused to evoke—imitate?—genuine regret. Had Tommy ever wept over what he'd done? It was a question Mack couldn't answer and never figured out what he wanted the answer to be. Even before re-connecting with Tommy's wondrously twisted mind (for Christ's sake, *Bob Hope* as America's spokesman)—Mack scanned the letter twice to make sure he hadn't missed some mention of Janice. During the early, phantasmagoric stays at Passavant, he'd tried to wring out a picture of Janice Kilkenny from all those melting, re-forming images.

He had planned to get the lowdown on Jan from Tommy when they painted the town red. Was she seeing someone else? Did she ever talk about him, the spiritual son of Victor Schlegel? He didn't plan to use the word "freak."

After he finished flight school, Tommy did get the week's leave he'd been promised, but his ancient grandmother passed away, so Tommy—and Jan too—spent the week in their mother Ellen's hometown of Oyster Bay, Long Island.

When he and Jan finally did get together after the last release from the hospital, they tried to pick up their love affair or unbridled lust or whatever the hell it was. Jan said she hated hospitals and hadn't visited. Her explanation didn't even sound like a well-prepared lie.

# Chapter 6



*May 1941*:

The first time Mack met Leopold Belgian, the foreman beat the hell out of him. Mack had convinced the employment office at the Steckel Avenue defense plant that he really did want any available shop-floor job. The fat, professionally friendly woman on the other side of the desk tried to steer him to an office job in personnel or public relations. "It looks like the best fit for someone with your level of education and your, uh, physical condition."

"No," Mack more or less replied, "I've pushed around enough papers as a grad student. I want something on the shop floor. Something real—and you can rest assured I won't be getting drafted."

The hiring-office lady hemmed and hawed. Some of the things she said without actually saying them: "You have no factory skills whatsoever. From our point of view, you really can't do anything. We're not looking for someone to teach American History or produce scholarly treatises on Thomas Jefferson's economic theories."

Completing the application paperwork, Mack realized that his arrival at the Steckel Avenue personnel office stemmed from the disappearance of Walter Clinckscale a dozen years before. At Camp Ojibway in the Michigan Northwoods, where Sim exiled his wayward son for six weeks each summer, there was, of course, one kid all of the other thirteen-year-olds picked on—Walter Clinckscale.

Walter didn't seem an obvious target at first. Walter didn't wear glasses, wasn't notably fat or skinny, and he didn't have a voice squeakier than average for a boy staggering toward adolescence. It was, Mack decided, the sum of other, smaller traits that made Walter the camp scapegoat. His neck was too long, his Adam's apple too prominent, his large ears angled, wing-like, from a balloon-shaped head that sat uneasily on a frame that seemed too small.

Mack and the other boys short-sheeted Walter's bunk bed, threw his clothes and towel into the water as he swam spasmodically, and put fish from Lake Ojibway under his pillow. Walter's fey, overly dramatic gestures of anger and complaint only worsened the abuse. The counselors told him to tough it out. Walter's parents were out of reach, traveling in Europe. (This was a rich boys' camp.) Then, on a late-July Sunday near the end of the camp session, Walter Clinckscale vanished. The counselors tried, with utter lack of success, to keep things quiet by talking individually to the boys in Walter's cabin—Mack was one—and swearing them to secrecy. The campers went home and heard nothing more about the investigation. The Lindbergh baby had not yet been snatched, so a potential kidnapping was not necessarily a headline story.

Several weeks after returning home to serve out the rest of the summer in Winnetka, and completely by chance because Mack wasn't a newspaper reader, he spotted a story at the bottom of the *Tribune's* front page headlined "Missing Lad Turns Up in Detroit."

Walter's name appeared in the lead paragraph. He'd hitchhiked the 200 miles from Camp Ojibway to Detroit and somehow managed to get a job on one of Henry Ford's assembly lines. Walter had saved his meager pay, rented a room, kept to himself, and was apparently happy in his work. A Clinckscale uncle visiting Detroit on business spotted him from behind the wheel of a Pierce Arrow touring car. Uncle Clinck nearly got arrested when he tried to force his nephew into the car as the boy loudly denied any connection to the Clinckscale clan. The *Trib* reported that, after a stay in a Detroit hotel, "the sullen-faced lad reluctantly returned to Lake Forest in the company of his parents."

Mack never saw Walter again, but the sullen-faced lad became a hero to him. A model of how to stop losing battles, not just by leaving the battlefield, but by resigning the position of one-who-must-fight-battles. After Mack had sufficiently recovered from the accident, he decided that he too would live out the proletarian escape of Walter Clinckscale.

The Steckel Avenue plant could be more selective before Pearl Harbor, so landing a job wasn't a sure thing. Back in those days, Roosevelt was still battling the America-Firsters and cajoling the nation to dip a toe into the ice-cold pool of war by building up the nation's pathetic arms industry—a move Sim denounced at the time as "another New Deal takeover."

Now, with the USA jumping into the fight up with both feet, the plant was gearing up to run three shifts 365 days a year, they'd probably take even a one-eyed guy with no skills and fucked-up depth perception and stick him on the Engine Assembly line.

More hemming and hawing from the Personnel lady made mention of "working alongside Negroes." In fact, the lady had pointed out, "It happens that everyone in Plant Cleaning is a Negro—not that there's any formal rule or anything." She took off her glasses and peered myopically across the scattered manila envelopes on her desk. "You know how it is."

The next day, Mack waited, as ordered, outside the darkened employment office where Leopold Belgian was to pick him up at the start of the graveyard shift. It was obvious no one had bothered to tell Leopold anything about his new man.

His sleepy eyes, which Mack quickly learned weren't

the least bit sleepy, widened. "You *sure* you my new Plant Cleaning guy?"

Mack nodded and introduced himself. As they followed a twisting path through the labyrinthine plant, Leopold spat out a couple of questions—"Where you from, my man?" Mack answered truthfully but briefly. As they picked their way along a darkened row of drill presses, Leopold tapped Mack's shoulder and gestured toward a shadowed spot between the machines. He grabbed the lapels of Mack's brand-new denim work shirt and pulled his face close to his own. "You nothin' but a motherfuckin' reesh boy, and you takin' a job from some black man, maybe a guy with a wife and kids that lives around the block from me!"

His right hand slipped away but came back hard, an open-handed slap across Mack's jaw. It felt as if someone had picked up a piece of plywood and whacked him. Mack slid to the floor, too taken aback to resist. Mack had been on the sending side of bullying more often than the receiving end.

Had Walter experienced something like this in Detroit? Was it a hazing ritual for all new factory workers before sliding into the anonymous routine Mack was after?

Anger and adrenaline surged through him, fists clenching to hard balls. Mack recalled from a psychology lecture that he was experiencing the fight-or-flight response. As the smell of hot oil filled his nose, he hunkered down into a three-point lineman's stance, looking for an opening to fire out and cut the bastard's knees out from under him. He'd done that once to a big Polack lineman from Michigan who'd been playing the Anvil Chorus on the head of the UofC Maroons' quarterback. Tommy, at halfback, hit him high, while Mack cut-blocked him across the knees. The Maroons lost by five touchdowns, but they carried the guy off the field on a stretcher.

With Tommy at flight school in California, Mack had no help this time. Leopold pulled him upright and then off his feet. He shook Mack's chest. "Look here, Reesh Boy, if you playin' some fuckin' game here—gonna write a half-assed story for the newspaper tellin' 'the true story of the Negro worker' or any bullshit like that—I'm gonna use this-here drill to put a hole in your head! Just like drillin' for oil or whatever your daddy and his rich buddies did to get so fat. You got that?"

He set Mack down, and swung a massive elbow into his ribs, driving every molecule of air from his lungs and sending him staggering against the nearest drill press. The glass eye started to slide out of its socket as if a large, overly friendly beast—a chimpanzee, perhaps—was sucking on Mack's face. Starting to retch, Mack reached up with both hands to stop the ocular prosthesis from popping out and rolling across the oil-stained floor, a scene, he felt, the Marx Brothers would surely have used in a movie if they'd thought of it.

"Whatchew doin' there?" Leopold bent down as Mack caught the glass eye just before it sucked itself all the way out. "Good God, Reesh Boy, you got just one eye!"

"Good God, you're right!" Mack's anger began to drain away. No football block would have had much effect on Leopold Belgian, but Mack also understood that Leopold was taking a colossal risk in laying violent hands on some unknown white "reesh boy." His amazing courage or self-confidence or whatever it was had to be respected.

"How the hell that happen?"

Mack explained. Then, ignoring the official eleven p.m. start of the shift, Leopold told him how he'd changed his name from Bellejean to Belgian because "the damned cracker Yankees up here couldn't say it right."

He looked Mack straight in the face. "I come to this goddamn town 'cause my brother Charles was here. He knew Louie Armstrong, played his sax in the same jazz joints in Bronzeville where Louie played before they both left for New York. My wife Francine hates it here. Cold and mean is what she calls it. To remind her of New Orleans and her mama, she makes her own andouille."

As if replying to Mack's open-mouthed look, Leopold rolled his eyes. "How you be so ignorant, Reesh Boy? Andouille's Louisiana sausage, best in the world, spicy enough to make a grown man sweat while he begs for more. When Francine makes gumbo and jambalaya with it, the angels weep from jealousy."

# Chapter 7

As Mack returned from his memorable first day at Steckel Avenue, he found Tommy's next letter in his mailbox at Mrs. McLady's rooming house. As Mack read, he almost saw Tommy's grinning mug across his crumb-encrusted kitchen table. The letter didn't mention Janice.

*May 12, 1941*
*Larkin Air Field*
*Butler, California*

*Dear Cyclops,*
*As you can see from the salutation, I did manage to clean out the goddamned "p" on our typewriter before it drove me to distraction—army typewriters and bombs must come from the same defense plant!*

*I may have given you the idea that Larkin is a million miles from anywhere. Actually, we're only about 100 miles from LA, although it usually seems as far away as Chicago or Palm Beach or Mars. The rattletrap bus that heads down to Hollywood-Land three times a week takes the whole morning to get there, and just as long to get back here to Dante's Inferno.*

*The father of my co-pilot Pete Winogrand is a lawyer in Frisco—not a plutocrat like your da', but doing well nonetheless. He drove down a few days ago when Pete and I each had a weekend pass, and he took us to the big city in style, in a big Packard touring car instead of the bus, which makes every twist of the mountain roads seem like Death's Door. Pete and his dad filled the time with family talk that actually made me miss Ellen and Blarney Bob.*

*Pete Senior mentioned that one of the clients he was seeing in LA was Michael Romanoff, the crazy immigrant who runs Romanoff's restaurant in Hollywood—you know, the joint that Hedda and Louella always write about. Romanoff claims to be a long-lost member of the Russian royal family, and he never breaks character.*

*Any-hoo, Pete asked his dad if he could get us into the place. And sure enough, he did. It only took a quick whisper to the doorman or bouncer or whatever they call the big, cauliflower-eared galoot blocking the door. Romanoff's isn't very impressive inside—there are plenty of Chicago restaurants that make the place look like a dive. But, on the other hand, you don't often run into Humphrey Bogart at the Pump Room or Berghoff's. Bogie was sitting at a table drinking a martini with a not-too-attractive woman who may or may not have been his wife. (Obviously, I'd have applied my UofC scholarly skills to Hedda Hopper's column if I'd known we'd stop by Romanoff's!)*

*The food was the usual steak-joint stuff. Their claim to fame is a soufflé they serve in a ramekin, like a little dish of ice cream—bloody big deal, as Blarney Bob would say. Romanoff himself stopped by our table and said in his fake accent, "Oh, eet's PEE-tair, my favorite tovarich!" His meat purveyor is looking for a bribe, he says. Then he asks Pete Senior, "Dat ees deductible, yes?" If you ask me, Count Michael is a better actor than most of the movie-colony types who hang out at his place, bogus accent not-withstanding.*

*The high point of the evening was spotting Veronica Lake. You know, the looker who stole the show in* I Wanted Wings, *that phony picture about us flyboys-in-training.*

*(That's what we all say: I want wings! I want wings!) Ve-
ronica, wearing a mink stole in spite of the heat, waltzed by
our table on the arm of some lounge lizard, easy to spot
with that peekaboo hair covering half her face. There was
some whispering and pointing, but apparently leaping up
and asking for an autograph is frowned upon at Romanoff's. She's stacked like a pile of library books, but boy, is
Veronica short! She tops out at about four-foot-ten, shorter
even than my Grandma Boswell, who was almost a dwarf.
They must put her on an off-camera milk crate, or she'd
make all the other actors look like giants.*

*I've learned that the only way to get along in the ser-
vice is to take it one minute, one hour, one day at a time—
forget what happened before, like we all did after Burnaby's
crash. But seeing Veronica Lake shook me up. I can't push
away the thought that I'll never see her again, not because I
don't go to the movies or never get back to Hollywood and
Vine, but because I'll never get back at all. Remember Shel-
lenbarger's Civil War class? How McClellan's and Grant's
soldiers pinned slips of paper with their names inside their
uniforms? Let somebody—mother, father, bride, kids—know
I died in the war, that I'm not just one of the "missing." We
have dog tags for that now, of course, so we won't go to our
reward anonymously. But walking past the Neanderthal
bouncer on the way out of Romanoff's, it hit me that it's
possible, maybe even likely, that none of us from our bird
will come back.*

*When we're shooting the bull in the mess hall or the of-
ficers' club, we all tell each other that it'll be over before
Uncle Sam gets in. The Krauts and the Limeys will kiss and
make up before London is turned into one big field of rubble, and that'll be it. The fight is officially declared a draw.
We all go home, grow old, tell our kids about Dad's adven-
tures flying planes around the Mojave Desert, and maybe
someday get around to talking about Burnaby and his crew.*

*But now I don't think that's how it will go. Instead, it
feels like we're all on a train—it's a night train, rolling*

*through the dark, and the thing is, it's picking up speed, but nobody knows where we're bound.*

*This is getting morbid again, Cyclops, so I'll end now. Sorry I didn't just leave you with Veronica Lake!*

*Brothers to the end,*

*Tommy*


Trapped on a night train to war. To Mack, the vision signaled their divergence since the accident. He was slowing down, retreating into one-eyed life as Mack the Hermit, a novice at one of those monasteries that demand you burn all your worldly goods. The flyboy was speeding up, hurtling away toward…what?

Even as they headed in opposite directions, Mack saw that he and Tommy were united by a surrender of the will. No more planning for the future. From now on, life would be the random cycle of boredom and terror for the flyboy, the servility of a bottom-rung factory drone for the self-proclaimed hermit.

Not wanting to undermine the morale of a service man, Mack decided not to share this dazzling insight with Tommy. His next letter to Tommy was simply a Grand Tour of his digs at Mrs. McLady's rooming house: the ragged brown rug, with irregular patches stained a darker shade by years of spilled coffee; the rose-pattern wallpaper yellowed by the rainwater that trickled down from the roof even when it wasn't raining; the torn leather easy chair Mack had retrieved from the pile of battered furniture in Mrs. McLady's cellar and clumsily patched with masking tape; the sagging purple couch abandoned by the last tenant—a mysterious Mr. Burgos, who fell fifty bucks behind on the rent, departed one morning for his job at an Oak Park funeral parlor, and promptly disappeared.

"How can you be happy hiding out like that?" Tommy answered back. The surprise question brought Mack up short. After a few months at Steckel Avenue and Mrs. McLady's, Mack decided he *was* more or less satisfied, or at least accepting of the life he'd been thrust into, or thrust himself into. Servile or not, he had come to like clocking in and out at work—the metallic click of the time clock recording his arrival at the place he was supposed to be then noting the completion of his appointed rounds. He enjoyed getting home when everybody else was leaving for work then paging through *Life Magazine* or the hyperbolic grumblings of the *Trib* before, most of the time, drifting off to sleep.

The humble job at Steckel Avenue provided not just a hermit's retreat but a contribution to the defense effort. Dirty lavatories spread disease, Mack argued, and sick workers couldn't create the Arsenal of Democracy. Of course, he mistrusted his own arguments. If there was one thing he'd learned at the UofC, it was to convincingly take any side of any issue.

The job did offer the mindless comfort of serving as an unquestioning cog in a larger machine, a feeling he hadn't experienced since his football days. "Machine" was a stretch for the Chicago Maroons, guys who lost every game by thirty or forty points and celebrated like they had won the Rose Bowl when they scored a touchdown.

An unexpected Steckel Avenue benefit was working with Leopold Belgian and the rest of the Negro janitors. Warned off by Leopold, not a single one ever mentioned Mack's eye, or lack thereof. They were fellows he would never have met in a thousand years if the accident hadn't flung him off Ralston Road—and off the rich-boy's track he hadn't noticed he was on. A Hope-Crosby road picture with a nihilist twist. Call it *The Road to Oblivion*.

Mack tried to get this "sweet are the uses of adversity" bullshit across to Tommy, but he didn't buy it. He replied with a brief scrawled note: "I'll be mad as hell at myself forever for what happened to you, Cyclops, and I can't believe you don't feel the same. But I know the goddamned auto wreck was the best thing that ever happened to *me*. The accident, you getting hurt so badly—it was also a chance to get the hell out of my fucking, pre-ordained life. It pushed me to enlist, and that got me up in the air. I'll never stop flying."

Then he compared Mack to Simeon Stylites, the ascetic who achieved sainthood by praying and fasting his life away on top of a pillar. It was a classic History Department jibe, usually aimed at those who feared venturing beyond UofC's fake-Gothic citadel.

Mack wadded up the letter and tossed it in the trash, the only letter from Tommy he didn't keep. He raised a spotty kitchen glass and downed a sip of lukewarm tap water, a toast to Walter Clinckscale. Long live the patron saint of proletarian hermits!

Mack planned to initiate Tommy into the cult of Saint Walter the next time he came home. But when he was deployed to the Philippines later in the summer of '41, the army air Corps bollixed things up. Tommy's B-17 and her crew were sent straight across the Pacific from San Francisco, no leaves allowed.

# Part 2

# Men on a Mission

I am a stag: of seven tines,
I am a flood: across a plain,
I am a wind: on a deep lake,
I am a tear: the sun lets fall,
I am a hawk: above the cliff,
I am a thorn: beneath the nail,
I am a wonder: among flowers,
I am a wizard: who but I
Sets the cool head aflame with smoke?

I am a spear: that roars for blood…

*~ From the "Song of Amergin" (eighth-century Ireland)*

# Chapter 8



*Spring, 1942:*

Mack thought of the gasping Model A as a scuttling beetle. It crawled eastward across the city then north on Lake Shore Drive and Sheridan Road, creeping block by block toward Winnetka. He knew he was late. With gasoline in short supply—and talk of rationing in the air—it was a bitch to get anywhere these days. He'd bummed a ride to the Steckel Avenue plant and taken the bus to the eye doctor's office, all to have enough gasoline to nurse his ancient auto to Chez Les Simmons. Sim Simmons, of course, had no trouble acquiring gas for his Cadillac, no doubt an insider's reward for serving on several war-related boards and committees, all very, very important. But would dear old Dad come to him or arrange some more convenient meeting spot, maybe his office on LaSalle Street? Of course not.

The lack of traffic continued to amaze. Not only was gasoline hard to get, but the act of driving had become unpatriotic. The Ford coughed, sputtered, and nearly died as it rolled past the half-finished white wedding cake of the Baha'i Temple. Mack down-shifted and nudged the accelerator. As the Ford's metallic heartbeat grew stronger, he speculated on the outlandishness of a Moorish dome arising on the North Shore. What next? A pagoda at State and Madison to honor our Chinese allies?

Winnetka, he had to admit, still looked comfortingly familiar: The elm trees had leafed out in a happily pre-war fashion. No old-money mansion had been replaced by a war plant or anti-aircraft battery. No barrage balloons in sight above the Lake Michigan whitecaps. He turned into the long driveway lined with poplars, which helped shield the house from passers-by on Sheridan Road. Good thing—the very sight of his rusty old Ford might compel the neighbors to call the cops. Mack smirked as he pulled on the emergency brake and strode between the white columns bracketing the front porch. Mr. Dineen swung the door open before the bell's throaty chimes stopped echoing.

"It's good to see you, sir," Mr. Dineen said, a broad smile spread across his aging-leprechaun's face.

"It's wonderful to see you too." Mack had been afraid Mr. Dineen, who clearly thought of the Simmons family as his own after twenty years of service, might greet him with the disdain of P. G. Wodehouse's Jeeves. Mack stuck out his hand, and the two shook heartily. The old man's hand felt warm and dry, but frail and thinner than he remembered.

"I'll tell your father you've arrived," Mr. Dineen said evenly before disappearing down the middle corridor leading out of the broad entrance hall.

When his father had called to set up—make that "order"—this particular command-performance visit, he complained that the only servants left at the Simmons manse were Mr. Dineen—never called anything else, as if "Mister" were his first name—and Lavinia, the cook, no doubt still in shock at having to take up the duties of the now-departed maid. Flighty young Eloise was joining the WACs—proof, Sim said, they'd take anybody.

This was the latest in a series of command performances. After the getting-suspended-from-Lake-Forest-Academy talk, there had been the discussion of "how did you get arrested on a drunk and disorderly charge?" Mack's explanation for that episode was simple: "Tommy and I started drinking our way across the Loop and didn't want to stop." They were the words, he saw now, of an arrogant "reesh boy." Bailed out of jail by his furious father, Mack recalled staring into the mirror during that get-together, still in the throes of a hangover that made death seem a serious alternative. The blood congealed around his nostrils, and the livid purple shiner both came courtesy of a Chicago cop's angry fist. The cut on his forehead took a dozen stitches to close. He had no idea how he'd gotten it.

Was that early episode part of the story-line that led to joining Tommy on their ridiculous drunken excursion to find Minnie's road house? Had he *really* wanted to die that December night, swim away from his life? A death wish? (Thank you, Dr. Freud.)

Certain his father would keep him waiting from force of habit, Mack wandered over to the row of portraits mounted on the right-hand wall of the entrance hall. Apparently, America's entry into the Great War had ended the portrait fad among the First Families of Winnetka, all the paintings dated from the early years of the century. The hawk-like face of a slender young Sim, just graduated from Yale Law, gazed serenely from behind a wide, empty desk. The brass nameplate on the ornate frame identified him by his official moniker, John Mackenzie Simmons II. As the third to bear the name, Mack wondered if this gave the lie to the old saw about good things coming in threes—or was it bad luck that came in triplicate?

In the next portrait, Uncle Frederick, always called "Stubby" by friends and family, smiled widely, his book-lined study in the background. There seemed to be a rule that the more prominent the family, the sillier the nick-names. Mack returned Uncle Stubby's smile as he thought of Chauncey Something, Something the Fourth back at Lake Forest Academy. Called, of course, Froggie.

Mack glanced at his battered work shoes. They were steel-toed. The Safety Department at the Steckel Avenue plant required everyone working on the shop floor to wear steel-toed shoes at all times. That made sense if you were installing carburetors or manifolds on the massive B-17 rotary engines as they inched past, dangling like steel carcasses from the assembly-line chain. If your job involved sweeping cigarette butts off the floor and cleaning toilets, it seemed less likely that a foot-crushing piece of steel would come hurtling down at you.

His father would no doubt see the heavy, oil-stained shoes, along with his greasy khaki work pants and rumpled denim shirt, as some kind of insult, yet another facet of Mack's rebellion. But he'd had to leave for Winnetka right from work.

"Please follow me, Mr. Simmons."

Mack started at Mr. Dineen's quiet words, which came from directly behind his right ear. The butler turned without waiting for Mack and headed down the corridor to the elder Mr. Simmons's study.

Mr. Dineen left Mack in front of the heavy oak door to the study. As the butler padded down the hall toward the kitchen, Mack wondered if the butler might tip-toe back to listen at the door but rejected the idea as unworthy of a man in Mr. Dineen's position.

Mack tapped twice on the door and gently pushed it open. Bookshelves filled top to bottom with leather-bound law volumes took up the whole wall behind Sim's surprisingly small roll top desk. Pen in hand and his familiar yellow legal pad on his lap, Sim looked up. His expression never changed.

"Hello, Mack," he said in a neutral-sounding tone. He looked Mack up and down twice.

"Hello, Father. How have you been?" Mack replied without acknowledging his father's inspection, though he did register that Sim wore his usual tie and vest.

Sim didn't favor the question with a response. Mack understood the inquiry was completely perfunctory. His health was always perfect. He expected to outlive his great-grandfather Edward, who fought in the War of 1812 before leaving the family's hardscrabble New Hampshire farm to make a fortune in railroads and real estate in booming Chicago, where he died at age 101.

Mack filled the silence before it became too awkward. "Can you solve a mystery and tell me why you asked me to come this morning?" He omitted the phrases "out of the blue" and "for no apparent reason."

"I can understand why you're wondering," Sim replied, in a softer tone Mack didn't expect. "It's too complicated to discuss over the phone. Have a seat, and I'll explain." Sim gestured toward the overstuffed chair by the wall.

Mack tugged the chair across the carpet to face his father's desk at an angle that allowed him to see around the raised roll top. As he sat down, he waited for the familiar exhalation of air from the cushion, a sound identical to a fart that had always sent Mack and his sister Felicia into uncontrollable laughter. The old chair, which served as Mack's perch for most of Sim's lectures, began its leathery fart. Mack grinned then glanced up into his father's angry eyes.

"Yes, your mother is well enough, the same as she was when you last deigned to visit. Thank you so much for asking."

The sudden injection of acid caught Mack off guard. "I would've asked after her if you'd given me the chance. I thought you were about to plunge right into the matter at hand. Whatever the hell it is."

"A gentleman would have naturally asked about his own mother, especially after not seeing her for such a long while."

*I refuse to go for that bait*, thought Mack, who simply said, "I'm glad she's all right." He shifted in the chair and waited.

Sim opened the wooden box on his desk and went through a lengthy sniffing-and- clipping ritual before filling the silent room with Cuban cigar smoke. Mack followed the rising plume as it further obscured the spring sun struggling to shine through the window high on the opposite wall.

Sim exhaled a satisfying stream of smoke. As always, smoking seemed to calm his father down. "Mack, this seems to be the one vice you haven't tried. Aside from Reverend Ogilvy, you're the only man I know who doesn't smoke." The friendly, conversational approach seemed practiced.

"Another failing, I guess," Mack replied in what he hoped was a jaunty tone. "I don't like vices you can practice all the time and not get arrested." He didn't say that all you got from smoking tobacco was the need to smoke more of it. He also didn't mention the reefer Chocolate Slim handed out at work to make the graveyard shift pass more quickly. There was a vice with a proper payoff.

Sim chuckled. "Not get arrested. That's a good one!" Sim balanced the cigar on the edge of a crystal ashtray. "You look well enough. I mean the eye and all. You're still seeing Dr. Bennett?"

"I saw him last week. He said there's no more infection, no need for a pirate's eye patch." That, at least, was a humiliation neither wanted. A surrender, as Mack saw it, to the permanent status of freak.

Sim slid a thumb across his thick white mustache and seamlessly shifted to a more urgent tone, "I have important news, and it's about someone you know." Mack was certain his father had written the words on the legal pad.

*Okay*, thought Mack, *the undercard is over. Here's the main event, Joe Louis versus Max Schmeling.* "And who might that be?"

"Thomas Kilkenny. He died in combat." Mack felt himself choking. He couldn't speak. He understood his father's legendary skill in court—dance around a topic, lull the opposition, then plunge in when least expected.

Mack struggled for breath. His oldest friend, connoisseur of catastrophe, the author in some insane way of his one-eyed condition. Would there really be no more secret laughter? No more inside jokes that drew stares from those outside their magic circle? Forever?

Sim drew again on his cigar. "No one thought such a headstrong young man would last two months in the military, let alone two years." As he spoke, the smoke flowed from his mouth. "Thomas made quite a success in the air corps. It's common knowledge MacArthur picked only the top men for his air wing."

Sim shook his head. It was a gesture Mack knew his father used in laying the groundwork for the main point, marshaling his arguments before both a jury and his wayward son.

Sim waved away the cigar smoke. "But that's water under the bridge. Top men or not, MacArthur's air force has failed just as miserably as the rest of his command."

"Tommy's dead for sure? Not missing or captured, really dead?" Mack squirmed in pain. Weep later—don't cry in front of him. Like a child, he bit his lower lip, hard. Mack's shoulders began to shake. Tears pushed into his right eye—the real one. The empty eye socket seemed to remember weeping and threatened to replace tears with blood. Mack squeezed his hands into fists and kept squeezing until the shaking stopped.

"I know this is difficult, but there's no sugar to make it go down more easily. Take a deep breath, son, so I can go on. What I've got to say is important."

Mack complied, as much to curb his anger as his grief. So Tommy's death *wasn't* important, you horse's ass?

"What happened was quite extraordinary. It was on the island of Mindanao. For once, they were opposing a Jap landing. Thomas was the lead pilot of a flight of B-17s trying to bomb the Japs' landing fleet. The usual disaster occurred. The other planes were shot down almost immediately. Captain Kilkenny's bomber was on fire, several crew members dead. He swung back over land, so the survivors could bail out. God knows what happened to them, probably Jap prisoners and wishing they'd died too."

Sim stopped and shook his head, a gesture Mack recognized as an effort to convey sadness and sympathy.

"Then," Sim continued, "Captain Kilkenny turned back to the Jap fleet, flew through anti-aircraft fire, and crashed his burning plane into the Japanese flagship, a cruiser. The ship was blown to pieces, several others damaged, and the landing stalled, no doubt the strongest blow against the Japs in the whole damnable campaign. Those who witnessed the event, including veteran military men, called Captain Kilkenny's actions the most heroic they had ever seen."

His father's words struck like a hammer, but a small part of Mack's brain started reasoning again. "Wait a minute!" Mack sat upright. "How is it that you know all this? There hasn't been anything in the news."

"Quite true. Stateside, there are perhaps a half-dozen people who know anything about this. One is the president. Now, you're part of the group."

"Well, thank you for telling me. It's about the worst news I've ever heard, but I'm glad to know it." Sure now that he wasn't going begin weeping, Mack began to rise from his chair.

"Please sit. This conversation isn't over."

Mack paused, hunched over halfway between sitting and standing, then eased himself back into the farting chair.

"Where to begin?" Sim muttered, glancing down at the legal pad, appearing to be talking more to himself than to Mack. Then he fixed his bottomless black eyes on Mack again. "The war's going badly—thanks to the censors, much worse than you know. With the Philippines, Malaya, Singapore, and the East Indies, the Japs have built one of the world's great empires in record time. Australia may be next. Despite the defense buildup, our army's still training with wooden rifles and trucks marked 'tank.' There's no way we can lick the Japs anytime soon, let alone the Nazis. My God, their U-boats are sinking our tankers within sight of shore!"

"First you tell me my best friend is dead, and then follow up with a history lecture. I majored in history—remember? I *know* all this."

Sim chomped down on his cigar and returned it to the ashtray. "Of course. I'd forgotten what a well-educated man you are—no doubt your current employer's only janitor with a University of Chicago degree." Mack saw that his father was struggling for control. Even so, he couldn't seem to resist going down that all-too-familiar road.

"Just get on with it, will you? I need to go home and get some sleep." Mack stretched and yawned—with more sound effects than warranted—reflexively provoking his father, a childish camouflage. Why did he have to keep doing that?

"If this weren't so important, I'd throw you out of my house. Now, keep quiet for once and pay attention!"

Eager to end things, Mack grunted a quiet, "Okay."

Sim leaned back in his chair and firmly grasped his right forearm with is left hand, seeming to throttle himself back. "The isolationists didn't simply disappear after Pearl Harbor. They're still all around us, howling for revenge against the Japs like everyone else. But they're still waiting to turn the country into some ridiculous Fortress America if the war goes badly for too long. Why, just the other day, that horse's ass Skipper Blanchard claimed over lunch he's got 'inside information' that Roosevelt and Churchill engineered the attack on Pearl Harbor to get us into the war. Idiocy!"

Sim squeezed his arm harder, and it seemed to soften his tone. "Mack, you've got to understand the country's on a knife edge right now, hungry for any kind of favorable news, something to convince people that we can win this war. Hungry for a hero."

Mack stared blankly at his father enthroned behind the roll top desk.

"That hero can be—must be—Thomas Kilkenny."

A scalding laugh boiled up Mack's throat. "Tommy, a national hero! Jesus, if he weren't dead already, he'd die laughing at the thought!"

"Perhaps," said Sim quietly, "but he has no choice in the matter."

"Well, go ahead then. Fire up the propaganda machine and make him a hero if that's what you and the other Powers That Be want. It's no skin off my nose."

"It's not as simple as that. We have to deal with his family, especially his father. I know you've met him a number of times. He even visited you in the hospital."

"Blarney Bob! I can see him accepting the Congressional Medal of Honor on Tommy's behalf." He couldn't stop thinking about ridiculing the whole situation over beers with Tommy.

"Robert Kilkenny is a loose cannon. There are so many contradictory stories about him, it's hard to know the truth—and believe me, I've tried to find out. If he's just another Chicago Machine politician, we can live with that. Roosevelt and the Mayor are political allies, and we can turn Blarney Bob into a hard-working public servant. Or at worst, a character out of Damon Runyon."

"Damon Runyon is right as far as I know," said Mack, leaning forward in his chair, becoming interested in spite of himself. "Tommy loved to mimic him—'Thomas, me boy, kiss whisky lightly. 'Tis the elixir of embarrassment.' I'd laugh so hard I thought I'd pee in my pants!"

Sim leaned on his elbows, moving ahead. "On the other hand, if the allegations are true that he's not just a machine hack but connected to organized crime—'the Outfit's man in City Hall' and all that—then it's a whole different situation. If he's involved in crimes related to war work, shaking down the unions or trucking companies or some such, it could bring down the whole project. Colonel McCormick and the *Tribune*, the isolationist politicians, would trumpet it to the skies—a golden opportunity to embarrass Roosevelt."

"I suppose I understand. But besides losing the best friend I'll ever have, I don't see what I've got to do with this."

"You have everything to do with it. You must visit the Kilkennys, offer your condolences, and find out the truth about Blarney Bob. You know them all. You and Thomas stayed close to Ellen after the divorce, and you've dated their daughter Janice. We know they have no real allegiance to Blarney Bob. If you ask the right way, they'll tell you what they know, things he said only to them, most likely when soused. But *you* are the only one who can approach them."

Mack felt anger rolling over him, for the moment drowning out his grief. "Goddamn it! You've sent out private detectives, haven't you? Your divorce-court gumshoes! I won't be forced into this."

This time, Sim remained quiet for a few seconds. He leaned back, reaching toward his mustache, but stopping just before his index finger touched it. "Refusal is simply not a possibility, Mack. My people were unable to learn much about Robert Kilkenny's activities, now that we're in the war. I even had them look again into the Schlegel affair. And except for reminding me that the murder and your accident occurred the same night, they couldn't come up with anything beyond what was in the papers. That's suspicious in itself."

"Schlegel! Victor Schlegel was nothing but a crooked ward heeler who got himself killed. The fellow was an Outfit guy from top to bottom, a bag man. There were dozens of people who wanted him dead—that's what the police said, not just the newspapers!" Mack slapped the chair's cloth-covered arm, startled by the tiny dust cloud at the point of impact.

"The man was a crony of Alderman Kilkenny," Sim replied. "Supposedly the fellow charged with preventing him from talking too much in public when he'd been drinking. And the alderman apparently was the last person to see Schlegel alive. For the record, Thomas saw him that day too."

"Victor Schlegel told him about a roadhouse in the suburbs. That's where we were going that night."

Sim drew on his cigar.

"Look," said Mack, voice rising as he conjured up another dust cloud, "I don't care if Blarney Bob whacked Schlegel with Lizzie Borden's axe. I won't get involved in this!"

"In contrast to Robert Kilkenny, it was quite easy to find out what *you* have been doing these days." Sim's voice dropped to just above a whisper, and Mack couldn't help leaning toward him. "For example, I've learned that you and your Negro friends on the janitorial staff are using dangerous, illegal drugs, probably selling them too, at an important defense plant. You will do as I've asked, or I will have you all arrested. Even in your present situation, the courts will be lenient with you. They won't be so gentle with Negroes. The foreman Leopold Belgian, that fellow Benjamin Atkins who's called 'Chocolate Slim'—I can guarantee they'll go to prison for ten years, minimum."

Mack felt his face flashing red and white like a traffic warning. His muscles tightened, wanting to strangle this jaded, presumptuous man who was inexplicably his father. Mack stood and took a step toward the door of the study. Coercion, he thought bitterly, was always his father's fallback position.

Sim relit his cigar. "Two days," he said quietly between puffs. "You have two days to get moving and get back to me with the results. And remember, everything I've told you remains strictly confidential."

Mack found himself behind the wheel of the Ford, though he didn't remember how he'd gotten there. All he wanted was to be left alone. Let the catastrophe of war pass by, a flight of B-17s far overhead, their engine-throb muted by distance.

He knew Sim would pull it off. Loyalty. His father understood the structure of loyalty the way a taxidermist understands the structure of dead animals. Sim's own loyalties were to his family (at least in the abstract), to the law (as long as he won), to his class (though he would never acknowledge belonging to one), and, Mack had to admit, to his imperiled country.

Mack's loyalties were more tangled and obscure, but Mack knew the loyalties he'd taken on were as firm as his father's. Loyalty to the Negro workmates he'd fallen in with and befriended—Sim had hit the mark there. Loyalty to the mystical brother who'd half-blinded him, maybe pushed him to drink too much ("This is one race the Irish always win, my Anglo-Saxon friend!"), and become a goad and life line in his hermit's existence. Tommy dead—dead! A hero.

Forcing back tears, Mack adjusted the choke and coaxed the Model A into reluctant life. He drove slowly home to try to sleep.

☙❧

Once Mack slammed the office door, Sim stared at the glowing tip of the cigar. His anger at his son was a pot always on the boil. He couldn't turn it off, even for such an important conversation. And the miserable, demeaning janitor's job—why couldn't he stay away from bringing it up? Why were he and his son like those chemical elements that explode when mixed? He placed the questions in a compartment of his mind reserved for such upsetting thoughts.

Sim had always liked Thomas Kilkenny. He recalled without rancor that the young man might've become his son-in-law, though an imperfect one on account of his notoriously corrupt father. Sim was saddened by Captain Kilkenny's death—no doubt, an early casualty among thousands, perhaps millions, yet to come. But the circumstances of his death provided a unique opportunity for Sim to bring forth the hero necessary to ultimate victory.

What he couldn't ever say out loud was that Thomas's death offered one last chance to pull in Mack—uniquely connected to the necessary hero—and begin to rebuild the splintered Simmons family, fill in the holes in his life. True enough, he'd almost bungled the opportunity with his son, but, Sim concluded, it still existed. He would then move on to the larger enterprise of re-connecting with Katherine—his wife, a word he rarely used to describe her, even to himself. The grand project was now entering a critical phase. Today, Sim knew that, in spite of his missteps, he had won a key victory on both the public and personal fronts.

# Chapter 9

At Mrs. McLady's rooming house on Austin Boulevard, Mack reached into the top drawer of his battered dresser and unfolded a letter from Tommy—one of the last he'd received. Mack sat on the battered purple couch and riffled through the onionskin pages, numbly running his eye over the familiar, neatly spaced words. Mack once wondered why recipients kept letters—it seemed an outdated practice. Now, Tommy's letters were all Mack had left, a realization creeping over him like the onset of a debilitating disease.

The thin, tightly-packed sheets crackled faintly as he paged through them. Tommy's handwriting flowed along evenly like waves on a pond after you throw in a pebble. Mack's own handwriting was terrible, the stuff of legend. His teachers at Lake Forest Academy joked that he was destined to become a doctor. Tommy claimed to agree with the nuns at St. Thomas the Apostle Parish School: Protestants failed to recognize the beneficial self-discipline required by good penmanship.

"Just look at your chicken scratches," he said. "Most people wouldn't even call it writing at all, compared with my fine Catholic hand." Tommy held up the thick fingers of his Irish potato-digger's hands. "Obviously, you could use some whacks with a wooden ruler from Sister Mary Immaculata—and I don't just mean your handwriting, buster!"

*June 17, 1941*
*Clark Field*
*The Philippines*

*Dear Cyclops:*
*We've settled into the typical boredom of military life, so I have another chance to write—but no typewriter! We've finally gotten all the planes and men of our Air Wing shipped over here. It's been like elephants fucking—a slow, cumbersome job, with lots of possibilities for accidents and damage. We were lucky to get here just before the rainy season. It started a couple of weeks ago, and it's as if God suddenly turned on the spigot—a Chicago thunderstorm that won't end! With all the rain, the jungles and rice paddies show every shade of green you can imagine—maybe Luzon is the real Emerald Isle. (Mention that to Blarney Bob the next time you see him!)*

*Clark Field is in the middle of the Filipino equivalent of Nowhere, forty or so miles from the dirty sprawl of Manila. It's only some hangars and barracks, with a couple more bomber-length runways still being bulldozed. The airfield is the biggest thing going in these parts, and we've got the whorehouses to prove it! The nearest town—called, in an irony you'll appreciate, Angeles—has the biggest red-light district I've ever seen.*

*In case you're wondering if I'm speaking too freely, don't worry. We're officially at peace over here, of course, and that means censorship is nearly nonexistent. A fat, alcoholic major named Willard is the official censor of our mail, but everybody knows he doesn't actually read any of our letters before sealing and posting them. The rumor is that anything not addressed to Tokyo or Berlin goes straight through without a look. (If you hear that I'm in the brig, you'll know this barracks rumor ain't so.)*

*Now that all our crews and bombers are present and accounted for, and at the service of His Majesty Douglas MacArthur, we were honored by a visit from the King Him-*

*self. He sauntered past us with his honor guard of flunkies and yes-men while we stood at attention for two goddamned hours, sweating through our uniforms. (It stopped raining just as he arrived, which must've made MacArthur feel even more certain he's the Lord God Jehovah.)*

*If Joseph Conrad were still writing, he could do a lot with what's happening over here—especially us bearers of the White Man's Burden, with all our heavy weapons and self-destructive politics, lording it over a bunch of brown-skinned folks we're convinced are inferior. The Filipinos are hard to figure out. They smile and nod a lot, and they appear loyal to the good old USA, but the old hands here remember how tough they were back in the Philippine Insurrection days. The women are beautiful, like perfect little dolls. It's all sort of an updated version of* Lord Jim, *with overtones of* Heart of Darkness.

*It's your fault I'm thinking like this, Cyclops, in particular, your talk of becoming buddies with your Negro colleagues (in your honor, I'll use the polite words) at the Steckel Avenue plant. But if you develop a taste for watermelon and chitlin's, I'll start worrying! Have you not considered the oddity or "historical congruence"—whatever the hell we'd call it at the UofC—that your plant builds the engines for the planes we're flying?*

*Flying is the only interesting thing I'm doing these days—a lot of flight exercises, practice bombing runs and such. Other than that, maybe because we're stranded here on the other side of the world, the boredom is even worse than back in California. It's like a tropical disease that saps your strength and brings out whatever madness you have hidden inside. It's worst for the fellows who are married or have fiancées or steady girlfriends. Men will literally stare, hypnotized, at a woman's photo for hours at a time.*

*One day, I was on Field Street, the main drag of the red-light district. Women and girls were working the street everywhere, with their little beady-eyed pimps watching them—they all have shivs in their boots, so even the MPs leave the pimps alone. I had finished my own business and was strolling along a back street lined with little wooden or sheet-metal shanties, trying not to step in puddles or pig shit.*

*I heard a loud ruckus around the corner, screams and punches. In the middle of the mess was the bombardier from my crew, a skinny Swedish kid from Duluth named Sorenson. He was whaling away at a girl, no more than fifteen. Things like that happen all the time on Field Street, so a lot of people were watching, but nobody stepped in.*

*I didn't want Sorenson to get knifed, or arrested by the MPs, so I tried to pull him away. I'm much bigger than he is, but it took all my strength. He got in a couple of hard punches to my chest that still show bruises, and the girl was a bloody mess. I pushed her into the arms of an older woman who seemed to know her, shoved a couple of dollars in their direction—a lot of money over here—and told the older woman to take care of her.*

*Sorenson never said a word, but as I walked him down the street to where he could catch a ride back to Clark Field, I looked past the blood, dirt, and tears into his eyes— they're the same vacant shade of blue as your Cyclopean one! I knew the girl didn't deserve the beating, but I could see in Sorenson's eyes that it wasn't all his fault either. It was a crime, not of passion, but of longing. He attacked the girl in a fury, not because he hated her or because she'd tried to rob him or anything, but only because she wasn't his girl back in Duluth.*

*Her name is Helen. At Sorenson's insistence, we named our bomber after her—"Hellacious Helen"—and I had our navigator Jack Smithfield paint a big busty blonde on the side of the plane. Sorenson knew for a dead certainty that he might never see her again in the flesh, or that Helen might leave him for some other fellow before he gets home, if he ever does. It was eating him alive.*

*Thank God, I'm free of all that. You've heard me solemnly swear off marriage, or anything close to it. Maybe it's because of the way my folks' Holy Union came apart. Blarney Bob Kilkenny and the eldest daughter of the Long Island Boswells—the most mismatched pairing since Rasputin shagged the Czarina.*

*I want to see blood on your next letter. An oath signed in blood that you'll never enter—to quote the Father of Our Country—an "entangling alliance" with a woman (even my sister!), and that you'll have me shot if I ever violate my oath again. So help you God, buddy.*

*Brothers to the end...*

*Tommy*


Mack folded the letter and put it back in the drawer next to his last pair of clean socks, allowing his friend's voice to wash over him. Every time he read the letter, an automatic pang reverberated in his heart at the mention of Janice, however backhanded. This time, the pain was stronger, almost nauseating, as he thought of facing Janice and her mother, pulling them in the hero project.

He thought of Sorenson too. Had he died in the anti-aircraft barrage, forever cured of his fevered love for Helen from Duluth? Or had Tommy's flying skills allowed the bombardier to bail out and survive? If so, Sorenson's frantic devotion would serve as either torture beyond even his captors' imagination or an iron defense against their cruelty.

Had some horny Jap gunner caught sight of Hellacious Helen on the side of Tommy's B-17? Mack imagined bare legs, tight bathing suit, and huge painted tits, all headed straight at him. Had the gunner become distracted, his aim thrown off just enough to allow Tommy to complete his suicide mission?

Tommy had to know that's what it was. Was he wounded? Most likely—burned maybe, but not blinded. (He always seemed to have luck in that department.) To blow the Jap cruiser to smithereens, he must've been able to aim his burning plane right at the ship's ammo magazine. Or maybe the bombs stacked in the plane's belly like bottles in a vending machine had done the job by themselves. Maybe Tommy was already dead when the impact came. Just a lucky hit. If "lucky" was the right word.

Now, Tommy was about to embark on the next leg of that last flight—not as a pilot but as an elite, though deceased, passenger on Hero Airlines. Where did that leave Mack? Part of the ground crew maybe. It was a role he might have volunteered for if his father had granted him breathing space to decide for himself. Instead, he had peremptorily coerced him, drafted him, into the job.

His father was like the racetrack fixer Blarney Bob once tipsily described to him and Tommy. "We called the fella Old Belt-and-Suspenders, a man who left nothing to the idle whims of chance. He drugged the other horses then bribed the jockeys as well!"

# Chapter 10

Sleep had been hard to come by, but at least the brief spaces of unconsciousness hadn't been interrupted by dreams. Driving to work by rote along North Avenue, Mack, though technically awake, dreamed himself back to the Bijou movie theater when he was twelve.

He and three childhood friends from Winnetka had gone to the Saturday matinee—a cowboy movie, cartoons, and a newsreel, all for twenty cents. Jazzed on soft drinks and candy, they were noisy and pushy to begin with. When the Western included too many love scenes and not enough riding and shooting, the boys made smooching noises and threw popcorn at the screen. A flashlight-toting usher found his way to their row. He waved his bouncing beam along the line of blinking kids, illuminating trampled kernels of popcorn and a congealed oil slick of spilled Coca Cola.

The usher, scarcely older than the boys themselves, said in a harsh whisper, "All right, that's enough. Get out!" Mack's three fellow troublemakers, all good Winnetka kids, obediently left the theater. Seated four seats in from the aisle, Mack sat still for a second. Then, he decided to hold his ground, try to look pleased the disruptive element was gone. The rest of the movie, Mack happily discovered, included as much cowboy action as anyone could want.

The fury of his friends amazed him. How could he stay when they had to leave? They'd all been doing the same things—Mack was, if anything, louder and had thrown more popcorn than the others—yet *they* had to suffer, while he got off Scot-free. It was fate, Mack said, using the word for the first time. Nobody said anything when he led the way in and wound up in the fourth seat. No one fingered him when the usher convinced himself he'd gotten rid of all the troublemakers. Which was true—Mack hadn't made a sound during the rest of the movie. Obviously, the usher was an instrument of fate—acting on a tiny stage, but a minister of fate nonetheless.

Fate, he decided now, was an empty word, a way of pretending to explain something unexplainable. Fate could fall on you from the sky, completely unavoidable. Mack tried to convince himself the accident was like that. Not a Freudian death wish, but a riff on the canard, "character is fate." According to this reading, being Mack Simmons, he couldn't have decided *not* to stop by Chester's that night and quietly stayed home to read de Tocqueville. Nor could his father have failed to imitate Old Belt-and-Suspenders and drag him into the hero business.

On the other hand, maybe you could create random bits of your so-called fate by exploiting pure, usher-dodging luck. Tommy could have bailed out with his crew, but he *chose* not to, right? Or was Tommy acting out his own character, some innate sense of invulnerability?

Had Tommy been acting that out the night of the accident too? There was a twist of fate for you. Uninjured Tommy enlists and gets himself killed in heroic fashion. Poor Mack, that self-pitying freak, is labeled 4F. A fair trade? No military service for the one-eyed guy, no chance for heroism, assuming he ever wanted to be a hero. What if Tommy had been injured in the rolling Buick and *he* had been thrown clear?

War was nothing but a vast agglomeration of supposedly fateful chances leading to more unanswerable questions, fate kicked in the ass and sprinting full speed ahead. Bend over at the right instant—the bullet misses. Stand up, you're dead. Do I steer the plane infinitesimally to the left? A bit of shrapnel rips through the fuel line, and the aircraft vanishes into a ball of flame—no survivors, not even any remains to bury. Stay on course, and the line is only nicked, leading to a small fire and a still-flyable B-17. The door suddenly opens for an act of heroism, impromptu or not.

Accidents cause heroes. Heroes cause accidents.

Mack turned automatically and found his way in the dark to the plant parking lot. Steckel Avenue was one of the first defense plants built during the reluctant pre-Pearl Harbor buildup. That pre-war date meant a big parking lot. With loyal Americans now urged to car-pool, something Mack had so far avoided, a parking spot was always available. As usual, he was barely on time. Mack parked as close as possible to the nearest employee entrance and headed for the door at a trot.

Next to a light standard, dark now, either as an electricity-saving measure or simply because the sleepwalking Maintenance Department hadn't gotten around to replacing the bulb, he collided with a man standing in the shadows. He was almost exactly Mack's height, made slightly taller by a battered fedora tipped back from his forehead. The collision caused both men to lean forward inadvertently, and they almost butted heads. The fedora dropped to the sidewalk. The guy, a skinny son of a gun, shook himself like a wet dog and continued bending over awkwardly to scoop up his hat. He straightened up slowly, in stages almost. Facing one another, he and Mack muttered half-heard apologies.

Mack hurried on, leaving the guy standing like a gaunt statue next to the lightless light pole. At this time of night, people were hurrying in or out of the various plant entrances, not hanging around the parking lot. Luckily, no other employees were ahead of him, fumbling with their time cards. He punched in exactly one minute before the eleven o'clock start of the shift.

His first task was sweeping up in Parts Fabrication. The metal-bangers didn't have a graveyard shift because they built up a parts backlog large enough to feed the Engine Assembly operation through the late-night shift. In the spartan Engineering Building across the parking lot, an efficiency expert wielding a stopwatch and clipboard was surely figuring out how to speed up the production line so they could start a graveyard operation in Parts Fabrication too. Production Will Win the War—that's what the banner over the main entrance to the plant said, the motto placed above a crude cartoon of a Flying Fortress dropping its bombs one by one.

As Mack pushed his wide broom past the silent, half-lit rows of lathes, drills, and punch-presses, a more detailed picture of the man he had run into came into focus, a photograph in developing solution. A sunken, haggard face, as deeply lined as Abe Lincoln's. A worn, ill-fitting jacket, too short at the wrists, a perfect match for the ratty fedora. A guy you'd see in a soup line or, these days, applying at the Steckel Avenue employment office.

He was someone Mack had seen before. Where? At his father's office downtown, maybe a year ago. The man had been leaving as Mack arrived for a typically uncomfortable lunch with Sim, who'd mentioned in passing that he had just hired a "private operative" to shadow an unfortunate husband. The fellow's wife, represented by Simmons, Burgoyne, and Altfelder, was about to sue him for divorce. Maybe the skinny operative wasn't a snarling, leather-coated Gestapo agent from the movies, but he was a spy, nonetheless, one Sim had surely directed to watch his wayward son and his reprehensible, drug-dealing work mates. Did staying faithful to Tommy's memory require submitting to his father's all-seeing eye?

Mack pushed the gritty, orange-red sweeping compound, thickly leavened with butts and gum wrappers (no condoms so far tonight) into a wide-mouthed dustpan and emptied it into the rubbish bin next to the Parts Fabrication shipping bay. A pair of overall-clad workers strolled past, a fat guy in his fifties and a girl in a red bandanna who couldn't have been more than seventeen, returning to the assembly line after a bathroom or smoke break. The fat man turned to the girl. He pronounced two words Mack had come to recognize: "White nigger."

Mack had gotten used to the blank, empty looks when he rolled his squeaking janitor's cart past teams of machinists drilling out carburetors or de-burring manifolds. Their eyes said, "I'm looking through you as if you were a pane of glass or the oil-smelling air itself." For Mack, though, the bored stares gave way to shaking heads and muttered slurs. "My God, you're a white man, an ofay janitor! An albino darky, maybe? Nope, a genuine white janitor." Hard, squinting eyes asked: What are you doing, pushing brooms with a bunch of chitlin'-eating jigaboo night fighters? Why the hell aren't you in the army, like a standup American white man?

Mack didn't recognize either of the line workers. Were they part of his father's spy network too? He chuckled at his snowballing suspicions. The Steckel Avenue plant was hiring dozens of new employees every week. Maybe it was all part of his father's master plan. Victory through paranoia? An even better question—could he ever turn off the Question Machine?

To while away the hours of the graveyard shift, Mack mentally composed letters to Tommy. In the weeks before the meeting with his father, Mack attempted to get across his half-invisibility as the sole Caucasian janitor. Tommy's response was a reference to Amos and Andy on the radio, another case, he wrote, of white men pretending to be Negroes. Mack wasn't surprised. Before Steckel Avenue, their only contacts with blacks had been the usual Pullman porters, waiters, and bellhops backed up by Aunt Jemima and Scarlett O'Hara's Mammy.

The break-time bell sounded. Janitors gathered from across the plant to meet at the informal coffee stand by the loading dock in Shipping. Mack dropped a nickel in the cigar box on the chipped tabletop and poured himself a paper cup of strong black coffee. A half-dozen janitors sat on folding chairs, drinking coffee, smoking cigarettes, gazing at the empty loading dock. Mack blew on his coffee and pulled up a chair next to Leopold Belgian. "…and that's when we had to pull up stakes right quick and leave Ophelia, the day my daddy marched up to the courthouse to register to vote. The year nineteen-and-nineteen it was, Daddy in his doughboy's uniform after gettin' gassed in France. And those redneck bastards beat the hell out of him!"

Mack had heard this story before. Ophelia wasn't a woman but a town. Depending on Leopold's mood, the little Louisiana burg was either Paradise on the Mississippi or a sweltering corner of Hell. Leopold had left the place as a kid to move, or flee, as this particular telling had it, to New Orleans. The foreman slid into his story as Mack sat down, though he made it sound as if Mack had arrived in the midst of the tale.

Leopold swirled his tan coffee-with-cream. It was the same color he was. "See, Reesh-boy, that's what I'm tellin' you," he rumbled as if Mack had been sitting there all along. "That's why I'm pullin' for the Japs now that they've declared war on white folks—and are kickin' your skinny butts around the block, if you got brains enough to see through the bullshit and figure out what the papers is really sayin'. 'Strategic retreats,' my ass!"

The coffee cup looked lost in Leopold's big hand. Heavy-lidded, with a shaved head and protruding belly, he resembled a statue of Buddha. Leopold was the biggest man Mack had ever known, bigger than Stevie Wolek, nicknamed "Moose," the heaviest lineman he'd played next to on the University of Chicago Maroons.

"Amen, brother," said Chocolate Slim, as he pinched the end of the marijuana cigarette he'd just rolled. A couple of the other janitors nodded and muttered. The rest remained silent.

Mack glanced around the half-lit shipping dock, hoping his father's operative hadn't hidden among the piles of wooden planks that surrounded them. When the shipping department was going strong, an army of carpenters banged out crates to ship Steckel Avenue's engines to the aircraft assembly plants in Michigan and California. The loading dock included a siding for the railroad flatcars that transported them. The place was silent now.

"I know you don't really mean that," said Mack for the ump-teenth time, knowing Leopold was goading him. "The Japs may not be white, but they're fighting alongside the Nazis, the same guys that said Joe Louis is 'inferior' because he's not part of their goddamned Master Race. The Japs've already slaughtered thousands of women and kids in China—" Chocolate Slim lit his smoke and inhaled deeply. "—and they'd surely kill *all* of us, whites and Negroes, if they had the chance!"

Leopold clapped his thick hands together in slow applause. "That's good, Reesh-boy! You almost had me believin' you." Two or three other janitors clapped too, though their smiles took the edge off. The "reesh-boy" moniker Leopold bestowed on him included, of course, a recognition that Mack could always return to the cocoon of a wealthy family. But to Mack's grateful surprise, his workmates never brought it up.

When the janitors first started with this talk of wanting the Japs to win the war, Mack was horrified that anyone could believe such a thing. He seriously told them victory by the Japs and the Nazis, who were probably even worse, would lead to a new Dark Age. Mack had gotten pretty far into the Churchillian history lesson before he understood they were pulling his leg. Letting him know they weren't a bunch of dumb Steppan Fetchits.

That was, he realized, what he wanted to convey to Tommy—that Negroes put on one face for their white "superiors" and an entirely different one among themselves and the occasional ofay workmate. He'd never quite got it right, never sent the letter. Leave it to a UofC graduate to close the connection with his closest friend with an unsent letter.

The harsh metallic bell rang again, ending break time. Mack headed back to work. As he passed, Chocolate Slim held out the burning cigarette, called a "spliff," Mack had learned. Mack hesitated taking it long enough for Slim to look up at him with a slightly puzzled expression on his mahogany-colored face. What the hell? His father already knew they were sharing spliffs, though he'd never comprehend the odd Jamaican word. The supposedly pro-Jap sentiments presented a bigger potential problem. But he couldn't imagine Sim's keyhole-peeper hiding close enough to hear them. Mack grabbed the marijuana cigarette and inhaled greedily, holding the smoke in his lungs as long as he could, as Leopold and Slim had taught him. Then he did it again.

The pleasant buzz was more subtle than drinking booze. It made lavatory duty, which took up the remainder of the shift, slightly more bearable, along with making his three a.m. cheese-sandwich breakfast…or was it dinner?…taste better than it had any right to.

Driving home half-blinded by a cloudless sunrise, Mack, clear-headed now, tried to sort things out, overcome his numbing grief. The nameless Abe Lincoln look-alike was surely sent by his father, following through on his hero plan, grabbing the loose reins of fate and random catastrophe for his own purposes.

At Mrs. McLady's, Mack kept a close watch on the wall telephone in the upstairs hallway. When the coast was clear, and knowing Sim hadn't left yet to catch his morning train downtown, Mack called his father at home.

Mr. Dineen answered on the second ring and put Sim on the line five seconds later. "When are you meeting with the Kilkennys?" Sim asked with no greeting or introduction.

"I haven't set it up yet," Mack replied angrily. "But I did, quite literally, run into someone you know, a long, lanky galoot. I saw him once at your office, and I'd bet the rent money you sent him to spy on us at Steckel Avenue."

The chuckle at the other end of the line set Mack's teeth grinding. "I didn't send him just to keep an eye on you. I told him to make sure you saw him doing it. I guess he wasn't very subtle. And the fellow's name is Graves! He looks like an undertaker, and he's called Graves!" Sim chuckled again.

Vasili, the scrawny Greek who lived down the hall, opened his door and saw Mack on the phone. He pulled his head and wattled neck back inside, a sluggish turtle retreating into its shell. The sight took the edge off Mack's anger.

"I guess I've got no choice but to visit the Kilkennys and try to get the inside dope for your hero campaign. Tommy deserves the honor, though I still can't believe he'd go along with it if he were here."

Sim interrupted, not chuckling now. "So stop delaying. Go see Ellen and Blarney Bob. We must move ahead on this."

"But I can't just barge in on them and start nosing around. They must be devastated—and in mourning. They've lost their only son. Janice has lost her brother."

The prolonged silence on the other end surprised Mack. Was his father actually paying attention to what he was saying? He tried to recall the last time *that* had happened.

Sim's voice, slightly subdued now, came back on the line. "Our last meeting ended so hastily, I didn't mention it to you…"

"Mention what?"

"I told you only a very few people are aware of Thomas Kilkenny's death and the circumstances surrounding it." He let out a little cough. "The members of the Kilkenny family are not among them."

The terrible truth and his father's voice registered at the same moment.

"*You* must inform the Kilkennys of their son's death."

# Chapter 11

Following his shift the next morning, Mack drove along North Avenue, his brain spinning. What could he possibly say to Tommy's family? How, when, and where to say it? The turn onto Austin Boulevard toward Mrs. McLady's came and went. Mack continued on across the city to Lake Shore Drive.

Marveling at the thin streams of auto traffic as the Loop's business day got underway, he was drawn south past Kenwood and into Hyde Park. Maybe he should individually inform each member of the Kilkenny clan of Tommy's death, arrange face-to-face meetings with Janice, Ellen, and Blarney Bob. That way, he could use a different pitch, spiel, line of gab with each one.

The brick mansions and grimy courtyard buildings of Hyde Park showed their age like Hollywood actresses sliding past their prime. At Promontory Point, the shifting color wheel of Lake Michigan had landed on emerald green with dollops of white foam. A blustering wind whooshed in from the east, pulling the temperature close to freezing, cold even for a Chicago spring. Steering like a robot pilot, Mack rolled past the green swath of the Midway and on to South Shore, domain of Blarney Bob.

Mack came to a stop across 75th Street from the Kilkenny house. It was a quiet street, not far from the toney South Shore Country Club and lined with comfortable brick homes surrounded by broad lawns, Winnetka for the Irish and the Jews. The grass was a reluctant pale green. The shoots apparently didn't want to venture into such an uncertain spring. Even as he pulled on the emergency break, Mack saw the folly of trying to talk to the Kilkennys individually, whatever creative BS he came up with. Surely, whoever he spoke with first would feel duty-bound to inform the others: you couldn't extract a vow of secrecy for something like this.

What had drawn him to the house? Tommy, of course, though he'd never return to this place. One of their UofC profs once quoted Sophocles—lines from a play full of dead warriors and weeping women—on how the demands of the dead become stronger than the needs of the living. Absence, at least when it's terminal, trumps presence.

A rusted-out truck, its bed surrounded by rough wooden slats, rattled into the Kilkenny driveway. A skinny young Negro in denim overalls and an unbuttoned plaid shirt climbed out and went to the front door. A few seconds later, a bald, heavy-set man in a black woolen sweater emerged from the house. Dominic O'Nore—Blarney Bob's bodyguard, or butler or handyman or whatever you called his jack-of-all-trades position. He spoke briefly to the young man, more words than Mack had ever heard from him. Dominic lifted open the garage door then returned to the house. Inside the garage stood a shiny black Cadillac, the replacement for the Buick Tommy had so memorably demolished.

A couple of cars passed by as the man from the truck methodically raked the front lawn, scooping dead grass and leaves into a cracked bushel basket. He bent up and down from the waist like a pump handle.

With no one paying Mack the slightest attention, he stared at the house and wondered if he would ever set foot inside again.

He pictured each room. The leather chairs and stone fireplace of the living room gave it the look of an old-fashioned men's club. He and Tommy had killed off many bottles of Blarney Bob's Irish whiskey there.

The second-floor window above the front door marked Janice's bedroom, full of lace curtains, satin sheets, and frilly pillows. When he and Janice made energetic love there, Mack imagined the room as part of a high-class bordello, in New Orleans, maybe. After the accident, he and Janice had attempted to re-unite on the canopied bed, but their hearts weren't in it. He said, inaccurately: Don't worry, the glass eye won't come out. She said: You lost your eye, buddy, nothing lower down.

As for the house's owner, until Mack saw the old photos, he'd viewed Robert Kilkenny as, well, "Blarney Bob," the bloated, red-faced cartoon politician the *Tribune* so relentlessly lampooned. Mack couldn't imagine him ever being different, a first impression extended back in time. Ironically, the photos sat on a shelf in Ellen Kilkenny's Astor Place duplex. All taken the same day, the framed pictures showed a slender, smiling young man in a tweed suit and dark tie, jet-black hair, a bit wavier than Tommy's, slicked back from the forehead. Young Robert stood with a foot on the running board of a fancy car—a Duisenberg perhaps, though the front end wasn't visible in the photo. The young man's long arm looped around a beaming, fur-clad Ellen Boswell. He appeared in a full-on portrait that showed off his engaging smile and full lips, again, not quite a carbon copy of Tommy, but close.

Ellen had come up behind him as Mack stared at the photos. "He was a dream in those days, wasn't he?" she said in a husky voice. "The handsomest man on the South Side—that's what they called him. Even Ginger Callahan said so, and he was always so jealous of Robert."

Mack chuckled as he recalled trying to cover his shock with a cough that turned into a hacking fit when he swallowed the wrong way. By sheer force of his legendary charm and the gift of gab that added "blarney" to his name, Robert Kilkenny, just off the boat from Dublin, personally salvaged the reputation of Ginger Callahan, the "bootlegger alderman" often seen, and photographed, with the likes of Dion O'Banion and Al Capone. Callahan eased into an early retirement in '27. His other options were said to be an extended trip to Stateville Prison or a more extended stay at Queen of Heaven Cemetery, courtesy of an Outfit machine gun. Young Mr. Kilkenny, already married to socialite Ellen Boswell in a legendary runaway match and the father of two beautiful children, was the natural choice to succeed him.

The door of the house swung open again. A tall, stooped figure peg-legged across the lawn, leaning heavily on a thick black cane. Like Babe Ruth late in his career, the barrel-shaped stomach seemed too large for the thin legs. It had become a cliché to note how much damage Irish whiskey, long lunches at the Bismarck Hotel, and fifteen years' service on the Chicago City Council had done to Robert Kilkenny. He put an arm on the Negro gardener's shoulder and shook his hand. Mack was too far away to read his lips, but he'd heard the script before: Where do you live? Oh, ho, that's Alderman Whosis' ward! Tell him—and your ward committeeman and your precinct captain—I said hello and give them all my kindest regards. Tell the alderman to stop by my office. We'll share a bit of the hair of the dog. If Blarney Bob Kilkenny followed any consistent, lifelong rule, it had to be: never stop campaigning.

Would he still be so glib after he learned of Tommy's death? No, Mack corrected himself, after *I tell him* of his son's death. Bob limped back to the house. The yard man stood still as a skinny African statue. His elongated shadow stretched across the lawn to the edge of the driveway.

*Where is Tommy?* That would likely be Blarney Bob's first question. Bob claimed he'd attended more wakes, funeral masses, and graveside services than anyone not in the burying business. He'd surely want the full-Irish treatment for Tommy.

Bob had once shown the boys a drawer in his desk full of nothing but Mass cards, some yellowed, others recently collected. Even if they hate my guts like Satan, Blarney Bob told them, the wives and kiddies are always glad to see me. "Alderman Kilkenny, could ya put in a good word for us down at City Hall," he'd said in a mocking falsetto. "Now that the Mister's gone, Paulie needs a job the worst way."

Tommy was gone too, but where *exactly*? In simple physical terms, he was "missing" in the most profound sense, nothing but ashes mixed up with the sooty fragments of the Jap sailors from the cruiser, all drifting down together, black snow dissolving in the tropical waters of the Philippine Sea. The ultimate peace of entropy: dust thou art to dust returneth.

*Maybe that's really why I'm here*, Mack thought. *Not so different from Blarney Bob at all, seeking an earthly spot to pay last respects, to remember the hallowed dead.*

At a more abstract level—as Mack started the car, he chided himself on his typical UofC thinking—in the abstract, Tommy, formally buried or not, was about to create a bigger stir than he ever had when he was corporeally alive. Many more people would know his name and dwell upon his deeds than had ever known him in life. Like Crispus Attucks, the Negro man shot down in the Boston Massacre, or Nathan Hale, the unlucky spy who famously regretted he had "only one life to lose for my country."

Why stop there? Tommy was a fallen warrior. Like the heroes of *The Iliad*, his death occurred in public, in front of his admiring fellow soldiers. Mack's own role in this epic was like Cassandra's. The difference was, she foretold events to come, and no one believed her. He was doomed to describe what had already happened, events nobody wanted to accept. Mack pictured himself in some flowing, stage-director's vision of Cassandra's costume. He laughed until his ribs ached as he retraced the route back to Lake Shore Drive.

❧❦❧

Dominic O'Nore grinned when the yard man glanced up and spotted him looking from the window. He bent to his task with a will. Dominic's grin widened. The yard man was the last trace of Victor Schlegel. The blackbird was connected to a numbers runner who'd been on Schlegel's payroll. When the morning's work was done, Dominic would quietly slip the skinny fellow an extra twenty and order him, in compelling fashion, not to ever come back. Blarney Bob would be none the wiser.

More than two years on, the thought of Victor Schlegel still stood up the hairs on the back of Dominic's neck, even on a quiet morning troubled by nothing more pressing than watching from the front window to make sure the bloody black fellow stuck to his rake.

Dominic's eyes came to rest on a rusted wreck of a car parked across the street. A friend waiting for the yard man? A relative who wanted to borrow the blackbird's truck? Dominic, who'd acquired a certain pride of place, tut-tutted that neither vehicle belonged in South Shore. The old jalopy stirred a faint recollection, reminding him of the wheezing auto young Thomas's bosom companion—what was his name again?—had stopped 'round in. Stopped 'round to see young Janice as well, he remembered, though he still couldn't bring to mind the fellow's name. Across the deserted street, the Ford jalopy pulled away.

# Chapter 12

Practice. The word was cruel, but Mack couldn't get it out of his head. After visiting South Shore, he knew it was impossible to simply ring the doorbell and stroll in with the news that would send the Kilkennys' lives swerving in a new and hated direction. Before approaching the Kilkenny family, he had to practice, tell someone else first. It had to be someone who'd cared about Tommy.

That could only be Felicia.

He didn't need to make an appointment to see his sister. These days, she rarely went anywhere, staying in the carriage house with their mother, pretending that their father lived somewhere in darkest Africa or the Australian Outback instead of a few steps away in the main house.

Parking in the wide alley behind the Simmons home was illegal, but the law was never enforced by Winnetka's lackluster police force. The Ford's engine sputtered to a halt, and Mack climbed out. He tapped the brass knocker against the heavy oak door opening onto the alley. The coach house now had its own mailbox. The nameplate read "Mrs. Katherine Simmons," as if his mother were a widow or divorcee. It must've been Felicia's idea. Their mother would never have posted such insulting words on her own.

It was during his first semester at Lake Forest Academy, early in grammar school, when Mack came to realize his classmates' parents didn't live in separate houses. The first words he remembered hearing about his mother were "sickly" and "that poor invalid." They became as much a part of his sense of her as the word "mother" itself. Once he understood that his parents' relationship was different from those of his friends' mothers and fathers—mostly living together, a few divorced and apart—he learned that Katherine was "frail." Her "blood was thin." She had a "nervous disorder." She appeared at the children's birthday celebrations, or at Thanksgiving or Christmas dinner, nodded, and smiled, dutifully praised the cake or the turkey or the decorations, patted the children on the head, then tottered back to the coach house on the arm of one of the maids.

Hearing nothing from inside, Mack clicked the knocker two more times. The door swung open at the second click. Felicia was tall, like their mother. She wore a white skirt and a red, short-sleeved blouse, too summery for a chill Chicago spring. The wind the door let in swirled the skirt around Felicia's slender legs. It was easy to see Sim's high cheekbones and jutting chin beneath her strawberries-and-cream complexion.

"Mack, it's you," she said in an unsurprised tone, her voice already furred from years of smoking. A cigarette, no doubt a Lucky Strike, the brand she'd smoked since high school, burned in her right hand.

"You're right, it is," he replied in a neutral tone that mocked hers. She didn't get his joke. Brother and sister hugged in the hesitant, perfunctory way of the Simmons clan, Felicia raising the cigarette above her head to keep from burning him. She stepped aside and ushered him into the snug living room.

"Mother's in her room, of course," Felicia said. "I'll get her. She'll certainly want to see her long-lost boy. And maybe we'll even discover why you're here." She took a final puff of her Lucky, stubbed it out in the overflowing ceramic ashtray on the coffee table, and headed upstairs.

Mack sat down in the easy chair by the fireplace. Did he want their mother present when he told Felicia his news?

Let fate decide, he concluded, feeling his unintended little smile.

The mantelpiece was empty except for one family photo in the center, a head-and-shoulders shot of the four of them sitting in a row. Katherine must have insisted on keeping it. The framed picture was too far away to see clearly, but Mack didn't need to. It'd been taken at Christmastime in 1930, just before "Depression" came to define the period, even for the Simmons family. Sim, his hair several shades darker, sat on the left, black eyes intent, mustache bristling. Katherine smiled benignly into the studio photographer's camera, seeming to know a secret none of the others were in on. Her blonde hair cascaded down to her shoulders. Dressed in a black tie and a tweed jacket with an itch he could still feel, Mack glared at the photographer, thin lips barely curled into a tiny smile. Pig-tailed Felicia, age ten, showed all her front teeth in an un-self-conscious grin.

Younger by three years, Felicia hadn't been as good a student as Mack. After her required debutante ball, which she tried to escape even as the servants pulled on her gown, Felicia plunged into sorority life at Northwestern. She thrived for a while.

After an October football game, Mack had brought home a certain halfback from the University of Chicago Maroons, one Thomas Aloysius Kilkenny. If it wasn't quite love at first sight, it was surely love after a few long looks. During his and Tommy's senior year at the UofC, which was Felicia's party-filled freshman year at Northwestern, the two became inseparable. With Tommy as her date, Felicia was soon the envy of the North Shore sorority set. The two disappeared for long walks along the lakefront and quiet dinners at the Drake Hotel. Sim commented that he saw more of Thomas Kilkenny than Mack. Talk of marriage was in the air.

Mack was seriously dating Janice Kilkenny by then. Tommy commented—mockingly, of course—that not one, but two Simmons-Kilkenny weddings would be the events of the Chicago social season. He'd noted that a Winnetka connection would help remove the Kilkenny stain from the Boswell name, while Blarney Bob could provide the firm of Simmons, Burgoyne, and Altfelder with a useful "in" at City Hall. It all seemed incestuous to Mack, well into incoherent rebellion against his family, his station in life, his future, and God knows what else. But then, after Tommy spent spring vacation at his family's place in Palm Beach— actually his mother Ellen's family's place—he inexplicably stopped seeing Felicia.

All Tommy would say by way of explanation was to quote George Washington's famous line about avoiding "entangling alliances." Admittedly, Mack didn't probe very hard. He only played the pedant and informed Tommy that it was Jefferson, not Washington, who coined the phrase, although, he said archly, "many ignorant members of the general public mistakenly attribute the term to President Washington."

After she was dropped by Tommy, some gravitational force gradually pulled Felicia toward home. Following graduation, taking care of their mother became her full-time career, with additional time allotted to blaming Sim for her mother's mysterious malady. Whatever Katherine's condition was, its symptoms swung between exhaustion and a grotesquely child-like dependence.

Katherine appeared in the living room on Felicia's arm. As usual, she looked nothing at all like a reclusive invalid. Her wide-shouldered navy-blue suit would've done Joan Crawford proud, and she even sported a fancy feathered hat—every inch a North Shore lady off to her bridge club or a Red Cross fundraiser. But of course, she wasn't going anywhere. The words echoed in Mack's mind as he hugged his mother, her cool forehead pressing against his neck.

"It's good to see you, Mum," he said softly in her ear. "It really is."

Katherine stepped back and looked him in the face, her pale blue eyes coming into focus. "My own Mack—it's really you!" She gently touched his cheek below the ocular prosthesis. "One can hardly tell which eye it is. We were so fortunate to get you one of the very best ones. It was just before this terrible war made them impossible to obtain." She didn't add "to obtain from Germany." Tommy delighted in pointing out that his German-made ocular prosthesis gave Mack a decidedly Teutonic, maybe even Hitlerian look.

Felicia sat on the couch, and Katherine followed suit. Mack returned to the easy chair opposite them. Felicia shook out another Lucky from the dark green pack on the table and struck a light from a nearby matchbook. She let out a long stream of smoke from the corner of her mouth and pointed her cigarette at the pack. "This is one of the last green packs they'll make. The green ink is supposed to have some chemical that's vital to the war effort."

"Lucky Strike Green Has Gone to War!" Mack and Felicia quoted the advertising line together. They both chuckled, as Katherine looked on, bewildered.

"You're still working at Steckel Avenue?" asked Felicia. For this Winnetka visit, Mack had time to change from his work clothes into a more respectable dark sweater and slacks, no steel-toed shoes.

"Yes. We're busier than ever, rolling out those bomber engines. It would be even better if the planes could get close enough to Hitler and the Japs to actually bomb them."

Felicia studied the burning end of the Lucky Strike. "Wouldn't it be an interesting coincidence if Captain Kilkenny were flying a bomber with engines made at your plant?"

"Well, I don't know…"

"It's certainly possible. I was thinking about it just the other day. Mother was asking about what Tommy was doing in the war. I reminded her he's flying B-Seventeen bombers for General MacArthur. He's still doing that, isn't he?"

Mack felt the situation spinning out of control. "Can

we have some coffee? I'd really like some coffee. In fact, I'll be glad to make some." He started to stand.

"Oh, no," said Felicia with an overly bright smile. "There's still coffee in the pot. I'll get us all some."

As Felicia bustled off to the little kitchen of the coach house, Mack eyed his mother sitting primly on the couch and cast about for something to say. "You're looking well, Mum" was the best he could do.

"Thank you, Mack," she said quietly. She removed her hat, looked at it with a small look of surprise, and set it on the table next to Felicia's cigarettes. "I am the same as ever. Still frightfully tired. Why, getting up in the morning and putting my clothes on often leaves me so exhausted that I have to go back to bed."

Mack nodded but had nothing to say. Katherine nodded back. "You know how it is."

Mack nodded again as Felicia returned carrying a silver tray with a tall blue pot and assorted coffee paraphernalia. She set the tray on the table with a metallic thump. "I shall 'pour out.' That's what Tommy's dad always said, that crazy Blarney Bob. It means pouring out the tea and milk and such, but with him it was usually Irish whiskey!"

"It sounds like you've been thinking a lot about Tommy lately." The words spilled out by accident.

Felicia cocked an eyebrow. "Maybe so, but it's only because he's the one man I know personally who's actually in the war. Have you heard from him? He'd certainly be more likely to write to you than me—Miss Ancient History." She took a hard drag on her cigarette, the bright orange flare seeming to substitute for angry words.

"No," said Mack in a half whisper, "no letters since last year, before Pearl Harbor." He raised the gilt edge of the delicate cup to his lips and took a long drink of black coffee. At least it was better than the brew at the janitors' coffee stand. "Not much time to write when the Japs are attacking, I suppose."

Felicia nodded noncommittally. Katherine stared and blinked.

*Why the hell not?* Mack cleared his throat. "As a matter of fact, I do have some news about Tommy." He swallowed and felt his Adam's apple bob up and down. "It's not good." Silence filled the room like fog rolling in from the lake. Mack savored it for a few seconds. "Thomas Kilkenny died in combat in the Philippines," he finally said. Somehow it seemed fitting to echo Sim's words and use Tommy's formal moniker. "He died a hero's death, more heroic than any American so far in this war."

Mack put down his cup. "His plane was damaged." He couldn't bring himself to say "on fire." "Tommy got the other crew members out and then went after a Japanese cruiser. He crashed his bomber into it and blew it up. People said it was the bravest act they'd ever seen."

Felicia began to sob softly, something Mack had seen perhaps twice before, once at the death of their beloved collie Honey when Felicia was twelve. "I stopped listening when you said he was dead," she said in a strangled voice. "I don't care how he died. He might as well have been hit by a bus or walked into the propeller of his plane."

Silence descended again. "You men with your wars and heroes. All it means is young men—ones who could've done great things—dead long before their time, killed while they're still boys!" Felicia buried her head in her hands, while Katherine softly stroked her shoulder.

Mack felt himself choking up too, the finality of Tommy's death hitting him hard again, a sucker punch. He cleared his throat. "You're right, Felicia. Of course, you're right. But we can take comfort—we *have to* take comfort— that he died a hero. He could have bailed out with his crew, but he chose to attack that ship, to do his duty and much more. That's important. It's how we must remember him— not just as a brilliant, funny, lovable guy who's gone, but as a man we loved who died a hero. It's all we have left."

Mack hardly knew where the words came from. Was his father controlling his speech, like the man behind the curtain in *The Wizard of Oz*? Was it possible he believed any of what he was saying?

More proof of his father's power.

Felicia was deep into sobbing now. Katherine still rubbed her shoulder, fingers working wrinkles in and out of the thin red silk of her daughter's blouse. Mack rose, dodged around the coffee table, and slid onto the couch next to Felicia. He found himself embracing her, harder than he ever had before. "It's all right, Kitten," he said, using Sim's nickname for her as a toddler. "It's all right. Just cry."

Felicia's sobbing filled the room. Tiny droplets flowed down her palms onto her wrists. Sliding his arms away, Mack knew she was struggling to compose herself and shut off the tears, which he hadn't expected, because the Simmonses did not cry in such circumstances. Felicia unfolded a napkin from the coffee tray, dabbed at her flowing eyes, then less demurely blew her nose. She sniffed back one final sob and reached for another cigarette, the signal Mack was waiting for.

"There's one more thing," he said in a voice notable for its noncommittal tone.

"Oh? And what would that be?" Felicia shook out the flame from her match and fixed now-dry eyes on Mack. Katherine stared at him too.

"I told you he died a hero, the biggest hero the country has. And we need heroes right now, with the war not going well." The time for beating around the bush was past, not that he'd proven any good at it. "The government wants to publicize what Tommy did, how he died—make him famous like Sergeant York or that chaplain who shouted 'Praise the Lord and pass the ammunition!' at Pearl Harbor."

Felicia puffed on her cigarette and said nothing. It was Katherine who spoke up. "That sounds like a fine idea! He certainly was a hero, wasn't he? He can help win the war even after he's gone—that's a fine thing!"

Felicia's eyes turned to narrow slits. "Maybe they don't want heroes whose fathers are referred to in the newspapers as 'the Outfit's ambassador to City Hall.'" She was catching on, anger at Sim flowing back, displacing any residual feelings she had for Tommy. At least for now. Mack was sure she would weep again later, in private.

"Isn't that right?" Felicia's voice became louder. "Isn't that why nobody—nobody at all—seems to have heard about Thomas Kilkenny's heroic death?"

Mack took a breath to reply, though he didn't know what he was going to say.

Felicia didn't give him a chance. "And that's why you're deigning to make one of your rare appearances here in Winnetka."

"Well, that's part of the reason—"

"Wait a minute—not so rare after all! Mr. Dineen mentioned you were here just the other day—a 'short meeting' with Father, he said. That has to have something to do with this visit. That son of a bitch *ordered* you to come to find out what I know about Blarney Bob—and for some reason you've agreed! What did he do, finally offer you so much goddamned cash you couldn't turn him down?"

"Felicia, your inveterate smoking is bad enough." Katherine shook her head solemnly. "But if there's one thing I have tried to teach you, it's not to use profanity. It's not something ladies do." Both her children ignored her.

"No, Felicia, I was not *ordered* to come, and I wasn't bribed either. I wanted you to know what happened to Tommy." For a moment, he hated himself for hiding behind such flimsy rags and patches of the truth.

"I knew Father was behind this somehow, with all his goddamned citizens' groups and businessmen's committees." Felicia's voice dropped, as if she was talking to herself. Then, she turned toward Mack again. "It's amazing, isn't it? After all those years of calling Roosevelt a crook and a Communist, he's become a patriot's patriot—Uncle Sam's favorite son, Mr. Win-the-War! But tell me, Mack, even though you're here for the kindest of family reasons and all that, it would still be fine if I had information about Blarney Bob, wouldn't it?"

"Yes, yes, I admit that it would. Whatever you think of Father, though, you've got to understand that this is more important than our family squabbles."

Felicia hurrumph-ed dismissively. Mack guessed she really couldn't understand, in any interior way, matters that didn't involve her, face to face. "Okay, I'll see what I can remember hearing about Blarney Bob's business or his connections or whatever the hell it is you want. But I doubt I'll be able to come up with anything."

"You can't think of anything now?"

"So, Dear Father is in a hurry, is he? Why doesn't he just send somebody to talk with Ellen and Janice? They won't be shy about incriminating Blarney Bob if there's anything behind the rumors about him."

Several different answers started to form in Mack's brain, ranging from blunt truths to outright fabrications.

"Just a second, wait one goddamn second—" Thrusting her arms toward the ceiling like a revival preacher, Felicia spoke before Mack could pick out a response from those on offer. "He's sending *you* to interrogate Ellen and Janice!" She pointed both arms in his direction, a carnival barker now, introducing a prize attraction. "My God, if it isn't money, Father must really have something hanging over you! Did you get some bigwig professor's daughter in the family way? Run somebody down while you were smashed? That would be ironic, wouldn't it?"

Mack squirmed on the couch next to her. Felicia surely knew she was onto something and couldn't resist twisting the sarcastic knife she wanted so much to use on their father. "It's not either of those things," Mack said without anger. "Let's just say there's something Father can do that I don't want to see done and leave it at that."

Felicia flashed him a self-satisfied look. Not quite a smile but heading in that direction.

"Well, Felicia, there are those guns you told me about, the ones in Robert Kilkenny's basement." Katherine picked up her North-Shore-lady's hat from the coffee table and straightened the long pheasant's tail feather so it lay flat. Felicia and Mack stared at her, speechless at last.

"You said there were pistols and ammunition in wooden boxes, hand grenades and what looked like shotguns. That's not something one would expect to find in a respectable person's basement, is it?" Katherine plopped the hat onto her head and tucked in a strand of faded blonde hair near her left ear. "You mentioned that Bob was seriously in his cups at the time."

As a kid, Mack liked to hang around the big kitchen of their house, watching Marjorie, the fat English cook, and her assistants. One morning, as he sat quietly in the corner, a big pot on the stove suddenly overflowed with a loud hiss of steam and an acrid burning smell that quickly filled the room. It may have been oatmeal, part of every Simmons family breakfast, or maybe custard or white sauce. Felicia's and Katherine's shouts—"You promised never to tell anyone!" "But Mack's part of our *family*!"—brought Mack back to Marjorie's banshee screech: "Bloody 'ell, Lavinia, you damned fool!"

Mack rose from the couch and stood over the two gesticulating women. Katherine's hat tumbled to the floor. Mack bent down and returned the hat, still slightly warm to the touch, to the coffee table. Mother and daughter turned to him.

Mack folded his arms across his chest. He unexpectedly had the upper hand. "Okay, this particular cat is out of the bag," he said in what he hoped was a reassuring tone, "and there's no putting the little beast back. So you might as well tell me about it."

Inevitably, Felicia reached for her Lucky Strike before answering. "I don't think this has anything to do with

Tommy. He didn't even know about that stuff in the basement. That's what Blarney Bob said."

"See," Katherine chimed in, "I told you it wasn't a bad thing to tell."

Felicia glared at her.

"And of course, Blarney Bob Kilkenny always tells the truth, especially when he's 'seriously in his cups.'" Mack silently kicked himself for sliding into sarcasm, his usual tone with Felicia.

She didn't notice. "Bob was tipsy—he always seems a little bit drunk—but he was scared too. It was like this crazy need to impress me about having those guns and things was at war with his fear of saying anything about it."

"How did you find yourself alone with an unseemly fellow like Robert Kilkenny? You never did tell me." Katherine's question wasn't phrased exactly like the one forming in Mack's mind, but it was essentially the same query.

"It was back when Tommy and I were still 'such a lovely couple'—three or four years ago, just before Mr. Thomas Kilkenny vanished from sight, or from *my* sight at least—"

Her voice caught, as if Tommy had materialized in front of her. She cleared her throat then did it again, and stared at the empty fireplace. "We were in the middle of one of our ritual Sundays, brunch with Ellen at Astor Place, then to South Shore for a typically bizarre supper with Blarney Bob, just the three of us served by that goon bodyguard of his, Dominic O'Nore."

She nodded, as if Tommy were encouraging her, then went on in a matter-of-fact tone. "Anyway, we'd just arrived at Blarney Bob's house, and of course, we were having a drink. The phone rang, and Tommy beat Dominic to it. He said it was a buddy from the university whose car had broken down or something, and he had to help him. Before he left, Tommy took me aside—it was really Ellen with some trumped-up problem: her toilet wouldn't flush, just a ploy to get him away from Bob. They were always playing those games."

Mack and Katherine nodded, marionettes on strings.

"Blarney Bob and I sat in the living room, sipping whiskey and not even making small talk." Felicia seemed to view the scene on the opposite wall. "Then he suddenly stood up and said in that stage-Irishman's brogue of his, 'Come, my girl, I've something to show you, a sight you've likely never set eyes on before.' I'd had enough whiskey to go along when he hustled me off to the cellar."

She took a deep drag on her cigarette. "He found a flashlight and took me downstairs. We walked past the furnace and the coal closet, past old chairs and couches—things 'that witch Ellen had no use for when she left me high and dry,' he said. Then we went along a little corridor with a ceiling so low we had to bend over. At the end of the corridor was a battered wooden door with a padlock. Blarney Bob fumbled out a key and unlocked the door—"

"And that's where the guns were!" Katherine grinned like a child listening to a favorite fairy tale.

"Yes, Mother, that's where they were—in a cubby-hole of a room with a bare bulb hanging from the ceiling. Weapons stacked against the wall, flat wooden boxes piled on the floor. The top one was open. It was full of bullets. I couldn't find any words to say. Blarney Bob didn't say anything either. I heard him gulp, like he was getting scared. Then he said in a voice I could hardly hear, 'All for the boys. I came here to be a hero to the boys.'"

"A hero to the boys! What the hell does that mean?" Mack hadn't intended to break the spell of Felicia's tale but couldn't help it.

"That's exactly what *I* said, but Bob wouldn't say any more. 'For the boys.' That's what he kept repeating. Then, getting really scared, he made me promise not to tell what I'd seen. I thought it was safe to tell you, Mother. But clearly, it was not."

"Who in hell are 'the boys'? Is the Chicago Outfit going to war with the New York mob?" Mack paused. "But this was a couple of years ago, right? There haven't been any gang wars. Nothing but Victor Schlegel's murder, and everybody, including the cops, was glad he was out of the way."

"'For the boys,'" repeated Felicia. "That's all he said."

# Chapter 13

Mack whiled away the first hours of the graveyard shift trying to figure out why Robert Kilkenny would hoard weapons in his basement. Logical questions came first. How the hell had he gotten his hands on such armaments? Did he still have them, or others? What "boys" were they for? The Irish Republican Army came to mind, though he'd never heard Blarney Bob mention them. He wracked his American-History-stuffed brain: Wasn't there now an Irish Free State? What was left for the IRA to fight about?

A few puffs on one of Chocolate Slim's spliffs replaced sober reasoning with nuttier thoughts. Was Blarney Bob planning to arm his neighbors in case a Jap amphibious assault came ashore at 79th Street Beach? Did he believe the rumors—retailed by the *Tribune*—about German bombers in occupied Norway preparing to fly over the North Pole to attack Chicago? Diabolically clever Nazi saboteurs were said to parachute from these remarkable aircraft.

Mack spread orange sweeping compound across a narrow aisle lined with drill presses. It was unused during the graveyard shift, a popular spot for cigarette breaks. As he pushed his extra-wide broom down the empty aisle, reasoning of at least a semi-sober variety returned as the effect of the reefer gradually wore off. What about the timing of Felicia's visit to the Kilkenny basement? Victor

Schlegel's spectacular murder had occurred only a few blocks away. Admittedly, Felicia's visit was months prior to Schlegel's death—but, still, could there be some connection?

✑✑✑

The second half of the shift drove away all such theorizing. On top of their regular cleaning duties, the janitors were conscripted, with no warning, to move a dozen lathes and drill presses, part of the efficiency experts' quest for more production. The project resembled cartoons where the housewife orders her henpecked husband to lug the couch over here—no, no, over *there*.

The Engineering Building geniuses in their white shirts and dark ties, grasping clipboards, stood around and smiled uncomfortably at the sweating, grunting janitors.

"Lordy," snarled Chocolate Slim, wiping his brow, "it's like bein' back in the goddamn cotton field."

Leopold, who tried to make sure the janitors didn't complain too loudly about anything, shot him an angry glance.

Slim muttered, "Leastways, the pay's better than sharecroppin'."

Finally, after spreading out a blueprint on the factory floor and clucking over it for several minutes, the engineers ordered all the machines moved one more time and bolted down right where they'd been in the first place, confirming the janitors' firm belief that everyone who wore a shirt and tie at Steckel Avenue was an idiot.

Still feeling the lingering effects of a spliff followed by pointless labor on a par with building the pyramids, Mack staggered with exhaustion when he made his way home to Mrs. McLady's. His thumping footsteps across the front porch stirred up tiny slivers of crumbling white paint. The place shed paint like dandruff.

Approaching his room on the second floor, Mack fumbled for his key. A voice sounded behind him, a fluty feminine voice simultaneously familiar and amazing. "Mack! I've waited so long for you to get home!"

The words barely registered. He knew it was Janice Kilkenny before he could turn around. His response was as completely involuntary as articulated words could be: "Janice, what the hell are you doing here?"

Janice's short, compact form emerged from the darkened hallway. She was hatless and wore a nicely tailored gray suit that he blurrily recognized as one of her favorites. "Well," she said, "as long as we're going to eliminate polite chit-chat, Felicia called me yesterday and gave me your address. She said you had something important to tell me. Something I need to know right away but have to hear from you." Her tone was light, showing no anger at his rudeness.

Mack stared at her, paralyzed, still gripping his key.

"Why don't you show me in to your spacious digs, politely pull up a chair, maybe get us some coffee? Then you can tell me this all-important news that apparently only your lips are capable of relating."

Mack, the zombie, succeeded in unlocking the door and ushering Janice inside—the first time she'd seen where he lived. Janice's dark eyes danced around the room. She bit her lower lip, clearly striving to hold back derogatory comments about his accommodations, which, except for a couple of new masking-tape patches to the torn easy chair, hadn't improved since Mack's letter had given Tommy a Grand Tour of the place.

"So this is it, eh?" Janice said in a determinedly neutral tone. "The cave where the hermit retreats."

The hermit reference—just like Tommy's—made a fleeting impression as Mack collapsed onto his sagging purple couch, receiving a sharp jab in the butt from the broken spring near the right armrest.

"Janice," he said in a voice that sounded fuzzy to him, "I have to close my eyes for a while, or I'm going to retreat into a permanent coma. Make us some coffee, and we'll talk in a few minutes."

He leaned against the back of the couch and slid his rear away from the broken spring. The couch's subtly moldy aroma, tinged with a faint smell of garlic, was the last thing he sensed before falling asleep.

The dead black of his empty, timeless sleep turned with surprising speed into an erotic dream: shoes and pants slipping off, soft kisses moving from forehead to lips, tongues sliding together. He swam to the surface. Janice was on top of him, he was inside her, and waking up didn't seem like a bad thing after all.

They each came with moans that Mack thought must be audible all up and down the hall. Perhaps that's what drove the mysterious Mr. Burgos away, the cries of ecstasy sounding through Mrs. McLady's paper-thin walls. Some landladies enforced a strict prohibition on visitors of the opposite sex. Ruth McLady, half-blind and pushing ninety, could hardly care less. Mack knew his concerns were absurd—their moans only felt loud to him.

Mack and Janice collapsed together in a tangle of arms and legs, with various articles of clothing: Mack's sleeveless undershirt and stained work pants, Janice's garter belt and one of her stockings, scattered on the shit-colored carpet or dangling over the back of the couch.

"See, my silly single-eyed boy," said Janice in a little-girl voice that exaggerated the s-sounds, "the whole thing was, you were thinking too much. You needed somebody who understands the element of s—s—surprise." She lightly drew a sharp fingernail across the outside of his thigh.

*Just like Janice*, he thought, as thought became possible. The petite, well-tailored rich girl, slightly on the plain side of pretty, was adventurous in bed. At least that was Mack's opinion. He wasn't exactly virginal, but not, he had to admit, all that experienced either. Was it pure instinct? Something she'd tried with other lovers? Had Janice peeked through the bedroom keyhole to spy on Ellen and Blarney

Bob? Her gestures and speech patterns resembled her mother's. Maybe Ellen liked to surprise Blarney Bob too. No one could know these things, even if they wanted to, which Mack decidedly didn't.

When they'd climbed back into their clothes—Janice insisted that Mack change into a clean shirt and a respectable pair of dark slacks—she said, "I've made us coffee, as Your Lordship commanded." She reached around him for the gray jacket of her suit, which lay over the armrest, and gestured toward the kitchen with her other hand. "In fact, coffee is about all you've got in there. Don't you eat?"

Mack stretched and let out an explosive yawn. "I usually go to the little diner down the street. It's close by and cheap."

"Uck! You mean that greasy-spoon joint on the corner? I was afraid I'd get ptomaine poisoning just driving by!"

"Morty is a true artist with Chicago hotdogs and five-way chili. I'll prove it. We'll have some of your coffee and then go there for lunch—and we can talk—" He scooped Janice's wristwatch off the rickety table next to the couch. "—assuming lunch is the next meal of the day. Two-thirty—that's two-thirty pm, right?"

Janice smiled and nodded, her fingers gliding across the back of his neck.

"It's a little late for lunch, so Morty's won't be crowded. You'd be amazed how customers line up around the block to get in. There are shoving matches, fistfights. The police have been called. It was all over the newspapers. You didn't see the story?"

Janice laughed, and Mack kissed her softly on the neck. He always liked her laugh, a let-it-loose guffaw that seemed to start at her toes and come from a much larger woman. At parties in the old days, he'd made it a point to glance around to catch the surprised looks when Janice laughed.

He kissed her more fervently, but the news he had to impart won out over thoughts of making love again.

As Mack and Janice approached Morty's arm in arm, the harsh wind had moderated to a gentle spring breeze, almost warm. As their reflections appeared in the plate glass front of the pawn shop next door to the diner, Mack noted that they made a handsome couple, more attractive together than either was individually. Tall, raw-boned, blonde-haired guy, demure dark-haired girl whose large breasts sneaked up on you. In his imagination, the wide window turned into a movie screen filled by a newspaper headline that screamed: *WAR HERO THOMAS KILKENNY DEAD!*

Mack's stomach performed a sickening dive off the high board. He inadvertently pressed Jan's forearm—she was back to "Jan" in his head by now—and she turned toward him in slight surprise. She glanced toward the dusty red-velvet pawn shop display, which held nothing but a badly tarnished tuba. Jan smiled, perhaps thinking he was signaling the comic incongruity of the oversized instrument. Pawned by a heavily-in-debt oompa-band musician drafted and sent away to a distant boot camp? Jan massaged his arm gently.

Part of Mack remained back in Mrs. McLady's rented room, a ghost or *doppelganger*, slowly vanishing. His fingers still cupped Jan's warm breasts. The skin of his forearm slid frictionlessly along her chest. The force of remembered passion was seeping away, replaced by heroes, war, death caused by a violent return to elemental matter. The lost-wax method—soft wax driven away and replaced by molten metal as a commemorative statue, hard and permanent, takes shape. *For Christ's sake*, thought Mack, *do all the images in my mind come from some goddamned UofC lecture?*

Morty's flickering neon sign, which simply said "Diner" in cursive script, was hard to miss. Jan and Mack made a sharp left, and Mack yanked open the dust-smeared glass door. The smell of frying onions rolled over them, a comforting fog. A dozen booths lined the putty-colored walls of the long narrow diner, occupied now by just two patrons.

Near the front was an older guy—that is, at forty-five or so, past draft age, the true division between young and old nowadays. He wore a gray, oil-stained shirt and matching trousers, maybe another graveyard-shift worker from Steckel Avenue or some other defense plant. The fellow probably hadn't worked steadily in years—now he was racking up overtime beyond his wildest dreams. Mack the Historian delaying the inevitable. Gripping the spoon in a clenched fist, the worker slurped in noisy gulps from a steaming bowl of chili. A layer of oyster crackers floated on top, lily pads in a volcano.

At the left-hand booth nearest the cash register sat a scrawny old woman in a black-cloth coat, probably a neighborhood widow gone nuts when "the Mister" died, her kids and other relations all angry, in jail, drafted, moved away. She poked a fork at a slice of Morty's legendary Dutch apple pie, seeking to while away as much of this slow spring afternoon as possible.

Mack yearned to join her—clean the gutters, take down the storm windows, repair the front porch. Anything to avoid relating his news to Jan.

He steered her to his usual seat, third booth on the right. They slid across the ancient leather banquette, worn to a soft sheen by decades of sliding butts. As the door from the kitchen swung open, Morty himself bustled out and waddled toward them, cardboard menus in hand.

"Mack, my favorite boy!" he shouted in an accent that was either Greek or Yiddish—Mack could never determine which. He waved and breathed a silent sigh of relief at the brief reprieve.

It lasted only long enough to order a toasted cheese sandwich and iced tea for Jan and a bowl of chili and a Pepsi for Mack. Morty slid a white chef's cap to the middle of his balloon-shaped head and mopped his brow. He headed back to the kitchen with a fat man's rocking steps, detouring to pick up the older guy's empty bowl. The weight of his task squeezed all the words out of Mack's head.

Jan said, "Some French writer talks about the sadness that follows love-making: *la tristesse d'amour* something, something. Is that what's bothering you? Or has the cat just got your tongue?"

A Negro waiter in a white apron, scarcely more than a boy, emerged from the kitchen with their tea and Pepsi on a small round tray. He silently placed the drinks in front of them. Mack sucked down half his Pepsi in a single gulp, almost collapsing the paper straw, coughing as the bubbles tickled the back of his throat.

"So," he said, finally finding his voice, "Felicia didn't tell you anything except that I have news for you? Nothing else?"

Jan squeezed a couple of drops from a lemon wedge into her tea. How long, Mack wondered, still playing for time, until lemons would be rationed and available only on the black market?

"Nothing else. She was very mysterious. It seemed like part of her wanted to tell me and another part didn't." She took a tiny sip of tea and gazed steadily at Mack. "Are you two pulling a prank on me?"

Mack picked up the sweating glass of Pepsi and drank it off, tipping the bottom until a small avalanche of ice cubes rattled against his teeth. He swallowed and wiped a sleeve across his mouth. The metal man, the statue, came forward.

"Tommy is gone. He died in the Philippines fighting the Japs."

He blurted out the words before he put down his glass. He owned the story now. That was why his father had told him in the first place, pulling Mack into his orbit the way the Earth's gravity controls the Moon. *At least*, he thought, *there's hardly anyone here to see her become hysterical.*

Jan kept staring for a couple of beats. "I know," she said quietly, running an index finger up and down the moist side of her glass. "Or at least I sensed it, like seeing a shadow but not the thing itself."

Mack looked into her dark eyes. Blarney Bob's black Irish ancestry had given both his children the eyes of Gypsies. The waiter's return with their steaming lunches barely registered.

"He knew it too," Jan said in a voice grown slightly husky. "Tommy sensed he was going to die."

Mack waved away the steam rising from the chili bowl. His mouth started to form empty words, maybe something about Tommy's night train to war, but Jan continued before any of his words came out.

"I got a letter from him a few days ago. It was dated this past New Year's Day. God knows how many hands it'd passed through by the time it got to me. Tommy wrote that after Pearl Harbor, there was no way the navy was going to risk the ships they still have to save the Philippines."

Jan's tone was matter-of-fact. Had she really done her weeping after receiving her brother's weirdly prophetic letter? She and Tommy hadn't talked to one another a lot, at least not in front of Mack, but they shared a silent language of quick glances and tiny smiles, an unspoken connection beyond anything that existed between Mack and Felicia.

"That was the logical part," Jan continued with a calm precision that amazed Mack. "Tommy said he'd had one of Dad's 'Irish visions,' this one about his own death. He never believed in that stuff before. 'Nothing but goddamned Mick BS and moonshine,' that's what he always said about Dad's tales. His stories were usually about some humble potato digger from Connemara who received a visitation from St. Brigid, the patron saint in charge of prophecies, and then saw into the future. But now, Tommy wrote, he knew what Blarney Bob was talking about. It was like seeing a movie, one with a lot of gaps and splices, but where the plot was clear."

Mack and Jan leaned toward each other across the table. Stifling a lover's urge to leap up and embrace her, comfort her, Mack could only lay a quivering hand on top of hers. Jan didn't seem to notice. Mack struggled toward logic, trying to fathom how Tommy could experience, or imagine himself experiencing, this kind of Old Country peasant's vision. He wanted to know more, but he bit his tongue. Jan's hand was cold. Her face had gone pale.

"Tommy wrote that they knew they were on their own, with no reinforcements on the way, whatever that bastard MacArthur said…"

She began to cry in deep gasps, as if the general's name had freed a dammed-up stream. Jan lifted her cloth napkin and buried her face in it, her whole upper body convulsed with sobs.

Solidly logical Mack melted away—the lost-wax method in reverse. This time, he did leap up, step around the table, and wrap his arms around Jan's shoulders. The sobs continued as she reached up and grabbed his arms with shaking hands.

The defense worker paid his bill and headed toward the door. His eyes, narrow slits in the red slab of his face, darted suspiciously at Mack and the weeping Jan.

As the door opened and closed, a piece of dirty wind swirled past, picking up and dropping the hem of Jan's skirt. The movement seemed to signal an end to her crying jag, the stream dammed up again. She gently slid his arms away, wiped her eyes, and quietly pointed to Mack's side of the booth. Jan took a large bite of toasted cheese sandwich. A yellow string of American cheese swung for a moment like a slack rope between the U-shaped bite and her lower lip.

While she methodically chewed, Mack slid back into his seat. Had his embrace really comforted her? He could think of nothing better to do than attack his chili. At least for now, Jan didn't seem to despise him for making love to her and then—oh, by the way—suddenly informing her of her brother's death.

Mack swirled a spoonful of spicy ground beef (heavy on the cumin), stewed tomatoes, and squishy kidney beans around in his mouth. Nothing, he decided, had ever tasted so delicious. He spooned chopped onions and grated cheddar on top and devoured half the bowl by the time Jan finished swallowing. They simultaneously reached for their glasses and washed down the food with gulps of iced tea and watered-down Pepsi.

Mack swallowed one last time and forced himself to mouth the by-now-familiar words about Tommy's heroic death, sounding far too much like Sim when he noted that Tommy's actions had temporarily stalled the Jap landing in Mindanao. He heard himself calling it the only success of the doomed campaign. Like it or not, the hero trade was becoming Mack's business now.

"Fire," Jan interrupted in a barely audible whisper, as if the tears might flow again. "Tommy saw himself dying in fire—a lot of pilots must think about that. But, in his vision, he saw it through to the end. It was all over before he got burned. There was a hot white light like huge flashbulb popping, he said. Then it was over. That's how Tommy's 'Irish vision' ended."

Mack waited patiently for more, while Jan took another hungry bite of her sandwich then daintily wiped the grease from her fingers on a dry corner of the napkin. "He wrote it was a relief to know, really know somehow, that he would never be taken prisoner," she said evenly, fighting off crying.

Her eyes widened. "Why are *you* the one telling me this?" She took another sip of iced tea. "I can't believe Mother or Dad didn't say anything. I've seen both of them over the last couple of days."

He told the Blarney-Bob part of his father's hero story, leaving out Victor Schlegel and the hidden weapons. Jan had never ridiculed her father within Mack's hearing, as Tommy so often did. But she was clearly embarrassed about being "the crooked alderman's kid." Blarney Bob was said to have arranged a substantial contribution to Northwestern to guarantee Jan's admission to the university—not exactly a route to social acceptance. Jan hadn't even tried to pledge a sorority. It was a tribute to Felicia that, even after her passionate affair with Tommy ended, she'd remained a steadfast friend to such a social outcast. Jan had fooled everyone by proving herself a diligent student and graduating with honors in journalism.

Mack got to the part of his tale about how the America First-ers and other steadfast isolationists would capitalize on any crooked wartime dealings by Blarney Bob.

Jan interrupted him again. "How can I put this politely?" she said in a rising tone. "Your father is crazy! He's right about the country needing heroes right now—but nobody, absolutely nobody, will care about Tommy's family when they find out what he did. And I'm not just saying that because he's my brother."

"But the *Tribune* and Colonel McCormick—"

"Would be insane to smear the reputation of a genuine hero, especially one from Chicago. Even if he was Al Capone's love child!"

Jan's head-bobbing vehemence caught Mack off guard until it became clear that she was employing the same tactic he was—talk about, think about, anything but Tommy's death.

He joined her in evasion: Was Sim's command performance really some sort of ruse? Nothing more than a plot to bring *him* to heel, really nothing to do with win-the-war patriotism?

If so, his father was going to a lot of trouble, throwing his weight around to short-circuit the ritual of formally notifying the loved ones of a fallen soldier.

"But there *is* something to it, something that doesn't seem connected to Bob's..." He coughed, seeking words that wouldn't upset the delicate balance Jan had achieved. "...connected with your father's questionable associates. He has, or at least did have, ammunition, grenades, and guns squirreled away in his basement. Felicia saw them."

"Felicia saw weapons in *our house*?"

"In the cellar, she said."

"Where, exactly?" Her voice grew more forceful as she

escaped more deeply into the role of a reporter pursuing a scoop.

"Felicia said they were in a cubby-hole of a room, past the furnace and coal closet."

"My God, Tommy and his pals from the neighborhood used to play in there, pretending it was a robbers' cave or secret hideout. I was frightened to go in, too dark and spooky." She brushed away an invisible crumb from the corner of her mouth. "It got to be the place we stored old tricycles and kids' books and my doll house, things we didn't need anymore, but couldn't bear to part with."

"So, after you and Tommy grew up, and Bob and Ellen divorced, it'd be the perfect place to keep the guns and grenades your father showed Felicia."

"*But why?*" They spoke the words together.

"All I can think of is the Irish Republican Army," Mack continued more quietly, fingertips straying to the unshaven cheek below his false eye. "I don't know much about what's happening over there now, except that the Irish have declared their neutrality. But if the IRA is using the war to finally get ahold of Ulster, and working with the Nazis to do it, and Blarney Bob is still helping them, it could be worse than any connection to the Chicago Outfit."

"Your father doesn't know about this, the weapons in our cellar?"

"Not yet. Felicia certainly never told him. I know for a fact, though, that he's got at least one investigator snooping around, and likely more. He's a man obsessed. You're right about how crazy this all is. My father's pushed his way into this war-hero business to make himself feel important and maybe to get to me somehow. He can hurt—and I mean badly hurt—everyone connected with this, including people you don't know."

Morty waddled out from the kitchen and deposited a check in front of Mack. "Good, yes? Nice to see people enjoy their food!"

Mack and Jan looked down to see that every morsel of

their lunches had disappeared without a trace. Mack nodded and forced a wan smile. "Thanks, Morty. Everything was delicious, as usual."

As soon as Morty was out of earshot, Mack said, "Did Blarney Bob ever mention the IRA? I think they call themselves Sinn Fein in Gaelic." He bit his tongue at his pedantry. Jan surely knew this.

"Never a word. He almost never talked about real things happening in Ireland, just the fairy-tale stuff. Visions and dreams and banshees, stories about Cuchulain and the Red Hand of O'Neill—he's the guy who chopped off his hand and threw it on the shore to be the first to claim Ulster. Tommy said it was all typically Irish: look reality straight in the face, not like what you see, then start making things up." A thin smile curled the corners of her mouth. Tommy's smart-aleck ghost holding off grief?

"How did your dad come to America?" A good, logical question, one Mack had never thought of before.

"There was never a word about it. A few years back, though, he talked about the day he arrived in Chicago—it was around May Day in 1916. There was a big labor parade downtown, all fine Irish union men, Dad said. He knew his long journey across land and sea had come to an end."

Hearing Blarney Bob's tale-spinning tone in Jan's voice, Mack inadvertently smiled. In spite of everything, Jan followed suit.

"I mentioned it was just after the Easter Rebellion. Dad took a long sip of Jameson's and corrected me. The right word, he said, is Easter *Rising*, 'the nation rising like Christ from the tomb, more than a rebellion against the damned bloody Brits.' Leaving Ireland then was a lucky coincidence, more proof of his 'natural good fortune.'"

Mack slid out a buck from his wallet and some change from his pocket. He put two quarters on top of the bill so it wouldn't blow away. He helped Jan from her seat. They left the diner without another word.

Mack and Jan quietly wept together, arms around each other's waist, as they walked through Columbus Park, still not speaking, trying to be absorbed in the unfurling spring leaves. Back at Mrs. McLady's, Mack pulled the Murphy bed down from the wall. For the rest of the afternoon, he and Jan made love more gently than before.

It was a wonderful anesthetic, better than spliffs or booze. Not enough, though, to drive away Mack's thoughts of Tommy and what must be done to assure his friend, his blood brother, became a hero.

# Chapter 14

The country was waking up. Mack felt it palpably turning into something new, no longer the beaten dog of the Depression, whimpering for a little food and comfort. It was angry now, still incoherent and unsure after only a few months' wandering in the dark forest of war, but ready to destroy—what? We don't know yet. Japan, Germany, and Italy, of course, but what the shape and dimension of their destruction will be, we don't know yet. But it will be revenge like nothing ever seen before—Mack could see it in the faces of the men in their khaki shirts and denim overalls, crowding through the gates of the Steckel Avenue plant, jostling one another as they clocked in. Jostling, not excusing themselves but not angry either, much less chattering and laughing than you'd expect. Their faces were hard and determined. *Ready,* Mack thought, *to do what's necessary. Justified.*

He could see the change in the women too, as if they'd been caught up by a new religion. Women at the Steckel Avenue plant had approached Mack, actively propositioned him with a directness that would've shocked the supposedly free-thinking females at the UofC—at least during the rapidly receding pre-war era.

In a hermit's activity never undertaken by the likes of St. Simeon Stylites or Walter Clinckscale, Mack had taken a plant girl home to Mrs. McLady's, their hands all over each other on the drive along North Avenue. She was just up from a West Virginia holler to find work and adventure in the big city, but she couldn't hide her disgust at his glass eye. It hadn't slid out or anything, only rolled around a little in the socket as they'd fucked.

"It ain't natural!" she screeched, in what Mack deemed a dazzling glimpse of the obvious.

He'd then popped out the ocular prosthesis and dropped it into the metal cup on the table next to the bed. It made a little splash when it dropped into the antiseptic liquid. The mountain girl had taken a cab home.

Later, a gentle, soft-faced welder from the South Side—a blue-eyed blonde with an unpronounceable Polish surname—had caressed his forehead with soft fingers after they made love on the squeaking Murphy bed. "My poor boy," she cooed. "My poor sweet boy." When he approached Magdalena at the plant, she said she'd quit that day to marry a neighborhood boy from Back of the Yards. "Andy just got drafted. He needs me to keep his spirits up so he won't get killed. I couldn't say no."

Magdalena had offered comfort Mack sorely missed, the warmth and contact as much as the sex. Had he found this powerful comfort again with Jan, permanent this time? He hoped so, deeming "hoped" a weak term to describe his awakened need for her.

☙❧☙

Mack and the other janitors got to witness the first shift pouring into the plant on account of the morning's War Bond rally. It wasn't an official order, but everyone on the graveyard shift was expected to punch out then stay an extra unpaid hour to attend. The all-white first shift clocked in and attended the rally before going to work. They did get paid, a fact not lost upon Leopold Belgian's team of janitors.

"So who's this honky they got jawin' at us?" asked Chocolate Slim. "Tryin' to find another way to separate a workin' man from his hard-earned cash." Leopold threw him the stink eye.

"It's Stan Hack," answered Mack, quoting from the notice on the bulletin board.

"Who the hell is that?" Slim growled back.

"Some ballplayer from the Cubs," said Leopold in a stage whisper. The small cluster of janitors stopped at the outer edge of the expanding crowd. Workers from both shifts gathered in front of an impromptu wooden stage set up inside the cavernous entrance lobby. The "Production Will Win the War" banner had been moved indoors and mounted on the wall above the flag-draped stage.

"How come they still playin' ball with this goddamn big war on?" Slim asked.

"President Roosevelt says we need baseball to keep our morale up on the home front," replied Mack, in the know-it-all tone he usually managed to avoid with his workmates.

"That got to be it," said Slim. "My mo-rale be shot to shit if them Cubs ain't playin'."

The shambling group on the bare stage included Ferdinand Gisbourne, the plant manager, who nervously puffed on a cigarette and looked uncomfortable in a navy-blue suit that strained against his paunch. Always called "Fat Ferdie," Gisbourne normally roamed the plant in rolled-up shirtsleeves and loosened tie, bellowing orders like a football coach in a tight game: "Coffee break's over. Time to get back to work! Let's go get 'em!" Most Steckel Avenue employees seemed to ignore him like the grinding gears of the trucks passing by outside, nothing but background noise.

Mack would've recognized "Smilin' Stan"—as well known for his movie-star looks as his extra-base hits—even if he weren't wearing a Chicago Cubs cap along with a well-cut gray suit. Fat Ferdie began speaking into the echoing PA system, but the buzz from the crowd never let up. Three women in tight headscarves, the fashion recommended by Veronica Lake to keep hair like hers away from spinning drills and whirling belts, pushed their way to the end of the stage where the tall, black-haired third baseman stood. After a couple more unintelligible comments by plant bigwigs, Stan Hack strode to the silver pedestal microphone at center stage. The crowd quieted. People shush-ed those who were still talking.

"I know a lot of you have watched me play ball at Wrigley Field—"

A roar echoed off the gray cinder-block walls. Stan Hack raised his right hand as if blessing the cheering crowd.

"Thank you, thank you, it's always great to meet fans of our team. But the whole country, the whole USA, is our team now, and we're up against a tougher enemy than those Yankees who beat us in the Series back in 'thirty-eight."

Scattered boos arose.

Stan smiled benignly. "That's right, the Japs and Hitler's Nazi sluggers make Gehrig and DiMaggio look like midgets! But you're the team to beat 'em. The bombers you're helping make here are like beanballs that'll knock Hirohito and Mussolini and that paper-hangin' Adolf right out of the batter's box—"

More cheering.

"Then, we'll come up to bat and blast their outfield fences with some long line drives!"

"You tell 'em, Stan, you're the best!" A female voice cut through the din. "Can I take you home? Hubby works the night shift, and he's a White Sox fan!"

Smilin' Stan grinned, waiting for the laughter and cheers to quiet down. "You may have seen my mug on that box of Wheaties last year. You may not remember, but also on that Wheaties box was my pal George Myers. He's an army air corps pilot and as big a hero as any ballplayer. George is a flight instructor, and he's training bomber pilots right now, right this minute, to blow those yellow-belly Japs to hell!" Yelling over the crowd, Stan shouted, "And they're flying bombers with *your* engines in 'em!"

The place went wild.

Was Stan Hack's Wheaties box-mate the guy who taught Tommy to fly? Whoever the instructor was, he did a superlative job, harnessing Tommy's swift reflexes and eye-hand control (the loaded phrase again!) that had made him such a skilled football and tennis player and directing them to the life-or-death craft of military flying.

Mack clenched his fists. The goddamned flight instructor did his job too well. If Tommy hadn't been such a gifted pilot, maybe he'd have bailed out with his crew, maybe made his way back to the States somehow to finish out the war as a flight instructor himself. Mack forced the thought, and its fast route to insanity, out of his head and focused on their celebrity visitor.

"There's one sure way," Stan Hack continued, "to get that hitting streak started against the Japs and the Krauts—and that's War Bonds. They're like a good Wheaties breakfast for a hitter, building up his strength." He pantomimed an uppercut homerun swing. "Getting strong, so he can sock 'em a mile!"

Stan took off his Cubs cap and waved it in the air, as the workers roared, including Mack, Leopold, and Chocolate Slim. Fat Ferdie came over to shake the ballplayer's hand then leaned close to whisper in his ear. Stan covered his mouth with his Cubs cap, and the tumult gradually subsided.

"My friend, Mr. Gisbourne here, has reminded me to remind *you* that all you have to do to start buying a bond is stop over by Personnel and fill out a payroll deduction form. Those deductions are like eating one peanut at the ballpark, so little you won't even know it's gone!"

Mack and the other janitors joined in the explosion of laughter.

"Better yet, if you sign up this week, your name goes into the hat for a drawing. The winner gets two tickets to Wrigley Field for our first game with the Cardinals. They're not as bad as the Nips or the Nazis, but we still hate 'em. I promise you the Cubs will knock the stuffing out of 'em!" He stuck his Cubs cap on Fat Ferdie's balding head and walked off the stage, arms raised like a triumphant boxer. Gisbourne reached up in surprise and touched the cap. He left it on and squeezed his thick fingers around the microphone like a strangler. The workers began to disperse before he started talking.

*Bread and circuses,* thought Mack as he headed for the parking lot. Keep us whipped up and cheering. We'll not only work harder, but pay for the privilege with War Bonds. That cynical strategy had worked for Hitler for years now—maybe it could be used to defeat him. But, Mack had to admit, cheering the Cubs' star third baseman alongside his workmates had made him forget his aching back, sore leg muscles, and the dozens of garbage barrels he'd emptied during the graveyard shift.

Mack slid behind the wheel of the ancient Model A. As he slid the key into the ignition, he heard breathing from over his right shoulder, a faint tick of inhalation stopping. He grunted and twisted to look behind him. His chin almost touched the smiling face of Janice Kilkenny, now sitting up on the edge of the back seat.

She began talking before Mack had turned all the way around. "Sorry to scare you! I dozed off…"

Mack took a deep breath, preparing to shout at her for nearly frightening him into a pants-wetting seizure. He stopped short when Jan continued: "We're going to Dad's house. Mother will meet us at your place, then we'll all go together in her car. She's got a full tank of gas." She paused and looked him full in the face. "That's what you wanted, isn't it?"

Mack tried to sort out his thoughts. "How did you get in here?" Best to start simply.

"I took a cab over here an hour ago. It was easy to find your wreck of a car—there are so few cars in the lot!—and I knew the lock's never worked right."

She opened the door, climbed out, and joined Mack in the front seat. Sliding in next to him, she continued without a pause. "You didn't come out at seven o'clock. Where were you anyway, working overtime? I got in the back to rest my eyes. I guess I fell asleep."

Mack began to speak again, still caught between a reprimand and a kiss, but Jan interrupted. "Start the car, and let's go! We can talk on the way."

Jan patiently answered Mack's tumbling questions. Yes, she'd told Ellen about Tommy's death. In the best stiff-upper-lip tradition of the Boswell clan, she'd gasped but not wept, leaving the tears to her daughter. "I should've known," Ellen had whispered then phoned Blarney Bob, who sounded badly hung-over, and told him only that she and Janice would be stopping over in the morning to "discuss a family matter." And no, Ellen did *not* hold Mack responsible for Tommy's unexpected enlistment after the accident.

Behind the wheel of a twin of Blarney Bob's black Cadillac, Ellen waited in front of Mrs. McLady's when they pulled up. A wartime appointment, dictated by whichever party had sufficient gasoline and reliable enough tires to make the trip.

On a thermometer of emotion, climbing into the back seat behind Ellen Boswell Kilkenny—she'd kept her ex-husband's name "so the children and I would have the same last name"—resembled entering a walk-in freezer. Sim had taken him inside one when Mack was seven. Their mission then had been to pick out a Thanksgiving turkey from a fancy meat purveyor. Like the frozen mist swirling through the freezer, Mack could feel the chill of Ellen's grief flow through the car. All that was missing was the plucked and naked birds and sides of red meat hanging from hooks.

Ellen and Jan stared straight ahead as North Avenue's stolid brick bungalows and courtyard apartments zipped by. It was the quiet cusp of the morning, after the working adults had left but before the noisy wave of kids headed to school.

When they turned onto Lake Shore Drive at North Avenue Beach, still empty as an abandoned Arctic outpost, Mack could stand the silence no longer. "Ellen," he said in a half-choked voice, "I'm sorry for your loss." He knew as soon as he heard himself that his words were empty as the forlorn beach, empty as anything Blarney Bob had recited at one of his political wakes.

"I know you are, Mack," replied Ellen in a voice much more calm and controlled than his. Neither she nor Jan turned around as Ellen took the Cadillac out of gear and rolled to a smooth stop at the Chicago Avenue traffic light. A half-dozen other cars had pulled up around them when the notoriously long light finally changed.

The code of chilled silence remained in force as they pulled into Blarney Bob's driveway in South Shore. The brick house loomed up still and silent. The slamming doors of the Cadillac echoed off the house front. Tottering on high heels, Ellen went straight up the front walk and rang the doorbell, which chimed faintly inside.

Mack was the last to reach the front porch. He stood behind Jan, lightly touching her shoulder. Despite Jan's assurances, he remained convinced that Ellen, with the iron logic of mothers, blamed him for somehow compelling Tommy to join the air corps. Now, would they *all* come to hate the sight of him for being alive when their beloved son and brother was dead? The question took Mack by surprise. He felt the hairs on his forearm stand up under his sweat-stained work shirt. Was Tommy's death to mean the death of everything he'd loved and connected with? His best friend—his once and, he hoped, future lover. He would even hate to lose Blarney Bob, touchstone for the muddle and buffoonery of the generation before his. Was it all at an end?

Jan reached for his hand and lightly squeezed it.

Ellen rang the bell again and followed up with a couple of hard raps on the door. "If that man's passed out on the couch, I'll kill him! I wonder why Dominic didn't answer."

She turned the knob. The door swung open with a mousy squeak.

"That's odd," said Jan. "Dad's motto has always been, 'Be a friend to all—but lock your doors!'"

Even Ellen gave out a small, half-suppressed giggle, as they stepped into the front hallway.

Jan called out, "Dad?"

Ellen called, "Bob?"

No response.

"Dominic, are *you* here?" shouted Ellen in a louder voice sharpened by impatience. The only answer was a slight echo off the curving staircase leading to the second floor. "Jan, you look for him upstairs. I'll look down here. If that man's been drinking, there's no telling where he wound up! Maybe Dominic's passed out too."

"That would be a first," said Jan, trotting up the stairs. Her mother turned left toward the living room.

Left alone in the front hall, Mack glanced around for a second or two, moves picked up and multiplied by the tall, gilt-edged mirrors on either side of the entranceway. Mack blinked at himself in the nearest mirror. He knew where he would search for Blarney Bob.

In a dozen strides, he was through the kitchen—the only sign of life there was a half-empty bottle of Jameson's on the counter—then down the creaking basement steps. He called out Bob's name, mostly to sell the notion that he was actually looking for him, not magnetically drawn to the basement by pure, un-hermit-like curiosity. He found the furnace amid Bob's collection of discarded furniture, including the scratchy faux-velvet couch where he and Jan had first kissed and later, surprised by their passion, made love.

The corridor past the coal closet was cramped as a mineshaft. Mack's shoulder bumped against a splintery support beam; he felt a tiny rip at the elbow of his shirt. The door at the end of the corridor was open an inch, revealing a light on inside. A padlock hung askew in the latch.

Mack pushed the door open the rest of the way. The light from a naked bulb in the ceiling socket revealed, not crates of rifles or machine guns, but a long-limbed, dark-haired man in a wrinkled black suit. Arms thrust forward, he lay face down on the coal-stained floor.

Mack stared as if claimed by rigor mortis. He gasped in as much air as he could hold and let it out slowly then stepped over to the man and tried to turn him over. His hands slipped away from the shiny surface of the cheap suit coat. It was like maneuvering a sack of wet cement. At last, on his hands and knees and breathing hard as if he'd been in a wrestling match, Mack succeeded in turning the man over, though one bent arm remained stuck under the small of the back. In the middle of the man's high, wrinkled forehead, brushed by a lock of scraggly brown hair, was a single round hole. Forcing his eyes away from the ragged red circle, Mack looked into the clenched, dead face. Mr. Graves, first name unknown, his father's detective.

# Chapter 15

Mack sank into a scuffed leather couch in Simmons, Burgoyne, and Altfelder's dingy waiting room and caught his breath. Waiting for his father. How many hours of his life had been spent doing that? Months, probably.

Back at the Kilkenny house, Mack's first instinct as he manhandled the body—an accurate phrase if there ever was one—had been a hermit's response. Forget about Graves. Let someone else find the body. It was none of his business. If Bob and Dominic had gone off somewhere, it could be days or weeks until some South Shore neighbor or neighbor's dog noticed the smell. Mack's reviving hermit side argued that the world was being eaten up by war, thousands perishing every day. What meaning could conceivably be attached to Graves's death?

Unexpectedly, a second internal voice spoke in opposition. Wasn't hearing voices in your head supposed to be a symptom of schizophrenia? Mack dismissed the question as overly analytical and listened to the second voice, which said with surprising eloquence that *every* death, grandiose or obscure, creates ripples, damages lives beyond the departed.

Was Graves's sketchy occupation the sole support of a wife and kids, an aged mother, a feeble-minded sister, all now plunged into poverty and desperation? Mack knew he couldn't walk away. He—and his father—would have to deal with the death of Mr. Graves.

The immediate decision not to contact the police had required only a few seconds, less than the time it took to switch off the light in the Kilkennys' basement room and close the door behind him. He was careful to wipe the handle with his handkerchief first and grab it along the edge with his fingertips. Mack convinced himself that he and Jan—and most likely, Ellen too—had nothing of substance to tell the cops anyway. The fact that weapons may have been in the room long before the body turned up there was probably a coincidence. It had to be, right?

In the waiting room, Mack crossed and uncrossed his legs and glanced over at Jan and Ellen, gazing absently at the opposite wall. The two women appeared transfixed by Sim's full-size reproduction of Trumbull's stagy painting of the signing of the Declaration of Independence. The chipped frame had gathered dust as long as Mack could remember, the painting's bleached-out colors growing fainter over the years. By now, several Founding Fathers seemed to be wearing tan Burberry trench coats. Simmons, Burgoyne, and Altfelder—Sim had bought out his partners long ago, but the three-headed name endured—had no reason to impress anyone with its office decor.

At the house, Mack, Ellen, and Janice had quickly formed an efficient team. Mack informed them what he'd stumbled upon. The women didn't flinch or question him— or ask to see the body of Mr. Graves for themselves. Jan and Ellen speedily searched the other rooms. For more corpses? Weapons? Other, more unexpected clues? Whatever they were looking for, they didn't find it, assuming they were really looking and not just trying to evade, for a while at least, the concrete, unchangeable fact of Mr. Graves' earthly remains in the cellar. Perhaps, after losing Tommy, they were able to cope with only one death at a time.

Mack had wrapped his handkerchief around the telephone and dialed his father's office. When Miss

Lincecombe, the ancient receptionist, came on the line, Mack briskly informed her that he had to see Sim right away. He'd be there in half an hour. When her shocked, old-lady's voice started to interrupt, Mack ordered her to tell Sim it was connected with the assignment his father had given him then hung up.

When they arrived at the LaSalle Street office, Miss Lincecombe had given Mack a dirty look over the half-glasses perched halfway down her witch-like nose, offended by his oil-stained shirt and shoes and hopelessly wrinkled work pants. She reluctantly revealed that Sim would see them shortly. Please have a seat.

The grimy windows of the waiting room overlooked the massive Corinthian columns of Continental Illinois Bank, the vainglorious edifice Tommy always called the "Temple of Mammon." The words, spoken in Tommy's put-on Irish brogue, caused Mack to smile and nearly cry at the same moment. Tommy, the about-to-be hero, was the mystical opposite of the anonymous Mr. Graves. But each was now the naturalized citizen of a country where fame and anonymity were equally useful—useful as a catapult to a cat, a shoehorn for a legless man. One more time, Mack wiped his hands across the front of his shirt. Fear of leaving fingerprints replaced by the primitive terror of contamination by the dead?

*Tommy* was the reason he was here, a true statement in more ways than Mack could count. If Tommy hadn't rolled the Buick and left him short an eye, this moment in time would've found him somewhere else, far from Chicago, LaSalle Street, and this ugly, dark-paneled waiting room. Mack would be in boot camp or, more likely, at Officer Candidate School, living up to his family bloodlines by learning to be a fearless Leader of Men. He pictured himself and Janice hastily marrying as he went off to war. They'd keep joking and joshing until his troop train rolled out of Union Station.

Moving independently of his roiling brain, Mack's left index finger scratched a tiny itch just below his ocular prosthesis. On Miss Lincecombe's desk, the spear-like minute hand of the brass clock clicked ahead for the thirty-fifth time since their arrival.

The oak door of Sim's inner sanctum swung open. Sim himself stepped into the waiting room. "Please come in," he said in a noncommittal tone. Sim showed no surprise whatever at the presence of Jan and Ellen. Ignoring his son, Sim gave a little bow in their direction. All three visitors simultaneously rose from their seats.

They arranged themselves on leather chairs, less battered than the waiting-room furniture, arrayed around Sim's Napoleonic mahogany desk, empty except for a leather-edged writing blotter and squat black telephone. Ellen took the middle chair and began talking the instant her fanny touched the seat.

"Mr. Simmons, you appear to have taken ownership of my son's death—and his memory." She spoke directly, in the plummy tones of a Long Island aristocrat, sounding a little like Eleanor Roosevelt, still no sign of tears.

Sim spread his hands on either side of the blotter. "Desperate times call for desperate measures," he said and curved his bristling mustache into a small, kindly smile that took the edge off his words. He continued in a sterner tone: "I haven't taken your son's memory, Mrs. Kilkenny. I am giving it to the nation, allowing his memory to live on as an inspiration that will help us win this war."

"But you never told me—"

"That was Mack's job, and apparently he's done it."

Three pairs of eyes swung in Mack's direction. He refused to look away. Dr. Bennett the ophthalmologist had told him after the accident that he was lucky—not a word often used to describe his situation—because he was an adult when it happened. "When a child loses an eye," the doctor explained, "he'll inadvertently turn in the direction of the missing eye and appear to look suspiciously away from those he's talking to, usually an unbreakable, lifelong habit. You're grown up," Dr. Bennett said. "You already know how to look people in the eye."

Jan nodded in Mack's direction with an expression he took to be sympathetic. Ellen placed a strand of coiffed hair behind her ear and fixed him with a searing look that rivaled Superman's X-ray vision.

Ellen finally looked back at Sim and began to complain. You could tell it was going to be a complaint by the twist of her mouth and widening of her pale eyes.

Mack spoke first: "I may not have told you the story myself, Ellen, but I know Jan told you most of it."

He turned to his father, who hadn't moved a muscle. "And there are several things even you don't know." Sim clenched his fists. *Don't be sarcastic*, Mack told himself, not an easy task when talking to his father. Sarcasm was the only language they shared, the essential Simmons family dialect. "I haven't come up with any criminal connections for Blarney Bob that might hinder the war effort. There's something else, though. I have it on good authority—" He made a snap decision to leave out Felicia's name. "—that Robert Kilkenny was involved in smuggling weapons— guns, grenades, and such—most likely bound for the Irish Republican Army. They were stored in a room in his basement."

"My God!" said Ellen in a whisper. "In *our* house!"

Sim pounded his fist against the leather-edged blotter. "The blasted IRA, some of them are in cahoots with the Germans! They've even set up some kind of ridiculous Irish fascist outfit."

"They're trying to bring back the Blueshirts as an ultra-nationalist group," said Jan primly.

She and Mack inadvertently smiled at her journalistic precision, each of them, Mack thought, waiting for the other to bring up Mr. Graves.

"Blueshirts, what nonsense!" snarled Sim.

"Stop all this phony political talk—it *is* nonsense!" Ellen's voice, grown shrill now, echoed off the wood-paneled walls.

Mack decided Ellen was right: they were drifting into a grad-student lounge conversation on current events in Ireland. "There is more, Father. That's why we're here," Mack said. "We were at Blarney Bob's house this morning. He wasn't there, and neither was his right-hand man Dominic O'Nore. That's a mystery in itself."

Ellen looked on the verge of yelling in frustration.

"But," Mack continued, "in the same room where the weapons had been, I found a dead body."

He had his father's full attention now. Sim's hands gripped the arms of his chair. He looked ready to leap across the desk.

"It was your detective, Mr. Graves. Somebody put a bullet into the middle of his forehead. You sent him around to spy on Blarney Bob in case I wasn't up to the job. Isn't that right?" Mack looked down at his open palms splayed across his lap

"Of course, I did. This is too important to leave in the hands of one person, especially *you*. You left the body where it was?"

Mack winced then nodded. Without another word, Sim picked up the phone and was put through to someone named Detwiler. Between decisions about which "operatives" to use, Sim turned to Mack. "Is the house locked?"

Mack whispered, "No."

Sim returned to barking orders to the mysterious Mr. Detwiler then hung up and leaned back in his chair. "At least the immediate situation is being taken care of. Assuming no one has called the police, which I doubt, Otto Detwiler's men will bring around a furniture truck, carry in an empty box that looks like it contains a table or an armchair, and then bring the body out in the same box. Graves—I never did know his first name—will likely turn up in an alley somewhere."

Mack marveled at his father's ruthless efficiency. He'd

always been that way, but Sim's ability to blast through obstacles was heightened now. Don't you know there's a war on?

"When this episode is over," his father continued, "I'll have Detwiler slip some cash to his family, if he has one, to make sure they don't talk to any reporters."

Lord Bountiful at work. Mack was about to acknowledge this grudging charity toward Mr. Graves's theoretical family—surely the right thing to do, even if done for questionable reasons. Then, another thought arrived uninvited. *He's only telling this to Jan and Ellen to pull them in, conscript them into the same Hero Brigade I've been forced to join.* Mack imagined a grainy photo of Mr. Graves—it was fading away in the blinding light of Tommy's heroism.

Jan shuddered. "It sounds like you've done things like this before, Mr. Simmons."

"One does what one must."

Mack saw the shadow of a smile pass across his father's face. He was enjoying this. The stage-managing, the dictatorial orders. He owned it all: his project, his office, this all-business meeting. What a horse's ass!

"Detwiler and his men will look for Robert Kilkenny, who I suspect is drowning his sorrows somewhere on the South Side. I'll give them a few days, then we'll announce Captain Kilkenny's heroic death. We have a press release ready to distribute with words from the president and General MacArthur on Thomas's supreme sacrifice. A posthumous Congressional Medal of Honor will follow."

"What about the IRA, and the Irish fascists and their Nazi friends?" Exasperated, Mack felt two or three moves behind.

"Now that we know about this possible arms smuggling, we can downplay it if it ever comes out, turn Blarney Bob into an innocent pawn. That's probably what he was anyway. And no one really cares about a bunch of Irish rebels. If the Micks ever got into bed with the Nazis, Churchill would send in the British Army in a minute. It wouldn't be pretty, but the Irish are small potatoes!" Sim snorted out a little laugh at his joke.

Mack had to admit his father was partly correct. If the Brits felt threatened, they would surely invade one more time, re-creating Easter 1916 with a whole new generation of dead patriots. During a long-ago night at Chester's, Tommy said most nations mark their history by famous victories and legendary kings; the Irish, in the Old World *and* the New, mark theirs by failed uprisings and martyred heroes. Who knew how Irish-Americans would respond to our closest ally crushing their native land and murdering more of their relatives? Mack gave an inward shrug and didn't bother bringing up the question.

"What's important," his father continued, in what Mack thought of as his blitzkrieg style, "is that we—the United States—must begin to win this war before the reality of it sinks in. Mack, your Uncle Stubby was in the Great War—the fool! He could've worked with the Munitions Board, or even with that bleeding heart Herbert Hoover—as if feeding starving Belgian children could make war into anything more than wading in blood. That's from Shakespeare, in case you still think I'm the boor you told me I was when you were an undergraduate at the University of Chicago. That's an institution I've paid thousands of dollars to—to train my son, the janitor, to turn his back on everything I've ever done and stood for!"

Mack felt his body and brain shrinking, sliding back to childhood. This was exactly the kind of rant that had turned Mack and Felicia into Sim's enemies and their mother into a near-imbecile. Jan and Ellen looked on, appalled.

Sim grasped his left forearm and squeezed hard, a move Mack had seen before when his father felt a need to curb his temper, throttle himself down. Sim went on more calmly. "My brother served on the Western Front, a major in the infantry. He was in the fighting for three months, long enough to almost destroy his mind. Nightmares woke him up screaming for years afterward—he saw doughboys with no legs or heads or faces, with their guts blown out and wrapped around their necks. That's all that war is for the men at the front, an ongoing nightmare."

He turned to Ellen. "You should be grateful, Mrs. Kilkenny, that your son died quickly and avoided that grinding horror—"

Ellen recoiled, as if she'd been slapped. Jan, stone-faced, never flinched. In his mind, Mack leaped up and stomped out of the office, loudly calling his father a horse's ass before giving the oak door a wall-shaking slam. The fantasy was profoundly unsatisfying. Mack remained rooted to his chair.

"—but this is a war that must be won, gruesome nightmare or no. We are the nation that tells soothing stories about everything. Love, marriage, politics, crime—and especially the nightmare of war. That's why we must have heroes, to tell the story of this war the way it *must* be told. Otherwise, the reverses we're experiencing will poison morale, the fighting spirit of the so-called 'masses.' Like it or not, it's the duty of us all to finish the job of making Thomas Kilkenny a national hero."

☙❧

Mack took the Chicago Avenue streetcar across the city. Despite the sparks and clatter, he dozed most of the way, once almost slipping out of his seat and into the cigarette-butt-strewn aisle. He'd turned down Ellen's and Jan's offer of a ride home. Drained by the day's events, everyone seemed relieved. They'd all seen enough of each other.

Ironically, the silence of Mack's room at Mrs. McLady's made sleep impossible. Second—and third—thoughts multiplied. Was he capable of serving as a foot soldier in a campaign that had already claimed one life? His father's reasons for pushing him into the role were so tangled they made the Gordian Knot look like a kid's twisted shoelaces. Mack smiled, in spite of himself: you didn't need a University of Chicago education to come up with an analogy like that, but it surely helped.

*Stay away from kings.* That was Eddie Fryman's wise-ass answer. Their English instructor back at Lake Forest Academy—a guy right out of college, younger than Mack was now—had asked the class, "What can we learn from Shakespeare's tragedies?"

"Stay away from kings!" piped up Eddie, creating a tag line repeated to choked-back giggles the rest of the semester.

Maybe Tommy was the real force behind all this, not the author, the Shakespeare, more like Hamlet or Macbeth, who spun their schemes and power-grabs with no regard for the fate of the other characters in the drama. For a little while, it all made crazy sense. From childhood, Tommy's doting parents had told him he was Destined for Great Things. *Tommy may never have tried to seize his royal destiny, but,* thought Mack, *the bastard still turned me into fucking Horatio, the sad-sack buddy, fated to talk about goddamn Prince Hamlet till the end of time.*

Modern-dress Shakespeare faded, as Mack's mind turned into a debating society—a full-scale parliamentary shout-fest. Remember Tommy any damned way you want, opined one caucus—the reformed Hermit Party—but stop acting like a secondary character in your own scarred life. Refuse to speak to Sim. Make a clean break. Quit the job at Steckel Avenue. Elope with Jan. Head west, find a new job, a better one. Have kids, find a little place with a white picket fence. Mack was—as the idiotic saying put it—free, white, and over twenty one—as well as 4F. He could do whatever he pleased.

Another brain-faction painted its own compelling picture. Mack, Sim, Jan, Ellen, maybe Felicia too, proudly cutting a ribbon at an army hospital to open the Thomas A. Kilkenny Wing. In a Chicago suburb, cars streamed along

Thomas Kilkenny Boulevard. The Friends of Tommy gathered on the South Side, breaking ground for the Thomas A. Kilkenny Elementary School. The Mayor and Blarney Bob were the featured speakers. Tommy was receiving well-deserved recognition for his heroism, some small recompense for a tragically brief life.

The politicians were spouting the usual self-serving hogwash, the Hermit Party faction shouted back. And what would any of it matter anyway? The Kilkenny name would become one of the historical ciphers "immortalized" by Halsted Street and Steckel Avenue or the Evans behind Evanston. Who were those stiffs anyway? No different from the half-anonymous Mr. Graves, whose full name no one could recall.

As he drifted off to sleep, Mack saw that his internal debates were meaningless as the proceedings of the Chicago City Council. The fix was in. He'd labored under the delusion that his father had chosen to go into the hero business then dragged in Mack. In reality, the hero game had chosen them all, Tommy included. Stay away from kings—too late for that.

# Chapter 16

When Mack finally woke up, he wasn't sure how long the knocking had been going on. Like most night workers, he'd gotten used to blanking out day sounds when he slept, although, after more than a year on the job, he still experienced the occasional sleepless afternoon. The knocking tapped out a steady staccato, not angry pounding, but a quietly insistent beat.

"Okay, okay, jus' a secon'." When he heard himself, Mack realized his half-articulate mutter wouldn't be heard, even through Mrs. McLady's pasteboard door. "I'm coming!" he yelled as he rolled out of the Murphy bed, fully awake now.

He ran to the mirror in the kitchen to make sure his ocular prosthesis was square with the world. He looked around for his slippers, couldn't locate them, same for his ratty blue robe. Then he spat out a frustrated, "Oh, screw it!" and shuffled to the door.

The man standing in the hall looked Mack up and down, his gaze shifting systematically from bare feet to coffee-stained gray pajamas to unshaven face.

"Mr. Simmons?" he said finally.

Mack nodded, already wary.

"May I come in? This should only take a few minutes."

Mack stared down at his wriggling toes, a stark contrast to his visitor's shiny black Oxfords. When he lifted his eyes, about to ask for a couple of minutes to get dressed, he saw that his unexpected visitor—a guy in a black suit and matching fedora who was noticeably taller and wider than Mack—held out a shiny gold badge. It showed an American eagle in full cry. Above were the words "Federal Bureau of Investigation."

"Agent Lars Neilsen, Chicago Field Office," the FBI man said with a nod of his watermelon-sized head. "And don't worry about getting dressed. I've seen a lot worse." Agent Neilsen didn't exactly smile, but his tone approached the border of friendly.

Joining the G-Man at the tiny kitchen table, Mack suppressed a grin at how the two large men absurdly filled the room, as if a pair of circus elephants had ambled in and made themselves at home. Neilsen carefully placed his hat on a crumb-free corner of the tabletop and slid a spiral notebook from an inside coat pocket.

He flipped a few pages and jotted a couple of lines in a quick scrawl.

"I need some information about an individual, someone you're familiar with—" He fixed water-colored Scandinavian eyes on Mack and sat back in Mrs. McLady's rickety chair.

Mack's internal debating society declared itself in session. Nominations were brought to the floor: Blarney Bob, some radical UofC prof or shady journalist friend of Janice. Maybe even his father.

"—Dominic O'Nore."

A true dark-horse candidate.

"You mean the guy who works for Blarney Bob Kilkenny? The alderman?" The Secretary of the Stupid Questions Committee will please read the minutes.

Agent Neilsen stared at his notebook. "Yes, that's correct. Alderman Kilkenny's assistant. Do you know his whereabouts?" Apparently, noted an antic member of the debate club, "whereabouts" was a term used exclusively by cops and people trying to sound like cops.

"As far as I know, he lives at the alderman's house. Isn't he there?"

"No, he's not."

"Have you asked the alderman?"

Agent Neilsen leaned forward. The chair twitched nervously, looking ready to collapse any second. "The Bureau has an urgent need to speak with Mr. O'Nore, and we're pursuing a number of lines of inquiry. That's why I'm here."

The mental photograph of the murdered Mr. Graves reappeared and refused to fade away. Mack felt an urgent need to step out of character, stop reciting the lines he'd been assigned in the hero script. He wanted to come clean, tell the whole story, leave out no detail. After all, this was the FBI—America's top crime fighters, now the scourge of Axis spies and saboteurs.

When he and Tommy had faced drunk-and-disorderly charges after their campaign to have a drink in every Loop saloon, Sim had teetered between defense lawyer and furious protector of the desecrated Simmons name. The lawyer won. Answer only the question you're asked, his father advised, offer nothing more. The boys' brief answers had sufficed, as Tommy's broad smile and political connections charmed the Chicago cops. That charge was quashed. This new intrusion might be pushed away too.

The FBI agent found several ways to ask about the last time Mack had seen Dominic O'Nore. Mack put forth all the charm he could muster, finding different ways to reply that he'd last seen O'Nore a few days ago, when Mack had dropped by the Kilkenny home. No, they hadn't spoken— they never had, as far as he could remember. Dominic was the same as ever, that is, silent and expressionless. Mack described Dominic's bulky black-wool sweater. Dark slacks too, he thought. The interview petered out. Neilsen retrieved his hat.

As Mack reached for the doorknob to show the G-Man out, Neilsen pulled a business card from his coat pocket. "If you remember anything else, Mr. Simmons, call me." Stepping into the hallway, he gave Mack a squinting look. "You know, I'm remembering something about *you*. Did you ever play football? For Chicago, wasn't it?"

"Yeah, I started at guard for three years for the Maroons. You play?"

"Tackle at Minnesota. We played against each other—in 'thirty-eight maybe. Strange game, hardly anyone at Stagg Field. We beat you something like forty-nine to nothing."

"We lost so many games like that, I can't keep track. UofC was getting ready to drop football. We didn't have any players."

"Well, you were pretty good, gave me some bruises I remembered for a while—and that halfback of yours, big Irish kid. He could've started anywhere in the Big Ten. You remember his name?"

"Yes, I do. Thomas Kilkenny."

"Same as the alderman. There's a coincidence for you. Any relation?" The agent shrugged his wide shoulders under the taut suit jacket.

"His son. A good friend of mine."

"Where is he? He's not on my list, but maybe he knows something about O'Nore's whereabouts."

"I doubt it. He's overseas, in the Philippines." Not lies exactly. Call it an edited version of the truth.

"Not likely he's got any information, I guess."

Mack watched for any hint that Neilsen knew about Tommy's fate, but he appeared to be nothing more than a thorough investigator, a quintessential FBI man.

Turning away, the agent muttered, half to himself, "A Big Ten school dropping football. Sounds un-American."

Mack heard unspoken questions: How did you go from the University of Chicago to a dump like this? Something to do with the glass eye? Mack was mortally certain everyone noticed it eventually.

Mack called after Neilsen as he was about to disappear

down the stairs. "You wouldn't happen to know what this is about, would you?"

"Nope. A Bureau matter, that's all Hoover and the higher-ups will say. They never tell us Field Office mopes diddly-squat."

He took a step onto the staircase then turned and stepped back to the second-floor hallway. The agent gestured toward Mack with an open, fleshy hand. "Hey, buddy, come here for a second, would you?"

Mack shuffled his bare feet across the hall carpet, faded to a vague oatmeal shade from some unknowable original color. They met next to the pay telephone, halfway between Mack's door and the stairs. The FBI man leaned close enough for Mack to inhale his coffee-flavored breath.

In a hoarse whisper, Neilsen said, "I shouldn't be telling you this…" He paused. Mack gaped. "…but this is big. We've got a dozen agents on the street looking for this fellow O'Nore, and those are just the ones I know about. The scuttlebutt is the director himself is personally running the investigation. Whatever the hell they're investigating."

"O—h—h—h?" The muttered half-word did a good job of conveying the message, "I understand what you're saying but have no reply whatsoever."

"What I'm getting at is, watch your back. Like when the other team has a goon who hits after the whistle." The friendly, footballers-together tone shifted. "Don't leave town. Don't go to any unusual places—you know what I mean."

Mack didn't.

"Keep things quiet. Ordinary. And let me know if you hear even a peep about Dominic O'Nore. Anything at all."

Neilsen paused, and his voice dropped again, as he fixed his eyes on Mack. They were so pale they seemed of no color at all. "Look, brother, I'm playing it straight when I tell you I don't know shit about why Hoover is calling out the troops. But whatever's going on, civilians have got to stay out of Bureau business. If you play Sam Spade on this, you're risking your ass—along with that one good eye. This isn't a goddamn football game. Remember that."

Mack said he'd remember and blinked hard to make sure both eyes were in place.

Neilsen walked quickly down the stairs, pulling down the brim of his fedora. Mack recognized the move from William Powell's *Thin Man* movies,

Mack returned to his room, closed the door, and thought about what to do next. Getting dressed and making coffee looked like good first steps.

Finishing his second cup and feeling the caffeine seep into his brain, Mack headed for the pay telephone. His first thought was to call Jan—certainly, an ordinary thing to do—to warn her that she could be on the FBI's list too. His nickel was almost in the slot, but he pulled it back. Why was he really calling her? From a ridiculous knight-errant's desire to play the protector?

Jan's core of self-sufficient independence—her *not* needing protection like some stereotyped movie heroine— that was why he loved her, wasn't it?

If G-Men came calling, Jan would handle it, answer only the questions asked.

Mack checked his watch, something he still had to do to get his daytime bearings: Three-thirty. He reluctantly concluded there was an FBI target whose responses were less dependable. He released the nickel and called Simmons, Burgoyne, and Altfelder. Miss Lincecombe answered on the second ring. When Mack asked to speak with his father, her response was actually polite: "I'm sorry, Mack, but he was called away."

"Do you know when he'll be back?"

"Well, that's the strangest thing." Her voice was tinged with…surprise? Concern? "He got a call on his private line—I heard it ring through the door. Hardly anyone's got the number." Mack was not a member of that select circle. "Then he marched out of the office without a word. He never said where he was going or when he'd be back." In the realm of Simmons, Burgoyne, and Altfelder, this was the equivalent of the eruption of Mount Vesuvius.

"Well, okay," Mack replied, shaking his head. "Please have him call me as soon as he returns." He read the faded number in the center of the dial. "It's a public telephone, but I'll stay close by."

Miss Lincecombe, her world clearly reeling, agreed.

Mack moved a kitchen chair near his door, poured another cup of coffee and, leaving the door halfway open, settled in to wait. Was Sim's unexpected departure a coincidence, unconnected with the tangled paths of Mr. Graves, Blarney Bob, and Dominic O'Nore? Maybe the call was from a desperate client threatening to shoot her unfaithful husband? Not likely.

Footsteps sounded from down the hall. Mack leaped up as if his butt had encountered a pitchfork. His neighbor Vasili fed a coin into the phone and dialed. If a wind had been blowing through the hallway, the guy's sweat-stained tee-shirt would've flapped in the breeze. Whoever was on the other end must've answered on the first ring. Vasili spat out a stream of rapid-fire Greek. Then his side of the conversation became "Nay!" stridently repeated seven or eight times. Ironically, noted a tiny pedant in Mack's head, the word means "yes" in Greek.

He opened the door all the way, ready to tell Vasili to please hang up—he was waiting for an important call. Vasili glanced in his direction, emitted one final "nay!" louder than the others, and hung up before Mack could take a step. He returned to his post by the door. Sounds leaked up to the second floor: doors opening and closing, voices that couldn't be held in by the thin walls, the rumble of traffic from Austin Boulevard. No ringing telephone. No assurance that it wasn't pure paranoia to imagine Vasili had been recruited by the FBI to keep an eye on him.

Mack opened the door a foot wider and, suddenly starving, went to the kitchen to make a bologna sandwich. He desperately wanted a beer or two or three to wash it down, but he never kept booze in his room. He wasn't an alcoholic. Mack told himself he could drink, but he wanted to push temptation away. Get thee behind me, Satan. Then take a couple of steps back.

Noting that his loaf of Wonder Bread was getting stale, Mack washed down his wretched sandwich, mustard, no mayo, with another cup of black coffee. Death seemed all around, a new component of the atmosphere, but stubbornly invisible. Then a shape congealed out of the transparent air. Dominic O'Nore—heavy-set, hairless, dressed in black, scowling. Who else could've murdered Mr. Graves, who just happened to be in the IRA armory? Why else would Dominic have disappeared? Mack tossed down a gulp of bitter coffee. He reminded himself how unlikely it was that the FBI knew about Graves or his death. Yet the G-Men were mustering an army of agents to find Dominic.

Everyone, himself included, possessed a few jigsaw pieces, but nobody, not even the FBI, could see the whole puzzle.

For Mack, the fragmented picture included Tommy's night-train-to-war letter and the Irish vision he shared with Jan. Mack had tried to convince himself they were nothing but romantic morsels that escaped the irony with which Tommy branded such thoughts. Now, Mack wasn't even sure about that. He couldn't sense what Tommy had claimed to see—no phantom rail journeys, no Irish peasant's look into the future. Did the approach of death enable you to see such things?

Mack's own brush with quick mortality had produced a lot of weird sensations but no images of the Destroying Angel, Grim Reaper, Four Horsemen of the Apocalypse, or less traditional avatars of doom. Perhaps that meant he was destined to live a long time, delivered to longevity courtesy of Tommy's drunken driving and the resulting 4F status. Maybe, Mack thought with a grin, he should pray to Brigid, patron saint of prophecies, to learn what she had to say about *his* future. She'd probably spoken only Gaelic, but canonization transcended language, right?

He forced down a last bite of bologna and stale bread. Wistfully, Mack wondered how one of those individual soufflés from Romanoff's would go down for dessert.

# Chapter 17

John Mackenzie Simmons II (never Junior) stared at the telephone on his mahogany desk as if the black hunk of wires and plastic had betrayed him. The phone ringing at all had been a surprise. Nearly every call to Simmons, Burgoyne, and Altfelder came through Miss Lincecombe, who then quietly rapped on his door—no intercoms were wanted at Simmons, Burgoyne, and Altfelder—and asked if he would speak to the party calling. Only when he acquiesced did she put the call through. This time, the telephone rang with, it seemed, the suddenness of a thunderclap. And it was on his sacrosanct private line.

"Is this Sim?" the youthful male voice had asked. Only relatives and friends, or at least acquaintances of long standing, called him Sim. Whenever he received a call or mailing directed to "John," he instantly knew the person was a stranger, someone who didn't really know him.

When Sim had reluctantly owned up to his familiar name, the caller identified himself: Agent Frank Washburn of the Federal Bureau of Investigation, Chicago Field Office. The Bureau had an urgent matter to discuss with him—in person, if possible. Would it be convenient to come over to the Federal Building, only a few blocks away, as soon as possible?

Sim was far more familiar with issuing orders than taking them, but he quickly agreed.

"Please don't mention this call or where you're going. Room six-sixty-eight. Thank you."

After rushing past the wide-eyed Miss Lincecombe, Sim walked fast, certain he could cover the short distance in less than ten minutes. Striding along LaSalle Street, he cursed the cold wind off the lake and the overcoat left hanging on the rack in his office. A stabbing thought brought him up short. What if this meeting had to do with Graves? Never thrown for a loop for long, Sim soon quickly reasoned his way through the brief moment of panic. Detwiler had called to confirm that his operatives had removed the body and that he was close to securing a safe, permanent resting place. So, it was unlikely the FBI knew—or for that matter, gave a damn—about Mr. Graves. Surely an unfortunate victim, but a nonentity nevertheless.

Furthermore, in the few cases where Sim couldn't keep law enforcement out of his divorce cases, the police always showed up unexpectedly to interview their target, usually a philandering husband driven to commit some foolishly illegal act. Sim put his concerns about Graves aside, but didn't dismiss them entirely.

In the creeping Federal Building elevator, Sim wondered if, like all his encounters with Outraged Authority over the past ten years, this had some connection with his son. However, by the time the elderly Negro man operating the elevator gasped out "Six" and yanked the lever to open the cage, that surmise had faded too. Sim was swimming in deeper water now. The call from the FBI must be related to his project, creating an authentic American hero, the nation's first in this failing war. Thomas Kilkenny.

He and his wife had always liked Thomas. When the possibility arose that he might marry Felicia, Katherine, in her supremely vague way, had been ready to welcome him into the family. Sim was positive too, but a bit less enthusiastic. But that was only because of the snide remarks Sim knew he'd overhear about acquiring an Irish Catholic son-in-law and a family connection like the notorious Blarney

Bob Kilkenny. He'd been much less positive about Janice and Mack. A pair of marriages between the families was too much, and Janice was too pushy a female for Sim's taste. Thomas, though, was a fine young man, especially compared to his own wastrel son. There was no accounting for their becoming such fast friends.

As Sim entered room 668, a sickly-thin, blond-haired fellow stuck his head out the door of an inner office, politely introduced himself as Agent Washburn, and asked Sim to have a seat in the waiting room—which was even grimmer than his own, featuring spotted, cement-colored linoleum instead of Simmons, Burgoyne, and Altfelder's respectably worn hardwood floor. The agent was barely older than Mack or Thomas Kilkenny. The realization brought Sim up short. Thomas, and all the other youngsters destined to die in this war, would always be boys. Forever.

Sim settled into the least stained of the three leather chairs jammed into the tiny room. Without quite knowing why, he asked himself the question again. At the end of the day, why am I doing this? He received the same answer, which always came as a surprise: I want my wife to love me again.

He would've laughed off the answer, or become angry, if anyone else had suggested it, most likely seasoned with a sarcastic joke about divorce lawyers. (After splitting up a thousand marriages, Sim Simmons—the hatchet man of LaSalle Street—is finally trying to save one.) But Katherine, he decided, was the underlying reason. Felicia, who'd made shielding him from his wife her life's work, was likely a lost cause. Reconciling with Mack remained a possibility. Involving him in the plan was going well. But Katherine could be his wife again, and through her, he could have a marriage and family again. He was sure of it. After so many years, Sim recognized that others would say it was impossible to shock or trick or tease Katherine back to the vivacious, loving woman he'd married in 1914. To be brutally honest, those nay-saying "others" would include every single person he knew.

His wedding to the Belle of Winnetka, as he'd thought of her, took place just after he graduated from Yale Law. Their wedding had been the North Shore social event of the summer. In a coincidence that had made no impression whatsoever at the time, Archduke Franz Ferdinand and his wife had been murdered at Sarajevo a few days afterward. Perhaps, in some incomprehensible way, the assassinations had somehow lit the fuse of his and Katherine's miseries just as they had for the world's larger troubles.

Sim viewed the scenes he wanted to see as if they were a motion picture—a beaming Sim and Katherine, arm in arm on a reviewing stand greeting the president and first lady at a flag-filled parade through downtown Chicago, the air filled with confetti and cheers. Armistice Day? The Fourth of July? In any case, the event had been organized by him in honor of Thomas Kilkenny, and the waves of love and gratitude were palpable, both from the cheering throng and the smiling, charming woman at his side. Sim would have preferred a Republican president, of course, but FDR was the only president available, and Katherine was an admirer of Eleanor Roosevelt.

The inner-office door swung open, and Agent Washburn stepped into the waiting room. He nodded at Sim and gestured toward the open door. Sim walked in, but Washburn didn't follow. In the dimly lit office, a solidly built man in a gray suit came into focus standing behind a desk cluttered with manila folders and stray coffee cups. A smile spread across the fellow's jowly face as he extended his hand.

"It's a pleasure to see you again, Sim!" The accent came from somewhere on the East Coast, but not the harsh New England tone of Sim's grandfather. It was softer, more Southern, maybe Virginia or Maryland.

Still awakening from his hero reverie, Sim knew full well he was presenting a flabbergasted look to his host.

"Sim, we're still indebted to you and the other members of the Crime Commission for advising us to keep the Chicago Police in the dark when we brought down Dillinger."

They shook hands warmly, and Sim, at long last matching an identity to the man's face, started to speak the name he'd finally found. But, as they finished shaking hands, the hearty fellow across the desk beat him to the punch. "J. Edgar Hoover, Director of the Federal Bureau of Investigation."

"Mr. Director, my apologies for not recognizing you immediately. I've had a lot on my mind lately." He breathed a small sigh of relief—if Hoover was involved, the meeting couldn't involve someone as insignificant as Graves.

Hoover smiled without exposing any teeth.

Buoyed by thoughts of the hero plan moving ahead, Sim's confidence flowed back like a balloon expanding. "And of course, you were not exactly the first person I was expecting to meet."

They sat down simultaneously, as if on command, and faced one another across the cluttered desk.

"I suppose not," the director said, the retreating smile still softening his voice. "I took the early train from Washington. No one outside the Bureau knows I'm here. Except, of course, you."

Sim nodded.

"Mr. Simmons—Sim—I recall being impressed by your patriotism and dedication, both before and after our men brought down that scum John Dillinger." He spat out the name like a mouthful of spoiled meat.

"Your men did a fine job, as usual." A minimal compliment seemed the best strategy for getting through the chit-chat stage and finding out what the hell this was about.

"It's always best to have honest citizens like yourself working with us. Of course, here in Chicago, it's not always easy to tell the honest citizens from the dishonest ones!"

Hoover chuckled at his own joke. The folds of flesh

beneath his jaw, which had grown more like a turkey's wattles since Sim had last seen him, wobbled rhythmically. Sim didn't like the slur on his native city. He resisted a sarcastic urge to point out that Washington, D.C. was, of course, a bastion of incorruptible honesty and truthfulness.

"So, Sim, I understand that you're working now to honor your friend Captain Thomas Kilkenny. My condolences for his loss, though, from what I've been told, he unquestionably died a hero."

"Thank you for your kind words, Director Hoover."

Suspicion rising, Sim noted that Hoover wasn't making even a minimal effort to sound sincere. Sim had never heard that the FBI knew about Tommy's heroic and still unannounced death, but it hardly surprised him. Sim had learned of it from his White House contact, Philip Gladwin, always called "Fix." He was a Yale classmate, now some kind of economic advisor with FDR's White House Brain Trust—whatever was left of it now that winning the war had replaced the New Deal. Fix called with the news of Captain Kilkenny's death and the vague plan to make him a national figure, the plan Sim had turned into his own crusade. Ever since, Sim had expected interference, admittedly, not from J. Edgar Hoover, but some bureaucratic effort to exert ownership of Thomas's sacrifice.

Hoover set his elbows on the desk and steepled stubby fingers in front of his chin. "The Bureau is in a touchy situation these days, Sim. Even before the war, we kept an eye on un-American groups—the German Bund, the Japs' 'White Chrysanthemum Societies,' and of course, we've always watched the Commies and their front groups."

Sim nodded again in a manner he hoped conveyed deep appreciation that the director saw fit to let him in on this inside information, even though he knew it already. With his boys'-adventure approach to crime-fighting and relentless self-promotion, Hoover reminded Sim of several flamboyant divorce lawyers he'd faced, publicity hounds with Hoover's instinct for mouthing a memorable line and getting in front of the newspaper photographers. It didn't matter whether they represented a wealthy husband or aggrieved wife. Sim always beat the hell out of them.

Hoover folded his arms across his chest, wrinkling the smooth surface of his vest, and continued in a more somber tone. "Now that Roosevelt's gotten us into the war, our job has gotten more complicated. We've got to keep track of foreign groups that oppose our so-called allies: Followers of that agitator Gandhi in India, Ukrainians and Lithuanians who despise Joe Stalin and the Bolsheviks."

"With good reason, I'll wager!"

"Amen to that! We'll be fighting the Russkies before this is over, mark my words." Hoover glanced down at his watch. "In any case, one of the outfits we've started watching more intently is the IRA, the Irish Republican Army."

Sim widened his eyes and dropped his jaw as if this were astounding news.

"Yes," Hoover said with a wise nod, "we were surprised too, thinking everything had gone quiet over there since the Micks finally got their own little country. But their bitter-enders, including some they've sent to America, want to use the war and Britain's troubles to seize the North, Ulster. And they're working with the Nazis to do it." Hoover pronounced "Nazis" the way Churchill did: Nazzies.

"I appreciate your taking the time to tell me this, Mister Director," Sim said, hoping the supplicant's tone wasn't too overblown, but then becoming convinced Hoover wouldn't notice. "Can you tell me if any of this has to do with Thomas Kilkenny? If so, my guess is that it's connected to his father. The alderman is certainly a prominent Irishman."

Hoover leaned back and smiled. "Indeed—he's prominent in a number of ways. We have quite a thick file on Robert Kilkenny. It includes bootlegging, gambling, tax evasion, aiding and abetting no end of illegal activities. But he's not the one we're investigating now."

Hoover paused, for effect, Sim concluded. "It's his

bodyguard we're after. Dominic O'Nore. Do you know him, Mr. Simmons?"

Sim cleared his throat. He was genuinely surprised. "*Know* is too strong a word. I've attended events with Alderman Kilkenny over the years—civic functions and such—and seen the fellow hanging about. Heavy-set, shaved head, indeterminate age. People commented that he looked like Mussolini. It's widely known that Robert Kilkenny has underworld connections and, most likely, underworld enemies, so it seemed wise for him to have an intimidating bodyguard. I'm sure I never exchanged a single word with O'Nore."

"We assumed that was the case."

"Why are you so interested in catching him?" Sim had played his role as the cooperative citizen. Now it was Hoover's turn to answer Sim's questions.

"He's a long-time member of the IRA, traveled back to Ireland a half-dozen times over the last few years, probably involved in smuggling arms—nothing we were much interested in. Now, we have information, solid information, that he's involved in something bigger. Much bigger." Hoover splayed his hands on the desk in front of him and went silent.

"So, I'm assuming you've told me all you can," said Sim after a few seconds, disappointed not to learn more about whatever cat-and-mouse game the FBI and the IRA were playing.

"You're correct. But, Sim, there is one more thing."

Sim leaned forward. *We've arrived at last*, he thought. *Appear to end the conversation, but save its real purpose for the "one more thing" stage*—Sim was a past master of the tactic. *Never use a trickster's own trick.*

"One more thing," Hoover repeated. "I must ask you to delay your campaign to make public Thomas Kilkenny's heroic death. Nothing can be done until we've picked up Dominic O'Nore. I will let you know when to proceed. And of course, we cannot predict when that will be. We must thoroughly interrogate the fellow."

The emphasis Hoover put on the word "thoroughly" convinced Sim that this would not be a short or simple process.

"Mister Director, you can count on me." Sim summoned up a look of friendly reassurance, something he did well, but he was already thumbing through a mental directory of operatives to locate Dominic O'Nore before the FBI.

Hoover's chair slid silently back from the desk, and the director glided upright. Sim stood too.

As they shook hands, more warmly than before, Hoover said, "I knew you would understand, Sim."

# Chapter 18

The border guard he'd killed near Strabane had taken the Devil's own time to die, coughing life away, blood filling his mouth, then emptying out and dripping down his cheeks like a teacup overflowing. A bloody long time—Dominic O'Nore smiled at his unwitting joke. As he pictured the dying man, really a boy of eighteen or so, Dominic recalled that he'd gone to school with the lad's older brother.

He couldn't remember if the pistols, rifles, and ammunition were going to or coming from Ulster when the boy-guard spotted them in the lorry. The border—the "bleeding wound of the nation," according to the IRA broadsheets—ran right through the muddy streets of little Strabane. The border post was supposed to be unoccupied, but there stood the lad in his oversized khaki uniform and wide leather belt, eager to do his duty—another failure of intelligence, as the higher ups laughably called it. When the guard came round to the front of the lorry, Dominic had no choice but to shoot him twice in the middle of the chest.

Unlike the guard, the damned snooping detective in the Kilkennys' cellar had become still and silent straight away. A fair amount of blood was connected with the recent affair too, of course, but not as much as Dominic had expected, considering the brain has so much blood coursing through, and he'd shot that fellow in the head.

When he and the bloated fool arrived at the Chicago safe house, the first question Lonegan had put to him was, "Did you clean up after?" He had indeed, Dominic had said, in a reply soaked in profanity. "I've brought along the rags so they'll find no blood. I'll return after dark and haul the corpse away to the river."

He cursed the police siren that sounded close by no more than a minute after he'd dealt with the tall fellow in the cellar. "I'm a detective," the man had muttered, the last words he uttered in this vale of sorrows. The great culmination—a word Dominic always liked—was too close to take chances. He'd thrown the satchel of papers, which now sat at his knee, into the front seat of the Cadillac, hustled the gibbering Blarney Bob and a pair of suitcases into the back, and flung the rags and the last box of weapons, mostly small arms, pistols and revolvers, into the boot. Then, breathing hard and telling himself out loud to drive slow and easy, he'd cleared out of the Kilkenny house.

"Now," he said to Lonegan in a more commanding tone, "go and burn the damned rags, and stop taking me for a bigger fool than this sodden fellow." He pointed to Blarney Bob, filled to the brim with whiskey and already snoring on the couch in the front room of the tiny Canaryville house. It was a shanty nearly as drafty and desolate as Dominic's own childhood home along the Falls Road. The stink of the Chicago stockyards flowed into the room every time Lonegan opened the door, an invisible fog flavored with shit. The place smelled worse than the Donegal pig farm where he and his mates hid after the Strabane incident. From Belfast to Chicago and all points between, are we destined always to live in foul holes not fit for rats?

He said to Lonegan, "The rags are in the boot of the car, which we must shortly be rid of. They're sitting next to the last of the goods from the cellar."

It felt good to be speaking to someone, even a nitwit like Hugh Lonegan. Dominic was not by nature a silent man, but that was the part he'd learned to play as dogsbody for the Right Honorable Alderman—he liked the feel of the title "alderman"—Robert Kilkenny.

He chuckled at the name. Offering a choice had been the fancy of Billy Farrell, sent out by Michael Collins himself to tell the blood-soaked tale of the Dublin Rising and get as many known rebels as possible out of Ireland before the Brits exacted their murderous revenge. Dominic had been present at the christening.

"And what shall your new name be, my lad?" Farrell asked the young Daniel McGuigan, an enthusiastic recruit from Bannacree, fresh from sending a British colonel to a long stay in hell and as handsome a black Irishman as he'd ever known. They were hiding in a mucky corner of the stables across the road from Kilkenny Castle, the very citadel of the enemy.

"Why, I choose Robert—a fine solid-fellow's name, I'm sure you'll agree—with the last name of Kilkenny, in honor of these swank accommodations."

Everyone laughed, a rare thing in those days and times, and the deed was done, with help from Higgins and his magical way with pen, ink, and British documents.

The Yanks had been fed so much rubbish about Ireland—the Olde Sod, the bloody Emerald Isle—they would've believed any name he came up with:

"I'm Seamus Goddamn Lake of Innisfree."

"And surely you are, sir!"

When it was Gerry Hearn's time to get out, he'd renamed himself Dominic O'Nore, after his favorite uncle and the lovely River Nore that flows through Kilkenny Town. He eventually followed Robert Kilkenny to Chicago.

At first, Dominic thought the icy winds would freeze him solid, and he never got used to a supposed springtime that swung crazily from snowstorms to the sweaty heat tormenting him now—nothing like the steady, creeping advance of warmth and green shoots he'd known in Ireland. But he persevered and reported over the years on Robert Kilkenny's rise to prominence. Sent hidden in packages of clothing and canned goods to shifting addresses in Dublin and Belfast, his dispatches were full of amazement at how far a bit of the old blarney could get you in America.

Lonegan, as thick-headed a fellow as ever walked the earth, clumped back in with the paper bag of bloody rags. "When you've stowed the goods, Hughie, bestir yourself to whip up some ham and eggs for the alderman and me."

"And what of this fellow, the alderman?" Lonegan asked with an overly dramatic gesture toward the couch. "I've seen his picture in the papers. Won't he be missed?"

"His wife and daughter scarcely ever visit, and she's no real wife anymore, in any case. And his handsome son is off fighting the Japs somewhere at the other end of the world." Dominic paused and chuckled to himself. "Besides, the Honorable Blarney Bob misses so many meetings at the City Hall they'd not blink an eye at his absence even if their bloody talking shop was open. If there's too much curiosity about the matter, I'll see that he's checked into Resurrection Hospital 'for observation.' If need be, we can arrange for poor Alderman Bob to take a sudden turn for the worse and require a resurrection of his own."

Lonegan, panting like a friendly dog, seemed satisfied and went out the back door again to the alley. Even parked out of sight off the street, the Cadillac stood out in this god-forsaken slum like a top hat on a hobo. He would have to use it to haul away the miserable detective's body, but Dominic surmised he was a man who would not be much noticed by anyone. In the scheme of things in this fallen world, the automobile was of greater concern. They must get rid of it, and soon. Maybe shove the car and its owner both into the stinking river.

He looked over at Robert Kilkenny snoring liquidly beneath the crucifix on the greasy wall. The red blood of Christ's wounds was the only color in the room. Dominic knew the grand enterprise he was embarking upon would likely leave him a bleeding corpse like the border guard, the sneaking detective, and Victor Schlegel, if not the Savior

Himself. But Dominic wouldn't let death take *him* by surprise. He'd take it on straight ahead, look death in the face, and use his sacrifice, if it came to that, to change the face of Ireland and the great world beyond.

೮ඨ೮ඨ

Rapid footsteps sounded from the hallway. Mack stepped from the little kitchen alcove into his laughably tiny living room. The door to the hallway swung open all the way, and Mack found himself face to face with his father. Sim's face was flushed. He breathed in fast puffs. He's run up the stairs, Mack concluded. Highly unusual behavior.

"Father, what are you doing here? Did you get my message?" His chairmanship of the Stupid Questions Committee remained secure.

"Message? I never received any message! I took a cab straight here from the FBI Field Office downtown. It's a good thing I remembered your address."

"Okay, okay," said Mack, seeking to calm his father down, not something he often did. "I wanted to warn you that a G-Man visited me today. But if the FBI's been talking to you too, the message doesn't matter anymore."

His life continued to be a farcical tale of missed connections, punctuated by banana-peel slips. Bernie Silverman, another UofC grad student, had introduced Mack to the Yiddish word *schlemiel*, according to Bernie, a guy mystically destined to always fuck up. I, Mack concluded, am the ultimate gentile schlemiel.

Mack gestured toward the purple couch and dragged over the crudely patched armchair. Both men sat.

Sim glanced around the room, which he'd never visited before. Mack braced for some pointed comment on his squalid living conditions. But Sim only stroked his mustache and said quietly, "Tell me about your FBI visit."

Sim straightened his shoulders under the jacket of his

dark-blue Brooks Brothers suit—the standard-issue uniform for LaSalle Street lawyers—and listened. To Mack's surprise, his father's only interruption was to make sure Mack's encounter with Agent Neilsen included no mention of the dead man in the basement.

"So, Father," said Mack, after fetching a glass of water for Sim, and checking to make sure the glass was clean before filling it, "the federal men contacted you too?"

Sim drained off half his water and leaned back into Mack's quicksand couch cushions. After a brief look of panic, as if he were falling down a well, Sim put the glass down on the battered end-table and appeared to reclaim his dignity.

"Yes, the FBI wanted to talk to me too, a command appearance—"

Sim paused, and Mack saw that it was for effect. He gritted his teeth. What was his father up to now? Recent experience had greatly expanded the realm of possibilities.

"You may recall my service years ago with the Crime Commission. Or more likely not, because you were too busy trying to get expelled from Lake Forest Academy."

Mack didn't rise to the bait, suppressing a grin at his hope as an adolescent that the Chicago Crime Commission was in the business of committing crimes…maybe Al Capone was a member?…and his disappointment that the group was dedicated to crime prevention.

"In any case," Sim continued, "the commission worked closely with the FBI, and I had occasion to meet with J. Edgar Hoover several times."

Mack reached down, pulled up his right sock, and sighed. His father would tell the story at his own pace.

Sim ran an index finger around the rim of the glass. "In fact, Director Hoover met with me privately this afternoon at the Bureau office in the Federal Building." Sim pursed his lips into a tiny smile.

"What…what did you and Director Hoover talk

about?" Mack knew his bafflement pleased his father, underlining that he was in charge.

"The director reminded me that I was the one who advised the FBI to keep the Chicago Police out of the Dillinger operation altogether."

Sim smiled again. "The director said the Bureau is keeping tabs on all sorts of organizations opposed to our allies: Ukrainians who hate Stalin and the Soviets, followers of that Mahatma Gandhi person agitating for Indian independence, that sort of thing. As if the Japs or the Communists wouldn't take over in ten minutes if the British ever left India!"

Mack caught on just before Sim continued. "The IRA! The FBI's watching the IRA and their sympathizers."

"Right, and they're becoming active now. Hoover said what we knew already—that some IRA factions are working with the Nazis. And they've planted agents over here."

"That sounds awfully general. Hardly worth a 'command appearance' before J. Edgar Hoover."

"That's what I thought too. Hoover was cagey at first, then he said something big is up. I figured it was connected with Blarney Bob—the director knows he's been involved in smuggling arms, but they're not interested in that—"

Seeing a need to shift the subject away from Felicia's discovery in the Kilkenny basement, Mack said, "I assume Hoover knows about Tommy and his Congressional Medal of Honor and all that."

"Of course he does. But the reason for the command performance was the same as the visit by your football-playing G-man. They're after Dominic O'Nore. He's surely an agent for the pro-Nazi wing of the IRA, probably intelligence received from the British. The FBI is scouring Chicago—and the whole country, for all we know—trying to find him. Hoover said we must stop the effort to make Thomas Kilkenny a war hero until they've caught and questioned O'Nore."

"Then, that's what we have to do. We don't know where Dominic is either, so we can't finger him for the FBI. Face it, Father, between the IRA and the FBI, your hero scheme is finished. Jan and her mother will be relieved to mourn in peace. Blarney Bob too—I doubt he'll care if his lost son is a hero or not. The only one who really cares is you!" Mack felt the joy of a reprieved prisoner. The hero game was releasing them.

"Nonsense!" Sim's shout rattled the windowpane and must've startled Mrs. McLady's tenants above and below. "This isn't finished, not by a long sight. We're not going to 'finger' O'Nore, as you so quaintly put it. But we—and that means you and I, along with others I'll be calling on—are going to find Dominic O'Nore, *before* the FBI gets to him."

"You still believe you're in control. You're as bad as MacArthur, thinking you're running things." Mack's arm swung in a broad horizontal wave that nearly knocked over his father's water glass. "This is war. Tommy's dead, so is Graves. There *is* no reason why, no grand plan. Nobody's in charge, not the generals, not anyone."

The thunderbolt Mack expected never came. "I won't defend our generals," said Sim, straightening his shoulders. "But this is one situation we can control. We *will* find Dominic O'Nore."

"Assuming we beat the G-Men to the punch, which is insanely unlikely, what would you propose doing with Dominic? By all accounts, he's a pretty formidable character." He was back to goading his father—it felt easy and natural, like dialing a telephone or pressing the keys of a typewriter. "Should we send him to Palm Beach? Take him to a ballgame at Wrigley Field?" A cartoon image of Stan Hack autographing a baseball for Dominic—or was it a grenade?—flashed through Mack's brain.

Sim refused to be goaded, a rare event that put Mack on his guard. "We are going to neutralize him. Make sure O'Nore, and Blarney Bob too, if he's in on it, cause no more harm to our British allies—and no more delay in inspiring our own countrymen with Captain Kilkenny's extraordinary bravery and self-sacrifice."

Mack wasn't entirely certain what he was hearing. But, as dawn broke, he felt the false drama of his words even as he spoke: "*Neutralize* him? Do you mean kill Dominic? Do you intend to kill him?

Sim petted the right half of his mustache as if it were a beloved puppy. "Yes, it may well come to that. It may well."

# Chapter 19

In his office at home, Sim attempted to mark up the documents related to the divorce of an annoying woman from Wilmette. It was the same old story—get the most out of her husband before releasing him to marry his much-younger mistress. Sim was proud of his ability to concentrate on the most mundane details. Now, though, he felt his powers waning as he waited for Mr. Dineen.

Sim snorted out an involuntary laugh. Wasn't Mr. Dineen supposed to wait on *him*? But Sim couldn't very well keep an eye on Felicia himself. Mr. Dineen had always gotten on well with Felicia. When she was a little girl, she rode around the wide lawn on his back, shrieking with delight, something, Sim was compelled to admit, she never did with him. Sim was curious about how the hidebound old Irish butler felt about tipping him off about Felicia's departure so he could visit Katherine. An illicit lovers' rendezvous with his own wife? Sim began to laugh again at the absurdity but stifled himself when a soft knock sounded at his office door.

"She's left?" Sim asked before Mr. Dineen had opened the door two inches.

"Yes, sir. The taxi picked her up in the alley no more than one minute ago."

A loyal Northwestern alumna, Felicia was bound for some sort of gathering of former sorority sisters. Sim shared

Mr. Dineen's disdain at all those foolish Greek letters and had no idea of the purpose of the meeting. All he needed to know was that Felicia had left and wouldn't return for several hours.

"Excellent!" Sim jumped up from his desk, almost tipping over his chair. He was already past Mr. Dineen and into the hall when a hasty thank-you got itself spoken.

Scant seconds later, Sim knocked gently on his wife's closed bedroom door. "Katherine, my dear Kate. It's Sim."

Soft scurrying came from inside the bedroom, but no spoken response. Sim extended his hand toward the silver doorknob, not touching it yet when the door swung open.

"Hello, my love."

"Hello," replied Katherine, in a tone Sim hoped included some level of recognition. As usual, her appearance belied her condition. Hair and makeup were in place, including a splash of dark-red lipstick that flattered her pale blue eyes and faintly pink cheeks. She wore a belted navy-blue robe that was slightly too big. Was Katherine losing weight? Sim stepped into the bedroom and wrapped his arms tightly around her unresisting shoulders, which seemed no more thin or bony than the last time they'd been together.

He eyed his reflection in the full-length mirror next to his wife's dresser. Sim rarely wasted time looking at himself, but current circumstances required making a proper impression. His tan cardigan and black slacks went well together, he decided, projecting just the look of off-hand relaxation he was after. When Katherine and Sim were first married, she'd helped him choose his clothes. Katherine claimed then he must be color-blind. Sim jokingly referred to himself as "color oblivious"—as long as his black or navy-blue suits were pressed, his shirts were clean, and his silk ties, always red or powder blue, were unstained, he normally didn't give a rip what he wore.

"Let's go down to the living room." He spoke quietly. The last time he'd been too loud and frightened her back into the bedroom, to be coaxed out like some exotic bird.

"All right," she whispered.

What he really wanted to do was strip off her robe and make love on the thick quilt folded across the bed. Sim knew it was too early for that in what he'd nicknamed "Operation Re-Connect," his campaign to win her back.

It was like courting all over again. There were a few differences this time around, of course—nearly thirty years of marriage, two troublesome children, an ocean of spent days and useless words. Above all, the current operation called for tact and delicacy. *And I'll be tactful and delicate if it kills me*, Sim thought, smiling at this flash of self-mockery.

His old law partner George Altfelder always said that lawyers must be like Cyrano de Bergerac, prepared to act as battle-hardened swordsmen or fulsome poets as the situation required. George, whose flowing mustache and military bearing gave him a startling resemblance to General von Hindenburg, had loved to quote Cyrano. Sim knew he'd ventured far beyond lawyer-ing now, but George's advice still rang true. Sim sought to temporarily suppress the side of himself that was ready and able to neutralize Dominic O'Nore and bring forth the poetic lover.

He steered Katherine down the curved staircase to the little living room of the carriage house. A pleasant room, he thought, without the clutter of the main house. Felicia had done a nice job of decorating, and not spent much money either.

Sim gestured toward the couch. As they sat down, he nonchalantly extended his arm to curve around her shoulder. Katherine didn't protest. He looked into her pale eyes but couldn't read what might lie behind them.

"How have you been, my dear?"

"Oh, I'm well enough," Katherine replied. "Not much change from day to day."

These meetings were like a game of Monopoly—one of the few games Sim had ever played with his family. So

many throws of the dice brought you back where you started.

Searching for something to say, he said, "Remember
when we all went to Mackinac Island and brought along that
Monopoly board. I think the game had just come out."

"Oh, yes!" Katherine replied, shaking her head and
surprising Sim with the vigor of her reply. "We played Monopoly in the evening on the porch of the Grand Hotel. You
won every game, Sim. You always put up your own 'Grand
Hotel' on Boardwalk and waited for us to land there. Mack
would get so mad."

This wasn't the warm family memory he was trying to
conjure up. "It was beautiful there," Sim finally said.

"It was!" Katherine replied with another enthusiastic
nod that shook loose a strand of hair. "We watched the sun
set over the water. It was like King Midas turning everything to gold."

Sim was charmed, more than charmed. The feeling was
even beyond another swirling urge to make love to her on
Felicia's sand-colored couch. Sitting quietly with his wife,
remembering past times together—he knew with renewed
certainty this was exactly what was missing from his life. It
was the same feeling he'd known when he realized he was
going to win a difficult case, that the judge or jury would go
his way.

"We used to walk together through the woods." Sim
choked out the words.

"There were flowers everywhere—violets, black-eyed
Susans, columbine." Katherine seamlessly picked up the
thread. "We walked while the children explored that huge
hotel. It was so quiet."

"They still don't allow automobiles on the island, you
know." Why couldn't he turn off the legalistic sector of his
brain that supplied this kind of trivial, *Encyclopedia-
Britannica* fact? Sim told himself to keep quiet and gave her
shoulder a soft squeeze through the terrycloth robe.

Katherine slid her head a couple of inches in his direction, gazing into his eyes at an odd, sideways angle. "Sim, my dear, I thought sure you were going to tell me about that young man who used to court Felicia—Thomas Kilkenny. Mack said the poor fellow died in the Philippines. Felicia wept when she heard the news. I wonder if she may still be in love with him. Then Mack said you were going to make Thomas the first American hero of the war."

A strange word…British, perhaps?…that he'd heard somewhere came back to Sim. Gobsmacked. Katherine's words left him gobsmacked.

Sim slid his arm away, as if Katherine had become someone he didn't know, and he might be accused of accosting a stranger. "*Mack* told you this?" He tried to compose himself. "I—I didn't know you'd seen him so recently."

"Oh yes, he stopped by and told us about poor Thomas. Felicia figured out that you were trying to make him a war hero. Then Mack said there could be problems with Thomas's father, that crude man Blarney Bob." She gave him an even wider wide-eyed look. "Is that right?"

"Yes, it is." Sim couldn't think of anything else.

Squealing brakes sounded from the alley. A car door slammed. One eye-blink later, the door to the carriage house opened. Felicia's voice seemed to enter the room before she did. "I left my cigarettes, so I had the cab turn around!"

Sim stood without realizing he'd done it. He felt like a kid caught smooching with his girlfriend, as he and his daughter, exactly the same height, faced each other eye to eye across the room.

"What are *you* doing here?" They said the words exactly together, with the same intonation.

Sim glanced down at his wife on the couch. She smiled slightly and didn't appear surprised at Felicia's appearance. Felicia, on the other hand, stared at her mother as if she were calmly reclining on the couch stark naked.

Sim recovered first. "I'm talking with Katherine. She's my wife, after all."

Felicia snorted then turned and looked back through the still-open door. "You can go now," she yelled to the invisible taxi driver. "I've changed my mind. Keep the fare." The cab roared away as the door swung shut.

Felicia stepped all the way in, eyes darting around the room. She put her black leather purse on the coffee table, straightened the padded shoulders of her dark-green jacket, and headed for the mantel, where an unopened pack of Lucky Strikes lay. Wishing he'd brought along a cigar, Sim watched as Felicia lit up, drew in an ecstatic lung-full of smoke, and emitted a thick cloud toward the ceiling.

"So, Father," she said finally, "is this an example of what happens when the cat's away, like the nursery rhyme says?"

"You have no right to ask that. This is my house as much as the main building. You only live here at my sufferance. I can come and go as I please."

Felicia took another drag on her Lucky and looked at him, not as angry as he'd expected, certainly not amused. Profoundly unimpressed.

"I thought he'd come to tell me more about Thomas Kilkenny," said Katherine, chiming in like a grandfather clock ringing the hour. "But you didn't get very far, did you, Sim?" Her tone was honey-sweet, no hint of irony.

Sim quietly said, "No, I didn't get far." The poet, or lover or whatever he was seeking to be, had come, succeeded for a moment, and then disappeared like a popping soap bubble.

"And I never got a chance to tell him about those things, the weapons, you saw in the Kilkennys' basement."

Katherine proceeded to tell her side of the story, and Felicia reluctantly filled in the details between cigarettes. Even though this was hardly how he'd imagined his rendezvous with Katherine, Sim was pleased and surprised at feeling that way. To the degree that she could become involved, Katherine was with him in the hero-creating business.

Felicia appeared willing to accept, albeit grudgingly, that Sim did indeed have the right to be with his own wife on his own property.

"I'm amazed a high-powered lawyer like you didn't invoke your supposed 'ownership rights' before now," Felicia said, lighting a fresh Lucky Strike. "And since you seem to have Mack under your thumb, I'll tell you about what I saw at the Kilkenny house—you'll get it from Big Brother anyway."

Felicia's strange tale proved to Sim that Blarney Bob's weapons smuggling was a bigger enterprise than even J. Edgar Hoover had realized. Graves's murder in the cellar likely meant that the IRA arms trafficking might still be going on, and that Dominic O'Nore, now the Number One suspect for Graves's murder, and likely the puppeteer controlling Blarney Bob, was a more dangerous man than he'd thought.

# Chapter 20

Mack was often slow to understand things the other workers at the Steckel Avenue plant seemed to know instinctively, but even he could tell right away when a posting on the bulletin boards came from the Plant Manager's office. The mimeograph machine there left a purple, thumbprint-sized smudge on the upper right-hand corner of each sheet.

All the workers, including Mack, recognized the oddity of the notice as soon as it went up. Everyone at the plant was to meet at two p.m. on a date a couple of weeks hence. The usual war-bond rallies, safety exhortations, and presentation of production awards were *always* scheduled for the start of the first shift on Friday mornings, with the notice posted the previous Monday.

This one went up on a Wednesday. And in stark contrast to the usual boilerplate, this notice closed with the words *Miss this meeting, and you'll be sorry! You'll regret it if you're not there!* right above Fat Ferdie Gisbourne's name and Plant Manager title.

Mack's first thought was that the meeting must be connected somehow with Tommy, but he swiftly accused himself of becoming infected with his father's monomania. Not *everything* had to do with Sim's hero plan. In their letters, Tommy and Mack had argued back and forth about which organization was more riddled with gossip and rumor: military bases or factories. They agreed, though, that the causes were similar, endlessly repetitive tasks and the excruciating boredom they engendered.

During their coffee break, the janitors seized upon the odd bulletin board notice like starving men given the keys to a delicatessen.

"Some high mucka-muck comin' to keep up our mor-ALE," grunted Chocolate Slim, "like that goddamn ball-player." Slim exhaled smoke from his spliff and mopped his brow with a handkerchief the size of a pillow case. The spring weather had turned hot as midsummer.

"Maybe MacArthur flyin' in for a victory tour," said Stevie Jay, except for Mack, the youngest of the group.

"Some goddamned victory," rumbled Leopold Belgian. "MacArthur's the biggest screw-up general since that old Frog who kissed Hitler's Nazi ass. What's his name again? Pet-something."

"Petain," said Mack. "He's the figurehead for the Germans' puppet government in Vichy." Mack took a deep puff on his own spliff.

"Knew *you'd* know, college boy. I guess you can still read your history books, even with one eye."

Mack's jaw locked in reflexive anger for a second, but the flare-up receded quickly. One-eyed jokes still hurt, but maybe not so much coming from his fellow janitors.

"Slim's right for once," Leopold continued. "Somebody high up is comin'. And I'll bet it ain't no goddamn, marchin'-around, gold-braid-wearin' military man. They too busy losin' the war to take time off, and the honkies 'round here so pissed they'd likely throw rocks and rotten eggs at the sumbitch!"

"It's probably the Governor or a Senator looking for votes, maybe some Congressman who was an isolationist just a few months ago," said Mack. It was a relief to think about something not connected with making heroes or locating murderous Irishmen. "Maybe it's the mayor trying to drum up support. Ed Kelly's not all that popular these days."

Coffee break ended, and the janitors scattered back across the plant. Mack happily whiled away the rest of the graveyard shift speculating about who might be visiting the plant—assuming a dignitary's visit really was the reason for the meeting. Vice President Wallace didn't seem to have much to do, proving his predecessor Cactus Jack Garner was right when he claimed the Veep's job wasn't worth a pitcher of warm spit. Maybe FDR was dispatching Henry Wallace on a make-work "fact-finding tour." More hopefully, it might be Veronica Lake stopping by to push War Bonds.

The lightness of mind created by the spliff made the drudgery of cleaning bathrooms easier. At one point, Mack even forgot to holler, "Janitor coming in!" when he entered the women's john by the engine inspection line—there were no female janitors to clean the "ladies' restrooms," as the genteel signs on the doors referred to the facilities. He startled a heavy-set woman in overalls who stood with a hand grasping the door of a toilet stall. The woman pushed past him, anger splashed across her flabby face, leaving Mack to wonder if she'd been on her way in or out of the stall when he blundered in.

The shift ground to a close. Neither the spliff nor speculating about the mystery meeting could keep away Mack's unease about his father and what he was getting himself into. Mack clocked out, an odd fish swimming against the current of first-shifters flowing into the plant.

He dragged his steel-toed shoes across the asphalt parking lot. Far more cars were parked there than when he'd arrived. The first shift was several times larger than the graveyard crew. The night had been hot and sticky enough, but the rising sun now added to the unseasonable heat. Mack reluctantly slid into the Model A, knowing it would be like a steam bath, even with the window down. He pictured his father's reaction if he were to drive directly to

Winnetka and meet him as he left to catch his morning train: Mr. Sweaty Workshirt versus Mr. Brooks Brothers.

Once, when Mack was maybe five years old, he'd impulsively—a term he knew applied to nearly all his youthful activities—climbed the apple tree in the Simmons backyard. There had probably been some juicy-looking fruit near the top, though Mack didn't know if he was making that part up. He'd gotten most of the way up the tree, getting poked all over by tiny, pointed twigs, when he changed his mind about the whole tree climbing project but discovered he couldn't find his way down.

Hanging on to knobby branches that began cutting his hands, he'd struggled not to cry but couldn't hold back. Just then, his father walked out the back door and looked up at him, hard black eyes staring like shiny lumps of coal.

Sim despised crying. Mack's first thought, which caused a new round of sobs, was that his father would simply look away, stride on to the carriage house or the alley or wherever he was going, and leave him to climb, jump, or fall down from the tree. Instead, Sim positioned himself below Mack and talked him down from his perch, coaxing him gently from one handhold to the next: "No, son, grab the branch by your knee. That's the boy!" His soft voice brought forth a warm wave of thankful amazement Mack could feel washing over him as he thought of it again.

When he'd gotten two or three feet above his father's reaching hands, Mack let go, feeling no fear as he dropped into his father's thin, wiry arms. Sim tipped him down onto the grass and, without another word, walked to the carriage house with the impossibly long strides of an adult.

As Mack steered the Ford, a rolling hothouse, against the flow of traffic, he saw their positions reversing. *I've been a bully*, he thought, *a spoiled brat. I'm a college graduate—with excellent grades*, he felt compelled to add as he twisted his UofC class ring. *If accurate, though, my curriculum vita would include lines for a going-nowhere-fast grad student and partly reformed drunk.* Now, as a one-eyed night janitor making less in a week than his father's hourly fee, Mack finally felt he was approaching adulthood. Despite the arrogant old man's bluster and detectives, Mack felt an aching, surprising need to protect his father from the deep waters he was afraid were about to engulf him.

# Chapter 21

Mack pushed his old-fashioned iron key—an item you'd associate more with the Bastille than a Chicago rooming house—into the rusting lock of the door to his room. The effects of the spliff were wearing off. They were replaced by waves of exhaustion that didn't wash away contorted dream-images of his father and Dominic O'Nore. The two dream-wrestled in the Kilkennys' basement, his father in a Brooks Brothers suit holding his own against the larger man in a tight black tee-shirt showing off bulging muscles and a shamrock tattoo. They fired revolvers at each other in a rat-infested dream-alley, where the corpse of Mr. Graves lay next to a dented, overflowing trash can. As an audience of tuxedo-wearing dignitaries looked on blankly, Sim and Dominic tried to grab Tommy's posthumous Medal of Honor. The bizarre gathering included Agent Lars Neilsen, sporting a top hat and cutaway coat.

Shaking his head to drive the images away, Mack twisted Mrs. McLady's clattery doorknob, which had likely begun working itself loose when Warren G. Harding was president, and pushed the door open.

As the hinges squeaked an uncertain welcome, a voice sounded from down the hall. "Mack, you're finally home!"

"Jan," he replied, after a second's surprise, "sneaking up on me is becoming a habit, and a nasty one at that." Mack immediately regretted his priggish tone.

He finished turning around just as she reached him, and they embraced. Her deep kiss drove away his flurry of irritation. "Let's go in," he gasped as they untangled.

Jan glanced back over the right shoulder of her filmy pale-blue dress, a sign of the sudden shift to warm weather. "Yes, we'd *both* like to come in."

A male figure, shorter and thinner than Mack, strode down the faded hall carpet. In the dim light of the bulb at the far end of hall, Mack recognized an army service uniform: tan shirt, black tie, tan trousers, carefully shined shoes. As the soldier got closer, Mack saw a narrow flight cap perched diagonally across a head-full of black hair, worn longer, Mack thought, than standard military length.

Jan turned and took in a breath, about to introduce her companion, as the lieutenant's silver bars twinkled. The smooth-faced officer—he was clearly Mack's age or younger—extended a hand before Jan had a chance to speak. "Lieutenant Peter Winogrand—call me Pete. Tommy talked about you so often, I feel as if I already know you!"

They shook firmly. Jan led the way into Mack's room and guided Winogrand to the purple couch. Mack pulled up short next to his single table lamp, chewing over the name as he contemplated the pattern of yellow water stains on the lampshade.

"Winogrand. You're Tommy's co-pilot—you must've parachuted from Hellacious Helen!" He plopped down on the other end of the couch as if he couldn't sit until he identified the name. Relief spread down from his chest and up from his ankles. He'd been afraid that Jan, always fearless and direct, was introducing him to her new lover.

Winogrand brushed back the coal-black cowlick dangling below the tight edge of his cap. "Exactly right. I was the co-pilot of Hellacious Helen. As far as the jump is concerned, I don't remember much. A Jap anti-aircraft shell from one of their ships exploded near our bird when I stepped off. Outside the cockpit, I'm scared stiff of heights, but the plane was on fire. The explosion knocked me out cold just as I pulled the ripcord." He related the story in the practiced tone of a man who'd told his tale before. "Some Filipino Army Scouts cut me down from the palm tree I was swinging from, rocking like a sleeping baby."

Jan was still standing next to the patched-up armchair. "Let's all have some coffee." She took a step toward the tiny kitchen. "And as my dad likes to say, I'd bet a flitch of fine Irish bacon who's going to make it."

The skinny lieutenant pulled a pack of Camels and a book of matches from his shirt pocket, lit up with near-automatic gestures, and blew a stream of smoke toward the kitchen. Mack thought of calling to Jan to bring out a saucer for Pete to use as an ashtray. Finally, the barbed nature of her Irish bacon remark sank in. He rose to get the saucer himself.

"You're from San Francisco," Mack said over his shoulder. "Tommy mentioned that in a letter."

"Palo Alto, but Frisco's close enough."

Mack grabbed an empty saucer from the counter and hastily emptied the bread crumbs that had somehow come to lodge in it. It was suddenly important—necessary—to seem a good host and a good man to Winogrand. Except for the black hair, the lieutenant, who could almost be called scrawny, and the tall, thickly muscled Tommy bore no physical resemblance to one another. But the airman had already become a stand-in, the closest he'd ever come to seeing Tommy again. Did Jan view the lieutenant that way too?

Winogrand stuck his cigarette between full lips and took a couple more deep puffs. "I know what you're both thinking: what the hell am I doing here?" The cigarette bounced up and down as he spoke.

Jan stepped in from the kitchen and looked at Winogrand without a word. He glanced up at her, removed the Camel from his mouth, and continued quietly. "You two are the ones closest to Tommy, so I wanted to talk to you, get to know you both. All of us on Hellacious Helen swapped home addresses, so I knew where to find you—at least you, Miss Kilkenny. Like I said, that's how I showed up on your doorstep."

Jan blushed. For a few seconds, the burble of the coffeepot was the only sound in the room.

"I only survived through a series of miracles," Winogrand finally said, "like Robinson Crusoe or Ishmael." He tapped off an ash into the makeshift ashtray and smiled shyly. "I majored in English at Stanford."

"Tommy circling back so you could escape was one miracle," said Jan. She ducked into the kitchen and came back with two cups of steaming coffee. She nodded toward Mack. Her clear message was that he could get his own damn coffee, and he did.

"Having him as our pilot was the real miracle. He was the best I've ever seen. He and the plane were like one big animal, a giant bird with Tommy as its brain."

Winograd took a tiny sip of coffee, which was too hot for a bigger gulp. "Before Pearl Harbor, we were on alert at Clark Field, not sleeping like those idiots in Hawaii. But we were idiots too, I guess, because our planes were parked wing to wing. When the Japs came, they couldn't miss. Just a few 'Seventeens' got away, and Hellacious Helen only made it because Tommy got us off the ground while the Zeroes were still strafing, and he managed to land at a rice-paddy airstrip the other side of Manila."

"How did you get out?" Mack bit his tongue after blurting out the words, a kid who couldn't wait to get to the climax of an exciting story.

Winograd sat at ramrod attention—it registered with Mack that his stiff military spine never grazed the back of the couch. Had he been injured parachuting from Hellacious Helen? Winograd stubbed out the Camel. "First, we made it down south in hops, flying just above the palm trees. We almost got shot down a dozen times, but we did at least a little damage to the Japs. Our nose gunner Teddy Gluck got pretty good at knocking out Jap trucks and staff cars from a hundred feet up."

Jan seemed to remember to sit down and folded herself into the armchair.

"When we got to Mindanao, General Sharp ordered us to attack the Jap fleet covering their landing. It was for show, by then there were just three bombers left. We never had a chance, but Bill Sharp didn't want to be accused of not using his so-called air force. The Zeroes got Mike Garside's Wicked Witch just as we took off. Then we got tagged right after Sorenson finished arming the five-hundred-pounders in the bomb bay. It was one of those moments that seems to go on forever but really must've taken only a few seconds. The plane was on fire, and we'd just seen Elmo Schlossmann and the Killer from Manila go up like a Fourth of July skyrocket. They were just off our left wing. Burning pieces of the Killer were flying all around us. You could hardly tell 'em from the flak the Japs were putting up. Hellacious Helen was bucking like a rodeo horse with a hot poker up its ass."

Caught up in the airman's tale, Mack followed WinograND's eyes as the man looked down at his empty hands.

"Schlossmann's real name was Earl or Edward, something like that. But everybody called him 'Elmo.' I don't know why. He was from Montana, a miner's son." WinograND's hands slid over his kneecaps as he took a breath. "The flames were getting closer to our cockpit. You could feel the heat, but there wasn't much smoke. Tommy yelled over the intercom, 'I'm circling back. Everybody out!' He took the ship upstairs and back toward the beach smooth and easy, like we were on a training flight. He turned to me and said, 'That means you, Wino. Get the hell out of here!' I strapped on my 'chute and got the hell out."

Mack suppressed a potentially embarrassing grin as he imagined himself chiding Tommy over his Famous Last Words. "You sure ain't no Nathan Hale!"

"Anyway, I came to when the Filipino Scouts were

lugging me back to our base. All they could talk about was 'Big blowup! Big blowup!' and then a lot of talk in Tagalog. I found out what they meant when I got back. Dago Ray—that's our waist gunner Ray Ianelli—and Swede Sorenson had got out of the bird too and managed to stay conscious all the way down. They had ringside seats to see Tommy find exactly the right flight path to bring the bird down amidships on a Jap cruiser, their flagship, with Hellacious Helen burning up around him. It was like he was bringing her in for a landing at our goddamned mud-puddle airstrip!"

Winogrand stopped talking. Maybe, Mack thought, it was a small, unspoken apology for his unseemly enthusiasm. He was, after all, describing the last seconds of life of his listeners' lost brother and closest friend. Jan blinked rapidly then rubbed her eyes with her fists like a child fighting off sleep. Mack saw no tears. For an unexpected moment, he felt a searing pain in his chest.

The lieutenant looked at Jan and Mack in turn. "Tommy had guessed right about where they stored the ammo and blew that cruiser right out of the water, along with a destroyer and a half-dozen landing craft. It was a victory, I guess, the only one we had. Everyone's spirits went up. But then, the next day, General Wainwright surrendered at Corregidor. And he surrendered *everyone*, even our Visayan-Mindanao Force down south. We were furious!" His snarl sank quickly to a more even-tempered, maybe weary tone. "Everybody knew the truth, of course: We couldn't hold out much longer without reinforcements—and there were no reinforcements."

Mack sought polite words to ask again about Winogrand *himself*. The lieutenant seemed to catch on and smiled faintly. "General Sharp showed up at my tent right after the surrender order came over the radio. It was just a short walk from his bivouac to our landing strip—which didn't have any planes left to land on it—but the general was still covered in mud up to his ankles. He handed me a leather pouch full of maps and documents, something a mailman would carry. He ordered a Filipino patrol to take me over the mountains to Lianga Bay, where there was a PT boat waiting.”

Winogrand shook his head. “I don’t know how we made it past the Jap patrols or what happened to the Filipino Scouts afterward. The PT boat rendezvoused with a sub bound for Australia. I rusticated for a day or two in Brisbane. Then, one of MacArthur’s court jesters stopped by the officers’ barracks with orders sending me back to the States to ‘represent our brave men who fought and died in the Philippines.’ The rear-area jamoke made it clear he especially meant Captain Thomas Kilkenny.”

Jan took a long drink of coffee and fixed her eyes on Winogrand. “So, is that why you’re in Chicago?”

Was she suspicious of Winogrand and his story?

“That’s what I thought,” the lieutenant replied. “I got to Washington after hopping across India, Africa, and South America. God!—for a while, I never wanted to get on another plane! Then the brass hats told me they were going to make a hero out of Tommy.”

He looked at Jan. “You know what he would’ve thought of *that*!”

Jan smiled, any suspicions seeming to vanish. Winograffnd had said exactly the right thing.

A dozen responses occurred to Mack, but remembered moments with Tommy flooded them out, especially the crazy, or maybe not all that crazy, historical theories that poured out from him after beer had been poured in. At this point, he’d have come up with several hundred well-chosen words on generals, propaganda, and heroes. Mack, though, couldn’t put anything into proper words, so he only nodded enthusiastically and attempted to smile.

“I caught a train to Chicago,” continued Winogrand, “with orders to check into the Blackstone Hotel and stand by. Plans for Tommy’s hero ceremony were underway, the public relations officer said. Now there’s a job I’d like to have! They were setting things up for the big announcement at a defense plant, he told me."

"Did they say which plant?" Mack tried to tone down the urgency of his question, but didn't succeed,

"Nope," said Winogrand.

"Pete, I want you to do us a favor," Mack said,

"Of course," Winogrand replied, lighting another cigarette. "Name it." He didn't light up with quite the robotic movements of Felicia. Maybe, thought Mack, he hadn't been smoking as long as his sister.

"I want you to let us know which defense plant you'll be appearing at. Call me—there's a phone right down the hall. Here's the number—" He waited for Winogrand to pull out a pencil and scrap of paper from a pants pocket and then began to rattle off the number.

"No," Jan interrupted forcefully, "call *me*. I have a real private phone, and you saw that I live in a real apartment." She looked up to see Mack's frown. "I'll let Mack know right away." She carefully enunciated her Astor Place number. Winogrand dutifully wrote it down, Camel dangling from his lower lip.

"So, Mack, you want to be the guy with the inside dope, eh?" Winogrand laughed out a cloud of smoke. "That's exactly like the air corps! Everybody one-upping everyone else." He balanced the cigarette on the edge of the saucer. "This is more complicated than it looks, though. When I got to the Blackstone, a guy from the FBI met me in the lobby. There's been a delay, he says, so stay close to the hotel and don't talk with anybody, especially anyone from the press."

"But you didn't—" Jan blurted.

"I don't take orders from PR officers, even when they out-rank me, or from a damn G-Man either. I was in Tommy's hometown, and I wanted to meet the people he'd talked about so much. All of us from Hellacious Helen felt the same way. Tommy could spin a funny tale as well as any actor or comedian, cast a spell over you with his words.

He got it from his father, he always said, then he'd get us all laughing 'til we fell down with a Blarney Bob story. I'd like to meet him too."

Jan blushed, which told Mack that she had found Winogrand attractive but hadn't acted on her feelings. A good sign, right? Of course—if you left out Jan's determination to make sure call-me-Pete had her phone number.

Mack tried to stop speculating, but he only succeeded in shifting to unspoken questions. Was Steckel Avenue Winogrand's secret Chicago destination? Was he the mystery guest at the all-employee meeting? Mack gave an internal shrug and leaned forward, drinking in the sharp profile of the slender man sitting so rigidly at the other end of the couch.

"What was Tommy like near the end?" Jan's voice caught hoarsely in her throat.

"At first, we thought it might be the 'long stare' you hear about from men who were in the Great War. My Uncle Frank said that in the Meuse-Argonne, soldiers would stare across no man's land, looking at nothing, or something invisible to everyone else. You knew they wouldn't survive for long."

"But Tommy wasn't like that." Mack's impatience spilled over again.

"Right. He was just, I don't know, in a different world from the rest of us. We all bitched about everything: the fucking Japs—excuse my French, Miss Kilkenny—the idiot officers, the mud that sucked you down and wouldn't let go, Mac Arthur strutting around and then leaving, the maggots in the tinned beef, the goddamned rain that wouldn't stop. Tommy never complained, just smiled at our bellyaching. It sounds like a joke to say it about a pilot, but Tommy seemed above it all."

*Thomas Kilkenny, meet St. Simeon Stylites*, thought Mack. *One above it all in a B-17 over the Philippines, the other above it all atop a pillar in fifth-century Asia Minor.*

Winogrand went on. "He kept telling funny stories, made us laugh in spite of ourselves. Whatever he saw at the edge of the jungle, or past the clouds after we'd dodged a squadron of Zeroes, it didn't hypnotize or frighten him. You could see him looking off into space. But when you asked if he was okay, or if maybe he was sick—those jungles are full of malaria and leeches and about every other kind of crud you can imagine—he'd laugh and say his brain was on a pub crawl with his buddy Mack Simmons. Without even having a drink."

Had Tommy spent his last days replaying the accident? Mack's ocular prosthesis inexplicably began to itch. Jan and Mack glanced at one another, and both grinned. If you looked at it from the right angle, the whole story was pure Blarney Bob, even though *he* never tried to convince any-one he hadn't been drinking.

თოთ

The three of them went for breakfast at Morty's, where Mack baffled Jan and Pete by ordering chili, heavy on the chopped onions.

"For breakfast!" they yelled in unison. Mack explained, not too coherently, as his exhaustion got the upper hand, that "breakfast" was a foreign idea on the graveyard shift. You ate whatever was available whenever you got hungry. They nodded politely when he dived into Morty's chili as Jan and Pete more decorously swallowed their ham and eggs. They were equally uncomprehending when he refused more coffee, which war workers were now downing in quantities sufficient, according to the rumor mill, to put java on the already detested rationing list.

"I've got to get some sleep," Mack finally mumbled, as he slid a dollar bill next to his empty chili bowl, feeling as if he, not Winogrand, was the long-absent visitor to a land that had become strange to him.

Mack was too tired even to pull down the Murphy bed from the wall. He collapsed onto the purple couch, impervious to its pointed spring. After a stretch of utter oblivion, his eyes slid painfully open. If eyelids could squeak, his would have, like fingers rubbing wet glass. They squeaked open wider when Mack saw Jan sitting in his armchair.

"So you think I was trying to make you jealous?"

A sensible reply in English was as likely as Mack spouting off a paragraph or two in Tagalog. Fortunately, Jan stepped over to kiss him without seeming to expect words in any language. Once again, her penchant for sexually ambushing him was wonderful and disconcerting at the same time

Afterward, as they lay like spoons on the Murphy bed, which Jan had thoughtfully pulled down while he slept, she broke the silence. "Now that we've established that I don't want to fuck Pete Winogrand, why do you care whether Pete's appearing at Steckel Avenue? Do you really want to lord it over the other fellows 'cause you're in the know?"

Mack propped his head on an elbow. "I didn't give a fig, as my Aunt Abigail, who's obviously far more decorous than you, always liked to say. But then the FBI came into the picture."

"Yeah, a G-Man waiting for Pete does seem strange." She brushed her fingers across his lips. "Maybe not so strange to you, Inspector Simmons. What gives?"

Before answering, Mack touched the skin next to his eye socket. Making love, at least with Jan, resulted in no embarrassment about the ocular prosthesis, but he still slid off the bed and went to the mirror that hung next to the tiny sink in the kitchen. Mack thought of adjusting his eye as getting straight with the world, able to look at it squarely in the face. Dr. Bennett, a surprisingly jovial fellow for someone who spent his days staring into damaged eye sockets, once told him about a one-eyed man who liked to surreptitiously pop in an alternate glass eye that showed a Confederate flag instead of an iris. Ophthalmologists' folklore.

Feeling straight and square, and somehow buoyed by the thought of the fellow with the Confederate eyeball, Mack sat on the edge of the bed. Not having to censor or edit the story of his visit from Agent Lars Neilsen and the talk with his father was a vast relief.

"However he talked around it, my father plans to kill Dominic O'Nore if he gets to him before Hoover and the FBI. I think Dominic will kill him first."

Jan rolled off the bed, pulled on her panties and slip, then urged Mack to help her with her bra. "You took it off fast enough, smart guy," she said as he fumbled with the hooks and straps.

Mack pulled on his own undergarments and stared at the articles of clothing still scattered on the floor. "Let's think rationally about this." Mack drew in a deep breath, trying to follow his own advice. "There are pieces floating around all over—the FBI and their dragnet for Dominic, your father's disappearance, Winogrand's trip to Chicago, which must be part of the Tommy Hero Show. But the pieces don't fit together. The only thing we *do* know is that the hero campaign is stalled. Otherwise, you and Ellen would have been officially invited to whatever ceremony they're planning."

Jan smoothed her skirt with a quick gesture Mack found particularly appealing. He leaned down and kissed her on the forehead. She leaned her head against his chest.

"Everyone's looking for Dominic," said Jan softly. "But we have to find him first and get Dad away from him, before your father and his detectives, or the FBI, starts shooting. Your father's men will kill Dominic in a minute, and they won't care who's in the way."

"Dominic will do the same," said Mack quietly.

They looked at each other in silence, realizing their conclusions presumed that Blarney Bob was, as he'd have put it, "still walking around on the top side of the grass."

"I'm afraid—scared to death, in fact," said Jan in a barely audible whisper. "I almost lost you. Then Tommy died. I can't bear to lose anybody else."

Mack had no answer.

# Chapter 22

Winston Bloody Churchill—that puffed-up bastard with the tree-trunk cigar perpetually stuck in his maw—if you asked Dominic, he was the one they should go after. Of course, nobody back in Belfast or Dublin ever did ask Dominic about such matters. With the Brits in the fourth year of an unsuccessful war, you'd figure that bloody Winston didn't point his nose outside Number 10 Downing Street without a battalion of bodyguards to light his torpedo cigars and preserve his arse.

But didn't some of the boys have a fetching way with dynamite and clockwork detonators? Surely, some hush-hush IRA man planted in London could pry loose the details of a politicians' banquet or hospital visit from a drunken clerk or lonely stenographer. A smile curled his lips as Dominic imagined a newsreel of the great event: Weeping Brits mourning the noisy end of their fat-arsed Prime Minister amidst the ruins of the exploded dining hall or hospital wing, whilst some hysterical BBC news reader pledged revenge against the devious perpetrators.

Ever since he'd first heard it, Dominic had filed away "perpetrator" as another favorite word. It sounded like "perpetual traitor" run together—and that's what the bold men of the IRA were pledged to be till our island's one again. *You knew they had you in their grip,* thought Dominic, as he felt the smile leaving him, *when your own brain churns out the words of their brainless patriotic hymns. By all the saints and all the snakes they drove away, did the doggerel words, "till our island's one again" really come to him on their own?* The men of the IRA truly held him in their proudly traitorous hands.

He couldn't appear a traitor over here, of course. He glanced in frustration at Blarney Bob, who'd returned to his familiar pose stretched out on Lonegan's sagging couch after wolfing down three fried eggs—"lightly done with plenty of free-running yolk, just as I like 'em!"—along with a half-dozen slabs of ham and a water-glass-full of Lonegan's whiskey. The fool hadn't even noticed that the whiskey was no better than horse piss—Lonegan was hoarding his bottle of Jameson's. Dominic felt the walls of Lonegan's tiny living room, with its dusty, rugless plank floor and furniture from Catholic Relief, squeezing him like a tightening vise. This bloody Canaryville, which he'd never visited, or even heard of before, was a right and proper shithole. He missed the posh house on 75th Street more each hour.

It was lucky, of course, that they had even a single safe house in what had once been the great Fenian cauldron of Chicago. Here, the Irish had become politicians, priests, coppers—and the entirety of the fire department and plumbers union—getting rich and forgetful enough to ignore the endless struggles at home.

The same thing happened in miniature to the rechristened Robert Kilkenny. For a few years, the former Daniel McGuigan of the IRA easily shared his good fortune with the boys back in Dublin and Belfast. When he arrived in the States, Dominic had been staggered by the life the IRA man was falling into as Robert Kilkenny—the life of a Sweepstakes winner or some foundling who becomes a bloody fairy-tale prince. Of course, such tales always ended before the handsome prince turned into a sodden sack of guts. Worse yet, as the aldermen cast his lot with the likes of Victor Schlegel, the sharing became grudging. The money piling up from the alderman's graft and his investments in speakeasies and whorehouses and bookie joints was needed, Bob said, by his children or for an election warchest, not a revolutionary one.

As Robert Kilkenny had gotten softer, Dominic's heart hardened. He'd barely noticed when the Free State was declared. Who gave a rat's hind end if the King still reigned in Ulster? The biggest part of the nation was free for the first time since Cuchulain wore short pants. We had won, hadn't we? But then, during the Civil War, a Free State murder squad shot down his brother Billy, barely fifteen and looking younger than his years. The lad was about to enter the seminary and bring joy to their Mum. Dominic joined the all-or-nothing boys of the bitter-end IRA. Insanely proud to be hunted by both the devils of the Free State militia and the bloody Brits in Ulster, he was no singer of rebel songs, but still a true believer in the Republic, United and Free.

With some reluctance, Dominic had given up, or at least postponed, the appealing idea of sliding both the cursed albatross of the Cadillac and its wastrel owner into the shit-colored waters of Bubbly Creek, which coursed its filthy way a few blocks over from Lonegan's hovel. No one could foretell when the auto might be found. Weeks away would be as good as years, but a discovery within days could ruin everything.

Restless, Dominic strode out the back door and down the creaking porch steps. He headed for the garage, nothing but a lopsided shack ready to fall down if a fellow sneezed inside its slanting, ramshackle walls.

As he'd expected, Lonegan was busying himself polishing the guns he'd unloaded from the boot of the car. He fingered a nasty-looking Luger P08 pistol.

"Hand me that fellow, will you, Hughie?"

Lonegan wiped a thick hand across a dirty plaid shirt and carefully placed the weapon in Dominic's strong-fingered hands, an altar boy presenting the blessed host to the waiting priest, something Dominic had done himself on many occasions.

"This is the one you should use, Dominic," said Lonegan in a hushed tone. "Small to the hand, not too much kick, but you don't have to be waltzing with the fellow you're after to do the job."

Dominic hefted the pistol, dropped it into a trouser pocket, then reached inside and yanked it out. His right hand embraced the surprisingly long grip.

"Hugh Lonegan, to be ferociously honest, you're not a man well known for being right. But I believe you're right as rain on this subject—a bit like the blind hen finding a bug in the grass. Perhaps you're embarking on a run of luck. You should locate a poker game with high stakes and make your fortune."

Lonegan grinned like a kid receiving a school prize and began oiling the barrel of a Mauser infantryman's rifle.

Dominic patted him softly on the shoulder. *When I leave to do the deed,* he thought, *perhaps I'll shoot this idiot between the eyes for target practice and burn this rotting hulk of a house down to its foundations.* Then, he took the plan a bold step forward: *make sure the equally foolish alderman is inside. Cadillac sunk in the river, Blarney Bob turned to ash in the house.* A brilliant idea, no doubt, but one that required a bit more consideration.

☙❧☙

In spite of himself, Sim had to admit a certain respect for Otto Detwiler and the way he never blinked at whatever Sim asked him to do. He never inquired about the shift from trailing wayward spouses to getting rid of inconvenient corpses. "So, no one has found Graves's body yet," Sim said. "Where did you dump it anyway?"

A twitch rumpled Detwiler's chubby cheek just under his right eye. Sim recognized the slight movement as the repression of an unseemly grin. "Well, 'dump' may not be exactly the right word."

Across the wide mahogany desk that dominated his LaSalle Street office, Sim leaned forward on his elbows.

"I know a fellow who has a cousin that works at one of the South Side mills. He's on the late-night shift, like your boy."

Sim was startled but refused to show it. Had he ever said this to Detwiler? Graves must have mentioned Mack's job to him. The detective had worked for Sim before joining Detwiler's agency, and Sim had still hired him independently. Not that any of it mattered now, but Sim hated people knowing things he didn't know they knew.

"I'm sure they'd have a lot to discuss if they ever met," said Sim dryly. He wanted a cigar but didn't want to offer one to Detwiler.

"Yeah, it's no picnic working when everyone else is in bed. Anyway, this cuz owed my friend a favor, a big one. So, the long and the short of it is that Graves is gonna be part of the hull of one of Henry Kaiser's Liberty ships, or maybe turned into a steel rail somewhere. You may be rolling over him the next time you ride on a train!"

Sim nodded approvingly. He tried to shut out his own wonderment at how easy the business of disposing of corpses and plotting murder was becoming. There were certainly aspects of settling divorce cases that, anywhere else, would be called blackmail, but those vociferous meetings—which usually came down to some version of "Pay, or I'll talk!"— were nothing like the calm discussions of crimes, serious felonies, that had become part of his life since he'd first learned of Thomas Kilkenny's death. *But*, he thought as that door in his mind swung firmly shut, *there's a war on. War means getting at the enemy any way you can and slaying him.*

"What about Blarney Bob and Dominic O'Nore?"

"Well, it's not as cut and dried as heaving Graves into the blast furnace." To Sim's growing frustration, Detwiler continued to enjoy his coup. "But we've made some progress on that front too."

Detwiler leaned back and grasped the lapels of his cheap blue-serge suit. Though he ran a successful detective agency, employing a dozen freelance investigators, it appeared to be the only suit he owned. And, thought Sim with an inward sniff, even when new it had cost far less than the silk tie Sim wore.

"A cop down at the Canaryville station house spotted a black Cadillac driving slow down Forty-Seventh Street—it was just like Blarney Bob's. At first, he thought it was a high-hat scouting for hookers. The straight-laced Micks around there can't abide that. The copper didn't have a chance to get the license number because a fight broke out at shift change at the Swift packing plant down the street, and he hadda go keep a couple of Micks who aren't so straight-laced from murdering each other."

"You have men checking around Canaryville?"

"Indeed we do."

# Chapter 23

"H ey! Hey in there—wake up! You got phone!"
Mack's first thought as he leapt out of his—currently single-occupancy—Murphy bed was, "What is this place? Fucking Union Station?

"Hey, guy! Wake up!"

He opened the door to confront Vasili from the down the hall, wearing his usual perspiration-stained undershirt and a sour expression.

"You got phone. Make it snappy. I got important phone coming."

Mack grunted out a guttural sound that resembled "Okay."

"Get phone now. I ain't no goddamn secretary." Vasili folded his arms and waited by the door, obviously intending to station himself there until Mack came to the phone.

"Okay," Mack repeated, more coherently this time. He pulled on his oil-stained work pants and followed Vasili down the hall, wondering if the important call he was expecting involved nylon stockings or counterfeit ration cards. Vasili, who didn't seem to have a job, was reputed to be a black marketeer.

Mack picked up the dangling receiver, but before he could say hello, Jan's voice sounded on the other end of the line. It had a tone of calm that sounded as if it had been hard to achieve. "Mack, you need to come over to Mother's place right away. Dominic O'Nore just dropped by for a visit."

❦

"He must've come up the back stairs," Ellen said quietly. "He knows the way." She came across just as Jan had on the phone, struggling for calm against a surge of panic.

"What did Dominic say? He didn't just hand you the envelope and run off, did he?"

Ellen fixed Mack with the patented Boswell glare that must have been perfected by generations of Long Island gentry. "Of course not," she said, leaving unspoken an implied "You idiot."

"As I told Janice, he muttered something about 'the alderman told me to give you this' and handed me an envelope with my name on it. Then he said more clearly, like a child reciting his lesson, 'He's going into a sanatorium for his liver troubles, taking the cure, but he wants no one to know. He asked me to leave the car for you—it's parked at State and Oak Street.' That's as many words as I've heard from him in the last five years. Then, he turned on his heel and left."

"What did the note say?" Mack spoke evenly, eliciting another glare. He found it comforting to play the detective

"I have not opened it as yet. I suppose I have no choice at this point but to share it with the two of you."

"So, the FBI man came right after Dominic left?" said Jan. "I must've been right behind him walking up the street with our groceries. It's like something from a French farce." She was relishing the mystery too—Mack guessed it was a way to push the darkness away for a little while.

Ellen clearly didn't appreciate the comparison but didn't comment as she turned to Mack. "It couldn't have been more than a minute later. I was standing in the kitchen, still half in shock, when there was another knock, this time at the *front* door. This very large man in a black suit showed me an FBI badge and an identification card with some Scandinavian name on it.

"Alderman Kilkenny's car had been spotted nearby, he said, and was he here by any chance? I said, 'Of course not!' and told him about Dominic. That really set him off, and he seemed to forget all about Robert. 'Which way did he go?' he shouted, and I led him to the kitchen and pointed to the back stairs. He thrust a card into my hand, told me to call right away if Dominic came back, and pounded down the stairs like a herd of elephants."

Ellen took a tiny sip from the china teacup that sat in front of her in the apartment's sunny kitchen. "You two obviously know more about this than you're letting on. Otherwise, Janice, you wouldn't have ordered Mack over here to listen to my tale."

Still enjoying the role of Inspector Simmons, Mack took a larger sip from his own cup. The savor of Earl Grey tea was a pleasant contrast to the bad coffee he was used to. "The FBI is extremely interested in Dominic O'Nore, but we don't know why. I'm sorry to bring up a terrible subject, but it may have something to do with Tommy."

Ellen looked up at him, no discernable expression on her face.

"Tommy's co-pilot, Pete Winogrand, made it out of the Philippines. He's here now, in Chicago, for some kind of ceremony that must be the kickoff for making Tommy a national hero. But the FBI visited him too and told him to sit tight."

"That's also got to be connected somehow with Dominic," said Jan, sliding into the role of Nora Charles to Mack's Nick. With her lustrous black hair, she did bear a faint resemblance to Myrna Loy.

Ellen walked over to the counter by the sink. Leaning against the wall was a small square envelope, the kind used for birthday and wedding invitations, the address side facing the wall. Ellen grabbed the envelope and tore it open. "I'm going to read this first," she said. "Then, if it contains nothing too private to share, we can go over it together."

Ellen unfolded a single sheet of lined paper that appeared torn from a school notebook. She read in stony silence. There was writing on only one side of the sheet. After perhaps a minute, Ellen slid the paper over to Mack. "Perhaps you should read it aloud."

Mack stared down at the paper. The writing was neat and legible. Tommy may have been right about the value of Catholic-school penmanship.

"'Dear Ellen:

"'I'm sending this to you by way of faithful Dominic on the assumption that the damnable wretches from the press will be pestering you in the near future, searching for Yours Truly. For the record, but not a record I want to share with anyone else, I am spending some time under a name that's not my own at a hospital that will also not be named. Upon the recommendation of my physicians, I've decided to seek further relief from the liver ailments that, as you well know, have plagued me for these many years.

"'Toward that end, Dominic and I are embarking tomorrow on a journey by rail to that spa we visited on our fugitive honeymoon so many years ago—the destination so beloved by the meatpackers of the South Side that goes by the surprising name of French Lick. The railroads these days seem to be the property of the US Army. But I don't wish to pull any strings to obtain a through-ticket that the bloody reporters might get a whiff of. The nub of the matter is that Dominic and myself will be incognito for several days as we make our slow journey to French Lick.

"'Tell our beloved Janice that I am well enough and praying to St. Brigid for better health. Let's all of us, every one, pray to the BVM and any other saint or spirit that might be listening, to preserve the life of our lovely, precious warrior son in this accursed battle against the heathen, back-stabbing Japs.

"'May all the blessings of sun and sky rain down upon you,

"'Your Former and (if God wills it) Your Future One and Only,

"'~ Robert'"

"Well," said Jan quietly after a few seconds of silence, "it sure sounds like Dad. He always said that if golden words were silver coins, the Irish would be the richest race in the world."

Ellen stared dreamily at the apartment's fancy gold-striped wallpaper. Bob's overblown words apparently provided her some brief solace.

Mack stared hard at the neat, evenly spaced words. Had Dominic written them out first to be copied? Did he dictate the note while pointing a gun at Blarney Bob? An image of Mr. Graves's contorted death's head forced further questions aside. "So," Mack finally said, "We can all agree the note sounds like Bob."

"Amen to that, in spades," said Ellen, a slight catch in her voice. "The handwriting is his, and I don't know who else would mention French Lick. Bob thought it was the funniest name he'd ever heard. He'd always say it with a wink and a leer, like Groucho Marx."

"And that *is* where you and Dad went on your honeymoon." Jan leaned back from the table.

"Yes, indeed," Ellen replied, mind still elsewhere. "Bob was all on his own, and my parents were dead-set against our marriage. Mother called Robert 'Mr. Nobody from Nowhere'—and of course, he was an Irish Catholic to boot. So we paid for our honeymoon with what little money we had between us. French Lick, Indiana, was as far as we could get, just a little spa resort in the middle of nowhere. It was wonderful, but we were so much in love, any place would've seemed grand!"

"Lots of wealthy meatpackers there, I suppose," said Mack, taking a sip of lukewarm tea.

"What?" said Ellen with a look of surprise. "No, I don't recall anyone like that." She reached over and picked up the note. After a quick look, she said, "But that's what he says, isn't it?"

Mack spread his hands in front of him on either side of his bone-china saucer. "Why do you suppose he wrote it then?"

Jan and Ellen shrugged in unison.

"Let's assume that Bob was kidnapped by Dominic O'Nore and that the note was written under duress. Those are both big, unprove-able assumptions, I'll grant you. So, maybe the meatpackers item is—if you'll excuse the expression—some kind of clue."

"I knew there was a good reason for calling you Inspector Simmons," Jan said with a smile that seemed forced. "But what kind of clue is it?" Her smile vanished.

"I'm stumped," said Mack. "Does Bob know people in the meatpacking business? Any Armours or Swifts on his Christmas card list?"

"He knows people in every business you can imagine, legal and illegal," Ellen said, shaking her head. "But you know Bob, he's got a thousand acquaintances, people he's happy to glad-hand and drink with—but very few friends. You never really know where you stand with him. Eventually, that applied to me too." She let out a long sigh. "But thank God, we know he's alive."

"Let's get back to the meatpackers," Jan said in a tightly controlled voice. Mack could see she was working hard to remain the observant detective.

Mack wanted to embrace and protect her, to fill the air with empty assurances that everything would be all right. The same bogus optimism people across the world were likely forcing upon one another at this very moment, in all the languages of wartime combatants.

"What could it mean?" Jan said in an earnest tone to which Mack couldn't assign a grade for sincerity. "A butcher shop? A steak joint? "

She paused, rubbing her index finger against the point of her chin. It was Jan's characteristic thinking-hard gesture. Mack saw the same struggle he was experiencing, logic and fear wrestling for control.

"Could he really mean the *stockyards*?" Jan said after several seconds. "If Dominic was looking over Dad's shoulder, he couldn't just write out where he is." Jan picked up her cup, stared at it for two seconds, and returned it to the saucer with a tiny click.

# Chapter 25

You gave Blarney Bob's note to the FBI. *Why the hell did you do that?*"

As Sim shouted, Mack heard scuffing feet outside the closed door of the office. The footsteps stopped—surely Miss Lincecombe deciding whether to knock on the door and ask what was the matter. Sim's index finger dabbed at a dot of shaving soap next to his mustache, but missed.

"The note from Blarney Bob is all nonsense," Mack replied, quieting his own voice. "He and Dominic are no more in French Lick, Indiana, than Hitler and Hirohito are there, taking the waters."

His father looked calmer but still dubious.

"Besides, we'd surely have committed a crime by not giving the note to the G-Men when it's supposed to be evidence. They've got to be watching Ellen's apartment— that's why the agent showed up so fast when the Cadillac was spotted. Imagine if she did or said something the FBI thought was suspicious. We might all be arrested, and that includes you!"

"That's at least possible," said Sim glumly. "The damnable note is surely counterfeit information—a stinking red herring to pull the dogs off the trail. It won't get anyone closer to Dominic O'Nore."

Mack nodded noncommittally. Jan's intuition had been right. His father's concern for Blarney Bob was about equal to his fellow-feeling for an ant tracing an unlucky path under the sole of his carefully polished shoe.

"Actually," Sim said. "from our point of view, there's more to it than just a red herring." He succeeded in wiping away the blob of shaving soap.

*Oh, oh,* thought Mack, *the ringmaster of the Hero Circus is moving center stage.*

"I keep remembering how the FBI froze the Chicago police out of the Dillinger affair back in 'thirty-four. They brought in local police from East Chicago, Indiana, but none from the city, a real slap in the face. I told the FBI to be wary of the Chicago cops, but I never expected them to act so arrogantly."

Well, if anyone knows about arrogance…

Mack struggled to suppress his rebellious thoughts and concentrate on Sim's words. It was much easier to support and protect his father when he wasn't in the same room with him.

"It would be just like Hoover to go storming off to French Lick."

"The Chicago cops won't try to stop him," Mack said, more involved now. "They'll never suggest the feds concentrate on the South Side."

"Not in a million years," Sim replied, in a tone approaching joviality. "The Chicago police are like the worst of the Irish rebels. They never forget, never forgive. The cops will likely stop looking for Dominic altogether and let the FBI play the fool."

With a hint of a smile, Sim leaned an elbow on the polished surface of his desk. "That clears the field for *us* to search for him here."

On the other side of the door, Mack heard Miss Lincecombe shuffle away.

A few days later at the Steckel Avenue plant, Mack glanced through the *Tribune* as he ate his three a.m. sandwich. At the bottom of page three was a brief item describing a recent raid by "Federal Bureau of Investigation officers" to break up an alleged "interstate gambling operation." The raid took place at the Springs Hotel and Spa in French Lick, Indiana. The FBI had taken Dominic's bait.

Back at Mrs. McLady's after work, Mack searched through his drawer-full of letters from Tommy, looking for one in particular. It was written from the Philippines the previous Fourth of July, on the other side of the border between Peace and War crossed so stunningly the following December. The epistle began with complaints about the tropical heat and stupefying boredom of the place: "Even the whores at Conchita's Casita can hardly get up from the couch. And they know they're going to be horizontal in a minute or two!"

Then Tommy sought in his own way to take in the fact that Adolf Hitler had unexpectedly turned on his erstwhile partner Joe Stalin and invaded Russia:

*The rumor is that army intelligence—if there is such a thing!—is working frantically on a Freudian analysis of Herr Hitler, as if science could penetrate those cubic centimeters of gray matter.*

*The tiny island within the skull is the last frontier, across the whole Earth, the last bit of un-explore-able wilderness. It's crammed with pure Tahitian, breast-baring innocence, along with ravenous dinosaurs eager for raw, bleeding meat, fantasies of vast booty and pillage and plunder. Imagination running wild, beyond all limits of what we desperately name sanity and civilization. At the outermost edge, that's where Adolf is, plundering and murdering his way across Europe, North Africa, now Russia, letting all his delusions loose, with a robot army of mesmerized Germans to make his fantasies real. No one knows where else or how far he'll go.*

Tommy, of course, had always been prone to such sweeping statements, which caused consternation among their more meticulous colleagues in the UofC History Department. And flying high in a B-17 had only expanded the scope of his high-flying pronouncements.

*But you and I, Cyclops, we're historians, not head-shrinking psychologists. We're part of a profession that dates back 2400 years to Thucydides, not a puny twenty or thirty years to Sigmund Freud and his disciples. To us historical analysts, Hitler's closest American analogue is good old Ulysses S. Grant.*

*That's not to make our bearded, beloved fellow Illinoisan—struggling to make his failing way in Galena—into some kind of Nazi. After all, Grant stood behind his suicidally brave black soldiers when the sainted Robert E. Lee sold his Negro prisoners of war back into slavery. No, the Adolf-Ulysses connection is pure historic circumstance. Two men of no consequence whatsoever, inexplicably riding the random waves of history to a prominence incomprehensible to every single person who knew them in their younger days.*

*As our estimable Professor Eckdahl expounded in our faux-Gothic Oxbridge classroom at the UofC—a time and place that seem as far away to me now as the Moon—there are always a few individuals who would likely have risen in any historical period: Leonardo, our own Ben Franklin, maybe conquerors like Napoleon or Alexander.*

*But then, I would add, there are the avalanche-riders—in our time, probably Teddy Roosevelt, definitely Mussolini and Stalin, in the past, the long roster of look-alike pauper princes, False Borises, Empress Theodora, the immortal Spartacus, and other whores, serfs, and slaves who crazily bobbed up from the dregs of society to the mountain top accomplishing great beneficence or staggering destruction. It was the avalanche of war, the ultimate catastrophe, that carried Grant and Hitler, both peacetime nonentities, to equally unexpected power.*

The letter was better than beer or whiskey, the perfect

antidote to a long night of floor sweeping and toilet cleaning.

*Professor Eckdahl hated this sort of stuff, of course. 'Barroom speculation,' he called it when I suggested the Hitler-Grant pairing in class one afternoon. It was the semester after the adventure that renamed you Cyclops. I was already second-guessing my twilight status as a pain-in-the-ass history graduate student, so I didn't challenge him. But I'm still convinced that, even though I did come up with my theory in a barroom, random catastrophe surely explains more than any number of excruciatingly detailed dissertations or a library-full of scholarly tomes. When I get home, I'm going to write a book establishing the Catastrophic School of Historical Thought. I may have already written the first chapter!*

As Mack re-folded the onionskin pages, he wondered if any faint irony about "Catastrophic History" had survived until Tommy's last flight, where some weird alchemy had transformed individual catastrophe into heroism. Another kind of avalanche riding? And if you bought into avalanche riders, you had to accept that the avalanches of history crush millions of less favored souls. That was as good a way as any of describing Mack's task now: Ride the avalanche carrying him along—admittedly a small one by Tommy's grand historical standards—and avoid getting crushed.

# Chapter 26

This was an opportunity Mack never would've recognized before. Now he could smell it in the air. He dutifully emptied the gun-metal gray wastebaskets and overflowing ashtrays of the executive wing of the Steckel Avenue plant.

The corridor of offices faced the street on the second floor, up a flight of steep steps just off the main entrance. The greenish paint on the cinder-block walls was still fresh, the black-and-white checkerboard of linoleum was barely stained. Steckel Avenue wasn't an old truck factory struggling to manufacture tanks or the famous soup-can plant now in the artillery-shell business. Less than two years old, the spartan, brick-faced plant was built specifically to assemble engines for B-17s.

A South Side draft board had taken a liking to Stevie Jay. So Stevie was now packing for a Negroes-only army boot camp. A couple of days later, Leopold Belgian had taken Mack aside and explained, finger jabbing into Mack's chest, that Petrocelli, the sumbitch dago Plant Engineer, nominally in charge of the plant cleaning operation, didn't want "another goddamn jigaboo" wandering through the executive offices in the dead of night. Leopold spat out the words.

The shop-floor workers enjoyed ridiculing Fat Ferdie Gisbourne and the plant's other top-management muckety-mucks. They certainly put in long hours, though. Every night since he'd started, Mack encountered Gisbourne or Halvorson the stone-faced transportation manager or Yarborough the safety chief, still at their desks, chain-smoking, guzzling bad coffee, poring over piles of memos, charts, and reports.

But not tonight. The whole row of offices was dark. Mack entered Fat Ferdie's domain and flipped on the light. As usual, the plant manager had filled his two heavy glass ashtrays to overflowing, every butt burned down to lip-scorching length. Mack dumped them into one of the rusty metal waste cans he used so he didn't have to wrestle his janitor's cart on and off the freight elevator to the second floor. As he swabbed out the ashtrays with the damp rag hooked over his belt, a little quiver of excitement worked its way toward his knees like a slow-moving electric shock. The feeling was familiar. Mack straightened up and tried to remember why.

Gisbourne's scuffed metal desk, probably scrounged from a government warehouse, didn't resemble Sim's burnished, handmade desk in his office at home. But Mack's quivering urge to tempt fate, to uncover secrets, however petty, was the same. Sim's desk, left unlocked in the security of his own house, hadn't revealed much, at least to Mack's fifteen-year-old eyes, mostly unintelligible documents about "divorcement." One was a copy of a bill for services rendered that Sim had sent to some lady in Lake Forest. Mack's ideas of wealth and money were sketchy at best, but he knew the sum was more than enough to buy the Duisenberg roadster he'd ogled in *Life* magazine. Some Hollywood actor—Cary Grant, perhaps—had stood proudly next to the sleek auto.

The file drawers of Gisbourne's desk were locked up tight. Not so the center drawer, which, when Mack gingerly slid it open, revealed a rat's nest of loose papers. Could there be evidence here that Steckel Avenue was to be stage for launching the Tommy-as-hero show? Mack grabbed the papers with greedy hands, lusting after secrets so intently he felt a vibration run through his dick. Disappointment grew as he ran his eyes over the documents. They were even less interesting than the papers he'd found in his father's desk years before. Shipping records. Work orders to repair broken-down drill presses and lathes. Mundane memos from officials with impressive titles at the War Production Board and General Motors, the nominal owner of the plant. No reference to any upcoming bigwig visit.

As Mack was about to return Gisbourne's papers, trying to recall how they'd been arranged, an odd brown shape in the right corner of the drawer caught his eye. He slid his fingers around the object, a leather-covered flask, larger than the one Mack and Tommy had shared the night of the accident. Mack placed the wad of papers on the desk and slid the flask out. He felt liquid slosh inside.

Mack licked his lips. His thumb and index finger found their way to the shiny metal cap, attached to the flask by a tiny chain. He ran his finger twice, three times, around the edge of the cap. The chain jiggled invitingly. He twisted the cap. It turned easily, almost opening itself.

Mack raised the open flask to his nostrils and sniffed. Bourbon. The sweet, pungent aroma was unmistakable. Gisbourne wouldn't miss one or two swallows from his liquor supply, would he? Mack gently shook the flask, imagining how the bourbon would taste as it traced its gurgling, stinging way past his tongue and down his throat. He pursed his lips around the narrow opening. A part of him was practically making love to the whiskey. Maybe whiskey on top of the adrenalin charge he got from rifling Gisbourne's desk would enable him to see the visions, or whatever the hell they were, that everyone was convinced Tommy saw before he died. It was exactly the sort of pathetic alcoholic's excuse he sought to avoid by not drinking anymore. He never tipped back the flask.

Panting from the effort of not sampling Gisbourne's whiskey, Mack replaced the flask, sliding it back to its corner. Then he spread the papers across the bottom of the shallow drawer, in more or less the original pattern.

*No Irish visions for me*, Mack thought, but he felt *something* acting upon him. His professors at the UofC would've thought him barking mad. They saw individual efforts to affect (capital H) History as crazier than King Canute commanding the tide. Canute at least was a member of the minuscule group with some morsel of worldly power. For everyone else, noted one Hyde Park scholar obsessed with the rise and fall of civilizations, the odds were even longer, akin to a drop of water leaping out of Canute's tidal flow and spontaneously building a dam. Yet, booze or no booze, Mack felt some force, like an unseen magnetic field, irrevocably pulling him away from the restless, empty, exhausting (it was, at least, a magnet for adjectives!) routines of living out his one-eyed hermit's existence.

Mack finished his cleaning duties in the executive wing. He didn't try any more drawers. Waste cans in each hand banged against the wall as he made his way down the stairs, where his janitor's cart waited near the main entrance.

Rolling the cart back toward the shop floor, Mack saw a figure enter through the main door. "Hello?" he called across the wide vestibule, not quite pitch black, but illuminated by only a couple of dim bulbs at each end.

The figure waved in his direction. "Hello, Mack," said a familiar voice. "It's me, Tom Yarborough. What the hell kind of job is this, coming to work at five in the morning? My wife says she'd see more of me if I was in the army!"

"Good morning. Welcome to the graveyard shift," replied Mack, returning Yarborough's wave while the safety director, briefcase in hand, began to trot up the steps.

Mack was opening the door to the shop floor when Yarborough's voice sounded behind him. "Mack, come over here for a minute, will you? I want to ask you something."

Mack parked the cart next to the door and returned to

the staircase, where Yarborough stood on the second step. The extra altitude put the squat little Southerner, a self-proclaimed "Kentucky farm boy," at eye level with Mack. Yarborough squinted.

"You're the fellow with all the fancy education, ain't you?"

Mack nodded and grunted, "I suppose so."

"Listen, Mack, when I first heard about you, I thought your rich papa had got you on our payroll to keep your ass out of the war, or that maybe you were some kind of agitator from that Commie university."

Mack winced. He'd hoped confrontations like this were a thing of the past. At least this one wasn't accompanied by blows like his first meeting with Leopold Belgian.

"Then," Yarborough continued, "I heard you lost an eye. My little brother Charlie lost his left eye after he fell under a combine—sixteen years old. It's nothin' I'd wish on anybody. I still don't understand why you want to work with niggers, but you work hard as far as I can see, and you keep your nose clean, so you're okay in my book. And by the way, that's the best-looking glass eye I ever saw."

Mack suppressed a smile.

"So, stop bein' so modest and answer my question. Like that big announcement halfway said, we have a VIP visitor coming in a few days. I can't say who it is, but it's a gen-u-wine VIP. I drew the short straw and got the job of organizing the goddamn visit on this end. 'You're the safety director, and we have to keep him safe,' Ferdie says. 'So the job is yours,'"

"Okay," said Mack, striving to sound serious yet non-committal.

"Trust me, Mack, the job is a pain in the ass, high, wide, and handsome. The worst part is the thing I need to ask you about. These days, every time the goddamn phone rings, the fellow on the other end is some desk jockey in Washington, screaming at me. First, it's a guy from the FBI telling me we gotta cancel the invitation for 'reasons of wartime security,' which they must say is the reason for every goddamn thing they want you to do or not do. Then, five minutes later, another government so-and-so calls and yells just as loud, sayin' he's from the Secret Service, our VIP wants to come, and the visit is on just as planned."

Yarborough put down his briefcase and pulled out a handkerchief. He wiped his brow, harder than necessary. "My job is preventin' accidents in this damn plant and getting the folks patched up and back to work when they do happen. I don't know who the hell has to kiss somebody else's ass in Washington. Here's my question: They tell me you're an American History expert, so who's the boss here? Who do I listen to, the goddamn FBI or the Secret Service?"

"Well, without knowing the details, I can't say who's in charge," said Mack, working toward an objective, scholarly tone. "The FBI's job is fighting crime at the national level—that's why they're the '*Federal* Bureau.' Nowadays that includes hunting for spies and saboteurs."

"Yeah," muttered Yarborough, "that Hoover fella will tell you about that every day of the week." His voice grew stronger, "Now, what about the Secret Service?" Yarborough yanked his necktie straight, covering a missing button on his shirt front, barely visible in the half light.

"Their main job is simpler. They protect the President of the United States."

Yarborough picked up the bulging briefcase. "Well, thanks. That's a good thing to know. I musta been playin' hooky the day they went over that stuff." Yarborough turned and trudged slowly up the stairs. Two steps from the top, he turned and looked down at Mack. "You ain't gonna say nothin' about the little quiz, are you, son?"

Mack reluctantly muttered, "I won't mention it," then returned to his janitor's cart. As he made his way to the shop floor and a final round of toilet cleaning, thoughts of chance, fate, and their hifalutin', avalanche-riding cousin Destiny criss-crossed his mind. Was FDR really coming to Steckel Avenue to proclaim Thomas Kilkenny a national hero and provide a stunning culmination to his father's project? Mack could almost hear the president's round, aristocratic tones, eulogizing Tommy as a "true A-MERI-can hero."

Sim had said that Roosevelt knew all about Tommy's death. Who better to elevate Tommy to the pantheon? What better place to announce his apotheosis than a defense plant in his hometown, a plant building the engines that powered the hero's plane?

After his shift ended, Mack found himself at the bottom of the stairs leading to the executive wing. The first shift had already arrived and clocked in. The only sound was the background thrum of spinning lathes and drills, punctuated by the pounding rhythm of the presses—production winning the war. He plodded up the stairs. The big bosses' workday usually began at eight o'clock, so, except for Yarborough's office, three doors down the hall, on the left, all the offices were still dark. Mack walked along the hall, slowly at first, then at a faster pace.

He knocked softly on Yarborough's open door. "Excuse me, Mr. Yarborough, sir." As soon as the words came out, he hated his kowtowing tone.

"Yes, what is it?" The safety director stubbed out a cigarette and flipped a stapled page of the report he was reading.

Mack took two steps into the office. "Did what I told you help you decide who to listen to?"

Yarborough leaned back in his chair and folded his hands behind his head. His gray suit jacket lay on top of a filing cabinet. The sleeves of his wrinkled white shirt were rolled up to the elbows. "Well, I'll tell you, son, that FBI fella, that high and mighty J. Edgar Hoover, is what we call a 'showboat' back home—the kind of player who always takes the last shot, even when another fellow is wide open. You've given me a chance to tell Hoover and the FBI to put it where the sun don't shine. Not in so many words, of course, but maybe it'll discourage Mr. Hoover from getting' in every damn newsreel you see. Not to mention his own strip in the Sunday funnies!"

"So Fat—I mean Mr. Gisbourne—is going to let you make the final decision?"

"Don't worry, son, we all call him Fat Ferdie too, leastways when he's not in the room. He's so afraid of the War Production Board and the big bosses at GM, he hates to decide *anything*. So, yes, with all this hootin' and hollerin' from Washington, he's gonna let me call the play on whether we go through with havin' Franklin De-LAY-no Roosevelt visit our little operation." Yarborough loosened his tie by another inch. "I say if the goddamn president wants to come and the Secret Service can protect his ass, then he should come. Besides, before the shit hit the fan in Washington, we set up the folks for somethin' big with that goddamn announcement. They won't be happy to see the damn mayor again, or even a big-league ballplayer like that Stan Hack. But Ol' FDR himself—what do you think of that?"

Mack's real thoughts had to do with whether the much-sought-after Dominic O'Nore knew about the president's visit. More accurately, how he'd place a large bet that Dominic was well aware of it and that was why the Feds were after him. *I have one last chance to put a stop to this*, Mack thought, *by convincing Yarborough that Hoover and his secretive G-Men—surely more secret than the Secret Service—may be right: the president is in more danger than the Secret Service is aware of.* Mack couldn't find the words. Like Mr. Graves before him, Mack was a soldier in his father's service now. They would have to deal with Dominic.

So all Mack said was, "That's terrific! Everyone will be excited."

"I'll bet a pup they will!"

As Mack backed out of the office, Yarborough said with growing excitement, "And we got niggers working here. Maybe Eleanor will drop by too."

Mack turned toward the hallway. "Remember," Yarborough called after him, "this has all got to stay a deep, dark secret, or both our dicks will be in the wringer!"

☙❧

Driving home along North Avenue, Mack saw a plane slicing across the sky, the airliner's silver wings glinting in the sun—n early morning flight from somewhere north or west beginning its descent toward Chicago Muni Airport on the South Side. Every time he saw a plane overhead, Mack cursed Tommy for the way he died. If he were simply missing in the usual sense, Mack would be able to wonder if Tommy might be on board the plane, miraculously flying home like Pete Winogrand. Mack wanted to imagine Tommy scribbling notes for his book of catastrophist history, the engines of the homebound plane roaring in his ears.

Tommy had robbed him, and Jan and Ellen and Blarney Bob, of even that ragged shred of possibility. He was irredeemably gone—that's what happens when you're at the center of an explosion, no barroom metaphor, but a real explosion transforming tons of flesh and steel into unidentifiable shrapnel. Were there volcanoes in the Philippines? If so, people miles from the Japs' landing site must've felt doubly cursed that day. First, invasion and war, now a sudden eruption of Mount Whatchamacallit.

From his father's point of view, this certain, unambiguous disappearance—with no possibility of an unexpected return like Walter Clinckscale's—was what made Thomas Kilkenny the perfect hero. Sergeant York had returned from the Great War, of course, shown his Medal of Honor to adoring crowds then vanished into the Tennessee hills. In general, though, you couldn't trust live war heroes. Consider Theodore Roosevelt. Had Thomas Kilkenny survived, he might have written the book he'd promised and many more. Tommy might've followed his father into politics. Mayor of

Chicago? Senator? The first Irish-Catholic president? All empty speculation now.

Franklin D. Roosevelt himself—Teddy's shirt-tail relative—would perform the secular last rites, proclaiming the flesh-and-blood self that had been Captain Thomas Aloysius Kilkenny was no more. In a story Mack had read as a kid, from a book of "true tales of the Old West," an outlaw tied up his victim in a rickety shack and set off three-hundred pounds of TNT. Charged with murder, the bad guy invoked *habeas corpus*. No body, no murder.

Mack laughed so hard the Ford lurched into the left-hand lane for oncoming westbound traffic. Fortunately, it was empty.

# Chapter 27

Why did you turn *this* way?" asked Jan, gesturing down Lake Shore Drive toward Hyde Park and points south. A couple of days after the meeting with Yarborough, Mack was still digesting the fact of the president's visit—reality now, not mere speculation.

Jan had met Mack in the Steckel Avenue parking lot when his shift ended. "The cabbies are getting suspicious about my one-way trips out here," she'd laughed. "God knows what they're thinking!" After a quick breakfast at Morty's, Mack had been driving her home until the unexpected turn.

"I'm not sure why I turned," Mack replied, sliding his fingers along the top curve of the steering wheel. "I want to look around your father's house one more time, and for you to look too. Maybe Dominic's returned to the scene of the crime. Maybe he's there now, and we can call the FBI to pick him up. I still have Agent Neilsen's card."

"And I have keys to the house and an excuse for being there," said Jan primly.

"Well, there's that too. Not much gets past you, does it?"

"Get used to it, buster."

They both laughed until Jan continued. "Do you think we'll find another corpse in the cellar? Dad?"

Mack shook his head no as they rode in silence past the Museum of Science and Industry and then into the quiet residential streets of South Shore.

Mack's theory was simple enough. If Dominic was planning—under orders from the IRA? the Nazis?—to attack the president in Chicago, he wasn't going to stay around afterward. That meant disposing of Blarney Bob, who raised the term "unreliable" to a new level of meaning. Jan had surely pushed through to this conclusion, too painful to describe out loud. Even before leaving the French Lick note, Dominic, obviously a resolute and resourceful fellow, may well have taken the alderman back to his house and murdered him there.

Mack didn't really expect to find Dominic at the Kilkenny house. Going there was his writ of *habeas corpus*. He certainly didn't want to find Blarney Bob dead, but he needed to grab hold of something *solid* to prove he wasn't struggling with ghosts and their familiars: letters, notes, words, lies.

Mack parked on Jeffery Boulevard around the corner from the Kilkenny house. "Let's go in through the back door, in case somebody's out front," he said. "The Cohens haven't built a fence, have they?"

"Not that I know of." Jan's breathy reply seemed equal parts fear and excitement.

They strolled down 74th Street, and Mack struggled for nonchalance. If anyone was watching, and no one appeared to be, they would've made an unusual pair. A grease-stained working man arm in arm with a well-coiffed, well-tended looker—a woman far too good for him.

The Cohen place, which backed the Kilkenny property, was a mirror image of Blarney Bob's house—there was no intervening alley. Mack recalled Jan's laughing reminiscence of playing spin-the-bottle with David, the Cohens' handsome only child. She'd admitted she had kissed him whichever way the bottle pointed, partly because she liked to feel him squirm and partly, she also admitted, because she had a seventh-grader's crush on him. Was David in the service now? Jan couldn't recall.

Jews and gentiles lived cheek by jowl in this part of South Shore. "Democracy for those who can afford it," as Blarney Bob liked to put it, a sociological insight that might have gotten him tenure at the UofC or Northwestern.

With a tiny pull on Mack's elbow, Jan signaled a sharp turn into the Cohens' side lawn. A side window squeaked open behind them. Jan squeezed Mack's elbow so tightly it still stung after she let go.

"Jan, I thought it was you! It's been ages! How's your father? It's been almost as long since we've seen him. Herb asked about Robert just last night at dinner. 'How come we never see the alderman anymore?' That's exactly what he said!"

Mack glanced back as Jan winced. Addy Cohen's gabby nature was legendary. Jan smiled and gave a stiff wave toward the window, where Addy bent over to talk through the open space above the sill—a shimmery silhouette behind the glass.

"Dad's not feeling well, so Dominic's taken him to a sanitarium, a place out in the country."

"Oh, that's too bad," said Addy. "I hope it's nothing too serious."

"We do too," replied Jan, in a tone both friendly and clearly intended to end the conversation. She took a short step toward the Kilkenny house and tugged Mack along with her. "I can't locate my front-door key, so we're going in the back way. To pick up some things...for Dad." She took another step and nudged Mack to do so too.

"Wait a second, dearie. Wait right there." Addy disappeared from the window without closing it.

Jan and Mack waited in silence. A long half-minute later, the Cohens' front door opened and closed. Addy bustled around to the side yard, flowered housedress flapping around thick ankles.

"Here," she said breathlessly, "I've been picking up the

mail ever since I saw your house was empty." She pushed a paper bag into Jan's hands. "It's mostly catalogs and flyers, but there are some bills there too. I was going to give them to Dominic, but he was never home either. That seemed strange till you said he's taken the alderman to the sanitarium." She reached up and gave Jan a quick hug, crushing the paper bag between them. "Oh—so Jan," Addy said, taking a quick step back. "I almost forgot to ask—what do you hear from that good-looking brother of yours? Still flying those big bombers?"

"Far as I know," Jan replied, not missing a beat. "Of course, the army doesn't give out much information these days."

"Neither does the navy." Addy's voice dropped. "David's finishing his training in San Diego. He'll probably be on a destroyer, he says, even though he's not supposed to talk about it." She looked into Jan's eyes. "Maybe they'll run into each other out there."

"Stranger things have happened," Jan said, shoving Mack toward the Kilkenny house.

"Anyway, it's nice to see you, you and your friend both…It's Mack, right?" Addy nodded, acknowledging Mack for the first time.

He nodded back, hoping his smile didn't look like a clown's painted-on grin.

"Come back soon. We'll have coffee!" Addy went on, her voice returning to her usual tone. She turned and trotted back toward the house.

Jan waved goodbye as she and Mack crossed the invisible line marking the boundary between the two lots. "Dad always said if Addy started on May Day, she'd still be talking when the birds fly south for the winter." She took a breath and said to no one in particular, "I hope David is okay."

The grass merged with the Kilkennys' flagstone patio—a favorite spot for highballs during the summer but now devoid of lawn chairs and folding tables. While Jan juggled Addy's bag of mail and fumbled for keys in her bulky purse, Mack gave the doorknob a sharp twist. The door popped open. Mack glanced quickly at her. Was it sloppiness by the FBI? Everybody knew Robert Kilkenny always locked his doors. And, thought Mack, people also knew Alderman Kilkenny had disappeared, although, as far as the press and general public were concerned, the lid on that particular news remained tightly in place. *Give the FBI a gold star for that at least.*

They stepped inside. After a quick look, the kitchen appeared undisturbed. Mack's closer inspection revealed the opposite: drawers not quite shut, a cupboard door left ajar, half a muddy heel print by the pantry door, the framed photo of FDR slightly askew on the wall.

Jan went through the contents of the paper bag.

"Any official invitations?" Mack asked. "Maybe one to join Lieutenant Pete Winogrand for some kind of gathering? Maybe at a defense plant?"

"Nope," said Jan, "only fliers and bills." She thrust a half-dozen envelopes into her purse and abandoned the bag on the counter.

Mack envied her for the normality of it—mail to sort, bills to pay, mundane, predictable. Unlike anything else in their lives at the moment.

Jan walked into the living room. Mack followed. Signs of a search were apparent there too, as Mack nearly tripped over a lace-edged silk pillow from the couch that had ended up on the floor. Jan stood in the middle of the room, clutching her purse as if someone were about to grab it. Mack felt the normality leaking away, as Jan's eyes darted around before looking Mack in the face. "I guess...I guess we had better check the cellar."

Mack nodded in agreement when they were interrupted by a booming voice from the dining room. *"I've already looked there!"*

To manage the sudden shock, Mack saw himself for a second as a Looney Tunes cartoon character literally leaping out of his skin to become a naked skeleton. Jan emitted a tiny, high-pitched scream. *It may have disturbed a passing bat*, thought Mack, surprise and fear still merging in his mind. Conclusion No. 1: The simple, in-and-out search of the Kilkenny house was no longer possible.

Mack and Jan remained rooted to the florid Oriental rug covering Blarney Bob's living-room floor. A stout man in a blue-serge suit strode from the dining room and stood in front of the stone fireplace.

"Who in the hell are you?" Jan and Mack said the same words, one beat off, their shouts ending in "—you-ou!"

The fellow stepped halfway between them, glancing at each in turn. "Well, as the swells like to say, 'I have the advantage of you, 'cause I know who the hell *you* are!" He folded thick arms across a protruding belly and rocked backed on his heels. The guy was enjoying the moment. Mack hated him for it.

"Okay, Sherlock, you can climb down from your high horse." Mack spat out the words. "What are you doing here? And by 'here,' I'm referring to this house, which belongs to Miss Kilkenny, the lady over there." Jan nodded as if she were being formally introduced.

Her ownership was perhaps not as binding as Mack was making it, but he was sure her right to be in the house was more legally solid than this impudent fellow's—exactly the phrase, Mack thought ruefully, his father would use.

"Miss Kilkenny, Mr. Simmons." The fat man nodded with exaggerated gravity. "I am Otto Detwiler, General Manager of the Detwiler Detective Agency." Thick fingers slid up to grasp the lapels of the cheap suit.

*General Manager—why not Generalissimo? Fuhrer in charge?* Mack didn't express his sarcasm out loud.

"I'm here on an assignment from a very important man in the city." He shook himself by his own lapels. "That man, young fellow, is none other than your father, Mister John M. Simmons!" He left off "the Second."

*At least,* thought Mack, *this self-important boob is nominally on our side.* Not exactly a comforting thought when one considered what happened when another of his father's foot soldiers—that would be the late Mr. Graves—dropped by Blarney Bob's place. "So, Mr. Detwiler, you picked the lock on the back door, and you've been snooping around waiting for Dominic O'Nore to come back."

Detwiler rocked back one more time, revealing more of the mud from his shoe he'd left on the kitchen floor. "Well, not to put too fine a point on it—that's correct."

Jan visibly relaxed and nodded toward Mack. "Proving our theory that everyone's looking for Dominic." Was she relieved Blarney Bob hadn't turned up dead in his own house? Mack couldn't tell.

"Look, bud," said Mack, finding a harsher tone, "you know as well as I do there's no point in holding out on one another. And you also must know my father's pulled me into this business too. So let's all stop playing Keystone Kops and share what we know. Like it or not, we're in this together."

Detwiler puzzled things over long enough for Mack to confirm the man was a dullard. Jan rolled her eyes. Finally, the detective nodded in agreement.

Under the unblinking gaze of FDR on the wall, they trooped back through the kitchen out to the flagstone patio. "In case O'Nore comes waltzing in," said Detwiler patting the pocket of his suit jacket suggesting the presence of a firearm, as if he were auditioning for a part in a bad detective movie.

Mack described the intensive FBI search for Dominic but couldn't determine if his father had shared the information with Detwiler. Jan paraphrased the supposed note from Blarney Bob to Ellen. Swallowing hard, Mack said, "There's one more thing. It seems that the President of the United States is coming to town, to the defense plant where I work. I'm not sure if the big bosses at the plant know it yet, but the reason for the visit is to honor Miss Kilkenny's brother Thomas for his heroism in the Philippines."

Jan glared at him. He hadn't yet told *her*.

None of it appeared to faze Detwiler. He was, Mack concluded, either trying to brazen it out and convey that *of course* he knew about the president, or was too slow on the uptake to comprehend the news. Slow-on-the-uptake won in a landslide.

"Okay, that's enough," said Mack, fixing his eyes on Detwiler's blank stare. "We've come across. Now, it's your turn. And you'd better not hold back."

This empty threat had a powerful impact on Detwiler, who rubbed nervous fingers across the dust-colored lock of hair above his sweaty forehead as he described the unlikely black Cadillac slowly exploring the streets of Canaryville, Blarney Bob's fancy car, now returned to his former wife. Or, Mack asked himself, to his widow?

"The Caddy's not been seen since," Detwiler concluded.

Mack tried to recall just where Canaryville was. North Side? South Side? He glared again at Detwiler and sternly asked, "Exactly where in Canaryville did the cop spot the Cadillac?"

"Forty-seventh or Forty-Eighth Street, near Halsted, by the big packing plant."

෴

As Dominic peered between the unlikely lace curtains framing Lonegan's smudged front window, he felt a wave of relief. The Cadillac had been a shiny black anvil hanging 'round his neck till he'd left it like an orphan child on the doorstep of that damned witch Ellen.

The move had meant one last terrifying drive, akin to the one with Blarney Bob to Lonegan's place and the solo trip to fetch the detective's body and dump it. He'd been gobsmacked at first when his flashlight showed the basement room to be bare as a newborn's bottom, as if shooting the detective had been part of a fever dream or a drunken man's ravings.

Dominic had got hold of himself after a few seconds of abject panic: someone else had found the detective and taken away his earthly remains. It didn't matter who or how as long as no bloody policeman could locate *him*. Dousing the light, Dominic had made his way by feel and memory out of the Kilkenny house, back to the Cadillac, and through empty, dead-of-night streets back to Lonegan's. The Yanks spoke of stealth as "walking on eggs," but never driving on them, which is what he did that night and then again in the daylight to Astor Place, where Cadillacs were, at least, thick upon the ground.

Dominic had been more than a little afraid to face Ellen, note in hand. No man had caused him such knee-knocking fear since Father Quinn had paddled the snot out of him at twelve with his twisted black-oak cane. But—perhaps on account of the draconian Sister Mary Gregory, whose glare turned Father Quinn's own legs to jelly—an angry woman was a more fearsome animal altogether. In fact, in a connection Dominic had not recognized before, Ellen bore a passing resemblance to the Sister, especially when the Missus pursed her thin lips and knitted her brows into a hateful harpy's look that bored an inch-wide hole into your forehead.

The two Kilkenny kids, Thomas and Janice, were hardly frightening but had been a mystery from the moment Dominic first set eyes on the pair of spoiled brats. Their done-up clothes, fancy toys, and gabbling Yankee accents made Blarney Bob's children as strange as citizens of the back side of the moon. The two were also familiar as a pair of old shoes. Both kids, with their smooth, pale skin and straight hair shining like polished ebony, could've wandered the muddy streets of Bannacree without drawing a second look—a seamless fit into the jumbled tribe of McGuigans who'd lived in that pig sty of a town since time out of mind.

The McGuigans fell into two lots—the ones ugly enough to stop a clock with their tangled eyebrows, potato noses, and sunken, famished cheeks, and the ones handsome enough to cause men to sigh and women to swoon when they passed. Like Blarney Bob, the kids, Thomas in particular, belonged to the handsome set. Strange how, as the great day approached, likely Dominic's last, his thoughts strayed so often back to Ireland.

It pleased Dominic to know things about Thomas and Janice's kin they'd go to their graves without ever guessing. Of course, it was a sure bet in the case of young Thomas. The handsome lad had died a hero's death, and everyone believed it enough to summon the president to Chicago, taking time off from his job of kissing Winston Bloody Churchill's arse.

The false note he'd left with Ellen would purchase a few days at most, though that would likely be enough. Dominic remained surprised at how, as they sat at Lonegan's chipped, food-stained table, he'd had to place the Luger right up against the alderman's head, just above the right ear, to compel him to write out a note to Dominic's specifications. He'd rewarded Blarney Bob with a plate of fried eggs and bacon, followed by a stiff whiskey chaser.

Then, as they'd stood up from the table, Bob pulled straight the front of his wrinkled shirt, which hadn't been changed since they'd arrived at Lonegan's.

"Dominic, I want to tell you something straight on, without any moonshine."

He spoke in a steadier voice than Dominic had heard from him in a long time, no sign of the tumbler of whiskey he'd just downed and with less of Bob's on-again, off-again brogue and more of the harsh Chicago voices that rubbed a rash on Dominic's ears every day.

"Whatever you think you're doing—and I don't have a tinker's notion of what it might be—I know you believe you're doing it for Ireland." He'd pointed a long finger at Dominic, who stared back with resolutely dead eyes. "But let me tell you something, boyo, something I've learned in my long stay over here. Ireland's fate is to act out the troubles of the world on a tiny stage. In this great warring globe, we're the Punch-and-Judy show of nations. An insignificant dunghill in a mountain of shit. "

Dominic had stared him down for several seconds, teeth grinding like millstones before slapping the traitor, as he now knew him to be, alongside the head with the Luger and had Lonegan drag his carcass down to the mildew-smelling cellar. They'd jammed Blarney Bob's stained blue-silk necktie down his throat then used a couple of yards of dusty clothesline to bind him to a forgotten wooden chair—a paint-chipped seat that hadn't received anyone's bum since the pope was an altar boy. Whether this would be the last day on Earth for the fellow born Daniel McGuigan was a question Dominic hadn't yet answered.

While Dominic watched from the window, no one passed by on the street except groups of screaming, tumbling kids bound for St. Gabriel's parish school around the corner—likely doomed to face another Sister Mary Gregory. He left his seat by the front window, a post where he could survey the street without being seen, and ordered Lonegan to watch from the porch, where his presence (as the neighborhood idiot, Dominic concluded) wouldn't be noted.

Tired from long staring, Dominic went to the kitchen and warmed his tea from the kettle on the stove. He sipped quietly for a few minutes. The front door squealed open and shut, and Lonegan joined him in the kitchen.

"Anything new on the street, Hughie?"

"Mostly quiet," said Lonegan, stirring a tablespoon of sugar into his tea. "Johnny O'Malley from the end of the street raced by, showing off his new De Soto. Lord knows where he got the cash. And just now, some fellow in a Ford jalopy that saw its best days before the stock market crash."

A faint recollection crept up on Dominic. "You didn't recognize the car then?"

"Some kid, I guess, wasting his da's gasoline roaming the streets with his girl."

"You didn't see the driver—the kid, I mean?"

"Only the girl, a pretty one indeed. She was on the side facing the house. Now that I think of it, they rolled by awfully slow, nothing like Johnny whizzing past in a race with the Devil. And the gal was staring hard. A pretty bit of stuff, black-haired, she was, but one of ours, I think, not a dago or spic."

Dominic sipped his tea and choked back an urge to strangle this lunkhead where he sat. Hugh Lonegan couldn't know if it was Janice Kilkenny passing by, of course. But even so, what kind of revolution was it that attracted such empty-headed fools?

"And you recognized neither the auto nor the girl?"

Lonegan poured the rest of the tea down his throat and raised his arms in an exaggerated shrug. In the way odd, buzzing thoughts will bang together, Dominic came upon the name of the fellow who'd courted Janice, the likely driver of the Ford jalopy. Mack Simmons, a damnable rich boy, meddling in the affairs of serious men.

# Chapter 28

The invitation arrived at the Simmons house in the afternoon mail, brought in from the mailbox as usual by Mr. Dineen. It was addressed to "Mr. and Mrs. John M. Simmons II." In his office at home, Sim leaned back in the desk chair and puffed on his cigar, chuckling to himself. He always enjoyed invitations addressed this way. Did it make Katherine "Mrs. II"?

The invitation was an anticlimax. Fix had let Sim know it was on its way. When he'd phoned Sim at his downtown office, they chatted amiably about fellow Skull and Bones alumni. Jack McGill had somehow talked his way onto the War Production Board, even though most of his experience involved producing bastard children. Bricky Hartle's boy— a West Point graduate, now an army major—had been taken prisoner on Bataan, and there was no further word on his fate, surely a bad business.

Fix said the president was determined to come to Chicago and present a posthumous Medal of Honor to the family of Captain Thomas Kilkenny. Live, fighting heroes were preferable to dead ones, of course, but Kilkenny's story was a godsend after the string of defeats stretching from the East Indies to Wake Island. FDR's speechwriters were working on his remarks, and the president appreciated the information Sim had provided. Franklin was looking forward to getting away from Washington, especially when it meant visiting a key defense plant.

The president had even chided Hoover, Fix related with a chuckle, "And you know *that* can be a risky proposition. 'What's that, Edgar, your G-Men can't catch one drunken Irishman? Well, you'll undoubtedly have him in hand before my Chicago trip. And if not, the Secret Service can surely handle things when we get there.' That had to cut to the quick. You know how Hoover despises anyone who tries to steal his thunder," said Fix, still chuckling. "The whole thing is pure Franklin, setting one bureaucrat against another—" Fix paused, and Sim let him collect his thoughts.

"Roosevelt believes in his own luck." Fix's tone had grown more serious. "At least since that little wop Zangara shot at him in 'thirty-three and killed your Mayor Cermak instead."

"If his luck ever changes," Sim had said, rolling his cigar to the other side of his mouth, "we'll have Henry Wallace in the top seat. That'd be a disaster."

"Absolute catastrophe!" Fix had replied with uncharacteristic vehemence. "There's already talk about what a mistake it was to put the Sage of Iowa on the ticket. I can assure you plans are afoot to be rid of him by 'forty-four. If we hadn't threatened to publicize Willkie's illegitimate child, the Republicans would've plastered Wallace's Himalayan mysticism and his weird guru across every front page. In his own way, the man's as crazy as Hitler. He admires Stalin, and he'd probably make peace with the Fuhrer if the goddamn swami told him to—"

As Sim opened the official invitation, he sent a cloud of cigar smoke rolling across his desk. He felt a stab of pain for the lost airman, but it passed quickly. After all, Thomas Kilkenny had taken an oath to defend his country even unto death, and he was defending it more effectively now than he had flying around the doomed Philippines.

Sim began planning how to prepare Katherine for the president's visit. There was no word yet about whether Eleanor was joining him in Chicago. It was an open secret, Fix had intimated, that the president's and the first lady's staffs hardly spoke to each another. A chance to meet Eleanor Roosevelt would've thrilled Katherine, but Sim couldn't wait to find out. His wife's physical appearance presented no problem at all, of course. Katherine was always every inch the proper lady. Complications would only arise when she opened her mouth, and the proper lady turned into a wayward five-year old.

Rehearsal before the event? Perhaps Mr. Dineen could play FDR—a role he'd relish—while Lavinia could be Eleanor. No, Sim concluded, it would only confuse his poor wife. The great moment was almost here. He couldn't take the risk.

❧❧

Ellen received her invitation the same day. Before tearing open the cream-colored envelope, she rubbed her index finger across the ridges of the Seal of the President of the United States embossed on the upper left-hand corner. She tossed the rest of the afternoon mail on the kitchen table, placed the envelope from the president's office squarely on a placemat, and sat down in front of it, as if beginning a religious rite. She knew there was a faint echo of the Roosevelt clan in her wide chin and high forehead, but Ellen had never heard of any connection with the Roosevelts. Not surprising. The Boswells, whose business ventures had long since risen to the realm of pure investment unconnected with any trade or profession, disdained relationships with politicians of any stripe—especially Chicago Irish-Catholic ward heelers.

With a reluctance that she recognized was born of simultaneously knowing what the envelope contained and not wanting to face it, Ellen slid her finger into the narrow space between the corner and the sealed-down flap. Very slowly, she tore the envelope open, keeping the torn slit as even as possible. The stationery inside had the same creamy texture as the envelope. The typing was neat, professionally done. The president will be honored if you would join him. Your son's sacrifice. Heroism. Must be recognized. Two p.m. The Steckel Avenue plant.

Ellen wanted to rip up the invitation then burn the fancy paper to ashes. Release the ashes to the wind, watch them dwindle to the same fragments her son had become. Motes of dust too small to be called anything at all.

Thomas had been a near-copy of his father. When she and Robert watched him climb the monkey bars in Washington Park or race his tricycle along the neighborhood sidewalks, Ellen joked she'd been only the carrier in this operation. Tommy and Ellen didn't talk often after he outgrew childish dependence on Mommy, and Janice came along to fill the gap. His rough games held no interest for Ellen, regardless of her son's athletic success. Cheering him on became Robert's task when he was sober enough to carry it out. Ellen always waited for Tommy to come to her. Sometimes he did.

They'd talked at Palm Beach, after she convinced him to join the family over spring vacation. "Let's get together one last time before you graduate from the UofC." The phrase "last time" caused Ellen's throat to constrict as she bent toward the table. It had been their last family gathering, period. One perfect, blue-sky day at the beach, women's looks glinting off Tommy's wet skin like sunbursts, he'd leaned toward her from his canvas chair. Water drops slid to the point of his chin but didn't quite drip onto the sand. In a hoarse whisper, Tommy said he was planning to ask Felicia Simmons to marry him.

Ellen had forgotten the exact words of her reply—purposeful amnesia, she admitted. Something about not being tied down, at least delay the proposal another six months, a year perhaps, keep open Tommy's unlimited future. Tommy nodded, droplets from his chin making tiny wet explosions in the white sand, and said no more. Too proud to admit he'd taken her words to heart. How like his father. In any case, Tommy stopped seeing Felicia when he returned to Chicago. Ellen had heard the poor girl, taking it hard, had turned into some kind of recluse.

People were naturally drawn to her son. They wanted to give themselves to him, the way strangers sent gifts to the president or the King of England, even when they understood that neither needed anything they could provide. After Felicia, Tommy went back to cutting his usual wide swath among the women in his circle, rarely dating anyone more than once or twice, an excellent strategy.

When the news came—from Janice, not Thomas—that he'd enlisted, Ellen had told herself military service would soon be a requirement for any successful political career. She'd thought—the irony made Ellen sick to her stomach as she grasped the edge of the kitchen table—the army air corps would get Thomas away from the wastrel Mack Simmons, who'd surely led the drinking expedition that winter night.

Mack had gotten what he deserved. Rough justice, but justice nonetheless, something she would never admit to anyone.

Right up to the end, she'd fought down another unspoken belief that re-surfaced now: Tommy's enlistment was adolescent penance for what he'd supposedly done to his bosom pal Mack.

Ellen carefully folded the invitation, wondering if the president had actually signed it or had a secretary with well-developed forgery skills. When Janice returned home, Ellen informed her they would both be attending the ceremony at the Steckel Avenue plant.

❧❧❧

As Hugh Lonegan entered the tiny living room with a

pair of envelopes in hand, Dominic subdued his smile of satisfaction. Lonegan handed him a plain brown envelope bearing Lonegan's last name and address and a Washington, DC postmark. Dominic calmly opened the envelope. Inside, as he well knew, had to be a fancy envelope bearing the invitation for Alderman Robert Kilkenny to attend the memorial service for his son at the defense plant.

Dominic never doubted their contact in Washington. Like the most useful spies back home, he was probably some bachelor clerk so gray and invisible he seemed made of smoke or fog, someone seen then immediately seen through. The fellow hinted he worked for a bigwig in the White House. It was surely a lowly job but one that put him in a spot to know about subjects of importance to the Cause, which now included young Thomas Kilkenny's heroic death. Dominic's brief coded notes to the D.C. post office box always got through. The knowing fellow on the other end followed every jot and tittle of Dominic's instructions, sending along details on the Kilkenny business and now the president's providential visit to Chicago, which eliminated the cumbersome chore of traveling to Washington to do the deed. Dominic smiled at how smoothly the IRA man diverted the alderman's invitation to Hugh Lonegan's out-of-the way address. Not everyone over here had fallen away like Blarney Bob, proof the Almighty was now in sympathy with the Cause after so many years of looking the other way.

Grasping another, much-handled envelope, Lonegan waited for Dominic to finish reading. He held up his own envelope festooned with bloody Free State stamps—a child showing a treasure to his da', thought Dominic. "It's a letter from my gran in Meath, but look here, at these postage stamps." He thrust the paper in front of Dominic's eyes. "See, there's Daniel O'Connor, the Catholic Liberator, and look, here's the one about the Easter Rising twenty-five years on." The stamp showed a tiny IRA man bearing a rifle, tiny face half-mad with patriotic fury.

"Hughie, you must always be aware that, in letting go of Ulster, the bloody Free State has left Ireland like a man with an arm and a leg cut off."

"But how would a man like that even know where his limbs had gone, let alone how to paste them back on?"

Dominic smiled, his usual fury at Lonegan's thick-headedness nowhere to be found. "No, no, our six lost counties haven't sunk into the sea. They are where they've always been, waiting only for us to show the cunning and strength to take them back."

"And that we shall do!" said Lonegan with a broad smile, taking his precious envelope into the kitchen.

Dominic's grin widened. For Lonegan to claim cunning was like a dog claiming to play the fiddle. Regarding his own greater task—the magnificent opportunity to make *him* the instrument for restoring Ireland—Dominic now knew the where and the when. The how was taking shape too.

Dominic had allotted a pair of bullets for the alderman and for Lonegan. But perhaps he would let them live, leave the bloody authorities to deal with their criss-crossing words hopping past like rabbits in springtime. The thought of some copper questioning Lonegan made him laugh, at first softly, then uproariously. He saw Lonegan creep, wide-eyed, into the living room then tiptoe back to the kitchen.

# Chapter 29

In the days before the president's visit, the newspapers were full of stories of starving Filipino and American survivors of the Bataan Death March straggling into the prison camp at Cabanatuan. The Wehrmacht pressed its siege of Sebastopol, which led to the capture of 90,000 Red Army prisoners. Rommel's Afrika Korps took Tobruk as the British Army retreated into Egypt. In northern China, Japan accelerated its Sanko Sakusen "Three Alls" program—Kill All, Burn All, Seize All—resulting in 250,000 deaths.

At the White House, according to Sim's friend Fix, FDR and Harry Hopkins decided against a motorcade from Union Station to the Steckel Avenue plant. The added attention to the president's visit might rile up Hoover beyond the breaking point, and there was no need to shore up support in Chicago, of all places. "If we can't win there," the president joked, "I might as well retire right now and turn the war over to Henry Wallace."

In Sim Simmons's LaSalle Street office, Otto Detwiler reported no sign of Dominic O'Nore or Blarney Bob anywhere on the South Side. He volunteered to look for them in French Lick, Indiana, maybe they hadn't yet arrived when the FBI raided the place. Barely listening, Sim replied, maybe later. He wondered what other operatives were available.

✑✑✑

In Lonegan's bare living room, Dominic tried on a nondescript black suit that had belonged to Lonegan's late brother, a long-time Chicago cop. The suit fit perfectly. The silver police captain's badge pinned to the lapel glinted in the sunshine streaming through the dirty front window.

"People see what they want to see, Hughie," said Dominic with a smile. "I never wear a suit or a hat, but I'll be sporting them at the presidential get-together, so they'll see a different fellow, particularly when the Right Honorable Alderman says I'm his personal copper." He slid a hand into the inside pocket of the suit jacket and scooped out a pair of sunglasses. Dominic slid them onto his nose and around his ears. Another perfect fit.

*No need for some Sherlock Holmes disguise*, thought Dominic, *no uncanny portrayal of a doddering granny or postulant in the Sisters of Mercy. And it's not one of their bloody Halloween begging costumes I'm looking for, either. Just enough to get in with no questions asked after a good word from the alderman. And I don't give a long-tailed Belfast wharf rat's ass about getting out.*

"Now," said Dominic, assuming a more business-like tone, "we must ensure we have a ticket into this splendid event."

"That packet from Washington said there'd be tickets, then?" Lonegan wiped his hands across the front of a sleeveless tee-shirt that Dominic concluded must have been unearthed in some long-forgotten cache of clean undergarments.

"Not precisely," said Dominic, still settling himself into the unfamiliar suit jacket like a boy on his way to First Communion. "The alderman himself shall be my ticket to enter. He'll need some cleaning-up before the day arrives, of course. And some softening-up too, so he'll play the part of a grieving da' with no false steps."

Lonegan gave him a blank look, such a familiar expression that Dominic barely noticed. "What we must do now, my lad, is go down cellar and speak kindly to your guest."

Dominic felt excitement rising, a quiver of the muscles making its way from calves to knees to thighs. It was more than excitement, a drug more powerful than drink or even the heroin Victor Schlegel and the Outfit peddled to the Negroes, the blackbirds, in Bronzeville. Patrick Pearse and Michael Collins must have felt it as they gripped their rifles and prepared to storm the Dublin Post Office on that Easter so many years back. They were heroes in the same way he was about to be, beyond simple courage, beyond the ancient jape that a hero was no braver than an ordinary fellow, only brave five minutes longer. True heroes were ready, willing, happy even, to abandon their families and lay down their lives, all small things compared to the Cause.

When he exiled the alderman to Lonegan's moldy cellar, Dominic had determined to have as little contact with him as possible. But Dominic began to fear that his prisoner might become too shopworn to perform the duties required. So, to keep him lively, Dominic brought his meals and whiskey down himself, chatted amiably even when Bob growled or cursed in reply, and allowed him to walk and stretch a bit before binding him to the chair again.

This time, he bade Lonegan do the binding up. The last time, Bob had complained that fucking Dominic was squeezing the life's blood from his arms and legs. When Lonegan looped the first coil of clothesline around the alderman's right wrist and started to pull it tight against the chair, Dominic said, "Hold off, Hughie, and give the gentleman leave to breathe a minute."

After taking a long sideways step that placed him in front of his prisoner, Dominic crossed his arms over his chest, the Luger softly coiled in the fingers of his right hand. "I know you're hating me now, Alderman Kilkenny. And it's my sad fate to bring you news that will surely compel you to hate me all the more." Dominic had practiced his speech and expected the opening lines to catch Blarney Bob's interest. But he might as well have been talking to the battered chair.

Having begun, Dominic was determined to keep going. "The news I have bears upon your fine son Thomas. He has perished in the heat of battle in the Philippine Islands. Died a true hero, I'm told on the best authority, and due to be honored for his sublime courage and sacrifice."

He had Bob's full attention now. The alderman's staring black eyes could curdle cream then heat up to melt lead. Yet his easy-working mouth remained shut tight as an oyster.

"Our young Thomas led an attack on those slanty-eyed heathen Japs and blew one of their big ships to smithereens, to atoms! Alone in his airplane, he was." For a moment, Thomas Kilkenny became a martyr of the Cause, with Dominic composing a ballad to honor him.

Blarney Bob spoke up, sudden as a man jerked awake from an unsettling dream. "You are truly the very scum of the earth, Dominic O'Nore." His words began slow and quiet but climbed in volume and force. Lonegan took two mincing steps away from the chair, as if Bob's voice might burn him. "But let's forget that vile false name and recall that you're no more than Gerry Bloody Hearn from the very arse-end of Belfast!"

Such words would ordinarily have enraged Dominic, but he was well beyond such feelings now. "Sir, I understand your fury, but I'm simply a messenger, no more than the postal carrier or a telegraph boy."

For a stretch of twenty seconds or so, Robert Kilkenny wept. It was a sloppy affair, noted Dominic, beginning with a gasping struggle to hold back the sobs, gagging like a man who's discovered his lamb chop's gone off, and concluding with a surrender to tears that came sure as the rain. Lonegan stepped toward the chair and rested his hand gently on the alderman's shoulder. Probably not knowing or caring whose touch he was feeling, Kilkenny grasped Lonegan's hand.

Dominic, who had some experience in comforting the bereaved, allowed the moment to run its course.

"As for my bringing you to this foul place, and the rough treatment since," Dominic continued, picking up the thread of his speech, "I am a messenger boy in that as well. I must tell you, Robert, that the hard men in Dublin are sorely worried you have turned against the Cause and are playing the traitor's part. Their suspicions were born when you climbed into bed with that foul Outfit weasel Victor Schlegel, and they've grown like weeds since—"

Dominic skipped a beat to look for some response from the alderman. There was none. "Grown to the point where I was ordered to bring you to a safe house 'til a full investigation could be concluded back home. I had to push things forward a bit when I caught a sneaking detective in the secret room—"

"A detective—in *my* house!" Blarney Bob's voice was back in operation.

"Don't worry, he was a private man. The local police wouldn't come near if you were shitting ten-pound notes."

A tiny smile gave a twist to the alderman's lips and quickly vanished.

"I sent the detective to play poker in Hell at the same table as Victor Schlegel. That's why we had to leave the house like thieves, in the dead of night."

Dominic studied the alderman's florid face, but it had frozen back into a hard mask.

"So, here, sir, is where we sit. The President, F.D. Roosevelt himself, is coming to commemorate your son's bravery. Other bigwigs will be there as well, the Mayor, other men you know, who will be expecting to see you. We have attended like ceremonies, though, sadly, none with the import of this one."

The alderman nodded solemnly.

"I'm bound to keep you under my eye 'til the investigation is sorted out and proves you to be a true Fenian—"

"Whatever I might have said, I am true to the Cause. You know that, Gerry. Dominic. You know I am!"

"I do indeed. And I want to bloody well make sure the rough boys haven't decided to take no chances and sent someone to stop your tongue for eternity. You need protecting more than ever, and I'm still the man for the job."

Dominic looked hard to see if the alderman was drinking in this long draught of moonshine. But his usually active face never changed. It didn't matter. Belief was all force and compulsion. "Compelling belief" was the phrase the bright fellows used, but it meant nothing more than whose hand held the gun. That's how the bloody Brits compelled belief in the Devil's doctrine that Ulster was still theirs, how that crazy fellow Hitler got the Germans screaming in unison at his mad speeches, spittle flying from his mouth.

Two murderous giants—turn the one already battling the Brits into the ally of United Ireland. That was the trick. The sainted Roger Casement had joined the Irish cause with the Kaiser's in 1916 and nearly brought it off. Now was the time to take hold of the weapon at hand and bend it to the Cause. Let the politicians label that weapon nothing but a bayonet wielded by some goose-stepping Nazi. Sean Russell and Seamus O'Donovan, lost heroes gone too soon, they had understood. We must pick up their fallen banner, seize the moment, and press home the advantage offered by the shifting fortunes of war.

"And what of the dead detective, then?" the alderman finally asked in a harsh whisper.

"There's a bit of a mystery about that. It seems someone has packed off the fellow's remains to parts unknown. And stirring the pot further, the authorities are looking to me to assist in their inquiries. There you have the reason why you'll see me in unfamiliar dress and with the badge of a Chicago copper as the great event unfolds to honor our Thomas."

Lonegan seemed to be a fellow at a mad tennis match, wide eyes swinging back and forth. His face unexpectedly broke into a broad grin. *Finally*, thought Dominic, *the idiot has heard something he understands.*

# Part 3

# "Miss this meeting, and you'll be sorry!"

"The superiority of the United Nations in munitions…must be overwhelming—so overwhelming that the Axis nations can never hope to catch up…This production of ours must be raised far above present levels, even though it will mean the dislocation of the lives and occupations of millions of our own people. We must raise our sights all along the production line…In this year, 1942, we shall produce…forty-five thousand combat planes—bombers, dive bombers, pursuit planes." ~ *Franklin D. Roosevelt, State of the Union address*

# Chapter 30

When Jan and Mack walked into Sim's LaSalle Street office, his father emitted a long, sincere sigh. This was unusual in itself. His father was down in the dumps about as often as a locomotive or steamroller. Low spirits, at least those visible to the naked eye, simply weren't part of his makeup.

Shirtsleeves rolled up, with no suit or tie in sight—another uncommon occurrence—Sim gestured for them to sit, silently convening a Saturday morning meeting of the Dominic-and-Blarney-Bob Search Committee. Mack briefly summarized their encounter with Detwiler and the fruitless drives along the byways of Canaryville.

"Well, Detwiler hasn't done any better—no surprise there," said Sim, staring at his reflection in the Napoleonic desk's mahogany surface. "If the fellow weren't terrified of me, I'd have my doubts he's really looking at all."

The thought of Detwiler cowering before him would surely bring a smile to his father's face. Right on schedule, it did.

He celebrated by lighting a cigar. After two thoughtful puffs, he glanced at Jan and Mack in turn and shook his head ruefully. "And," he said, studying the slowly forming ash, "it appears the FBI has stopped searching."

"But this could be a plot to assassinate the *president*," said Jan in the loudest voice yet used at the Search Committee meeting. "They can't just stop looking for the assassin!"

Sim exhaled a fog bank of cigar smoke. "I didn't think so either. But Fix, my old friend at the White House, tells me Hoover is absolutely livid about the president making the trip here against his advice—or perhaps 'his orders' is a more accurate way to put it."

"Maybe the FBI wants to step in at the last moment and save the day." The words rode an express train from Mack's brain to his mouth.

Sim placed the cigar in a ceramic ashtray at the corner of the desk and looked Mack in the eye. "Son, I'm not surprised it took your devious mind to think of that."

Jan smiled and nodded. Mack couldn't decide whether to feel insulted or complimented. Then he understood that his father's uninspired joshing was an invitation, long delayed, to enter his circle. He was telling him, we're on the same team now. We're working together—not exactly like law partners, but at least striving for the same goal.

The father-son moment was immediately challenged by the splinter parties within Mack's hopelessly divided brain-parliament. Each quarreling faction drafted its own resolution proclaiming that his father was a) monstrously egotistical, taking advantage of his son's protective feelings to weave the final spider-web strands to trap him forever; b) sublimely patriotic and selfless; c) utterly absurd, the consummate wealthy crackpot.

His father leaned back in his chair. "I wouldn't put it past Hoover to place the president's life in danger for his own ends. Therefore, it falls even more forcefully upon us to stop Dominic *now* and allow the ceremony to take place as planned."

Jan and Mack glanced at one another, both waiting for some acknowledgement of Blarney Bob, his undeniable role as father of the hero, and the danger he was in. None was forthcoming. The parliamentary debate raged on.

❦❦❦

As the presidential visit and Tommy's apotheosis approached, Mack felt time dribbling away. Random driving around Canaryville looking for Dominic or Blarney Bob seemed more and more pointless—and, Mack decided, might even push Dominic deeper underground if he recognized the searchers before they spotted him.

Mack asked around the Steckel Avenue plant for anybody who actually knew his way around Canaryville. My sister's marrying a fellow from St. Gabriel parish, he said, and I need somebody to give me the lowdown on the guy. Ironically, it was Leopold Belgian who introduced him to a real Mick from the neighborhood—a gentle first-shift machinist in his sixties named Mick Halloran.

Despite the fact that the Irish and the Negroes had been at each other's throats for decades, a mutual love of jazz brought Mick and Leopold together. They'd heard Leopold's brother Charles play tenor sax at the Grand Terrace Café in Bronzeville—a "black and tan club," Leopold said, where whites and Negroes could listen to music together "without starting a goddamned riot." For only a couple of bucks apiece, Leopold had parted with a pair of his treasured recordings by the Crescent City Five—that was Charles's quintet—so Mick owed him a favor.

"Outsiders aren't favored in Canaryville. We take care of our own, and the rule is 'live and let live.'" Halloran spoke in a thick Irish brogue as he and Mack sat in a dingy restaurant near the plant. "The only fellow in the know who might give you a sit-down is Father Goskowski, our parish priest—he's of the Polish persuasion." And, Mick related, even he had learned "there's no palavering with anyone who could be a copper of any stripe whatsoever, even if he's a lad from the neighborhood." Mack passed the information along to Jan, and the two came up with a plan.

Even so, when Jan said out of the clear blue sky that she'd been to see the priest, Mack's first, knee-jerk reaction was that she was pregnant and arranging a quick ceremony for Ellen's benefit. Jan had quickly added, "That would be your Father Goskowski—"

Jan looked at him for a second and smiled beatifically. "Don't worry your pretty head about me having a bun in the oven. You'll be the first to know."

Mack's all-too-glib tongue had no answer to her female mind-reading.

She fished a spiral reporter's notebook from her purse and flipped through the pages. "He's been at St. Gabe's since he mustered out as an army chaplain in 1919, spent the first five years convincing the Canaryville Micks his mother was Dublin-born and that he wasn't just 'some damned Polack.' His words." She flipped another page. Her black hair, which she'd just gotten permed, bobbed up and down. Mack's thoughts strayed to making a baby with her right on Morty's tabletop.

Jan glanced up. "Pay attention, lover boy. We'll attend to that later. I told the padre I was writing a magazine article on the local branch of the Irish Republican Army and what became of it. Father G, which he said I should call him, got interested in spite of himself. He's the unofficial neighborhood historian. Canaryville was thick with IRA sympathizers right after the war, he said. And when the Free State was declared, they had their own Irish Civil War with fists and knives instead of guns and bombs. When things settled down and the Partition had to be accepted whatever side you'd been on, the violent fellows all went to work for the bootleggers. One of them was Dad's old friend Ginger Callahan, who became so flush and so penitent that he donated the cash for a new sacristy at St. Gabe's."

Mack was about to urge on her story, when Jan continued, "But, as Dad always puts it, I digress. Except for a handful of diehards, Father G said, the IRA has vanished like mist before the rising sun. He is half-Irish, after all!"

"And who are the holdouts, the diehards?"

"Most of them actually have died by now. Father G came up with three or four names. Then he remembered that

'I buried Danny Leary last summer' or 'Oh, yes, Jack McClure had a stroke and moved in with his sister in Milwaukee.' The only IRA man—or at least a fellow who talks like one and who's still around—is named Hugh Lonegan." Jan tapped her notebook with an emphatic finger.

"And who might he be?" Mack took in an overly large guzzle of Morty's coffee. It nearly went down the wrong pipe.

"Not a very promising lead, I'm afraid. 'A simple-minded fellow' is how Father G described him. Spends most of his time polishing the old Chevy he drives to St. Gabe's every Sunday, even though the church is only a block away. He lives in a little house, almost a shack, on 47th Place."

"Forty-Seventh Place," Mack said, happy for a change of subject. "Didn't we drive by there during our Time of Aimless Wandering?"

"Yes, we did, and I'm of the opinion we should stop by for a visit with Mr. Lonegan, simple-minded though he may be."

The next day, near the end of Mack's shift, Mick Halloran stopped him as Mack emerged from a newly-cleaned women's lavatory. He glanced around furtively and asked Mack to tell Leopold he'd pay five dollars—"an overly dear price, by all that's holy"—for the record of Charles and the Crescent City Five riffing on "Harlem Nocturne." As an added sweetener, Mick passed along the name of a gas station attendant on Cicero Avenue who'd part with a few extra gallons at the right price. This inside dope plus Jan's (or Ellen's) cash allowed them to fill up Mack's Model A. The battered Ford would cause less of a stir in Canaryville than Ellen's Cadillac.

They'd almost waited too long. *Maybe*, Mack thought, *in one of Dr. Freud's non-accidental accidents, they don't want to find out what's happening in Canaryville—and be forced to do something about it—and subconsciously hope they'll run out of time.* In any case, after Mack called in sick at work and they spent a restless night on Mack's Murphy bed, they set out for Hugh Lonegan's place two days before the meeting at Steckel Avenue that no one should miss.

On the drive to the South Side, Mack craved silence, sick of all his internal wrangling. *This could be* my *test, like Hellacious Helen's last flight*, he thought. With no invading Japs or exploding shells in sight, he gripped the steering wheel and aimed the Ford south down Halsted Street. Rolling away from the hermit's life, a committed one-eyed warrior in the Thomas Kilkenny Hero Brigade.

Maybe to keep her own demons away, Jan wanted to talk: "The name Lonegan rang a bell," she said as they rattled past bungalows, saloons, and corner groceries, and the sky filled with rumbling storm clouds. "Hugh's brother was a cop, a captain, I think, on Ginger's payroll. He visited our house sometimes. Father G said the brother bought the house for Hugh and laid by enough cash for him to live on. The car must've been his too. Apparently, little brother Hugh couldn't even hold a job at the packing plant." She continued after an interruption by thunder muttering off to the west. "The captain—Kieran was his first name—reminded me of John Wayne, tall and deep-voiced. I had a crush on him as a kid. He died in a freak accident, hit by a squad car while investigating a bank robbery."

Mack nodded and drove on, pondering Jan's selective naiveté. What were the odds that Kieran Lonegan's fatal accident had been arranged by other cops on the take at the behest of some rival gangster? The alderman may have known it was in the works even as Captain Lonegan sipped whiskey in his living room. Tommy's ascension to national hero could be a kind of absolution, wiping clean the family stain of Blarney Bob's many, many sins. Mack felt the familiar pain of wanting to talk over these wild ideas with Tommy.

Up ahead, on the other side of a railroad viaduct, loomed the packing plant, a soot-covered brick citadel overlooking the vast Union Stockyards beyond. Just before the viaduct, they turned onto 47th Place, a decaying residential enclave tucked between 47th and 48th Streets.

"Seven-thirty-seven, that's Lonegan's," said Jan, pointing at a swaybacked shotgun house, even more ramshackle than the others on the block. Mack pulled over to the curb a couple of doors down, rousting a mangy yellow dog, who trotted slowly away, panting in the damp heat. No one else noted their arrival.

As they trudged up Lonegan's front steps, Jan looked over and wrinkled her nose in disgust. The neighborhood aroma of offal and pig shit was bad enough inside the car, but overwhelming outside. An armchair sat on the porch, stuffing leaking out from multiple wounds. Jan nodded in its direction. "Just the thing for your room. Ask Lonegan if it's for sale." Mack ignored her, banter-proof for once.

Jan rapped on the door, knocking off a shard of ancient gray paint. She wore a plausible female-reporter's outfit: pleated black skirt and no-nonsense white blouse. Mack wore a nondescript tan shirt and dark trousers—no work shoes.

Jan gave another double knock, louder this time. It brought forth a trickle of noise from inside—echoing footsteps, a muffled voice, maybe two. The door opened the tiniest of cracks.

"Mr. Lonegan?"

The door opened further, just enough to reveal a blinking eye and narrow slice of face.

"Mr. Lonegan, my name is Janice Boswell. I'm a writer. Father Goskowski gave me your name and said you might be able to help me." Father G's name worked the hoped-for magic, and the door swung open to reveal a scrawny, middle-aged fellow in a sleeveless undershirt and stained khakis.

Jan began by introducing Mack as her assistant Jimmy—thankfully, she didn't saddle him with the full moniker of Clark Kent's nitwit cub reporter Jimmy Olson. Lonegan nodded blankly.

When Jan first used Father Goskowski's term "simple minded" to describe Hugh Lonegan, Mack had thought the priest surely must be exaggerating. In reality, Father G was being kind. Lonegan—a cross between leprechaun and troll—informed Jan that he'd never heard of the Irish Republican Army, that the IRA were the finest fellows God ever made, that he would be proud to give his life for the Cause, and what were they doing here, anyway? This performance was accompanied by a symphony of nervous tics: finger sucking, dry coughs, and gargle-y throat-clearing. Lonegan's flat gray eyes darted everywhere in the bare room except the couch where Jan and Mack sat. From the crucifix on the wall, the sad eyes of Jesus peered over their shoulders.

Jan had to at least pretend interest. Once it became clear that Lonegan's responses were pure drivel, Mack listened hard for other sounds. There weren't many. A fuzzy noise from below. A rat in the cellar? Floorboards creaked. A death rattle of this collapsing hovel, or was someone else in the house?

Jan sustained the interview for a full thirty minutes before snapping shut her reporter's notebook and shoving herself up from the quicksand cushions of the couch. "Thank you so much for your time, Mr. Lonegan. If I have any more questions, I'll call you. What did you say your phone number was? I'm afraid I didn't write it down the first time."

Lonegan blurted out the number. He froze for a second, perhaps recalling that Jan hadn't asked him for it before, then jumped out of the chair he'd lugged in from the kitchen as if he was about to dash out the front door. "I don't know nothing about nothing."

"Nothing about any important visitors to Chicago?" Jan asked sharply. "Maybe somebody coming from Washington?" Agent Lars Neilsen couldn't have slipped the topic into the conversation more skillfully.

"No, no. Nothing about that. Nothing about Alderman Kilkenny either."

Mack almost tumbled back onto the couch. But Jan tucked the notebook under her arm without batting an eye. "Come along, Jimmy," she said primly. Mack struggled up from the couch, reaching a standing position on the second try.

After Lonegan slammed the door behind them, Mack touched Jan's shoulder and gave her the sh-sh-shush sign. They played Living Statues and listened. From inside came Lonegan's quavering voice saying words they couldn't understand, followed by another voice—low, growling, equally unintelligible. Mack couldn't think of anything better to do than point to his car and mouth the words, "We have to go."

Mack pictured Dominic, surely armed, standing on the other side of Lonegan's door. Was Blarney Bob standing next to him? Who knew? Poking around outside seemed a fast route to getting shot. They climbed into the Model A and drove a couple of hundred yards to a parking space in front of a tiny bakery on Halsted.

"Let's go to the police. Right now!" Mack felt Jan's struggle to hold back hysteria.

"We have to think this through." It was yet another effort to project a calm reasonableness Mack didn't feel. Jan's black eyes looked as if they could pierce steel. A sweating guy in a cook's cap and white apron slid a tray of fresh sugar cookies onto the counter. As he looked up and wiped the sweat away from his forehead, he gave the car a long, cold stare. The old Ford was sitting in the parking space reserved for customers.

"Now that Dominic knows we're poking around, he can go anywhere. Our best chance to stop him is to go where we know *he's* going—Steckel Avenue." As he spoke, they turned into the northbound lane of Halsted. "We'll raise the alarm at the plant tomorrow. It shouldn't be hard. The Secret Service will be there in force."

Jan looked blankly at the passing parade of shift workers from the packing plant. She remained silent the rest of the way home to Astor Place.

With some reluctance, Mack called his father from Mrs. McLady's rooming house. To his surprise, Miss Lincecombe put him through to the inner sanctum.

"I may have found Dominic," Mack said with no introduction.

When he finished describing their latest adventure in Canaryville, his father reached the same conclusion Mack had. "They could've gone anywhere in the city," he said. "We'll have to intercept Dominic at Steckel Avenue. Meet me at the plant entrance at one o'clock. I'm supposed to be on the podium, so you'll have to point out Dominic. None of my men know what he looks like."

☙❧❦

Dominic was going to kill the president. The rhythm of cleaning toilets jarred Mack into several more inescapable conclusions. The murder would surely jeopardize the country's nervous alliance with Churchill and the Brits—an alliance notable so far for racking up an unprecedented series of defeats. The Germans would show their gratitude by helping the IRA seize Ulster—at least Hitler and von Ribbentrop must've promised they would. *If this war has proven anything,* Mack thought, *it's shown that nothing, nothing at all, is impossible.*

As Mack returned to his janitorial cart, a newsreel played in his head. A giant headline screamed "FDR Shot!"—a news bulletin as shocking as Lincoln's assassination, but coming at a time of national defeat, not victory. War footage followed: scenes from the unexpected new front. Battles in ruined, burning Belfast and Dublin. Corpses in work shirts and suit jackets, all dead IRA men according to the Brits. Captured German paratroopers. British troops in flat helmets crouched behind tanks rolling through stone-fenced Irish pastures. Angry Irish-Americans marched, waving placards reading "Stop Killing Our People!" They faced hostile crowds with their own signs: "Don't you know there's a war on?"

Roosevelt had Irish America under his thumb: chieftain of the whole unruly Celtic crew of Machine pols, bloated union bosses, backslapping saloon keepers, red-faced bishops, teary Hibernian Society sentimentalists. Irish or not, no American would feel such a visceral connection with the new president. Henry Wallace's picture was on no one's kitchen wall. Mack's jumpy mental film showed nervous military types and queasy congressmen and cabinet members surrounding a befuddled President Wallace.

Present facts replaced newsreel speculation. Whether or not Dominic stayed the night in Canaryville, he would ride to Steckel Avenue with Blarney Bob, probably in Lonegan's well-polished auto: it would be a one-way trip. All the pieces fit together, a glass slide coming into focus under the microscope. Dominic kidnapping the alderman then murdering Mr. Graves, the French Lick note, Lonegan's unlikely mention of Blarney Bob—an unraveling thread leading to the president's Chicago visit. All Dominic's moves were aimed at positioning him within pistol range of Franklin Roosevelt. Dominic was like that doctor who shot Huey Long in the Louisiana capitol. Mack tried to come up with his name: White? Weiss? In any case, the guy was mowed down by Huey's outraged bodyguards. Like White/Weiss, Dominic, after hitting *his* target, wouldn't give a good goddamn about getting ventilated, as the true-crime magazines always put it.

Mack bumped the janitor's cart against the cinderblock wall and took in a long, slow breath. A teen-aged assembly-line guy heading for the men's room threw him an accusatory look.

"Hey, shit-picker, get to work. The place has gotta be clean as a whistle. We got a big shot coming through tomorrow!"

He was right. Leave it to a UofC type to establish a useless historical context for *anything*, including an upcoming presidential assassination.

The heritage of his lost friend (the hero), his father (the hero-maker), his lover (mother, he hoped, of his future children)—none were better off as a result of these historical insights. Tommy's catastrophes of history were exploding all around, as far from his control as an outbreak of spots on the sun.

Within a few hours, Dominic would be inside the plant, waiting near the president's podium, vouched for by a Chicago alderman—father of the honored hero. Mack decided to crawl into the back seat of his car, try to rest, and raise the alarm in the morning.

Usually, Mack was Johnny-on-the spot to clock out at seven a.m., but his historic speculations wouldn't shut off. He was the last man at the time clock and noted that he'd donated ten extra minutes to the war effort. The rusting Model A sat alone next to the parking-lot fence, as if other cars were mortified to be seen nearby. As Mack approached from the driver's side, a man dressed in black, a very large man, stepped around the ancient Ford. A wide-brimmed fedora obscured his face, but his broad shape looked familiar. Dominic O'Nore extended his arm toward Mack and into a shaft of light from a streetlamp on the other side of the fence. In his hand was a pistol aimed at Mack's chest.

"Now, Mr. Simmons, please be so kind as to hand over the keys to your fine car."

Mack pulled the keys from his pants pocket and handed them over—a mechanical gesture worthy of the Tin Woodsman of Oz.

"We shall be going for a ride, and you will be relieved of the trying task of driving." He poked the gun into Mack's side and steered him around to the passenger-side door.

"That's more words than I've ever heard from you, Dominic."

"Don't get used to it, boyo. Now, lean your arms up against the auto. Mind the dirt." He snorted out a short laugh. "Now!" Footsteps shuffled in the parking lot gravel.

They were the last sounds Mack heard for a while. He eventually determined that someone with a blunt instrument that seemed heavy as a log had clubbed him alongside the head.

# Chapter 31

When he awakened to a crushing headache that he thought might mean a concussion, the first thing Mack saw was Jesus looking down from the cross. Could he be attending his own wake? The surface underneath him seemed too lumpy for a coffin. As his eyes began to focus properly, Mack turned away from the crucifix on the wall. The room was familiar, especially the torn armchair where he remembered someone sitting not so long ago. The previous occupant had been Hugh Lonegan, a recollection that caused a throb of pain. The current occupant was Dominic O'Nore, still dressed in black but uncharacteristically grinning. Mack crow-barred his barely functional body to a sitting position, finding himself at eye level with the barrel of Dominic's pistol.

Steps sounded from the kitchen. Lonegan led a limping Robert Kilkenny into the living room, unshaven, wearing a wrinkled gray suit, and looking thinner than Mack remembered. Blarney Bob plopped himself down at the other end of the couch. Mack was happy to see he was alive and more or less okay, but becoming furious at himself for walking so blindly into this bloody mess.

It began with the oh-so-clever plan he and Jan had hatched, a casual approach from a Bob Hope film. Walk a swaying tightrope: stop Dominic, but keep out the compromised authorities. Of course, they had fallen off, a fall likely to prove fatal, not only for Mack, but for Blarney Bob and Franklin D. Roosevelt too. His father was right. Mack never considered the consequences of his actions, whether they involved short-sheeting Walter Clinckscale at Camp Ojibway, socking a Purdue lineman in the jaw as the Chicago Maroons were driving for a touchdown, or rolling cherry bombs under the family Packard. Now, his compulsive rashness was going to make history, in the worst possible way. Torn by these conflicting emotions, Mack gave Bob a pat on the back, which the old man ignored completely.

Dominic stood and waved his gun toward the kitchen. "Hughie, show some manners and fetch tea for the latest guest at your establishment." Dominic settled himself back in the chair and patiently waited for the tea to arrive. The gun remained in plain view.

While Mack and the alderman sipped tea from mismatched cups, Dominic carefully placed himself in the exact center of the room like Mack's father during their most serious confrontations. Mack's potentially concussed brain measured the distance from the couch to the front door, crazily wondering if he could make a break for it. No matter how he figured the angles, he realized he'd be dead before he could struggle up from the couch.

"Now that we've calmed ourselves," said Dominic, tugging at the neck of his black tee shirt. "We've all done a bit of deep breathing, sampled some tea, so it's a fit time to plan what lies before us. Mr. Simmons, you have likely never pictured me as a deep-thinking man. That's understandable. Perhaps your opinion will shift when you hear me out." His empty blue eyes stared at Mack and Blarney Bob in turn. "To be sure we're all reading from the same catechism, I believe all of us here know the tale of Thomas Kilkenny's heroic death—ah, so brave and so far from home!" Blarney Bob remained stock still.

"My sincerest condolences to all the family," Dominic continued, "and they are truly sincere. I always thought most highly of the dear lad."

Outside, a new line of early-summer storms rolled in, thunder sounding in the distance.

"It's most fitting and necessary that young Thomas receive the honors he bought with his life's blood. Thus, we must put on a brave face and attend the high ceremony tomorrow, which includes the president himself."

Words boiled up from Mack's throat. "You bastard! You're lying through your goddamned teeth. You're going to Steckel Avenue to *kill* the president. Admit it!"

Dominic shook his head, looking sad. "No, young fellow, my only task is to protect the alderman from the harm that's headed his way, and I believe the alderman himself is coming around to this opinion."

"What 'harm' might that be, Dominic?" Mack spat the words out, wondering why the alderman didn't speak for himself.

"Harm from those back home who believe he has gone soft and traitorous from the money and the friends he's made over here. The hard men know of tomorrow's meeting. What better way to send a message to possible traitors everywhere than put a turncoat out of the way under the eyes of the President of the USA?"

"How often must I tell you I've never played the rat?" Bob mumbled. "I've grown impatient with our lads back home and their incessant wrangling. And it's natural as the sunrise to turn to friends like Victor Schlegel, whose faces are in front of you and not away across the sea."

Blarney Bob rubbed his forehead with the palms of both hands. "On occasion, I have gotten loose-tongued from drink and said more than I should have. I've you to thank, Dominic, for keeping me straight—but I have *never* turned traitor!" He choked back a sob. "I have been as true to our cause as my poor lost son was to his!"

"That I know, sir," replied Dominic with an understanding nod. "That's why I shall be acting as your bodyguard one last time, and you will identify me as a sworn officer of the law when I give you the nod."

Blarney Bob gave a weary nod of his own. For all the world, he looked like a whipped dog, beaten into submission.

"What about the man you killed, Dominic?" Mack leaned forward on the couch. "The fellow you murdered in the alderman's basement."

"Didn't know him," said Dominic calmly—if he was surprised at Mack's knowledge, he didn't let on. "But the fellow had no business there. Perhaps a burglar, perhaps sent from Dublin or Belfast to spy on the alderman, or to murder him. Or skulking about for some other foul purpose. I had to take care of him, and I did." He drew a deep breath. "That's why I must leave tomorrow as soon as the meeting with the president is finished. Get myself back to Ireland. I know how to do it."

Mack's temper boiled over again. "You speak better than I ever thought, Dominic. Tommy was a brother to me, and *he* knew how to describe what you're saying. Pure blarney—Irish moonshine and bullshit! The man in the cellar was a detective. He was hired by my father."

Dominic's face grew hard, and he fingered the pistol. "You may believe what you like, Mr. Simmons, but we are playing by my rules here. You will do as I say." He scratched the side of his shaven head, rubbing red a patch of pale scalp. "As an insurance policy that all goes smoothly tomorrow, we are going to take a hostage just as we used to do during the struggles back home. That hostage will be you, Mr. Simmons."

Mack figured that he must've appeared more of a simpleton than Lonegan himself.

"The rules are plain and straight," Dominic continued, "and the alderman can verify my words. We'll hold you here, Mr. Simmons, treat you well enough, and set you loose once it's known the president's ceremony is done."

He looked at the alderman. "Am I correct in my description of the rules for hostages?"

Bob nodded impassively. "Yes, you are."

Dominic continued. "As a point of interest to both of you, I have contacted your daughter, Alderman Kilkenny, and your paramour, Mr. Simmons—both, of course, being Miss Janice Kilkenny. I gave her Mr. Simmons's college ring as a token of our having you in hand and of our willingness to release you when we know Miss Kilkenny has quietly attended the ceremony with her mother. She has been told that her beloved father is feeling better and that he will reunite with her and her dear mother after the alderman speaks at the great event. Not beforehand, since his health remains delicate, he must take things one at a time."

Mack checked his naked fingers. He hadn't noticed his UofC ring was gone. Hostages, stolen rings, gushing family reunions—it was all moonshine and bullshit. Mack saw no benefit in continuing to point it out, so he shut up. He glanced over at Blarney Bob staring down at his own gnarled hands.

Dominic's face hardened into a scowl. "But, I swear by all the saints and sinners who ever walked the earth..." His voice turned into a harsh monotone. "I swear that if the police or the FBI or any of Roosevelt's bloody guards show their faces here, at the house or on the street—anyone who's not known—you'll receive a bullet straightaway. It's the fate of the hostage when things go awry."

The gun still on display, Dominic watched as Lonegan prepared a surprisingly tasty supper. Ham, baked beans, soda bread. Even some chocolate ice cream for dessert.

"See," said Dominic, "hostages *are* treated well. There are men who make their living at it."

"Aye," said the alderman, wiping a touch of chocolate from the corner of his mouth. "Remember Tim O'Shea from Ennis—helped support five kids by serving as a hostage. Easier to call Tim than put the arm on someone not disposed to do it. And no one wanted to be the man that had to kill him, so the rough boys had an extra reason to pay their debts and resolve their differences."

The rain clattered as Mack seethed. Why hadn't he and

Jan just called the cops, told them a burglar was breaking in at 737 West 47th Place, or some such nonsense, then allowed events to take their course?

"This one and your own boy certainly made a set of terrible twins," said Dominic with a small smile, "and the gal makes a good match for her brother."

"Yes, it was many a scrape I had to bail those boys out of. Often, if you can believe it, their misdeeds were connected to strong drink."

Bob and Dominic shared a small laugh across the kitchen table, setting Mack's teeth on edge.

Lonegan fingered the pointed leprechaun tip of his right ear. "Drinking liquor—that's a thing I promised Ma I'd never do. Kieran held me to my word." A small cockroach crept along the baseboard.

The long late-spring afternoon wore on. Bob and Dominic exchanged more muttered reminiscences of Ireland, interrupted by more inane comments from Lonegan. A bottle of Jameson's appeared. Dominic poured out a small ration of whiskey for himself and another for the alderman.

Dominic glanced at Mack then eyed the bottle. Mack's mouth, tongue, and brain all recalled their obscene hunger for the bourbon stashed in Gisbourne's desk. Mack nearly gagged, and shook his head no. When the glasses on the table were empty, the bottle stayed close to Dominic's hand, no more for Blarney Bob.

Was the alderman still allied with Dominic and the IRA? Or was he waiting, however forlornly, to make a move against them? Listening to Bob as he sipped multiple shots of Jameson's had looked like the best way of finding out where he stood. When Dominic put the bottle back in Lonegan's kitchen cupboard, Mack's curiosity drained away. Even with no assistance from booze, his eyelids grew heavy from food and numbing boredom.

"All right!" said Dominic, giving the table a slap that rattled the dishes and caused Mack, Bob, and Hugh Lonegan all to jump from their seats. "We must prepare for tomorrow!"

The Luger appeared from Dominic's pants pocket. "We'll begin by getting Mr. Simmons settled for the evening."

Followed by Lonegan and Blarney Bob, Dominic shoved Mack down the stairs to the cellar and its collection of rotting cardboard boxes and broken furniture. Mack counted pieces from three different bedsteads stacked against the wall. Dominic ordered Mack into a chair by the rusting furnace. Then, Lonegan began winding yards of old clothesline around Mack's arms and legs, securing him tightly to the creaking chair.

Except for Mack's grunted complaints, no one made a sound until Dominic said, "Alderman, in light of your newfound cooperation, you'll be moving up to Hughie's couch tonight, after a better wash and shave than you've had thus far. Fortunately, I brought along one of your fine suits, just the thing for tomorrow."

# Chapter 32

s Mack sat alone in the basement shadows—Dominic had left on the bare bulb above the staircase—the first minutes bled into a blur of pain and confusion. He wiggled his fingers to keep the blood flowing to his wrists and hands. His bladder hurt, urine turning to wormwood. Lips and tongue, acting on their own, managed to move the rag Lonegan had stuffed into his mouth, shove it far enough forward to stop the gag reflex. Every sound was startling. Squeaking footsteps above. Little clicks from the furnace ducts as they contracted in the cool evening air. Screeches from neighborhood kids and swarming night birds.

A car roared around the corner onto Halsted. The sound swirled into a vivid cartoon from the latest round of war posters. The leering cartoon driver looked faintly Japanese and wore a swastika lapel pin. He was deeply unpatriotic, the poster said, squandering both rubber and gasoline.

From a half-remembered Eighteenth-Century Lit course, the wisdom of Dr. Johnson emerged. Nothing concentrates a man's mind like knowing he'll be hanged in the morning—some words like that, anyway. The hostage ploy was a ruse to get Jan and her father properly in place for the Steckel Avenue meeting. Had booze pickled Blarney Bob's brain to the point that he believed Dominic? Outside on 47th Place, a car with bad brakes squealed by.

A cricket chirped from inside the cellar. The rag in Mack's mouth slid down a quarter of an inch, causing him to choke until his tongue blocked the way. As sure as the sun rises in the east, he thought, Dominic had ordered Lonegan to kill him once the Steckel Avenue event was underway. Dominic must've presented it as the imbecile's chance to become an IRA hero. By that time, Dominic—with FDR either in his sights or already dead—wouldn't care whether his sidekick succeeded or not.

Mack's concentration waned. He didn't know for sure if he'd slept, but the time slipped away, punctuated by black interludes that might have been sleep. Eventually, little threads of sunlight stretched themselves across the concrete floor, bright lines drawn across the broken furniture and moldy boxes. The light may have come from a cellar window behind him, but Mack couldn't turn his head enough to look. The longest day of the year was approaching, so it was still early morning.

He slid back into a sleep-like stupor of indefinite length. The telephone rang upstairs, loud and sudden as an air-raid siren. Mack's limbs stiffened against the ropes, and the chair nearly toppled. Footsteps scuffled above. The phone stopped ringing, followed immediately by Lonegan's shouts. "Hold on, hold on a minute!"

Who could possibly want him on the phone? St. Peter welcoming him to heaven? Satan ushering him in the opposite direction?

Lonegan pounded down the stairs, almost losing his balance. "It's her! Miss Kilkenny!" He was still shouting, as if expecting Mack to jump up to take the call.

"Hm-mumph…a-mumph!" Mack tried to make his strangled grunts sound angry and decisive. Lonegan stared for too many seconds. Finally, he edged his way over, sharing his bad breath and warily undoing the clothesline binding Mack to the chair. The bindings finally became loose enough for Mack to shake them off on his own—a clumsy task for half-paralyzed arms and legs. Lonegan leaned close again and yanked the gag from his mouth. Lips twitching, Lonegan pulled a snub-nosed Police Special from his pocket and thrust it toward Mack's face.

"Hurry up," he snarled. "Miss Kilkenny's waiting for you."

A stray fact tiptoed into Mack's aching brain: Jan extracting the telephone number from the unsuspecting Lonegan. As a football player, he'd felt painfully stiff and sore after an afternoon of getting mauled by some gorilla from Minnesota or Ohio State, but hours of being bound and gagged left him barely mobile. Even with Lonegan's gun prodding him in the small of his back, climbing the half-dozen creaking steps to the kitchen felt like ascending the Matterhorn. Lonegan's telephone was in the kitchen. With his empty hand, Lonegan gestured toward the phone, which sat on a rickety table. Mack picked up the receiver from the narrow tabletop.

"Zha-a-n, are you dere?" He massaged his jaw and said it again more clearly.

"My God, you sound awful! What did they do to you?"

"I was tied up in the cellar. I'm okay. What the hell is going on?"

Jan took in a breath. "Mother and I just got here. I haven't seen hide nor hair of Dominic or Dad." Her voice began to race. "I told some of the men in suits that there are 'rumors that *Dominic O'Nore*'—I emphasized his name—'is using Alderman Kilkenny to get close to the president so he can shoot him. You better look into it when they get here.' All they did was smile and nod and all but patted me on the head. The bastards think I'm just a hysterical little girl!"

Lonegan mouthed Hurry Up, his sallow face turning red, leaving out only the earlobes and the tip of his pointed nose.

"Mother is so excited about meeting the president, she's forgotten everything else. I mentioned that Dad would be here, and she didn't even blink."

"Where are you calling from?"

Jan's breathing rasped over the line. "The Plant Manager's office—that's Gisbourne, right? I couldn't just wait around while Dominic played his Irish hostage game. He had me meet him on State Street late last night, like something from a spy movie. He had your UofC class ring! Did you know that?"

She didn't give him a chance to answer.

"When I told Gisbourne I needed to make a telephone call, he was so eager to please, he practically carried me up the stairs to his office."

"That's Gisbourne all right. So, your father isn't there yet?"

"Mother insisted we arrive early. They're still setting up the stage inside the main entrance of the plant. And everyone's saying the president will be late. That seemed to make your father mad. He's here with Felicia and your mother—Katherine looks great, by the way, like *she* could be first lady. Lieutenant Winogrand's here too. He walked in just as I was heading upstairs."

Her nervous, chatty tone became a staticky whisper. "Can you take care of that fool Lonegan and get out of there? I thought he wouldn't let you talk to me, but he's like an obedient dog. Talk to him forcefully enough and he'll obey. "

"Oh, I'm sure everything will work out fine."

"He's holding a gun on you, right?"

"Yes, indeed. That's a great idea!"

After a few seconds of silence, Mack said, "We should hang up now," trying and failing to sound unafraid. Dominic knew Lonegan as well as Jan. The obedient dog was going to kill him now.

After they rang off, Mack stared down at the squat black telephone, seeking to conjure up an image of Jan, thinking how desperate he was to see her in reality. When he looked up, he saw only the greasy gray wallpaper of Lonegan's cramped kitchen.

"Turn around, Mr. Simmons. Or maybe I should call you Jimmy now, like Miss Kilkenny did."

Mack turned slowly and found his natural eye looking down the barrel of the .38 Police Special. No doubt the weapon was once the property of Captain Kieran Lonegan—another instance of useless historical thinking.

The grinning Lonegan shifted the gun a couple of inches to the left. "Dominic said to look you in the face like he always did in sending the bloody Black-and-Tans to hell and then to shoot you in the false eye. He said I'd have to look close to tell which one it was, but it was a shot even I couldn't miss!"

Mack was about to yell something, anything, to distract Lonegan. Then he saw a ropy bicep twitch under the sleeve of Lonegan's yellow-stained tee shirt. Mack dove clumsily to the floor, bringing the rickety table and telephone down on top of him. The gunshot seemed to fill whole room with sound transformed into a massive electric shock, as if the house had been struck by lightning, a bolt Zeus might've hurled from Mount Olympus. Mack noted ruefully that at least the University of Chicago lobe of his brain was functioning normally.

Mack, still on the floor, ears ringing, grabbed the solid object nearest at hand, a leg of Lonegan's telephone table. He crawled toward the kitchen wall and shoved himself up, sliding against the greasy wallpaper.

Lonegan staggered in front of him like a drunken man, apparently as shaken as Mack at the impossibly loud gunshot. Mack gripped a second leg of the telephone stand, chiding himself for grabbing the world's worst offensive weapon. He pushed himself away from the wall, blinked automatically make sure the ocular prosthesis remained in place, and took a step toward Lonegan. Starting with a long backswing, he took a homerun cut at the bobbing head of the gaping Lonegan. The rickety little table shattered into uncountable pieces.

Despite the successful contact with Lonegan's skull,

the encounter with the table seemed to wake him up instead of knocking him out. Lonegan stared down at the Police Special and looked surprised to find it in his hand.

With Lonegan apparently ready and able to pull the trigger again, Mack flung himself at the smaller man. He chopped at the gun but failed to knock it loose. In fact, seized by Irish revolutionary fervor or maybe a simple survival instinct, Lonegan resisted with a strength far out of proportion to his size.

Lonegan gradually pulled his arm out of Mack's grasp, bending the hand with the gun back toward Mack's face. Mack rolled his shoulders and managed to turn both himself and Lonegan onto their sides, partially freeing up Mack's right arm. He found himself staring down the barrel again, as Lonegan's index finger groped toward the trigger. Mack wrenched his right arm all the way out from under Lonegan and clawed at his scrawny, leprechaun's face. Mack's hand slid through Lonegan's reddish hair and across his sweaty forehead.

Mack felt his thumb come to rest above Lonegan's fluttering left eye. His own functioning eye flicked back to Lonegan's quivering trigger finger. Mack levered his hand an inch above Lonegan's eyelid and extended his thumb. Then, with a guttural sound somewhere between a grunt and a shout, Mack shoved his thumb, hard, into Lonegan's eye. If there was pain involved, it seemed to take a long time to complete the short journey from eye to brain.

Lonegan's gun-toting arm went slack, as Mack stumbled up to a standing position and kicked the gun away. It spun across the floor, twisting to a stop an inch from the kitchen wall. Then, with no warning, Lonegan let out a wall-shaking yell and grabbed at his bleeding eye.

Looking down at the sobbing man, who was now crying in loud spasms like a child who'd thrust his hand into a fire, Mack's first instinct was to kick him in the head and keep kicking until all movement stopped. Mack even drew back his foot, still wearing a Steckel Avenue steel-toed shoe, prepared to deliver the first blow. Tommy, always confident of his instincts, would surely have killed Lonegan on the spot.

Mack decided later it must've been the blood flowing down Lonegan's left cheek that brought him up short. On the night of the accident, which felt several geological eras in the past, he must have looked like that to the ambulance crew that had scrambled down the snowy embankment to save him.

Pocketing Lonegan's gun on the way, Mack went into the kitchen and located a pair of reasonably clean dishtowels. He soaked one in cold water and dabbed away the blood, then tied the second over Lonegan's wounded eye. The bleeding stopped, and the eye looked to be intact. Mack ran down the stairs to retrieve the rope and gag.

"Kill me," Lonegan muttered as Mack tied his wrists and ankles to a kitchen chair. "I failed the Cause. Failed."

"Failed, because you didn't shoot me like a rat in the alley." Mack tightened the knot around Lonegan's wrists and shoved the chair back against the wall.

"'Look for the real eye then to the false one,' he said." Lonegan looked up at him, although Mack couldn't tell what Lonegan actually saw. "'Shoot him there…in the glass eye.'"

Mack stuffed the gag into Lonegan's mouth and pulled it part way out when he began to choke. His gurgled breathing returned to normal.

Mack placed the fallen telephone on the kitchen table and confirmed that it was working. Agent Lars Neilsen's card still nestled in his wallet, keeping company with a pair of greasy dollar bills. He gave the phone number to the operator.

"Chicago Field Office. Agent Morrison speaking," said a young man's voice on the other end.

"You're searching for the IRA assassin Dominic O'Nore. Or you should be." Morrison started to interrupt, but Mack didn't allow it. "He's with Alderman Robert Kilkenny, probably pretending to be a Chicago cop. Right now, at this moment, they're at the employee meeting with President Roosevelt at the Steckel Avenue defense plant. O'Nore is planning to shoot the president. You know this—now do something about it!" He slammed down the phone as Lonegan emitted a low moan.

If his father's White House contact was right, Hoover and the FBI had already washed their hands of Dominic, but Mack—back to full-time duty in the Hero Brigade and finding it a temporary antidote to his lingering terror—felt duty-bound to give it a try. He didn't trust the local cops and had no idea how to contact the US Secret Service. So, the next order of business was to get to Steckel Avenue—fast.

There was no automobile available. He couldn't wait for a taxi. Roving cabs were nonexistent in Canaryville, so he'd have to call for one. Did he know anyone the South Side to give him a lift? Some former grad-school colleague from UofC? Even if one of them answered the phone and didn't hang up on him, it would take the rest of the day to explain his situation, which, as Victorian historians would've put it, beggared belief.

Mack picked up Lonegan's Chicago phone book from the floor and riffled through the pages, a pointless exercise until Mack realized he did know someone on the South Side—Leopold Belgian. The address in the book was on 39th Street—the other side of the line walling off the Black Belt from the rest of the city but not so many blocks away. Mack hurriedly gave the number to the operator and sweated through five, six, seven unanswered rings.

Glancing around Lonegan's cramped, stained kitchen, Mack caught the eye of President Roosevelt, or at least his eight-by-ten photo behind a grease-slicked glass frame—a duplicate of the serene, fatherly portrait in Blarney Bob's much fancier kitchen and thousands more in every state— probably Leopold's too. Would they all soon be wrapped in black mourning ribbons?

"Hello?" A soft female voice came on the line. Leopold's wife...what was her name? Mack coughed. Not being able to identify her stopped his tongue. "Who is this, please?" A soft Southern accent, gentle as a floating dandelion wisp.

"Francine?" Mack knew his voice was much too loud.

"Yes, it is," she replied evenly.

"This is Mack Simmons. From the plant. May I speak to Leopold? It's an emergency."

"I'll see if he's left yet."

*Damn*, Mack thought, *I never checked the time*. The graveyard shift was expected to return early to the plant—unpaid, of course—for the big meeting no one should miss.

Mack felt himself sweat until Leopold's gruff voice sounded in his ear. "What's up, Reesh Boy?"

"Leopold, I'm on the South Side, and I need a ride to the plant. Can you pick me up at Forty-Seventh and Halsted? Right now. I know it's out of your way, but it's important—and too complicated to explain on the phone. Just pick me up, and I'll tell you about it on the way."

Several more seconds ticked by. "Okay, Reesh Boy, get your ass to Forty-Seventh and Halsted. Your story better be damn good."

As Mack stood up from the kitchen table, he felt the weight of the Police Special in his pants pocket. He pulled it out and stared at the ugly stump of a weapon. It looked like a prehistoric rodent with its nose chewed off. Using the gun to dispatch Dominic had a brutal, enjoyable irony, along the lines of grabbing John Wilkes Booth's pistol and putting Lincoln's bullet in his brain instead. Mack briefly appreciated the history-bending thought before sliding the gun into one of Lonegan's kitchen drawers. There would be more than enough armed men at the plant. He didn't want to give them a reason to turn their weapons on him.

When Mack stepped onto Lonegan's crumbling porch, all his planning and logic fell away. With the astounded vision of a newborn, he saw Canaryville, the sky (a dazzling summer blue), the whole bright, sun-warmed world. He jumped up and down, improvising an Irish jig, stifling the urge to knock on random doors and embrace Lonegan's disbelieving neighbors. He wanted to roll on the wet ground like a joyful dog, rubbing his shoulders back and forth against the rough grass of Lonegan's postage-stamp lawn, greener now after the rain.

*Thank God for Jan's phone call*, he thought. Without it, Mack's corpse would still be bound to the chair, bits of his ocular prosthesis and chunks of gray matter plastered against the cellar walls for the rats to investigate. He made a promise to himself: *If we live through the rest of this day, I'll ask Jan to marry me, make an honest woman of her, something her mother might say, and keep asking until she says yes. Soldiers who survive battle—from a nameless skirmish to Marathon or Gettysburg—must feel giddy elation like this,* Mack thought as his inner historian again took center stage. *Tommy must've felt it after safely landing Hellacious Helen, bouncing across a mud-choked Luzon airstrip. No Zeroes got us today. No machine-gun bullets or cannon shells shredded the wings or Helen's golden body on the fuselage. The 750-horsepower radial engines kept up their faithful heartbeat.*

Mack stood on the sidewalk, panting in the warm June air, grinning like an idiot. A rusty Plymouth chugged past and pulled up in front of the house at the dead end of the block. The bungalow was even tinier than Lonegan's, but more recently painted. A fat, red-faced fellow in overalls climbed out of the car, lunch pail in hand—another nightshift worker?

He gave Mack a searching look as he made his plodding way up the front walk. In the distance, a police siren sounded. Had even the live-and-let-live neighbors become suspicious after hearing the gunshot and then watching Mack cavort in front of the house? Mack headed for Halsted Street, trying not to walk too fast, rediscovering the neighborhood's slaughterhouse smell as euphoria drained away.

# Chapter 33

Traffic was light on Halsted. Standing on the corner, Mack ignored the passing truckloads of snuffling hogs but peered at each auto as it rolled by. Naturally, he didn't know what make of car Leopold drove and hadn't asked when he had the chance. He got quizzical stares from passing drivers. Was this jumpy fellow a hitchhiker? A self-proclaimed prophet preaching the end of the world?

A Model A, the same vintage as Mack's, pulled up. Polished black hood gleaming in the sunshine, it was in far better condition than Mack's rust bucket. From behind the wheel, Leopold jerked a thumb toward the back seat. As Mack climbed in, Chocolate Slim waved from the front seat. They all spoke every day at work, but Mack never realized Slim and Leopold drove in together. Approaching a stoplight, Leopold pulled off his hat and tossed it into the backseat.

"Put this on, Reesh Boy, and drag it low over your face. The cops see niggers and honkies drivin' together, they'll pull us over. Think we're some kinda Commie agitators."

The hat—a tan, wide-brimmed fedora—was a couple of sizes too big, making it easy to follow Leopold's instructions. The light changed. "Okay," growled Leopold, "what the hell you doin' down here?"

"Trying to save the president's life!" Mack blurted out the words—a line stolen from a Saturday-matinee serial?

"Shit, man," said Chocolate Slim, turning back with a toothy smile, "you gotta do better'n that, or you gonna have a long goddamn walk ahead of you!"

Leopold stared at the road ahead and gave out an annoyed grunt.

"Okay, okay, let me start again…" Mack told his story.

The only interruptions were involuntary outbursts from the front seat: "Hot damn!" muttered Leopold when Mack got to the IRA assassination plan. Slim's "Sweet Jesus!" came out an octave higher than usual. "Those sumbitches really tryin' to kill him!" By the time Leopold turned onto North Avenue toward the plant, the car had gone silent.

With employees from all three shifts gathering for the big meeting, the Steckel Avenue parking lot was jammed. Leopold found a spot near the fence. The three piled out, but before Mack and Slim could take two steps, Leopold blocked their path. Instead of denim overalls, he wore a starched white shirt and sharply pleated brown slacks.

Leopold pointed a leg-sized arm at Mack. "Look here, Reesh Boy, I named my boy after the president, likely the only Franklin D. Roosevelt Belgian in the whole damned country." He widened his stance and folded his arms. "No sumbitch Irish Mick killer is gonna shoot him. Not if I can help it."

Workers in denim shirts—and some in coats and ties—streamed toward the plant entrance, many with spouses and kids in tow. Slim said, "Word sure spread like fire in dry cotton about the president comin' to give a medal to that fool pilot who's already dead."

Leopold's caramel-colored face never changed expression as he and Slim stared at him. Both clearly waited for Mack to say *something*. "Fellas," he finally said, "I honestly don't know what we can do on our own. Just locate Dominic O'Nore and finger him, make sure the Secret Service knows who and where he is, try to make sure they get to him before he can get to the president."

Mack knew he had to do better than that, but the best he could come up with was a thumbnail sketch of Dominic: "Strong-looking, heavy-set fellow, about my height, shaved head, probably wearing a suit." Then, almost an after-thought, Mack added, "Oh yeah, he might be wearing a Chicago Police badge."

"Shee-it, man," said Slim, "you think the fuzz or those Secret Service guys gonna believe *us* 'stead of a honky with a badge?"

Mack shrugged. All he knew was that time was ticking away. "Let's just get as close as we can to where the presi-dent'll be speaking and see what happens." Like a football team getting the "hike!" signal, they all started running to-ward the plant entrance, receiving dirty looks and assorted un-original insults as they dodged their way through the crowd.

The crowd was thicker inside, forming growing circles as Steckel Avenue employees waved at familiar faces and introduced family members to their workmates. Mack soon lost sight of Leopold and Slim in the laughing, echoing mul-titude. The stage—a broad, low platform along a side wall of the cavernous entrance hall—was still under construc-tion. On the side nearest the main entrance, carpenters from the Shipping Department put the finishing touches on a broad wooden ramp, no doubt for the president's use. Be-hind the stage, the "Production Will Win the War" banner flapped high on the wall. A large podium of dark wood stood at center stage. It bore the circular seal of the Presi-dent of the United States—an American eagle, wings and legs so sprawled out it looked like a bird splattered against a windshield.

Wearing a somber navy-blue suit, Fat Ferdie Gisbourne hovered behind the podium. A sheen of sweat reflected from his forehead in the glare of the spotlights mounted on each side of the stage. "Testing! Testing!" he yelled. The mike responded with a harsh whine.

Pushing closer, Mack saw a row of folding chairs set up in pairs across the low-rise stage. Off to the left, sat Jan and Ellen, talking quietly. Mack waved in their direction, but they didn't see him in the writhing crowd. Mack pictured himself climbing onto the stage, grabbing Jan, and fleeing down the ramp and out the door. They'd flag down a cab and head for Union Station. Catch a train bound anywhere, change their names, have a kid or two, raise them in anonymity. Who cared who was president? America would win the war eventually. Who nominated *him* to save the world anyway?

*Okay*, Mack thought, *at least I have an answer for that one*. His name had been placed in nomination by one John Mackenzie Simmons II, a nomination seconded—in absentia—by Thomas Aloysius Kilkenny. The responsibilities of the position had shifted, but there was no doubt he was still the candidate.

Mack stared at the seated dignitaries. In a pair of chairs near the middle of the row, Blarney Bob and the Honorable Ed Kelly, Mayor of Chicago, talked animatedly, in their element. Wearing a blue pillbox hat and white gloves, Felicia sat a few feet away from the side closest to the plant entrance. A man in uniform reached over and lit her cigarette with a silver lighter. Lieutenant Peter Winogrand.

Near center stage, Mack's father and mother sat next to each other, quietly holding hands, looking for all the world like a typical well-connected, well-tended Winnetka couple, pillars of the community. Mack blinked, half-expecting the strange vision to vanish. The last time he'd seen them together in public was when the headmaster at Lake Forest Academy, Dr. Buckley Buchholtz, had insisted upon a conference with Mack and *both* his parents, the alternative being immediate and permanent expulsion. This happened after the lab-rats-in-the-locker-room incident at LFA's sister school Ferry Hall, which had followed an afternoon of drinking beer under the football stands. His father fought against the two-parent meeting, afraid of what Mum might say and how it would inevitably spread through the gossip-ridden institution.

To Mack's amazement, his parents brought it off, just as they appeared to be doing at Steckel Avenue. His father had taken up the challenge, using his courtroom skills to forcefully emphasize Mack's top-notch grades (at least in the courses he liked). Looking much as she did now on the stage, Mum in pearls and a dignified dress stated convincingly that she'd been ill lately, her son was high-strung, and he must have been reacting to the family situation through what she called "high school high jinx."

Whatever high jinx Dominic had in mind, he was nowhere to be seen. A dozen men in anonymous gray suits ranged in front of the raised platform, creating a five-foot-wide No Man's Land between stage and audience. Their eyes looked outward, away from the on-stage preparations.

Mack swam through the crowd toward the nearest presidential protector, a beefy crew-cut guy who bore a passing resemblance to his FBI acquaintance Lars Neilsen. Could some of these fellows *be* FBI men, planning to heroically come to the president's rescue on behalf of J. Edgar Hoover, humiliating FDR's feckless Secret Service agents?

Mack squeezed past a family: large mom, skinny dad, three tiny dark-haired girls. All five were dolled up in their Sunday best. Mack excused himself to Mama and received a civil-sounding reply in what he took to be Italian. The heavy-set Secret Service—or FBI?—man was three feet away.

*There's an assassin here you should know about.* Mack had practiced the line in his head. How about, "Ask Alderman Kilkenny over there about the killer he brought along with him today"?

Mack couldn't come up with anything to actually say to the guy, whose suspicious eyes were now looking hard in his direction, that didn't include such hair-trigger words.

Mentioning Dominic by name without being able to point him out would be just as bad. At this point, an encounter with the authorities would surely lead to a violent arrest. And worse was in store for Leopold and Slim if they spoke up. Mack looked around but couldn't spot them. The gray-suited guy gave him an even more searching stare before retreating back into the crowd. Mack received a friendly nod from the beaming Tom Yarborough. Mack responded with a tiny wave.

Turning back to the stage, he waved again. This time, he caught Jan's eye. She smiled, no doubt pleased at his continuing presence on the right side of the grass. She glanced nervously around and gave a quick little shrug.

Another screech echoed from the PA system, followed by Fat Ferdie's echoing amplified voice. "Okay, okay, everybody. Settle dow—own. President Roosevelt is on his way-ay. He'll be here-ere any minute. He's asked that we get started, so we don't miss any more—ore work!" Everyone laughed but Mack.

He slid behind the Italian family. Would they remember this day with the same horror as those in the receiving line in Buffalo when Leon Czolgosz shot McKinley or the theater-goers who laughed at *Our American Cousin* with the Lincolns?

On the stage, Felicia and Pete Winogrand gazed at each other, seemingly oblivious to the commotion around them. Then Mack noticed something else. The wide, low stage hadn't been built flush against the wall. There was a gap, perhaps a yard wide, between the edge of the stage and the wall. Mack began to inch his way toward the far end of the stage.

Looking for a possible hiding place for Dominic, and maybe a more direct route to the back of the stage, he peeked underneath. The stage was a checkerboard of smaller, table-sized units fitted together, making the underside a tight maze of metal legs. Mack continued his slow circuit around the low-rise stage. The presidential guards were all looking toward the main entrance.

At the corner of the stage stood a wooden easel. Mounted on it was a cardboard poster depicting a blown-up version of the Congressional Medal of Honor—a constellation of stars set in a vivid blue-ribbon sky, an eagle, wings spread majestically, sitting on a bar inscribed VALOR, supported by a five-pointed star and laurel wreath. Mack recognized the helmeted figure at the center of the wreath as Minerva, Roman goddess of Wisdom. Hard to see exactly where Valor and Wisdom intersected.

Fat Ferdie's voice echoed through the hall again. "Many of you know-ow by now-ow why we're here-ere today-ay!" He twisted the microphone from side to side, and the reverberations diminished. "As the president himself said when he accepted our invitation, the purpose of this great event is to honor a true American hero—"

An adjustable wrench poked out from under the stage. Mack scooped it up and rested the long handle against his shoulder. He slid Leopold's fedora farther down over his face. Just a Shipping Department guy off to make some last-minute adjustment at the back of the stage. Mack picked up his pace and promptly tripped over a supporting leg for one of the spotlights, but he managed to regain his balance without upsetting the spindly light standard.

Following a round of polite applause, Lieutenant Winogrand stood at the podium. He glanced back. Felicia threw him a little wave. Mack's pace slowed involuntarily. "I'm one of the luckiest—" Winogrand coughed into the microphone. "—one of the luckiest guys in the whole world. The reason for all that luck is simple: I flew with Captain Thomas Kilkenny. Tommy was the greatest pilot I ever saw. When our bird got hit, he made sure I got out, along with everyone else left alive. Only then did he go after that Jap cruiser and put it and about five hundred yellow bellies out of the war—for good!" The brief spell Winogrand had cast was broken, and the place erupted in cheers.

"I can feel Tommy here right now, among us." As the lieutenant's voice dropped, the crowd hushed. "He's calling on us to put more Flying Fortresses into the air and still more again." The crowd leaned forward, straining to hear. "And I can feel him doing quieter things too, like bringing me and the wonderful woman who was once his own fiancée together." He gestured toward her. Felicia waved again, more broadly. This time, the cheers included a counterpoint of gasps and sighs.

Mack stood paralyzed. Good God, was Winogrand to be his brother-in-law? Where in the hell did the fiancée business come from?

Winogrand introduced the Honorable Robert Kilkenny and turned back toward his seat. The alderman, walking with exaggerated slowness toward the podium, gave Winogrand a warm handshake. Blarney Bob stood at the microphone and took a deep breath.

"My friends, I am, as you can surely imagine, struggling with immense feelings on this occasion." His deep voice quieted the crowd. After a few steps toward the far corner of the stage, Mack slowed down again.

"On the one hand, Mrs. Kilkenny and I are in despair. Our dear son Thomas, the light of our lives, is gone, gone beyond retrieving, taken from us in a place called Minda-NAYO, so far off we'd not heard its name until we learned Thomas died there." Silence in the hall. Down the row of folding chairs, Ellen touched the corner of her eye. "But I am feeling something else as well, an emotion stronger than grief—"

The alderman paused, pulling the crowd closer. *Winogrand is an amateur*, Mack thought, *but here is a past master.*

"Pride," Bob continued. "I'm feeling pride today that's swelling my heart to the bursting point. In destroying our bloodthirsty enemies, those sworn to destroy *us*, Thomas died for Lieutenant Winogrand, for me, for all of you. Take strength from his deeds, never forget you're carrying on

Thomas's work every time you turn a bolt, every time you build an engine to power a bomber like Tommy's!" The crowd screamed its approval.

The alderman patiently waited for the crowd to quiet down. "My son was a busy fellow in the Philippines," he went on, nodding to acknowledge the applause and scattered laughter. "But he always found time to write home. His letters were filled with the highest praise for the airplane he and his crew flew. A sweet bird, he called it—"

More laughter and applause.

Bob's voice rose. "—with engines like a mighty heartbeat that cannot be stilled." He took a breath, and the crowd breathed with him. "Engines built with your own hands and sweat, engines that sent that Jap cruiser to the deepest pit of hell!"

Blarney Bob waved as the cheers echoing off the cinder-block walls became a tidal wave. Fat Ferdie walked slowly to the podium.

Another tidal urge swept over Mack: turn around, leave the plant, never return. Let Pete and Felicia get married. Mack and Jan would take over caring for Mum, who looked stronger than she had in years. They'd never leave the coach house except to pick up booze and other necessary supplies.

Mack fought the latest urge to run away and forced himself ahead, continuing his reluctant circuit around the stage toward the gap at the back. The production banner flapped above his head, the wing of a giant prehistoric bird. As the cheers rolled on, Gisbourne looked at the microphone, seemed about to speak, then appeared to think better of it. Mack turned the corner and looked into the long narrow space, which resembled a dark corridor with no ceiling. Barely within his range of vision, a silhouette came into focus. A man-shaped shadow, heavy-set, leaning forward, apparently drawn in by Blarney Bob's words.

Framed by a pair of folding chairs, Gisbourne put an arm around the alderman's shoulders. Ferdie brushed away a tear as his head swung toward the ramp. One of the gray suits in front of the stage pointed toward the entrance to the plant and nodded.

Ferdie leaned over the microphone, took a deep breath, and gave out an amplified cough. "Ladies and gentlemen," he shouted, "it is my honor and privilege to introduce to you…the President of the United States!" He gestured broadly toward the ramp, nearly smacking the alderman on the side of the head. "Franklin Delano Roosevelt!"

The crowd erupted all over again. A spatter of shouts and flashbulbs boiled up alongside the ramp. The gentlemen of the press, a smaller gaggle than Mack had expected. An open touring car rolled slowly through the wide-open doors of the main plant entrance and chugged up the ramp, stopping at the edge of the stage.

One of the car's back doors opened. A pair of broad-shouldered young men leaped out—were they a pair of the president's sons, who were often shown helping him walk?—and ran around to the other door. One reached in, and another broad-shouldered figure emerged, a grinning Franklin D. Roosevelt, grasping the arm of each helper at the elbow as he cast the legendary presidential smile across his audience like a spotlight. The applause and cheers thundered across the entrance hall. The president proceeded toward the podium at a rapid pace in spite of his rocking, stiff-legged walk.

Mack turned at an awkward angle and tried to run toward the man-shaped silhouette. The wrench slipped out of his hand, but he didn't hear it hit the floor. Mack had cut the gap between them in half when the guy thrust his arms onto the stage and clumsily heaved himself up, lurching walrus-like onto the stage, losing his hat in the process. As his large head thrust itself into the lights, Mack recognized Dominic at once. How could all the federal agents have missed him? The answer came just as fast. They didn't see Dominic. They saw Alderman Kilkenny's hefty bodyguard, a veteran Chicago cop, a colleague who knew the territory. Sure, Captain, go check the back of the stage one last time—great idea!

Dominic had begun to slide back off when Mack arrived. He put a violent hand on each of Dominic's shoulders, yanking him the rest of the way off the stage. Threads popped at the shoulders of his black suit. As his back thudded mushily against the wall, Dominic O'Nore stared blankly into Mack's face for a moment then blurted out a half-articulated "Wha-a-a-t?"

Dominic struggled to push himself upright, and for a second, the two men stood jammed together diagonally in the narrow aisle. Mack felt his strength drain away as he tried to shove his opponent to the floor. He'd had enough trouble with scrawny Hugh Lonegan. How could he handle an opponent twice as big and probably four times as strong? Dominic shoved him back, hard, and they became a pair of wrestlers grunting and shoving inside a telephone booth.

The applause and shouts subsided. A familiar voice sounded. "My friends, I cannot tell you how delighted I am to be heah—"

Dominic ripped Mack's hand away from his shoulder as FDR's aristocratically drawled "heah" echoed through the hall.

"—heah in one of my favorite places in all the world—Chicah-go!"

More thunderous cheers.

Dominic's right arm slid away from Mack's heaving chest and disappeared inside the suit jacket just below the silver police badge. When the arm reappeared, Dominic's fingers were wrapped around the barrel of a pistol, holding it like a club.

"…Congressional Medal of Honor!" Roosevelt's words led to more frantic applause. "But whether or not you receive a medal, you are *all* heroes—A-MERI-can heroes like Captain Thomas Kilkenny…"

Wishing he still had the wrench, Mack swatted weakly at Dominic's gun as it swung at his head. He missed and tried to dodge away but succeeded only in losing his balance, sending his head, now hatless, falling toward the gunstock, a baseball aimed at a swinging bat. The blow coldcocked him.

Even if you're knocked out for just a few seconds, Mack knew from the football field that you always wake up in a new world. This one included blood running down his forehead and cheek. He knew right away the ocular prosthesis was gone, no doubt ricocheting like a pinball under the stage. An ice pick seemed to thrust itself over and over into Mack's empty eye socket. He swam through the pain, observing a wavy underwater image of Dominic stepping over him. Was his good eye damaged too? Mack had never imagined full citizenship in the Kingdom of the Blind.

As Dominic clambered onto the stage, Mack struggled to his feet.

The president's words continued to cast their spell on the crowd: "…I could not agree more heartily with Alderman Kilkenny. Thomas Kilkenny's life—and his sacrifice—prove once more that no danger is too great, no enemy too powerful, no challenge too daunting, that it cannot be overcome by the united strength of the American people. My thanks for all you have done and—carrying the indomitable spirit of Thomas Kilkenny in your hearts—I thank you for all you *will* do to win this war!"

Mack launched himself after Dominic, slipping on liquid spilled on the tiled floor—his own blood, he soon realized. He wiped a sleeve across his face and hauled himself onto the stage. As his vision began to clear, Mack breathed a prayer of thanks to Minerva, the first immortal being that came to mind.

Dominic was several paces ahead. They both looked at FDR's broad back, which seemed to prevent the crowd from seeing the ruckus behind him. Gripping the podium with both hands, the president remained at the microphone, nodding and smiling. Blarney Bob, with Ellen trailing behind, headed back to the podium to accept the Medal of Honor on

Tommy's behalf. The alderman waved to the crowd. Mack saw Mayor Ed Kelly straighten his bright red tie and take a step toward the group at center stage. Winogrand smoothed the front of his uniform and began to stand. Dominic stopped, his legs spread wide. His right hand gripped the pistol. The barrel slowly rose.

"*No—o—o—o!*" Mack screamed, a feral caveman's shout, hardly a word at all. The only one on the stage who seemed able to locate the source of the cry was Blarney Bob. His rising eyebrows and dropping lower jaw gave the crazy impression that the fleshy red face was being stretched like dough. Did his look signal a horrified recognition that he'd brought the president and his killer together. Was it a joyous reflex at the history-shifting blow about to be struck by the Irish Republican Army?

Mack threw himself at Dominic. His shoulder connected with Dominic's left thigh, just above the knee. But, like a quarterback getting ready to throw a pass, Dominic had set himself well. He lurched forward, but Mack couldn't knock him off his pins. The gun in Dominic's hand fired. But compared to Lonegan's thunderous shot, it sounded like a kid's popgun, rapidly losing volume as the sound ricocheted off the concrete walls of the entrance hall.

Attempting to stand, Mack had barely gotten to his knees when Dominic gave him a perfect football straight-arm to the shoulder that left him sprawled face down in the middle of the stage. He found himself at eye-level with another prostrate figure. Blarney Bob lay on his back directly in front of him. The alderman's white shirt front dripped with blood.

*There's one hell of a lot of blood around here,* Mack thought. *The janitors, the cleanup crew—we'll have to mop it all up.*

Pete Winogrand ran toward the alderman. At the podium, two of the gray-suits were already at the president's side, kneeling beside him like supplicants. Mack finally managed to drag himself upright, eliciting gasps from the crowd—Boris Karloff's monster unexpectedly popping up.

Dominic sprinted for the front of the stage. He looked over at the president. As far as Mack could tell, Roosevelt was unhurt. Dominic didn't have a clear shot. He raised the pistol and fired into the air.

"He's got a bloody gun! He just shot the alderman!" Dominic shouted. He pointed to the badge on his lapel. "Captain Lonegan, Chicago Police. I'm going after the bastard!"

Mack wondered for a shaky moment if Dominic really *had* spotted some other IRA assassin. Dominic's effort to create confusion also worked well on those with less battered brains. Still waving the gun, Dominic leaped off the stage. Was he planning to turn and take the final, fatal shot from there? The crowd, even the federal men, parted magically, all apparently hypnotized by the police badge—the Red Sea giving way to Moses.

Pete Winogrand, with help from Felicia, cradled Blarney Bob's head. Felicia's white gloves had turned red. "What can we do?" Felicia asked in a quavering voice. "What can we do?" Winogrand leaned toward her. Jan stood over them, rocking back and forth, her face a Greek mask of tragedy. Ellen stood a few feet away, frozen.

Mack bent over as the alderman, looking amazed, stared up at Mack's face. In a barely audible voice, Blarney Bob croaked, "Better me than the president—much better. Tell Franklin I said that."

Mack staggered to the front edge of the stage. Down below, Dominic continued shouting: "One side, get out of the bloody way. You'll let him escape!" The Italian family, eyes wide as dinner plates, backed away.

"Not so fast, Dominic!" A Negro man in a white shirt, bigger than anyone around him, stepped out of the crowd and blocked Dominic's path.

"Out of the way, blackbird, or I'll have to shoot you, however in the hell you know my bloody name."

Leopold Belgian stepped up to Dominic as he raised his gun. Dominic hesitated. Leopold took another step forward until he was less than a foot away. Dominic fingered the badge on his lapel and seemed about to speak. With hardly any windup, Leopold smacked Dominic on the side of the head so hard he fell to the floor. Mack recognized the move. Leopold had greeted him the same way on Mack's first day at Steckel Avenue.

"That's Dominic O'Nore," Mack yelled with all his remaining strength. "The assassin—There on the floor. Goddamn it, go get him while you have the chance!"

Mack's shout seemed to galvanize the gray suits among the crowd. Three agents ran, guns drawn, over to Dominic and Leopold. Dominic lay on his side, pistol in hand.

"Drop the gun!" shouted the Secret Service man who looked like Agent Neilsen.

Mack's natural eye, though partially occluded with blood, became the lens of a Brownie camera snapping an unlikely wide-angle photo. At the center were Dominic's pale blue eyes as he looked down the barrel of his pistol, with Leopold looming above, huge arms folded across his chest. Moving outward: the stunned, staring crowd of Steckel Avenue workers and their loved ones; shouting government men, mouths stretched to the limit; the president, sitting next to the podium, tie askew, useless legs splayed out, the Medal of Honor gleaming in his hand. Mack's father ran to the front of the stage then wrapped his arms around Mack, staining his Brooks Brothers suit.

All frozen forever.

Dominic smiled a tiny Mona-Lisa smile, barely showing his front teeth. He thrust the Luger into his mouth. As he pulled back the trigger, Mack thought in a bizarre moment of clarity, that his smile became a kiss for death, full on the lips, open-mouthed. He has nothing more to say, returning to the silence that had defined him, at least the side he'd allowed the world to see. But the alderman made a statement—Mack had heard his words. "Better me than the president." Was it a proud, defiant placard thrust up through the roiling avalanche of history? Perhaps only the caption to a newspaper cartoon, one last bit of blarney from Robert Kilkenny's counterfeit golden tongue.

For Dominic O'Nore, though, silence remained sufficient. After he pulled the trigger, a column spouted upward, raining red droplets. The crowd around him—even the cops and Secret Service men—took a step back then another, and another.

Mack's mother joined his father at the front of the stage. She cooed her son's name, "Mack, my own dear Mack," and daubed at the blood running down his cheek with a tiny handkerchief that quickly became saturated. Her touch drew away some of the pain.

Mack's father went on patting his back and squeezing his shoulder. Seemingly, all he could do was to choke out, "I'm sorry, son, so sorry" over and over. Was his sorrow for Mack, for Blarney Bob, or Tommy or himself or all of them together? Mack didn't care.

Hearing Sim say it was enough. Mack felt something break inside the old man, nothing like a heart attack or stroke—something stuck for a long time that had worked itself loose.

In the vast entrance hall, the palpable silence exploded into shouts and more popping flashbulbs. A skinny reporter in a baggy linen suit lit the cigarette dangling from his lips, stepped away from his fellow journalists, and pointed in Mack's direction.

Mack slipped gently from his father's embrace and turned to look for Jan. He located her, still standing over her father and the widening pool of blood surrounding him. Jan was coming back to herself—shoulders at attention, white blouse tugged back into place. Looking back at him, Jan nodded and slid a comforting arm around Ellen's sob-wracked shoulders.

Still groggy, Mack understood they both had connected somehow with her brother, doing the necessary thing.

*Heroes cause accidents. Accidents cause heroes.*

# Chapter 34

*December 2, 1944:*

*T**O: Captain Thomas A. Kilkenny (no known address) FROM: Mack Simmons (Winnetka, Illinois, USA, Planet Earth)*

*Tommy:*

*I know you're dead and gone, and I don't believe in ghosts or in spirits looking down from Above, so this letter isn't an exorcism or a confession. Why am I writing you a letter then? Well, some part of you—probably just a heavy-duty memory (heavy duty like a blockbuster bomb)—is with me all the time. This is strange in itself because, when I re-read your letters, they now seem full of juvenile bravado and false confidence at a time when bravado and overconfidence can be fatal flaws. I recognize that now, not only because I'm alive and kicking and you're not. I'm also three years older than you ever got to be. Back to the original question—why write? Maybe I want to turn the repeated one-way communication of reading over your letters back into a two-way street, like we used to have with our back-and-forth missives, even if that street is now a dead end.*

*The idea of a letter first came to me as I buttoned the top button of my starched white shirt and knotted my tie. Over these past few years, I've become almost as skilled in the silk-tie-and-Brooks Brothers-suit routine as my father. It dawned on me how surprised you'd be at this news.*

*Jan taught me how to tie a Windsor knot on our wedding day—you and I are brothers in law now. Jan sneaked down to the basement of St. Mark's Episcopal Church—Winnetka's most prestigious nuptial venue—for an inspection before Father Constable joined us in holy wedlock upstairs. Showing that can-do Kilkenny spirit, she took one look at my slipshod knot and ripped off the tie, a sedate navy-blue number I'd borrowed from Father for the occasion.*

*"Refusing to wear a tux is fine with me," she said with a wide smile that showed teeth as white as her own unadorned dress. "But at least you've got to look like you've worn a suit before." She made me sit on a folding chair while she guided my clumsy fingers through the intricacies of the Windsor knot.*

*"Who tied your ties when you were a kid?"*

*She had to ask again before I admitted it had first been our cook Lavinia then Felicia.*

*Leopold Belgian—the Negro foreman of my old all-black-minus-one janitorial crew at Steckel Avenue—rumbled out a laugh. "Hell, Reesh Boy, back home, my momma made me learn to tie a tie when I wasn't but three years old. Couldn't put your nose inside our church without it." He slid oversized fingers along the sleeve of his tailored black jacket. "And I own my tux—just one reason the best man is gonna look so much better than the groom at this shindig!"*

*Our wedding was a small affair just after Easter of last year. Ostentatious weddings are frowned upon—wasteful during wartime. My choice of Leopold as best man was another reason it was a small affair. Father and Mum, to their credit, never batted an eye, while your own dear mother Ellen was so eager for us to wed before Jan "began to show," as she said at every opportunity, that she'd have welcomed a ceremony at the Baha'i Temple with a Buddhist monk officiating. Most of Winnetka society, though, had*

*out-of-town plans or were otherwise occupied on our wed-
ding day.*

*If they'd known that Leopold had stopped your old
family retainer Dominic O'Nore from taking a second shot
at the president or gunning down Secret Service agents at
the Steckel Avenue plant, where FDR was honoring your
heroic sacrifice, a few good Winnetka citizens might have
renounced their white supremacy for a day. But the War
Information Board—the same outfit that until recently pro-
hibited publishing photos of dead or wounded Americans—
suppressed the story of the assassination attempt. Not even
Father's White House connection knew who the real censor
was. Henry Wallace? J. Edgar Hoover? FDR himself? In
the official story, your da' was murdered by his crazed bodyguard for the madman's own inexplicable reasons. President Roosevelt remained only an interested bystander, not
the intended target. Along with the Information Board, both
the FBI and the Secret Service enthusiastically endorsed
this official, now-historical version.*

*Blarney Bob's last words—better for him to die than
the president—were spoken loudly enough for me to hear
and, so it seems, only me. I anonymously passed them
along, minus an admonition to "tell Franklin I said that,"
as the noble words of a hero. Already the stuff of legend,
they were invoked at the alderman's funeral mass at Holy
Name Cathedral, Archbishop Stritch officiating, Jan and
Ellen in the first pew. Mayor Kelly tried to prevail upon
FDR to attend, but the president wasn't available.*

*My own role in the Steckel Avenue events was dis-
missed altogether. Too inconvenient, I suppose. I was just
the nameless guy who tussled with Dominic before he carried out his mad mission. As we historians know, back in
'33, a Mrs. W. F. Cross, or maybe it was just a rickety folding chair, thwarted the simple-minded anarchist Giuseppe
Zangara. A shrimp, less than five feet tall as you'll recall,
but emboldened by the gun in his pocket, Zangara climbed
onto a chair when FDR gave an impromptu pre-*

*Inauguration speech from the back of his limousine. Giuseppe's wobbly perch, or a shove from Mrs. Cross, caused him to miss FDR and fatally wound the president elect's traveling companion, Mayor Anton Cermak of Chicago. The random bystander, or wobbly chair, that redirected the shot—that was my role in the grand drama of fate and capital-H History.*

*You surely would have presented a counterargument. Perhaps you would have cast me as Franz Ferdinand's chauffeur, that unfortunate fellow who got lost in the twisting streets of Sarajevo and struggled to turn around the Archduke's massive town car right in front of Gavrilo Princip, planning to use the revolver in his pocket on himself. The failed assassin, of course, found himself staring his target in the face. A sitting duck, however you say that in Serbo-Croatian.*

*Anyway... I pushed that necktie knot toward my Adam's apple and shrugged into my Brooks Brothers suitcoat. A few steps away, in the upstairs bathroom of the carriage house, Jan, in a satin slip, re-applied her lipstick for perhaps the tenth time. I couldn't convince her that makeup was about to be rationed. She rubbed her dark-red lips together, a gesture I must admit I always find attractive. I stepped behind her and massaged her shoulders, smooth as costly fabric from some exotic land. She gave a small, not-entirely-negative shrug.*

*"Not now, lover boy. We have to be in Waukegan by two, and we can't be late. You said that, remember?"*

*I slid my hands away, tracing a lingering path across her back. "Is Maeve still sleeping?"*

*"Yes. Lavinia can't wait for her to wake up, so she and Maeve can play." Jan and I were afraid Lavinia would balk at having a squally newborn around. I also feared she might be scandalized by a child born a scant four months after her parents' wedding. On the contrary, becoming Chief Nurse and Babysitter gave our ancient cook a new lease on life.*

*Jan chose our daughter's name, after Maebh, the warrior queen of Connacht, who famously stood up to Cuchulain. Despite the phonetic spelling, it's a lovely Gaelic name, hard and otherworldly at the same time, a sly, secret message from us to you and Blarney Bob, our child's lost uncle and grandfather.*

*Jan and I moved into the carriage house right after Mum returned to the main house and Felicia married Pete Winogrand—another unexpected brother in law. Unlike you, your co-pilot followed the Yellow Brick Road back home. Needless to say, theirs was a full-blown Winnetka wedding.*

*By the way, at my father's insistence, I've become director of the Thomas A. Kilkenny Foundation. Father was surprised I didn't put up more of a fight. He woke up one morning, a few weeks before our wedding, determined that I, not he, should head up the foundation he and Ellen were establishing in your name.*

*As usual, Father marshaled a litany of legalistic arguments. When we met at his home office, he was fully prepared. Suit and tie in place, especiale Cuban cigar fired up, points to be made arrayed in numbered paragraphs on a yellow legal pad. He looked up in surprise at my corduroy jacket, part of an outfit that would've easily fit in on the UofC campus, complete with leather elbow patches and pressed corduroys.*

*Father looked disappointed when I acquiesced after Point One, something about my age and "situation" making me a better ambassador to the wounded boys the Thomas A. Kilkenny Foundation planned to assist. When I accepted Father's invitation, I heard your laughing voice egging me on. "What the hell? Why not?"*

*Clearly, the decision wasn't as carefully thought out as Father's arguments. My clownish turn on the stage of History forever cast aside the cynical kid I'd been for so many years. I held onto that character, an over-age spoiled brat hiding out in a crummy, boarding-house room—my hermit's cave, as you called it. That way of living seemed the only cover, the only camouflage, for the scarred, one-eyed freak I'd turned into. A nasty, wise-ass, one-eyed hermit—there's a winning combination for you. Tasty as skunk-shit pie, a favorite line of the counselors back at Camp Ojibway.*

*The decision to head up the foundation was another case of my reaching a conclusion first and working out the reasoning later—perhaps an inversion caused by years of skewed, one-eyed vision. Or maybe the decision wasn't mine at all—maybe the vast catastrophe of war and the personal catastrophe of your death made the choice for me. You were among the first of hundreds of thousands of Americans to die in this war—with untold millions of all nationalities still to come. Your death had already been used to encourage blood drives and Victory Gardens, sell War Bonds, and manufacture bomber engines at an even more frenzied pace. Maybe the spectacular tale of your death could also be used to repair some of the war's damage—a triflingly small percentage, but some nonetheless.*

*Even in the midst of history's most catastrophic war— what for me will always be your war—I know now that your historical Theory of Random Catastrophe isn't the whole story. Catastrophe isn't always an inevitable fate we ordinary mortals can only deal with by hunkering down and waiting it out. Sometimes—when the stars or the gods or the inscrutable forces of the universe align just right—we can convert catastrophe into something that can, often at great cost, be managed. Not by your species of heroic sacrifice, the stuff of legend and Technicolor films, but by the steady efforts of anonymous functionaries, a group that now includes me.*

*After three years, the war has become our climate, the weather of every day. News of gruesome destruction doesn't get our attention the way it did in your day. Warsaw has joined Rotterdam and Stalingrad on the lengthening list of cities reduced to rubble. Berlin is next in line, maybe Ma-*

*nila too. B-29 bombers, larger and more fortress-like than your Flying Fortress, are burning Tokyo to the ground.*

*Jan and I drove along Sheridan Road toward Waukegan. There's more traffic now, as the grinding progress of the war gradually expands the gasoline supply. The day's mission for Jan and me is to formally present a new iron lung to the VA hospital, courtesy of the Thomas A. Kilkenny Foundation. With VA hospitals springing up across the nation, providing non-government-issue equipment like that is the Foundation's main function. We even bought a bungalow next door to a hospital near St. Louis and turned it into a free boarding house so the patients' families can visit with no hotel or restaurant bills.*

*We're looking ahead too, and I'm starting to redirect some Kilkenny Foundation funds to education. And believe me—when you combine the results of Father's shakedown of his LaSalle Street cronies, your mother's donations from various Boswell family trusts, and the envelopes from every state containing a buck or two and, usually, a prayer for you and even for Blarney Bob—we have a hell of a lot of funds.*

*Your anarchist brain was always, shall we say, dubious about the benefits of education, but you were dubious about everything except flying. That kind of cynicism would likely have made you a great politician, maybe even, as your mother so devoutly wished, a future President of the United States.*

*In any case, the Foundation is funding scholarships for the siblings and kids of the war's dead and badly wounded. I made sure our charter includes some legal claptrap about scholarships for "other individuals, at the discretion of the Foundation." That's why Franklin D. Roosevelt Belgian— already embarrassed by his presidential moniker—attends the University of Chicago Lab School. Leopold's still working at the Steckel Avenue plant, and he's organizing a janitors' union there. I'm planning to get him into the UofC too, as a part-time, special-admission student.*

*Between the Japs and MacArthur's army, dozens of Philippine towns have joined the ranks of flattened cities. So when the fighting's done, the Thomas A. Kilkenny Foundation will build some schools and hospitals over there in your name—a tiny recompense for all who've died and who will die as MacArthur triumphantly returns to the scene of his '42 disaster.*

*A far smaller post-war project involves a new ocular prosthesis for me. Mum insists that only a replacement from Germany will do. They've surely had a lot of practice making them, she says with impeccable logic, what with all the German boys who must've lost an eye in the war. While we wait for the war in Europe to end and the peacetime ocular prosthesis industry to revive, I've added a black eye patch to my wardrobe of silk ties and Brooks Brothers suits. No one asks if I'm a pirate.*

*When I visit a hospital, a wounded soldier, usually an achingly polite boy swathed in bandages, will ask if I lost my eye in the war. Father has encouraged me to say yes. It'll build rapport, he says, and, he legalistically emphasizes, my injury is a war wound or at least a war sacrifice. If it had never occurred, you wouldn't have enlisted so early and become a hero.*

*I can't do it. "Just an accident," I reply, "happened stateside, nothing to do with the war. Remember, it's the Thomas A. Kilkenny Foundation. He's the hero," I glibly tell them, "the one who died to bring off a small, necessary victory when retreat and defeat were all we knew. I just write the checks"—a line that usually gets a laugh.*

*If I'm the bookkeeper, Jan is the soul of your titular foundation. She's wept with the wives, sisters, mothers of the lost and maimed. She cuddles with uncomprehending fatherless children as joyously as with our own Maeve. Mum has accepted your sister as a second daughter. Father has fallen in love with his daughter-in-law. After months of grief and silence, your mother now makes powerful appear-*

*ances at our hospital visits, quietly acknowledging the cheers of the wounded boys—a secular Virgin Mary.*

*When the endless misery tour overwhelms us, Jan and I desperately clutch each other, gasping shipwreck survivors convinced, for a moment at least, that everyone else on earth has drowned. We're thankful beyond measure that we each have someone who comprehends our particular wounds, a bizarre definition of love likely to be shared more widely as more wounded souls come home.*

*In Waukegan, we park near the back of the vast, crowded lot. The hospital director offered a VIP space near the entrance, but I turned him down. "It'll do us good to walk," I told him. That's no doubt true for me: signing checks and pushing around papers instead of Steckel Avenue trash barrels has given me the beginning of a paunch. Jan, on the other hand, looks gray and queasy as we step into the crisp air, still unseasonably warm for early December.*

*She takes a deep breath and bravely waves at Father, who stands in front of the broad hospital entrance. He adores occasions like this and always arrives early to set up the easel and the enlarged poster of your posthumous Medal of Honor. He's flanked by Ellen and my mother.*

*Father asked Lavinia what she'd put in the morning oatmeal. It didn't agree with Janice, he said. I know different—she's pregnant again. Amid unending blood and death, another new life is heading our way, an undiscovered comet flashing across the constellation on your medal. Through an Irish vision Blarney Bob would have appreciated, I know the baby will be a boy and that he'll look like you, a definitive black Irish type.*

*Whatever Father's preference, there'll be no John Mackenzie Simmons IV, coupled with some arch, blueblood nickname. His name must be Thomas Robert Kilkenny Simmons. A proper public tribute, however unwieldy, to you and your da', each in your own way a fallen hero. Whatever*

*the hell that tattered travesty of a word means in this grave-*
*yard world.*

> *Brothers to the end,*
> *Mack*

THE END

# AFTERWORD

"We can't all be heroes because somebody has to sit on the curb and clap as they go by." ~ Will Rogers

# About the Author

An alumnus of Rice University, with graduate degrees from Penn and Buffalo, G. W. Kennedy was a college English professor at the University of Illinois-Chicago. After leaving academia, Kennedy worked as an editor and communications manager for several Chicago companies. He has published a number of short stories as well as articles and essays, including "op-ed" pieces in the *Chicago Tribune*. He is the author of the Professor Ben Barklee mysteries, *Purpose Pitch, Dead Arm,* and *Save Situation.*